KING ALFRED'S DAUGHTER

The remarkable story of Æthelflæd,
Lady of the Mercians, the heroine who
was written out of history.

KING ALFRED'S DAUGHTER

ÆTHELFLÆD, LADY OF THE MERCIANS

DAVID STOKES

The Book Guild Ltd

First published in Great Britain in 2023 by
The Book Guild Ltd
Unit E2 Airfield Business Park,
Harrison Road, Market Harborough,
Leicestershire. LE16 7UL
Tel: 0116 2792299
www.bookguild.co.uk
Email: info@bookguild.co.uk
Twitter: @bookguild

Typeset in 11pt Minion Pro

Printed and bound by CPI Group (UK) Ltd, Croydon, CR0 4YY

ISBN 978 1915603 197

British Library Cataloguing in Publication Data.
A catalogue record for this book is available from the British Library.

King Alfred's Daughter was written during the Covid lockdown. I dedicate it to all the Stokelings whose regular zoom sessions kept me going, and especially to Hal and Robyn who progressed from being bumps on a screen to real live babies during this period.

KING ALFRED'S DAUGHTER

Æthelflæd, Lady of the Mercians,
the heroine who was written out of history

Based on contemporary sources and archaeological evidence, her story is rich in drama, family conflict and historical achievement.

'I was hooked from the first chapter. I loved the action and the way the author fills in the history as the tale unfolds.'

'A vivid depiction of Anglo-Saxon society. The battle scenes are especially gripping.'

'An impressive combination of historical research and a good plot.'*

---

*Comments from beta readers

ABOUT THE AUTHOR

David Stokes was born in East Anglia and studied history at Oriel College, Oxford. He is Emeritus Professor in entrepreneurship at Kingston University and has published widely in the non-fiction field during his career as an academic. The Anglo-Saxons have been a lifelong interest, and he has combined this passion with his research skills to write historical fiction focussing on the early medieval period. His first historical novel, Angles or Angels? was published in 2019.

For more information about the author and the Anglo-Saxon period go to:

davidstokesauthor.com

ACKNOWLEDGEMENTS

Although any mistakes are my own, many others have contributed to the creation of this book. I am indebted to:

- *My 'editor-in-chief', Sue Gross, who scrutinised every one of the 100,000 words before they became final;*
- *The 'beta readers' who carefully commented on earlier drafts: Terry Faithful, Pam Palmer, Gillian Spencer, Anne Lawrence, Sheila Manson, Helen Roberts, Helen Fell, Carolyn Foster and Veronica Keywood;*
- *My mentor Laurence Darren King at Jericho Writers;*
- *The Book Guild for agreeing to publish my manuscript and their staff who have turned it into such an excellent edition;*
- *And to the spirit of the countless women who like Æthelflæd have found themselves written out of history. (I did the final edits of King Alfred's Daughter during the 2022 European Women's Football competition when I learned that the golden age of the women's game in the 1920s was buried by the men of the Football Association when they banned women from playing on their grounds for fifty years until 1971 – a reminder that the habit of writing women out of history was not just a thing of the medieval period.)*

CHARACTERS

These names from our story appear in the historic records, other than those in italics which are not documented. (See also Historical Notes at the end of the book.)

Ælfwyn	Daughter of Æthelflæd
Ælfweard	Second son of King Edward
Æthelflæd	Eldest child of King Alfred. Lady of the Mercians
Æthelgifu	Second daughter of King Alfred. Abbess of Shaftesbury Abbey
Æthelred	Husband of Æthelflæd. Lord of Mercia
Æthelwold	Son of Alfred's brother, Ethelred. Cousin of Æthelflæd
Alfred	King of Wessex (871–899), Æthelflæd's father
Anlaf	Danish jarl, nicknamed 'the Swart'
Athelstan	First son of King Edward of Wessex. Later King of England (924–939)
Cadel	Cadel ap Rhodri, King of Gwynedd, North Wales
Cadman	Irish monk, enslaved by Irish Norse

Cearl	Mercian soldier at Chester, old retainer of Æthelflæd
Cenwulf	Æthelflæd's uncle, brother of Ealhswith, her mother (actually his name was Æthelwulf but changed to avoid Æthel proliferation!)
Cormac	Irish monk, enslaved by Irish Norse
Cuthberht	One of Æthelflæd's military leaders
Cwen	Saxon taken prisoner by the Danes, daughter of the Reeve of Braydon
Beorhsige	Mercian ætheling, descendent of deposed King Burgred of Mercia
Beornoth	Mercian ealdorman based in Shrewsbury, father of Beorhsige
Ealhswith	King Alfred's wife, Mercian noblewoman
Ecgberht	Abbot of Chirbury, killed by Welsh King Hwgan
Ecgwynn	King Edward's first wife, mother of Athelstan
Edward	Eldest son of King Alfred. Later known as Edward the Elder, King of Wessex (899–924)
Eohric	Danish King of East Anglia, succeeded Guthrum
Eowils	Danish leader from Northumbria
Ethelred	King of Wessex (865–871). Alfred's older brother. (More properly, Ethelred was Æthelred but changed here to avoid confusion with Æthelflæd's husband)
Finna	Wife of Ingimund
Fintan	Irish monk, Abott of St Oswald's, Gloucester
Jokul	Son of Finna
Halfdan	Danish leader from Northumbria

Hæsten	Danish warlord of the 890s who fought Alfred and Æthelred
Hrotheweard	Archbishop of York
Hwgan	King of Brycheiniog, South Wales
Ingimund	Norse leader who fled from Dublin to set up a colony in the Wirral
Merewalh	One of Æthelflæd's military leaders, suitor of Ælfwyn
Merfyn	One of Æthelflæd's military leaders, from Gwynedd in Wales
Osferth	Son (unacknowledged) of King Alfred and confidant of Edward
Oscytel	Danish jarl from East Anglia
Osric	Saxon taken prisoner by Danes, merchant's son from Hertford
Plegmund	Archbishop of Canterbury
Ragnall	Danish leader in Northumbria
Sigewulf	Thegn of Kent, advisor/friend to Edward
Sigeholm	Thegn of Kent, advisor/friend to Edward
Thurketel	Danish jarl from Northampton
Thurston	One of Æthelflæd's military leaders, reeve of Shrewsbury
Wærferth	Old friend and advisor of Alfred and Æthelflæd. Bishop of Worcester
Wiglaf	One of Æthelflæd's lieutenants, reeve of Chester
Ysopa	Danish jarl from East Anglia
Wulfhad	Reeve of Worcester

- ● Townships
- ■ Burhs (associated with Æthelflæd)
- ✕ Battles

Æthelflæd's world – Kingdoms, burhs and battles 870's — 917AD

Æthelflæd's Family: from Kings of Wessex to Kings of the English

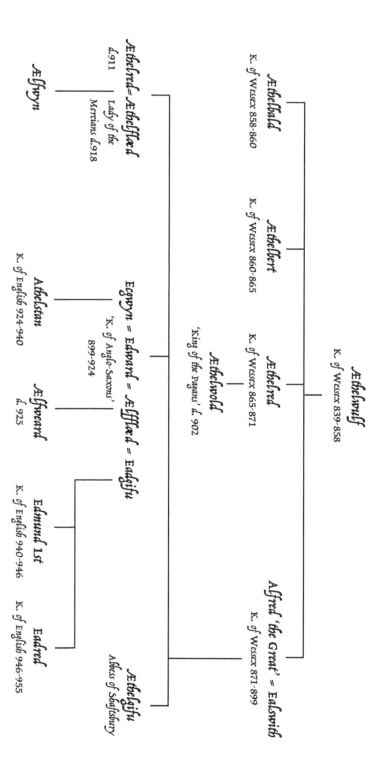

Æthelwulf
K. of Wessex 839-858

Æthelbald
K. of Wessex 858-860

Æthelbert
K. of Wessex 860-865

Æthelred
K. of Wessex 865-871

Alfred 'the Great' = Ealswith
K. of Wessex 871-899

Æthelred = **Æthelflæd**
d. 911   Lady of the
      Mercians d. 918

Ælfwyn

Æthelwold
'King of the Pagans' d. 902

Ecgwyn = **Edward** = **Ælfflæd** = Eadgifu
     'K. of Anglo-Saxons'
      899-924

Æthelgifu
Abbess of Shaftsbury

Athelstan
K. of English 924-940

Ælfweard
d. 925

Edmund 1st
K. of English 940-946

Eadred
K. of English 946-955

PROLOGUE

Do not read on if you prefer living quietly by the rules and staying out of trouble. Our lords do not want you to hear this story. It tells of a woman who brought the Angles and Saxons together to create Engaland. Yes, it was a woman. Not a king, nor a warlord, nor a magician. A woman.

There are men who want her story to remain untold so they can take the glory. Have courage. Turn the page. Read the truth.

Do not depend for the truth on chronicles written by monks. I should know. I am a nun. My grandfather, King Alfred, asked the brothers in his monasteries to write down his story so that they could be read by all. He wanted us all to know how he and his Christian warriors held off the pagan Danes to make sure that the Angle and Saxon kingdoms survived. His story has been well told. They call him a great king, and he was.

But when he died, his dream of a united land, under one ruler and one God, was very distant. The Danes held sway over much of Engaland, and the Angles and Saxons squabbled over who was to control what was left.

Until a woman was brave enough to stand once more against the pagan invaders.

How do I know? I am her daughter. She entrusted me with her story so that the truth would be known.

So read on and my brave mother will live again. When you have finished her story, don't just put it aside, retell it to your friends, or, if they are fortunate enough to understand the written word, beg them to read it too.

Ælfwyn,
Nunnaminster, Winchester, 927

ONE

Up ahead, I saw an oak outlined against the sky on the crest of a hill. The slope of its trunk and the contours of its bare branches looked familiar. I felt like smiling for the first time since I'd heard the news about father.

I was nearly home.

Although my horse was blowing hard after days of struggling through mud and sodden grass, I urged it on up the hill, my mind set on reaching that tree. Yet when I reached the top and looked down, the view puzzled me. I expected to see the smattering of wooden huts that I used to call home. Instead, a dense settlement surrounded by an unbroken protective wall lay in the valley. Houses, outbuildings and chapels were neatly arranged around a main thoroughfare criss-crossed by smaller streets like fish bones.

Maybe I was mistaken. The heavy rains had forced my small band of riders into detour after detour to avoid impassable streams and flooded fields. Perhaps the oak tree was not the one that I used to lean against as a child.

No, there were the unmistakeable white walls and tower of the Minster, the church that was once the centre of my world.

It had to be Winchester.

I slid from my horse and clasped my hands to thank the Lord for our safe journey, wishing I had more flesh on my body to cushion the hard saddle. I stared down at the imposing stone gate where a line of people and carts were waiting to enter the town. When I was young, I used to pass freely through that entrance.

I called to one of the riders struggling up behind me. 'Bishop Wærferth, why didn't you tell me that father had built so much? This is exactly what we need in Gloucester. Have someone draw it quickly before we descend.'

The man in flowing cleric's clothes, mud-spattered from top to bottom, did not dismount but drew level, both horse and rider panting with the effort.

'But Lady Æthelflæd, we are already late for the king's burial.'

I rolled my eyes. 'They must know there have been heavy storms ever since the news of my father's death. They will delay the funeral until our arrival. How many times have you told me it is better to serve the living than the dead? The king is already in the care of Our Lord, but our people need protecting by more towns built like that.'

I studied the layout of the streets, admiring the regular, interlaced pattern. The beginnings of a building in the centre caught my eye. 'What is that next to the old church?'

Bishop Wærferth sighed and lowered himself from his horse. His small group of companions took this as a general signal that they would be stopping for a while, and they likewise dismounted and tethered their horses. He squinted to make out the structure below.

'Ah, that is Edward's latest passion, the New Minster.'

'And what was so wrong with the old Minster that my brother has to build a new one? He could be strengthening other towns with that stone.'

'Why don't we finish our journey and ask him? He must be very anxious to see us.'

'I most certainly will. But I doubt he can justify building a new church when there is a perfectly good one right next to it.'

The bishop stretched his back to ease the aches of the hard ride. 'I am told it is a mausoleum for the royal family, m'lady.'

I could not believe it, not even of Edward. 'He is building me a tomb, just as I bury my father?'

'Why don't we descend and you can discuss his purpose directly with him, m'lady?' Expectantly, he took up the reins of his horse.

'Oh I will, you can be assured of that,' I said, beckoning a servant to help me back into the saddle. 'There is much I would discuss with my brother before he becomes king.'

*

The guards at the West Gate did not recognise me. It was not until the bishop came forward that they bowed and let us pass. I did not blame them. I had been a dazzling girl of sixteen when I had last ridden through the gate, my face widely known and admired. Now I was a timeworn woman of thirty, my once unlined skin creased by the anxieties of adulthood.

Impatient to see my father one last time before he was laid to rest, I gritted my teeth and tried to make my way through the townsfolk who milled casually about in the main street, impeding my route towards the church.

'Give way there,' I shouted to a group of merchants dragging a cart unhurriedly across the street. I almost lashed out at them with my riding crop when I saw their blank stares. Did they not remember the young princess who had been sent forth to help defeat the Danes? Those evil pagans had deposed every Anglo-Saxon king except for my father, Alfred of Wessex. His only friend was a dogged warlord called Æthelred who controlled what remained of Mercia. In order to seal an alliance with him, my father had offered me, his beautiful young daughter, to be his wife. I had dutifully accepted my role, but it had not been easy to leave behind everything I knew to live in a foreign land that had become a battlefield, with a warrior almost old enough to be my father.

It had been a long, hard struggle, but now there was peace. The pagans had agreed to live in their territory to the east, which they called Danelaw, leaving my father as King of Wessex and overlord of what remained of Mercia.

Now my father was dead, and everything he had fought for was at risk. The Danes would relish the chance to complete the conquest that he had halted.

And his daughter was forgotten in the town of her birth.

At last, I was able to turn into a side street that led to the Minster. I grimaced at the foundations of the new works that had begun alongside the towering structure of the original church. Why did my brother want to build his mausoleum so close? What was he trying to prove?

The area around the Minster was deserted except for an old monk tending to some rubbish in a corner of the graveyard. I paused by the grave of Swithun, a bishop of Winchester who had tutored my father as a young boy. He had chosen to be buried outside the west door of the church where ordinary people's feet would pass over him. That wouldn't do for King Alfred. He would be buried inside in a place of honour near to the altar.

The doors of the church were open and unguarded, the interior empty. I had expected my father to be inside, lying in an open coffin so his subjects could pay their respects. A shaft of light shone through a blue glass window onto bare flagstones. Not even a row of benches had been set out in preparation for the ceremony.

My stomach began to churn at the lack of activity in preparation for my father's funeral. I turned back to my companions who were reverently walking over Swithun's grave, as the old bishop had wanted. There were rumours that a cripple could be cured by standing on his tomb and now, it seemed, even the healthy wanted to walk on his grave.

I inwardly groaned at their distraction and looked towards the royal residence, tall wooden structures across the meadow. Several warriors in chainmail at the door were looking interestedly in our direction.

Guards everywhere. Father must be there.

I grabbed Bishop Wærferth and pushed him towards the palace. I did not want the embarrassment of being turned away by a zealous sentry who did not recognise the daughter of the dead king.

*

Fortunately, the guards seemed to be expecting us and announced our arrival by clanging a bell. We were shown into a small chamber that had been built onto one side of the great hall. I ran my fingers over the timber of the doorframe, remembering how, as a young girl, I used to peep through that very door to glimpse the raucous feasts of my father and his thegns. A sombre stillness now hung over the building.

The clatter of feet on wooden floors broke the silence. A slight woman in a nun's habit hurried in. We stared at each other in half recognition.

'Æthelflæd?' the nun asked.

'Æthelgifu?' I replied, shocked that I had hardly recognised my younger sister.

Æthelgifu rushed at me and seemed about to throw herself into my arms, but she checked when she saw Bishop Wærferth and bowed instead. We sat demurely together, and I gently patted her hand trying not to notice that she smelled of stale sweat. Æthelgifu asked about my journey from Gloucester to Winchester and sympathised over the problems I had encountered. I wondered at the lines in her face and the roughness of the hand that clasped my own. I remembered crying when I'd heard that my young sister was to be a nun. I had dragged her down from too many trees to know that her adventurous spirit would not be well suited to a nunnery.

Yet here she was, an abbess, and comforting me for arriving late.

'We all missed you yesterday.'

'Missed me for what?' I asked, suddenly concerned at her meaning.

'Why, for father's funeral,' she said.

Her words stunned me. My mouth opened but I was unable to speak.

Jumping up, I knocked over my chair. 'What's happened here? Where's my brother?'

I ran blindly for the door, just as it opened, and I had to hold out my hands to prevent it from striking my face. A squat figure with cropped hair bustled in.

'Edward!' I gasped.

'King Edward, if you please, sister. Welcome to our court.' He smiled as I staggered back, staring at the red robes that hung from his wide shoulders. 'You are late.'

'No brother, you are early.' My mind was racing at the certainty that I had missed my father's funeral and the possibility that Edward had already installed himself as king.

He seemed not to hear me as he greeted my companions.

'Welcome, Bishop Wærferth. And you must be Beorhsige,' he said to the tall, youthful warrior at my side.

'Yes, lord,' Beorhsige said, bowing.

Edward grunted. 'You must address me as king. I will forgive you this once as you have not yet taken your oath of allegiance. But remember from now on.'

Beorhsige gave me a sideways glance. 'Yes, lord king,' he said, bowing even lower. I winced at his discomfort. He was himself descended from a long line of Mercian kings so he must have found the reprimand particularly hard.

Edward turned his beady eyes on me. 'It seems you and I have some catching up to do. Follow me.' He flicked his long robe imperiously as he turned towards the door and swept out.

Bishop Wærferth gently touched my hand as I gritted my teeth and followed my brother.

*

Edward walked quickly, marching across the paved square towards an imposing door decorated with a golden cross. The area was much altered since my childhood, and I tutted at the extravagant new structures surrounding the old, thatched feasting hall. My brother had changed too; I was pleased to see that he was still shorter than me, but he had grown heavier with more muscle than the skinny youth I used to pin to the ground. Today, I would have to beat him with words, not fists.

I followed him into a room decorated with intricate carvings and draped with colourful tapestries. Edward sat on the high-backed chair in the middle of the chamber, leaving me to stand, feeling like a supplicant for his favour.

My lips trembled as I spoke. 'Where is my father?'

'He is temporarily buried in the Old Minster. We will move him into the New Minster as soon as it is complete.'

It was as though he was discussing an item of furniture. Tears filled my eyes. 'Why didn't you wait? You knew I was coming. I wanted to see his face one last time.'

'We spared you the pain. He was much changed in death. Besides we had urgent business that could only be done after the burial. And you were late.'

'I was delayed,' I shouted. 'Did you not notice the storms and floods that I have been travelling through? Of course not. You were plotting to make yourself king before anyone could blink. You could not wait to put him in the ground so you could sit on his throne.' My body shook with the force of my words.

Edward stood and glared. 'Have a care, sister. Some might think your words treasonous. King Alfred declared me his heir before he died.'

'Only the Witan has the right to pronounce who is to be king.'

'Which they have done. In my favour.'

I saw the same smirk on his face that I had seen in his boyhood when he returned from a hunt with a rabbit slung over his shoulder.

He took a step closer towards me, his hand on the pommel of his sword. 'The formal ceremony will be next year, at Kingston. It's not so far for you to travel, so try not to be late for that.'

Something in his look and the way he spoke finally took away what little composure I had left. Grabbing both his arms, I shook him as though he were a naughty boy.

'I am not late! You have disrespected our customs with your haste. You're not fit to be king.'

He struck me hard on the cheek. 'Why is Æthelred not with you? He should be here to control his wife,' he glowered as I staggered back.

In the old days, I would have pummelled him with my fists but something in the force of the blow and the cold look in his eyes made me hesitate.

I put a hand to my stinging cheek. 'He is ill, or he would be here to protect me from my brutish brother.'

'He needs to swear allegiance to me in person, not send his petulant wife,' Edward rasped

Before I could answer, I heard a familiar shrill voice behind me as the door opened.

'Will you two never cease your squabbling! Your father will be turning in his grave at the scene you are making.'

I twisted round to see a bent woman in a black habit scowling at us.

Edward exhaled impatiently. 'I'll leave you to make your daughter see sense.' He swept out of the room without a backward glance.

I ran to embrace my mother, Ealhswith, holding her tightly and feeling her bones under the thin covering of flesh. 'What has happened here?'

'Nothing that your father would not have wished. He is buried and his son is king. You must forgive Edward. He sometimes forgets his manners in his haste to rule.'

'He's a brute, mother, just like he always was.'

'He is your king, and you would do well to remember it.' Ealhswith stepped back, pulling a cloth from the folds of her gown.

'He's not my king. He does not rule in Mercia,' I said.

'He will demand Mercia's submission to his overlordship, just as Alfred did.' She offered me the cloth. 'Here, tidy your face. Your cousin is most anxious to see you.'

I dabbed at my eyes. 'Cousin?'

'Yes, Alfred's nephew, Æthelwold. But first, a word of caution. This is not the moment to complain of the king. Your father would have wished you to support your brother. And so do I.'

She had always favoured Edward over me. Giving birth to a girl must have been a great disappointment for her when her husband so needed an heir. I could still see the pride in her face when she had shown me her new-born son and I knew, however hard I tried, I could never make her feel as proud of me.

Later, I had tried to forgive her when I had realised how hard life must have been for her. Like me, she had been sent as a young girl to marry in a foreign land, except her journey had been in the opposite direction. She had travelled from Mercia to Wessex to marry an ætheling called Alfred, then the younger brother of the king. She was probably relieved at moving away from the ravages of the Great Heathen Army that had already invaded Mercia and deposed its ruler. But she got no respite. Within two years of her marriage, her husband's brother was dead, and Alfred was king – the only king left to fight the pagan invaders.

It was not long before she'd had to flee into the marshes with her husband and young family to escape capture. That was two long decades ago, but the anxious wrinkles in her face told me she was as determined as ever. She was not going to let a family argument undo all the good work she and Alfred had done.

It was a pity her first son was such a pig.

'Then you must restrain Edward. He is acting too hastily, without thought for others,' I said.

Ealhswith sighed. 'You think he listens to me? No, you are the one he used to respect, and you are the one to counsel him now.'

I snorted. 'Respect? You call fighting and arguing, respect? That's all I can remember of my time with him.'

'Yes, but you used to win. He still looks up to his big sister.'

'If hitting a woman's face is respect, then you're right. But I cannot bow to his bullying.'

Ealhswith reached out a hand to gently touch my face. 'The good Lord told us to turn the other cheek and swallow our pride. Will you not listen to Him, if not to me?'

'Blessed are the meek. But not the weak.'

Ealhswith shook her head. 'You haven't changed.' She took my arm. 'Come, there is one particular favour I would ask.'

*

As I followed her across the courtyard, I could not help but notice my mother's bowed legs and slight limp as she shuffled ahead.

She paused outside a small building with fresh thatch on the roof. 'I'm living here while they build the nunnery.'

'Nunnery? What nunnery?'

'Sorry, I keep forgetting we haven't seen each other for so long. I am building a convent to the east of the Minster. Nunnaminster, I call it. It will be my haven of peace.'

'Can I join you? I am tired of this violent world we live in.'

'No, your work is only just beginning. Mine is nearly done once...'

She waved me closer so that she could lower her voice. 'Once you have agreed to my little plan.'

As she opened the door, I peered past her, anxious to see who was inside. An elegantly dressed man and a young lad sat beside a fire that lit the gloom of a simple, sparsely furnished room. Both jumped up expectantly at the sound of the door creaking open.

'You remember your cousin, Æthelwold?' Ealhswith said.

I stared at the willowy figure who bowed towards me. I trembled at the memory of that tousled hair and those generous lips that I had come so close to kissing.

'But you won't know your nephew,' she said, indicating the boy who grinned, puppy-like, back at me.

'Nephew?'

'Yes, Edward's son, Athelstan.'

I blinked, thinking I had seen a ghost. The boy, who could not have been older than six, looked like an angelic version of my father, King Alfred. He had the same strong nose and piercing eyes, but his hair was curly and blonde, not straight and dark like my father's.

'Two fine young men. Both in need of your help.'

'Fine indeed,' I said, smiling at Æthelwold who had not taken his eyes from me since I had entered the room. 'How could I possibly help them?'

Ealhswith offered me a cup of wine and invited us all to sit around the fire. 'Maybe we can start with Athelstan. He needs a mother. A strong woman, like you.'

The boy looked embarrassed. 'What has happened to your mother, Athelstan? Is Ecgwynn unwell?' I asked.

'She is not here,' he replied. 'Father has a different wife.'

More news I had not heard. I looked to Ealhswith to explain but it was Æthelwold who spoke.

'He is forbidden to see his mother who has gone back to her parent's estate,' he said. 'Edward shuns the boy, so I am temporarily overseeing him. He is alone, as I was at his age when my father died.' He turned to look at Ealhswith. 'But I found a new family to belong to and a kind mother to guide me.'

'Yes, you were always like a brother to me,' I said.

Æthelwold's eyes narrowed into a fierce glare. 'And now it seems, I am to be disowned by your real brother.'

'How so?'

Ealhswith held up her hand. 'Athelstan, could you give us a moment? Perhaps you could take the dog outside.' As the boy prodded a longhaired hound from underneath the bench and dragged it out of the door, Ealhswith mouthed quietly, 'He does not enjoy hearing about his father. He has quite taken against him.'

I chuckled. 'I like the lad already.'

'Perhaps I can explain what has happened?' Ealhswith said. 'Around the time you were born, your father and his brother King Ethelred were hard pressed, fighting continuously against the pagan invaders, not knowing if they would survive from one day to another. So, they made a deal. If one of them should die, the other would take care of their family. Æthelwold, here, was but a babe in arms so he could not succeed his father and it was agreed that Alfred would take on the kingship if Ethelred should die before his son became a man. Soon after, King Ethelred was killed by the heathens, God rest his soul. Alfred became not only king but also guardian of his brother's family and steward of his estates.'

Æthelwold jumped up. 'And now that Uncle Alfred is dead, those estates should revert to me as the eldest surviving son. Except Edward convinced the Witan that my father intended to hand over his land to the future kings of Wessex forever, not just during King Alfred's lifetime. I don't even own the minster at Wimborne where my father is buried.'

I was surprised at the anger in his face. We had grown up together and I admired the gentle way he would detach himself from the bustle of the royal court whenever he could. Maybe it was the contrast with Edward's vulgar, aggressive habits, but I had always sought Æthelwold's company before my own brother's. We were close then; too close.

'What's to be done?' I asked.

Ealhswith put a hand on my arm. 'You need to work with Edward, help him to become a great king like his father. You could start by interceding with him on Æthelwold's behalf. Perhaps if you offer to foster Athelstan in Mercia, that might remove an embarrassment for him, and he might be better disposed towards Æthelwold's case.'

I studied my mother's wrinkled face. So that was her 'little plan'. Ealhswith had always worked behind the scenes to make good what she thought was wrong, and she obviously hadn't stopped. But the thought of working with a brother who had dared to strike me, sent shivers through my body. Edward would have to solve Wessex's problems for himself. I had come to Winchester not only as a daughter grieving the loss of my father, but also as the First Lady of Mercia on the death of our overlord. And taking on the new king's unwanted son and intervening in a Wessex land dispute might not best serve Mercian interests.

Besides I had a bigger problem of my own that I dared not let Edward find out about; not yet.

'No, I cannot work with Edward.' I stood to leave. 'You must sort out your own problems. I have enough of my own.'

At that moment, Athelstan rushed back into the room.

'M'lady Æthelflæd, there's trouble with one of your companions. Come quickly.'

TWO

Reluctantly, I put down my wine cup without taking a sip and followed Athelstan outside. Across the courtyard, I saw Æthelgifu looking flustered.

'What's the matter?' I called, running over to her.

'It's your companion, Beorhsige. He's in trouble,' she said.

'Where? What happened?'

'I was showing him to the stables in Market Street when it happened. Could a strong man come with me, please?' She smiled coyly at Æthelwold. There was something in her look that made me curious, but there was no time to speculate on that.

'Beorhsige's my ealdorman so I will come,' I said. 'Athelstan, wait with your grandmother. Æthelwold, come with us. Lead on, Æthelgifu.'

Æthelgifu took us quickly to a small gate, where a sentry opened a heavy wooden door that led into a side street. As I stepped outside, I felt small fingers touch my own and wrap themselves into my hand.

I frowned down at him. 'Athelstan, I told you to stay behind.'

'Can't I come, Aunt? It would be part of my tutoring to watch you,' the boy said.

'I am not tutoring you, nor taking you anywhere.'

He gazed up at me, his hand making a silent plea by tightening in mine. I could see his grandfather's resolution in those dark blue eyes, and I had no time to argue. 'Just this once. But stay close and don't say anything.'

It did not take long to locate the trouble. A crowd had gathered outside a large guesthouse, and we had to push our way through. A red-faced man lay on the ground tended by two women trying to stem the blood flowing from his nose. One guard held Beorhsige's arms behind his back whilst a second waved a long knife at his throat.

'Sheath that seax,' I snapped. 'This is my man. He will answer to me.'

The guard whirled around. 'And who would you be to order the King's Reeve?' he growled.

'If you do not know the sister of your king, the First Lady of Mercia, that makes you a badly informed reeve.'

The reeve lowered his weapon. 'Begging your pardon, m'lady, but this man has caused a disturbance by striking down the innkeeper, and the king has ordered us to come down hard on disturbances by anyone. I must take him away for the king's justice to be done.'

I might have known that Edward's insecurity was behind this. The king's justice, indeed.

'And how exactly do you intend to do this justice?' I asked.

'I am ordered to flog anyone caught brawling, no matter who,' the reeve said, throwing a cord to the guard who was struggling to keep hold of Beorhsige's arms.

'Does that include him?' I asked, indicating the man on the ground.

'He did not brawl, just got knocked down.' The reeve slipped the knife into his belt so he could help bind Beorhsige's hands.

'So, the king would have you punish the winners, yet not the losers. What is your account of this, Beorhsige? Did you have cause to hit this man?'

He was struggling to prevent the binding of his wrists and his words came in grunts. 'He insulted our ancestors, m'lady. Refused the coin I gave him. Said it was offal.' He managed to wrench his arms away from the guard and pushed away the reeve, to thrust a coin in the air so that I could see it.

I flinched. It was a Mercian coin with the head of King Offa on it. I would have struck the innkeeper myself for such an affront. I moved to stand between the reeve and Beorhsige. 'You are holding the wrong man. Arrest that one for insulting the royal family of Mercia.' I pointed to the man on the ground.

Æthelwold took advantage of the confusion to step into the fray, pushing away the guard to stand protectively with his back to Beorhsige.

Æthelgifu also ran forward, raising her hand with palm outstretched. 'I order you in the name of God to stop this fighting!'

The reeve looked confused and took a step back. 'It's my job to stop the fighting, Sister, not yours.' He reached for a horn at his belt which he put to his lips and blew three sharp blasts.

Æthelwold grabbed at Beorhsige's arm. 'Let's not wait for reinforcements.' He pulled the young warrior quickly through the crowd and together they ran off.

Æthelgifu shook her head at the reeve as she scurried after the two fugitives. 'You must learn to turn the other cheek.'

The reeve shouted orders at the guards who began to arrive, sending some in pursuit of the group disappearing along the street and others to attend to the injured man and the crowd around him. I was about to chastise him again but, feeling a small, warm hand in mine, I remembered I still had Athelstan by my side.

'Why did the man insult King Offa who died ages ago?' he asked.

I could not help smiling at his inquiring look and knelt closer to his ear to make myself heard above the buzz of the crowd.

'The people of Wessex hate to be reminded that they were once subservient to Mercia, that my mother's grandfather, King Offa was their overlord. Mercian power was felt throughout all of England from Northumbria to Kent in King Offa's time.'

'My father says he is going to take all of England back for the English,' Athelstan said, his eyes wide.

I smoothed his ruffled hair. 'For Wessex more like. Don't forget, the blood of the Mercian royal family is in you through your grandmother, and it comes from the great King Offa. He would have killed anyone who insulted his coinage, not just bloodied their face.' I nodded towards the innkeeper who was being helped to his feet, still clutching his injured nose.

Athelstan tightened his grip of my hand. 'Can you take me to see his dyke when I come to live with you? I hear it's as high as the Welsh mountains.'

I shook my head. 'Offa's Dyke is not quite that high although it was built to keep out the Welsh. And you're not coming to live with me. Don't believe everything your grandmother tells you.'

Athelstan dropped his head and said no more until we were back in the royal residences.

*

I was too exhausted from the journey and the traumas of my first day in Winchester to dine in the great hall. Besides, the thought of seeing Edward on the top table, enjoying the fawning attention of ealdormen and thegns keen to flatter their new king, made me retch. There was no news of Beorhsige and Æthelwold; probably drunk in some tavern on the outskirts of town where the king's guard did not dare to enter. I just hoped that Æthelgifu had returned safely to her nunnery. What had possessed her to run after those two, I could not imagine, but she had always been impulsive. I took my leave of Bishop Wærferth for the night and made him promise to make representations to the King for their exoneration and safe conduct home.

As I lay down to sleep, I little thought that a seemingly minor incident in Winchester's market street had set momentous events in motion.

*

I woke in the night from a dream. The theme was well known to me. I was suffering again from the agony of giving birth, although no dream could fully replicate the acute pain I had actually suffered. I had come very close to death the day I had pushed my daughter, Ælfwyn, from my womb. My husband had later confirmed to me that he had been told to expect the worst. In my dream, I relived that endless struggle to eject an infant from my body. Only this time, what finally emerged was a very large egg.

I woke, sweating and gasping for air. Relieved to find it had been a dream, I ordered a maid to warm water on the fire and I lay in a soothing bath, wondering at the meaning of my nightmare. I knew I could not possibly be with child. After that terrible labour, I had banished Æthelred from my bed for fear that I would die the next time I went into labour. To his credit, my husband had maintained a careful discretion over his use of concubines and whores in my place. His visits to them had diminished as he had aged and when he recently became ill, they seemed to have stopped altogether.

What was the meaning of the egg? I could not imagine. Maybe something new was about to hatch in my life.

I heard my mother stirring in the room next to mine, and soon Ealhswith stood at the door, clutching the small, leather-bound book that she always carried to prayers.

'A bath this early in the morning? You have learned some strange customs in Mercia,' she said, tidying the clothes that I had dropped on the floor.

'I was woken by a strange dream.'

'Tell me about it on the way to lauds. Be quick or we'll be late.'

Dressing hastily, I followed my mother out of the residence and across the field around the Minster. The sight of the old church's stone walls shimmering in the first light of day reminded me that I was in God's presence which helped calm my mind. I spoke to Ealhswith of the dream and the traumatic memory of childbirth that it had brought back to me.

She listened carefully and put an arm in mine. 'You have been brave and will need to be so again. That's the only message your dream is telling me. But let us contemplate on it during our prayers and the Good Lord may reveal his Truth.'

We hurried past the eastern end of the church towards the river until we reached a wooden chapel with a roof of fresh thatch. I admired the curved ending of the transept decorated with paintings of the saints and the golden cross above the ornate door to the nave. Although her nunnery was small, my mother had clearly not spared expense in building it.

'Soon, we will add some living quarters so I can live here with my fellow nuns,' she explained.

I blinked to see in the gloom when we entered. A sister was igniting the rush lights in iron holders on the wall, whilst other nuns knelt in the pews around the altar that was covered with a simple white cloth. Side by side, we joined them in prayer.

When the chanting had finished, Ealhswith beckoned me to follow her out of the rear door. She pointed at a newly dug pit surrounded by the beginnings of flint walls. 'This is where I will live. I shall finish my days here in quiet contemplation of the Holy Spirit.'

'It must be of great comfort to know your future with such certainty,' I said.

'The only certain thing in life is uncertainty. But I think I know what your dream was about,' Ealhswith said, resting on one of the walls.

'Do tell me.'

'It came to me during the psalm recital. An egg contains new life, a fledgling that will grow and learn to fly. So you will have such a fledgling in your life again.'

I was about to tell her the reasons why I was definitely not going to have any more children, but she continued.

'Except the egg was large, you said. So, it was in the likeness of a cuckoo's egg. It is someone else's chick that you will raise.'

Does her scheming never cease?

'No, Mother, Edward is not going to fledge his chick in my nest. He can find another unfortunate bird to do his work for him. I have enough mouths to feed, without his.'

I turned away so that she could not see the doubt in my face as I spoke. During prayers, I had experienced the very same premonition as my mother.

We were interrupted by shouts from across the field. Horsemen were riding out from the stables, seemingly in a great hurry as they spurred their mounts into a gallop towards the west gate.

There was a bustle of activity and an air of expectancy in the royal residence as we hurried back inside.

*

It was Bishop Wærferth who told us the news.

'Æthelwold has raised his banner over Wimborne Minster. He claims it is his family's ancient estate and should revert to him, not to the king. He is also claiming Christ Church for the same reason.' The bishop was clutching a large book adorned with a cross under his arm. 'He is appealing for other dispossessed landowners to join him.'

I gasped. 'He is rebelling against the king?'

'It would seem so, although the first reports are that only a small number have joined him, and they have barricaded themselves into Wimborne. The King has called the Wessex fyrd to arms and is preparing to march against him,' the bishop answered.

'He is raising an army against the threat of a few men?'

Wærferth could only shrug. Ealhswith's face had whitened, and she tugged at my arm.

'You must go and talk Æthelwold out of this nonsense. Edward will destroy him.'

'Mother, I hardly know Æthelwold anymore. Why would he listen to me? I cannot guarantee his safety. Only Edward can do that.'

'Then you must talk to Edward.' Ealhswith turned to Wærferth. 'Don't you agree, Bishop?'

The bishop studied his shoes for a moment. 'It will take a few days for the king to gather his army at Wimborne so there is time to intervene. Perhaps the church should mediate. Archbishop Plegmund has the ear of the king, I believe.'

I inwardly sighed with relief. 'Good idea. You know the archbishop, mother. Why don't you ask him?'

Ealhswith glared at me. 'No one listens to me anymore, but I will try.' She shuffled off towards her room.

I waited until mother was out of earshot. 'What news of Beorhsige or Æthelgifu,' I asked the bishop.

'None. They have not been seen in Winchester since…'

'Keep looking. I couldn't bear to think they are somehow involved with Æthelwold.'

'I will tell you as soon as I have news, m'lady.'

*

It took three more days to find Beorhsige and Æthelgifu.

I spent much of the first day in quiet contemplation and prayer with my mother. As the first Lady of Mercia, I had spent much of my time in either the frantic preparations for warfare or salvaging as much as I could from the aftermath. As a guest here in Wessex, I had little to do but wait and watch. The ealdormen and thegns went to join the army that the king was gathering in the southwest. The leading monks and churchmen packed their holy books and relics to follow and pray for a royal victory. A constant stream of servants and slaves drove packhorses and carts in pursuit of their noble masters.

The town rapidly emptied of virtually everyone I knew. Some wives and children remained in the royal palace, but most were strangers to me. I had not expected to feel quite so alone when I returned to my old home.

The town remained surprisingly busy considering so many of its menfolk had gone to war. When I did venture out, I noticed that the market still functioned and traders and farmers continued to arrive through the gates with wares to sell. The craftsmen on the alleyways that adjoined Market Street worked hard at their trades. But everyone returned my greetings with unknowing nods. It was not like the busy streets of Gloucester where everyone would greet me openly, bowing and waving as I passed. That was my home now, not here in the capital of Wessex where I was no longer recognised.

The next day, as I returned to my room after morning prayers, Athelstan was waiting expectantly, outside my door.

'Good morning, Athelstan. Is something the matter?'

'No, aunt, nothing wrong,' he said, shifting from one foot to the other.

'What then?'

'It's just that Æthelwold used to read with me each week on this day. Only he's not here.'

'So it seems. You'd best ask your tutor to read with you instead,' I said, about to walk past him.

'That's the Bishop Asser and he went back to his abbey at Sherborne when the king died.'

'I see. The bishop wrote a book about my father I believe?'

'Yes, m'lady. Asser himself read parts of it to me. It talks about your marriage to Æthelred of Mercia. It's very exciting.'

'I'm sure there are more exciting parts, but I am glad I am at least mentioned. There must be plenty of other monks to continue with your reading.'

'King Alfred wanted me to learn about everything. He said you were very good at learning. You could read when you were only seven, he said. Could you show me some new letters?'

I studied his plaintive smile, wondering if there was some guile behind his innocent look. It was as if he knew that I had always wanted a son. Not that I had wanted to please my husband with an heir. It would have been dangerous to establish a new dynasty in Mercia to challenge that of Wessex. No, I wanted a son for my own ambitions, someone I could mould in my own image so he would change the world in the way that I wanted. But Athelstan was the son of Edward. How could I shape him to my ways?

'I do find myself with less to do today. If you care to fetch something, we could read together. What do you have?'

'My favourite is the Shepherd's Book that King Alfred wrote.' He scampered off when I nodded, obviously delighted, and soon returned clutching a leather-bound manuscript.

I hardly needed to look at the neatly scribed letters. I knew the words almost by heart, but I used a pointer to show Athelstan which ones I was reading. My father had himself translated St Gregory's Pastoral Care, or Shepherd's Book as Athelstan had called it, into English and sent me a copy, just as he had to every ealdorman and bishop in Wessex. As I read, I could feel my father's presence, sitting with me as he had done when I was a child, patiently listening to my faltering reading.

I paused, suddenly struck by why Athelstan should own a book on how to govern the people, when he was still so young. 'You say my father gave you this?' I asked.

Athelstan looked up from studying the illustrated lettering.

'Yes. And a sword and a belt and a cloak.' He must have seen the disbelief in my face because he jumped up. 'Shall I fetch them?'

I nodded and once again he scampered away to his room. If the items were what I thought they were, it would be as if my father had left us a message before he died.

Athelstan returned wearing a faded scarlet cloak and a belt encrusted with tarnished jewellery. He held an old Saxon sword sheathed in a scabbard that he could scarcely carry. I recognised them immediately as the items given to Alfred when he was a boy of five. He had proudly shown them to me when I was a child, describing how he had travelled to Rome at his father's command where Pope Leo had received him and given him these traditional vestments of a Roman consul.

Athelstan was carrying the very same collection. It was a clear sign from Alfred that he expected this particular grandson to go on to do great things one day.

*

I was with Wærferth when a monk arrived with the news.

My mother had insisted that the bishop should bless the building of her nunnery with a visit and the three of us stood admiring the handiwork of the bricklayers as they busied about the walls. A brisk breeze made my hood fly from my head and, when I turned to adjust it, I saw the young man running from the Minster. I had a premonition that the news was not good and hurried with Wærferth to meet the messenger.

'The king sends word that Lord Beorhsige and Sister Æthelgifu are within Wimborne with the rebels under Lord Æthelwold,' the monk panted.

I had to strain to hear him in the wind. 'Where is King Edward?'

The monk looked at the wax tablet he carried to check his information. 'Badbury Rings, m'lady. The king asks you to come at once to his camp there.'

'Where is that?' asked the Bishop.

'It's an old hill fort that overlooks Wimborne. Edward must have picked the place to threaten Æthelwold and his band,' I said. 'I must go immediately if I am to rescue my ealdorman. Not to mention my sister and cousin.'

THREE

At daybreak, I rode away from the palace with three companions. Stars twinkled dimly in a clear sky, a sign that St. Christopher had listened to my prayers for a swift journey. It would be a cold but dry ride from Winchester to Badbury Rings.

Part of me eagerly anticipated the ride; I would be revisiting trails through open heathland where I had ridden often in my youth. But this journey was born of necessity, not pleasure. There would be no dawdling to enjoy the scenery, just a race to arrive in time to stop my impulsive brother from doing something stupid. Once we had clattered through the West Gate, I put my head low to the palfrey's neck and rode as fast as I dared along slippery, boggy tracks across the valley of the twin rivers that flowed into the sea at Southampton. My ancestors had defeated the Danes when they attacked that port many years before. Yet the pagans would return in their longships to wreak havoc on harbours such as this, if I could not reconcile the squabbling members of my family.

By midday, we had put the watery reaches at our backs and climbed to the drier region of the New Forest, where the Jutish people once lived. As the wooded valley gave way to more open scrubland, I called a halt to stretch aching limbs and rest the horses. The area had not changed since my childhood visits.

It used to be my favourite playground: the heathland, sparsely dotted with oaks, birches and beeches, was ideal for riding. The thin soil was not suited to tilling, so few villagers farmed the land but used it instead for grazing cattle and horses. I sheltered from the biting wind behind the thick trunk of an oak and stared into the distance.

I was close to the spot where the incident had happened – the incident that had ended my visits here.

How foolish I'd been! I was all of fourteen or fifteen years old and took my studies seriously, spending many hours reading and writing. But I loved riding even more. At every opportunity, I would saddle up and ride out with my friends from Winchester. When Edward was old enough, he insisted on joining me on his small pony and I soon became exasperated at his slow pace.

That had all changed when cousin Æthelwold had arrived at court to study under my tutors. He was born to ride. I remember gasping when I first watched him canter and gallop, his slim figure upright on his mount, his long blonde hair streaming in the wind. He performed manoeuvres the like of which I'd never seen before, ducking under the lowest branches, splashing though the deepest rivers, always with a smile and a flourish. His friends called him brave; I thought him foolhardy, but I fell under his spell even so.

We were soon spending all our spare time riding together. The image of his handsome, delicate features invaded my thoughts by day and my dreams at night. I found myself thinking less about the scriptures and more about my dashing cousin. That did not please my tutors. Nor did it please Edward who was used to having the sole attention of his elder sister and he would go into fits if I told him to ride with boys of his own age.

On that fateful day, I had plucked up the courage to tell Edward that he could not come with me. I said that I intended to visit a place infested with vipers. It was not a complete lie as I had seen one on a previous visit. For some reason, Edward was terrified of snakes, and he had complained loudly in his whining voice that we should ride somewhere else, or he would tell father. I ignored him and left early, before he had finished his work in the scriptorium. On our way to the New Forest, Æthelwold was the ideal companion, telling me all sorts of yarns and riddles and laughing in his infectious way.

Quite suddenly, a mist had blown in and become steadily thicker. Our mood changed abruptly with the weather, and we began blundering through boggy streams and thickets in the fog. Æthelwold did not seem too concerned at first, but even he had to finally admit that we were lost.

'We'll just have to sleep here until the morning,' he announced calmly.

I was far from calm. We had no provisions or tents. My parents would be furious and my little brother insufferable when we finally returned home.

These turned out to be the least of my worries.

With my help, Æthelwold had managed to light a fire and erect a flimsy shelter from brushwood and leaves. When he began spreading his cloak to make bedding for the night, it struck me that I would be sharing the bower with him.

The thought excited and worried me in equal measure. We often slept together as a family in tents when we followed father on his tours of the kingdom, so I knew it was customary to snuggle together to keep warm. At first, I lay on my back at Æthelwold's side but when I felt cold drizzle on my face I turned away and tried to sleep. But sleep was hard to come by. Acutely aware of his every twitch and turn, I felt him move closer and brush a leg against mine. A tremor of excitement – or maybe panic – ran through my body. I squeezed my eyes shut and prayed to the Virgin Mary for guidance.

Was he awake? What was he thinking? His breathing had slowed to a steady rhythm, and I could no longer bear the suspense. Gradually, I turned over to face him. I could hardly make out his face, so I propped myself up on one elbow and moved my head closer to his, irresistibly drawn towards his full lips. I was at the point of touching them with my own when a wisp of my hair fell onto his nose. His eyes flickered open and he sneezed abruptly. I felt warm snot on my cheek and recoiled, turning quickly away to feign sleep. I thanked the Holy Virgin for leading me from temptation and did not dare to stir again until morning.

When I woke, the light had returned and Æthelwold looked at me curiously as we prepared to leave, but said nothing. On the ride home, he was strangely silent.

When we finally made it back to Winchester, my irate father had begun in earnest to find me a husband. From thence forth, Edward insisted on always riding with me, 'in case you get lost', as he'd sneered.

Fifteen years later, I was once again facing the prospect of a night on the heathland. Darkness would come early on this winter's day and we would not get to Badbury before sundown. At least this time I had come prepared. I had my own tent.

*

My destination lay on the other side of Wimborne, the walled town that Æthelwold had seized as his birth right, against the king's wishes. As we skirted to the north of the town, I could see Badbury Rings rising up from the surrounding pastures, and immediately I understood why Edward had chosen it as the base for his army. In ancient times, the Celtish people had thrown up three concentric rings of earthworks to make a hillfort. The fortifications had stopped neither the Romans nor the Saxons from overcoming those who were encamped there. But to Æthelwold and his rebels in the town below, the sight of the waving flags and smoking fires of an army protected by those huge mounds must have looked very threatening indeed. It would take a large force prepared to accept heavy losses to attack Badbury Rings, and Æthelwold did not have that luxury. He was trapped behind the barricaded gates and walls that we studied from a distance as we rode past the town.

Soon, I noticed horsemen racing towards me, bearing the banner of Wessex. They were Edward's scouts who greeted me civilly and lead me towards the entrance between the first of the circular banks of earth that wrapped around the hill. The area bristled with warriors, some standing alert watching the trails, others pacing along the top of the mounds. Continuing to climb, we passed through the second and third lines of earthworks and up to the flattened top of the hill. I took a sharp intake of breath when I saw the orderly ranks of tents and fires crammed into the large circle protected by the embankments. It was not the camp of a warband but the base of an entire army. Edward was making a show of force to impress Æthelwold and anyone else that presumed to challenge his right to be king. I could not help but admire my brother for his decisiveness, but his overreaction to a minor protest risked inflaming the situation into a major revolt. Saxons could end up fighting Saxons whilst the Danes looked on and laughed.

Edward stood on top of the highest mound, gesticulating to a group of thegns. I knew he would have seen me approach from his viewpoint, but he ignored me for a while, continuing his conversation, or rather his tirade judging by the tone of his voice.

I slid from the saddle, rubbing the blood back into my aching bottom. 'Are you expecting a foreign invasion, brother, that you have gathered such a force?' I had to shout to make myself heard.

Edward swivelled round and glowered. 'Maybe. An ealdorman from Mercia is amongst the rebels and his lord, your husband, has yet to kneel before me.'

'When I last saw my husband, he could not have walked up this hill. Æthelred is sick, not seditious.'

'So why is one of your companions behind those walls, defying Wessex?' Edward wagged his finger towards Wimborne in the distance.

I looked down to hide my embarrassment. 'Beorhsige can be a hot-headed lad. Probably still recovering from being wrongly arrested by your over-enthusiastic reeve. But a valuable warrior nonetheless. I will go and speak with him.'

For some reason, Edward found that funny and laughed. 'This is not a game for girls. Men speak through their actions. By taking part of my estate, Æthelwold has said that he does not accept my kingship. Your ealdorman has joined him in rebellion. Tomorrow I will reply by battering down their barricade. What I want to know from you is how many more of your Mercian warriors will be joining them?'

As I feared, the situation was about to get out of hand. In my heart, I knew this was all a stupid misunderstanding. Yet it could easily escalate if my ealdorman was harmed in any encounter. With my husband so weak, it could easily lead to wider disaffection amongst other Mercian lords who resented being under the Wessex yoke.

I tried to deflect his question. 'And what I want to know from you is what our sister, Æthelgifu, is doing with them. Are you expecting more nuns to join the rebellion?'

Edward looked at me blankly. He never did have any humour.

'We need to get her out of there,' I said. 'At least, let me negotiate her release before you attack.'

'And exactly how do you intend to do that? Æthelwold has said that if he cannot live there, he will die there. Hardly a sign that he will negotiate. Perhaps you can fly over the walls like an angel of mercy,' Edward scoffed.

I looked towards Wimborne, wondering if Æthelwold was looking back to where I stood. 'He will listen to me.'

'Oh, sorry, I had forgotten he was a suitor of yours.' Edward curled his lip into a sneer.

'He was not, but he will listen. And our mother will never forgive us if we do not try to save Æthelgifu.'

Edward had always shown affection towards his mother. I had been saving this throw of the dice till last, and it proved a good one.

After some more haggling, he agreed that I should go to Wimborne that afternoon under a flag of truce.

*

Flying a white banner, I rode towards the town with an escort of four thegns. I halted before the barred gates where a line of sharpened stakes bristled at me like a hedgehog.

I looked sternly up at the figures crouching behind the palisade. 'I, Æthelflæd, daughter of King Alfred of Wessex, call upon Æthelwold, son of Ethelred, King of Wessex, to talk with me.'

My voice reverberated in the frosty air but was answered only by grunts and scuffling.

I could imagine Æthelwold on the other side of the gates, trying to make up his mind if this was one of Edward's tricks. My horse pawed the hard ground and I pulled my cloak tightly around me, wishing he had not chosen winter to make his stand. They probably had little food behind the walls. It must have all been a reckless impulse.

I frowned at the delay. What was taking him so long? Surely he knew I would never betray him.

A helmeted head appeared above the wall. 'The Lady Æthelflæd may enter. Alone.'

My companion thegn turned anxiously towards me, putting out a restraining arm, but I ignored him. 'Does the Lord Æthelwold guarantee my safe return?'

The head disappeared and, after more shuffling and mumbling behind the rampart, reappeared. 'Yes, providing you enter alone and unarmed.'

I shook my head as I unbuckled my belt. *They should fear the force of my tongue not my sword.*

As the gates inched open, I dismounted, gave my horse's halter to one of my thegns, and walked through the gatehouse and into a street on the other side. When I looked up and saw the dishevelled bunch of fighters manning the walls, I almost cried. They were dressed more like farmers than warriors and carried an assortment of weapons including scythes and hayforks. What had Æthelwold done? When Edward's troops beat down the gates in the morning, these young men would die for nothing.

Æthelwold stood watching me from a distance, no longer smiling as he once did whenever he caught sight of me. We locked eyes and I saw only desperation and fear where once had been fun and bravado.

'Follow me,' was all he said before he strode through narrow streets lined with the tall houses of the abbey of Cuthburga that sprawled through the centre of the town. He did not stop until he had reached the stone tower of the church that overshadowed the monastic settlement.

Pushing open the door, he stepped inside but did not turn to face me until he had reached the font, tapping his hand fretfully on the marble stone.

'Why have you come?'

'To stop a massacre.' My voice echoed around the high vaulted ceiling of the empty knave.

He snorted. 'So Edward sent you.'

'No, I have come to save you from becoming his sacrificial lamb. Edward would like nothing more than to start his reign with an easy slaughter that demonstrates that he will not tolerate any disobedience.'

'Then spare your words. I have already told Edward that, if I cannot live here, I will die here. This is my family estate. My father is buried right there.' He pointed to an engraved tombstone in the wall of the nave. 'I will give up my life before I give up my birthright.'

I loosened the golden neck-fastening of my cloak. 'Very noble. What of your men? Will those lads on the ramparts also have to sacrifice their lives for your birthright? What of my ealdorman, Beorhsige? What of my sister, Æthelgifu? Are they to be sacrificed because of your loss of land?'

He flinched. 'I expected you to understand…'

That angered me. 'Oh, I understand alright. You want your land back. You've made your point. Never mind that your beloved father died fighting against the Danes who will be the only winners from your rebellion. Never mind that Saxon mothers will soon be mourning their sons. Never mind that you have encouraged my ealdorman to break his oath. Never mind that my sister…' I paused, breathing hard. 'Where is Æthelgifu?'

He stared blankly ahead. 'In the monastery.'

'She must not be part of your noble sacrifice. Bring her here.'

Æthelwold closed his eyes and breathed out noisily, before walking to the door and shouting orders to a guard.

I followed close behind, knowing that I had shaken him. 'And Beorhsige? Where is he?'

'Gone.'

'Gone where?'

'Just gone.' He rounded on me. 'Look I did not plan it to be like…'

'You did not plan it at all, did you?' As a young man, he had lived spontaneously, moment to moment, and he obviously had not changed as an adult.

He shrugged. 'I expected more to come when I raised my banner. Your brother was not exactly a popular choice as king. But several of my so-called friends have broken their promises to me. So I will die here. Alone.'

'Then ask Edward for mercy, you oaf! He may be a brute but, if you surrender, he won't kill his own cousin in cold blood.'

'Maybe not, but how could I live with myself? I would be letting my father down.' He nodded towards King Ethelred's tombstone. 'Beorhsige got away before the main army arrived. Don't be hard on him. He was drunk when he decided to come with me and regretted it when he sobered up.'

I sighed. 'And Æthelgifu? How did she get mixed up in all this?'

He looked out of the door towards the nunnery. 'Ah, you didn't hear about us?'

'Hear what?' I followed his gaze and saw a woman making her way out of the monastery towards the church. She looked like my sister, but she was wearing a colourful flowing robe, not a nun's habit.

I stared at her in disbelief whilst Æthelwold spoke. 'When you were taken away to marry in Mercia, it left quite a hole in my life. Fortunately, Æthelgifu was old enough to ride by then, so…' The woman, who I could now clearly recognise as my sister, waved happily as she approached and Æthelwold half-heartedly returned her greeting. 'So we became companions, close friends, as you and I once were.' He turned to look at me. 'Only more so. Too close for your father. He sent Æthelgifu to a nunnery.'

I stepped out of the shadow of the church door and Æthelgifu started when she saw me. 'Æthelflæd! What are you doing here?'

'Trying to understand why a nun should dress in gaudy clothing,' I replied sourly.

Æthelgifu smiled sweetly at Æthelwold. 'Haven't you told her we are to wed, dear?'

He reddened and looked at his shoes. 'That's something we need to talk about. It seems that Edward is determined to… well that is, he will not accept my demands and when he brings his army here tomorrow, he will overwhelm us with numbers. You would be safer back in your nunnery.'

Æthelgifu's jaw dropped and she stared at him, then at me. 'Is this your doing, sister?'

I could see tears forming in her eyes. 'I am just the messenger, but hopefully one who can save your life.'

Æthelgifu buried her face in her hands, sobbing.

Æthelwold put an arm around her. 'It seems that the good Lord has not smiled on our union. You must go with your sister.'

She clung even more tightly to him. 'What will you do?'

'I will await my fate here. When Edward comes, I will ask him to be merciful to my men and to honour my family legacy in the name of his own father who always promised this estate to me.'

*

As the sun was setting, I walked back through the gate of Wimborne, arm in arm with my sister. Æthelgifu had donned her black nun's tunic and cloak once more, the veil pulled well forward to hide her puffy eyes. With the help of one of the thegns who had been patiently waiting outside the walls, she mounted up behind me. For some reason, Æthelwold had insisted she leave her own horse behind.

As we rode slowly towards Badbury Rings, I half turned my head so she could hear me above the wind that was rustling the trees. 'When did you two first think of marrying?'

I felt Æthelgifu tighten her arms around my waist as she leaned forward. 'Many years ago, when we were young, we used to ride together. Before I was sent to the nunnery.'

'I rode with him too but we never discussed marriage. Not between cousins.' I was suddenly taken back to that night on the heathland when Æthelwold and I had clung together for warmth and we'd been a heartbeat away from touching lips. 'Did he ever kiss you?'

'Of course he did. Other things too.' Æthelgifu giggled, and quickly added, 'but I was still a virgin when I took my vows.'

I felt my face redden. *Why did he kiss her but not me?*

I banished the thought with a shake of my head. 'You must say nothing of this to Edward. It will only harm Æthelwold's cause. And your own.'

I reined in my horse as the guards halted us at the entrance to the hilltop fort. After inspecting the newcomer behind me, they waved us through.

*

Edward was waiting for us on top of the hill, a banner embroidered with the half-dragon, half reptile wyvern of Wessex fluttering above his head. 'How sweet, my two sisters reunited,' he said. 'Come in and tell me of your adventures.'

He ushered us into a colourful pavilion where he offered us a bench to sit and mead to drink. 'What news of our cousin? Is he to join us for supper?'

I put a hand on Æthelgifu's arm to remind her of our agreement of who would do the talking. 'Like all our family, he is a proud man and does not surrender lightly. He is still aggrieved at losing the lands owned by his forefathers. But he will, I'm sure, ask for the king's mercy when you meet tomorrow.'

'You have arranged for us to meet?' Edward leaned forward, stroking his trim beard.

I swallowed hard. 'Yes, he will be there in the town with only a handful of soldiers, well more like farmers than soldiers. They don't intend to fight, I'm sure.'

'So why haven't they surrendered?'

'As I said, he is a proud man.'

'Please be merciful like the Lord Jesus taught us,' Æthelgifu blurted out, almost in tears.

Edward studied her face as she wiped at her eyes. 'You want me to be merciful to a man who abducted you, a nun, against your will? Did he or any of his men violate you?'

Æthelgifu's eyes widened. 'Oh no. He was a most… a…' She stopped as I squeezed her hand hard.

'What my sister is trying to explain is that Æthelwold did not harm her in any way. She was just a symbolic hostage. Our cousin did all this in a fit of resentment and now regrets it all.'

'And your ealdorman? Has he surrendered?'

'Beorhsige? It was all a drunken prank to him. When he sobered up, he slipped away in shame. He's probably back in Mercia by now begging forgiveness from Lord Æthelred.'

Edward went to a table and picked up a scrolled document which he waved at me. 'I have been reminding myself of the laws of our land. If he has broken the laws of Wessex, he should be punished here, not in Mercia.'

'I fear that killings and punishments of Saxons by Saxons, whatever their allegiance, will only serve to weaken us and strengthen our real enemies.' I stood and moved closer to him, lowering my voice whilst Æthelgifu snivelled on the bench. 'But there is a way we could use these incidents to unite us rather than divide us.'

'If that traitor Æthelwold has sent you to plead his cause, forget it. The estates he claims rightly belong to the kings of Wessex. Besides, I have already promised most of the land to some of his friends who might have been tempted to join him.'

So that was why so few had joined Æthelwold. My brother was more cunning than I had realised.

'I wouldn't presume to suggest how you administer your land. But I do believe we owe it to our parents to carry on their great work. To do that, we have to draw our family closer together. If we fall out amongst ourselves, we will fail.' I put my arm around Æthelgifu and sat next to her.

Edward looked puzzled. 'What exactly are you suggesting?'

'As I said, we need to keep our family together. So you have to forgive cousin Æthelwold. Make him your ally, take him into your household, reward him when he shows loyalty. Maybe give him back a small piece of his family's old land.'

Edward raised his eyebrows and shook his head. I had no choice but to offer him something more.

'Your son, Athelstan, also seems neglected and in danger of becoming prey to court intrigue. We should protect him from those who would plot against you. Maybe I should take him with me to Mercia for a while?'

A grin played briefly on Edward's lips. 'He's young to leave home.'

'He is old for his age, and his grandfather favoured him.' I did not want to mention Edward's new wife, the real reason why Athelstan had to leave Winchester. She was rumoured to be with child and anxious to see the back of her step-son.

Edward stared at me, unblinking, for several heartbeats. 'And you, sister, how will we keep you and your lord in our family?'

I feigned a smile. 'Why, by leaving us to rule in Mercia. Under your protection, of course.'

'Of course.'

*

Later that evening, I lay in my red calfskin tent staring at the pole above my head. I had hoped to fall asleep before the noise from the celebrating warriors became too loud. But Æthelgifu's gentle snoring had kept me awake and now the festivities were in full swing. Edward had decided to indulge his warriors before they marched on Wimborne in the knowledge that there would be no battle, so they were celebrating tonight. If all went to plan, the men of the fyrd would be free to ride back to their homesteads by tomorrow afternoon. Relief and concern flooded my mind in equal measure. I had rescued my sister, and my ealdorman was hopefully safely back home. I was certain Æthelwold would submit easily tomorrow and be taken back into the king's fold.

On the other hand, I would be returning home with someone else's child to look after. Ever since mother had suggested it, I had resisted taking on the needy son of my brother. Why should I pick up the pieces from Edward's womanising ways? Would I be expected to take on more of his children if he threw out their mother? Nor was I sure how my husband, Æthelred, would take to having a Wessex pup in his household. When I had renounced the nuptial bed, he had remonstrated that he wanted a son and that it was unnatural for a wife to desert her husband at night. Remembering our arguments about that, I chuckled to myself. I had used the example of the very same Cuthburga who had given her name to the church and monastery of Wimborne to justify my decision. Cuthburga was a Wessex princess who like me had been sent to another kingdom to marry its king. She had refused to have any intercourse with him and remained a virgin until the king's death when she achieved her wish in life and become the abbess of Wimborne. I had not gone to such lengths, but how strange that, in Cuthburga's very church, I had first thought of my plan to foster a child in order to achieve my ends. Æthelwold was too proud to surrender, but Edward had promised not to harm him once he saw that he could please his wife by removing his unwanted son.

I fell asleep, believing I had achieved something, at a price.

In the morning, I found that I had been deceived.

*

Edward ordered me to stay in the camp while he led his men to the gates of Wimborne. I was glad of the opportunity to wash and dress without the prying eyes of his army around me. Most of the guards he had left behind were happily playing dice, until one shouted and pointed towards a group of riders who were racing back to the camp.

Something was wrong.

I watched with mounting anxiety as they continued up through the earthworks and sought out my distinctive red tent.

The lead rider dismounted and ran towards me. 'The king requires your presence immediately in Wimborne, m'lady.'

'Why, whatever is wrong?' I asked.

'I'm not rightly sure, m'lady. The town was undefended when we entered.'

'Did Lord Æthelwold refuse to surrender?'

'No, m'lady. He was not there.'

FOUR

Once again, I was shifting uncomfortably in the saddle, my behind aching from a long mid-winter journey. Yet after the ordeals I had endured in Wessex, I felt greatly relieved to be returning to Mercia.

Despite the continued absence of Beorhsige, my entourage had grown from the small and lightly laden band that I had originally taken to Winchester. Packhorses struggled along the slippery trails under the weight of a host of treasures purchased by Bishop Wærferth including sumptuous copies of the Gospels and a tooth of St Alkmund and a hair of St Oswald, both safely locked in carved reliquaries. As agreed with Edward, Athelstan travelled with me guarded by a cohort of thegns, although I suspected that they also had instructions to report back to the king on what they found in Mercia. What little trust there had been between my brother and I had been shattered by Æthelwold's escape.

Edward maintained it was my fault, of course. If I had not assured him that Æthelwold was going to surrender, he would not have stood his guards down around Wimborne and brought forward the celebration for his men. How foolish he had looked when his warriors pushed at the gates of the town to find they swung open freely because there was no one to defend them. The place was deserted apart from terrified nuns and tradesmen. The king had sent scouts in all directions to find the fugitives, but they only found two farm lads who had got lost in the dark.

It made me blush to think of Edward's raving over my alleged part in Æthelwold's deception. My concession to foster his son in my own court troubled me more than ever. Whenever I looked at Athelstan sitting on his pony beside me, I was immediately taken back to the irritating outings I had endured as a young girl with my little brother dragging along behind me when all I wanted to do was to canter off with my friends. Maybe that was why I had not warmed to the lad. He was a constant reminder of his whining, self-centred father. Yet his politeness and calm temperament could not have been more different to Edward's behaviour at his age.

Athelstan smiled when he saw me looking at him and he steered his mount closer to me.

'I was wondering, m'lady, about Aunt Æthelgifu's mare,' he said, in his thoughtful way.

'Whatever for?'

'I was wondering why she left it behind in Wimborne.'

I was mystified. 'How did you know that?'

'She told me when I saw her in the stables, choosing another horse. She said she loved Saviour dearly.'

'Saviour? Who's Saviour?'

'Her mare. Why would she leave her behind if she loved her so?' Athelstan piped, his voice disarmingly child-like.

I studied him carefully. His question seemed innocent enough, yet it was one that had troubled me. It was Æthelwold who had refused to let Æthelgifu take her horse from Wimborne. In hindsight, I should have recognised that as a sign that he was planning to flee, not surrender. Otherwise why would he have needed an extra horse? But Athelstan could not have worked that out, could he? Maybe an old head was sitting on those young shoulders.

'We had to leave quickly so it was easier for Æthelgifu to share my saddle,' was all I could think of saying. Once in Gloucester, I would make sure that Athelstan got the education his bright mind merited.

When we did finally arrive in Mercia, my thoughts were rapidly diverted away from the new youngster in my household and towards the older male at its head.

*

I suspected something was amiss when Ælfwyn and Cenwulf came to greet me outside the walls of Gloucester. Ælfwyn, my daughter, fruit of the labour that had almost killed me, looked older in the saddle than her thirteen years. Her straight back and noble face already gave her the bearing of a lady and the golden ornaments at her neck and waist reinforced the impression of a mature woman. Beside her, Cenwulf looked wizened, his shoulders stooped and his beard flecked with white. He was my mother's brother, ealdorman of the Mercians and the man whom I respected above all others in my adopted home. They remained tight-lipped as we drew near.

'Uncle Cenwulf, Ælfwyn, how good of you to meet me. What...' I began.

'A word in private please, mother. Before you enter the town.' Ælfwyn glanced towards the riders struggling up the hill behind me.

I held up my hand to halt my followers and rode forward to join my daughter and uncle. 'Whatever's the matter?'

They had both dismounted and waited for me to slide from my horse.

'It's father. He's ill,' Ælfwyn said.

'He was ill when I left which is why he didn't...'

'No, this is not the fever. The physician says it's the palsy.'

The word hit me like a hammer. I had seen old folk half-paralysed or dribbling and trembling uncontrollably with the palsy. I embraced Ælfwyn to hide my tears.

'Are you sure? What happened?'

She held me tightly and spoke quietly in my ear. 'The elves attacked him in bed and he woke in the morning with a useless arm. The healers mixed crushed coriander with woman's milk and poured it into his ear. But he has not improved. His speech is weak and he cannot hold anything in his right hand.' She sounded matter-of-fact, as she generally did.

I felt the blood drain from my face. 'How long...?'

'Soon after you left,' Ælfwyn replied. 'We sent a rider but they couldn't find you in the storms.'

I tried to recover my composure and looked towards Cenwulf. 'Who else knows of this?'

'No one, yet,' the old warrior said, watching my followers who were all waiting patiently, looking expectantly in our direction. 'There's unrest enough with the death of the king, without giving cause for more.'

I nodded. 'I will inform no-one but Bishop Wærferth. We will need the prayers of the Church.'

I shuddered to think what Edward would do when he heard that Æthelred was really sick.

*

I tried to look calm and unhurried when I dismounted before the royal residences in Gloucester, gently thanking my horse for carrying me safely home as I handed her over to a stable lad. A gaggle of servants and thegns came to welcome me, no doubt hoping for snippets of news, as I strode into the long feasting hall. This is where I would normally come to meet my lord after an absence and, although I realised that I would not find Æthelred there, I did not want to do anything unusual. I turned down an offer of hot broth from the cook by the fire and made my way to our private quarters as calmly as I could. The guards stood aside as I swept through the door.

Even though I was half prepared for what I saw, it still came as a shock. The Lord of the Mercians was slumped in a high-backed chair, his head lolling on his chest.

Is my big bear really so ill?

He was always so brutishly healthy, his huge presence dominating every room that he entered. But seeing the grey pallor of his skin, the drool around his beard, and the arm that hung limply at the side of his barrel-shaped chest, I knew that he was not just sick, but seriously ill. Shooing away the girl who was hovering beside him, I knelt to dab at his brow with a cloth. When he didn't stir, I closed my eyes in prayer, begging every saint I could think of to help my husband overcome the evil spirits that had possessed his body. Just as I was beseeching St. Cuthbert, I heard a whisper.

'Is that you?'

I was used to his hearty bellowing so I hardly recognised the faint voice.

'Yes dear, it's me. I'm back.'

'Good.' His eyes glimmered but his lips hardly moved. 'You been far?' He was straining hard to make an audible sound.

What's going on in that hairy head?

'I've been to Winchester, to my father's funeral.'

He furrowed his brow, as if straining to drag back memories that were just out of reach. He had never been the sharpest thinker, preferring action to contemplation. Yet he would never have forgotten the death of the king he admired so much.

'Course you have. I'm not myself since I woke with this arm all numb.' He used his left arm to drag the right one across his body. 'Not much good for a shield wall, is it?'

I could hardly stop the tears at seeing my giant of a husband so weakened. I kissed him on the cheek and hugged him as hard as I could without crushing his limp arm.

Childhood memories of my father, doubled over in pain, flooded into my head. King Alfred's torment had occurred regularly, debilitating him for days on end. It was punishment, he said, for impure thoughts and deeds in his youth. But it also went away, leaving him untroubled for long periods. The palsy was different. It rarely disappeared.

'I will pray for you,' I whispered, running my fingers through his thick beard.

He nodded and stretched his lips into a faint smile.

I called to the guard. 'Fetch Lord Cenwulf, Lady Ælfwyn and Bishop Wærferth.'

It did not take long before they hurried into the room.

'My lord is much changed,' I said as calmly as I could. 'What do the healers say?'

Ælfwyn raised her eyebrows and glanced meaningfully towards her father. She obviously did not want to discuss his condition in front of him.

'I think we all need to know the truth,' I said. 'And that includes Lord Æthelred.'

Cenwulf nodded. 'They say that he may improve, but slowly. He may be like this for some time.'

'And what is the custom in Mercia when the lord is like this?'

Cenwulf shrugged. 'There is no custom. In the days when we had a king, the Witan would pick someone to take over whilst he was disabled. Now that we are under the King of Wessex, I suppose we should ask Lord Edward, if he is to be the next…'

I held up my hand. 'No! Edward is already king and waiting for just such an excuse to take direct control of Mercia. And he has added reason to doubt our loyalty.'

I hesitated, realising that I should not say too much in front of Æthelred. He had fought alongside Edward and had considerable respect for him. I gently put an arm on his shoulder and looked into his staring eyes.

'You are still strong enough to rule if I help you, aren't you dear? And Cenwulf here can take over military matters for a while, don't you think? The Bishop will advise me on administrative matters. King Edward will have many more important matters to concern him, so we will manage without bothering him, won't we?'

Æthelred nodded and whispered something that sounded like yes.

I stood back and smiled. 'There, you were all witness to that. Tell the Witan that their lord is indisposed but they can refer matters to me until he improves.'

'Stay with your father a while, will you?' I asked Ælfwyn, as I followed Cenwulf and Wærferth from the room.

Once outside, I spoke to Cenwulf in a low voice. 'Have you any news of Lord Beornoth's family?'

The ealdorman looked puzzled. 'Why no. Beornoth will be at the family estate, I believe, and his son, Beorhsige, was with you, wasn't he?'

'He was.' I quickly told Cenwulf the story of Æthelwold's revolt and Beorhsige's part in it. 'Can you see why we can't tell Edward of Æthelred's illness if Beorhsige is with the rebels? If my brother thought Æthelred was not strong enough to keep Mercia loyal, he would bring his army here immediately.'

'Surely he would trust his sister,' he protested.

'Right now, his sister is the last person he would trust,' I said quietly. 'And the feeling is mutual.'

I went back into the room where Ælfwyn was dutifully wiping her father's face. I watched, wondering how much was going on inside his head as he stared vacantly whilst she cleaned his beard.

'I brought you a present from Winchester,' I said to Ælfwyn.

Her face brightened. 'Thank you, mother. What is it?'

'He's a new playmate.' I tried not to chuckle at her hopeful expression. Being the daughter of Mercian royalty restricted her freedom and she had few friends.

'Who is he, mother?'

'Mmm, let me give you a clue. Try this. His grandfather fought the Danes and his father fought his mother, dismissing her from his bed and inviting in another.'

Ælfwyn winced. 'You and your rhyming riddles. Just tell me who he is.'

'At least have a guess.' I concentrated hard and continued. 'His name rhymes with 'man', yet he is but a boy. He could be our next king, so don't treat him like a toy.'

Ælfwyn sighed impatiently. 'I have no idea. I give up.'

'He is Athelstan, your cousin from Winchester. Let's hope his stay with us is not too sinister.'

I was so pleased with my rhyming that I burst out laughing. Æthelred let out a shrill wheeze, rocking forward in his chair. We both span around and joined his merriment, giggling and clapping our hands, delighted to see him so amused.

*

That evening, I knelt in the small chapel near the feasting hall for longer than usual. My guardians on earth seemed to be deserting me so I needed my Protector in Heaven more than ever. I had so many requests and questions that my bony knees were aching by the time I stood to leave. Not that I ever found decision-making difficult. On the contrary, my mind was usually made up long before most people even knew there was a decision to be made. But today, for the first time in my life, it was my judgement that would count. It was the turn of the Lady of the Mercians to have the final say. I had learned a lot from many years of watching men doing things not quite right, but I still needed God's guidance.

When I woke the next morning, my head was buzzing with ideas. As I washed and pulled on my clothes, my thoughts gradually clarified. By the time I had finished a meagre breakfast of bread and cheese, I had ordered my thoughts into plans. I knew what had to be done.

I sent servants scurrying around the royal residences to find the people I needed. Not wishing to disturb Æthelred who was still resting in our chamber, nor have my meetings in the main hall that was too public, I requisitioned a simple hut that was normally used for storage. I had it emptied and a trestle table installed.

The first to arrive was Cenwulf, whose gait was stiff, his face pained as he hobbled in.

'My lord, are you not well?' I asked.

'My old bones take a while to wake. I will be fine shortly,' he said, easing himself into a chair opposite me at the table.

I got straight to the point. 'What are the men of our army doing at present?'

Cenwulf looked taken aback. 'It's winter. The men of the fyrds are home with their families. Lord Æthelred's thegns are about the hall, practicing for battle, mending weapons, I shouldn't doubt. Collecting taxes when the weather permits.'

'Good, I have more useful labour to keep them occupied. A hundred or so strong men, wouldn't you say? Enough to start rebuilding Gloucester.'

'Rebuilding? Thegns aren't stonemasons or carpenters. We've already moved the walls to the line of the river and we've put in strong gates facing every direction.'

'True, but we have done little to improve what lies inside the walls. The streets are still full of rubble and waste. You cannot walk from one gate to another without clambering over crumbling buildings and dung heaps. No wonder no one is keen to live here. It is not at all like Winchester,' I said.

'No, but the Danes did not camp in Winchester, as they did here. They just sailed up the Severn and walked in. They couldn't do that today,' he said.

'But that was years ago. We have to clear up the mess. So I would like you to ask our warriors to use their muscle to remove the clutter. We need to make space for new streets where merchants can trade and artisans can work.'

At that moment, Bishop Wærferth was shown in, puffing and flustered.

'M'lady, I trust all is well?'

'I have called you and Lord Cenwulf here to help me.'

'What's to be done?'

'What's to be done is the reconstruction of our towns and the building of new ones.'

The Bishop gave Cenwulf a puzzled look. 'Reconstruction and building? Surely it is for the Witan to…?'

'The Witan decided some years ago to erect strongholds across our lands to defend us against the pagans, to build burhs that would protect the local people, just as my father did in Wessex. But all we have done is to strengthen Gloucester and Worcester. Where are the new burhs?'

Bishop Waerferth blanched. 'But these are military matters that should not concern …'

'Military matters concern us all, Bishop. The pagans do not just kill our soldiers.'

Wærferth dragged over a chair, realising that this was not going to be the quick meeting he may have hoped for. I had to raise my voice above the scraping on the wooden floor as he made himself comfortable.

'Our people live in defenceless homesteads scattered around the countryside, easy prey to long ships raiding up the rivers or warbands crossing the border.' I stood to contain my agitation by pacing about the room. 'Yet we know how to protect them. We build strongholds at regular intervals so that they can flee inside when the raiders are sighted. And if they take their livestock with them, the heathens have nothing to eat and soon go away.'

'We've made a start,' muttered Cenwulf.

'A start? Where?'

'Oxford, Cricklade.'

'Just two burhs on the Thames, close to Wessex and built at King Alfred's insistence, as I recall. What about further north?'

Cenwulf and Wærferth looked at each other. The Bishop shrugged. 'We've emptied the treasury fighting wars.'

Cenwulf grunted his agreement. 'Find us the coin, and we can build more burhs.'

I studied my advisors closely, knowing they would not deceive me.

'I will find you the coin. I need you to tell me where to start. King Alfred built burhs to protect river entrances against raiders' ships, but we also have heathens coming over our borders from the Danelaw, not to mention the Welsh from the west. Where should we build first, Lord Cenwulf?'

The old warrior scratched his beard. 'Some places just need strengthening. Maybe start with them.'

'Can you make a list for me to look at tomorrow?' I noticed Cenwulf's frown. 'Unless you have more important matters?'

'No, m'lady, nothing more important. I'll do it now.' Cenwulf stood to leave.

Wærferth struggled to his feet to follow.

'Another thing,' I said, putting a hand on the bishop's shoulder. 'Can you find me builders, carpenters and stonemasons to begin the restoration of Gloucester? And I particularly need your help to persuade the people living outside the town walls to move inside. We need them here, around us, to make the town alive. And to defend it if neccessary. Spread the word that it is God's will. Oh, and I need a monk with a fine eye for drawing layouts of streets and other details. Do you have someone at your abbey?'

The bishop wiped his brow, looking tired at the thought of all that he had to do.

*

Later, I was in the same room, my eyes sore from reading the pile of manuscripts that the clerk had brought me. Understanding how much wealth I had at my disposal was not an easy task. I smiled at the memory of Æthelred bawling at the unfortunate monk because my husband could not understand such detailed documents. That reminded me that I should go and see how he was faring.

I found him alone in his room, eating a meal of boiled pork and cabbage with his one good hand. My heart skipped a beat when I saw that his face had more colour. Although I had banished him from my bed, I was still very fond of my old bear.

'Feeling better, m'lord?'

He managed a half grin. 'Yes, still have to shout to make a whisper. More like a mouse than a man,' he rasped.

'But we know you are still the powerful, strong man you always were. Just your voice is weak.' I sat beside him, removing the remains of cabbage caught in his beard.

'Apart from this,' he said, trying to move the right arm that flopped at his side.

'The healers can help with that.'

He humphed. 'Pouring potions in my ear? What good is that?'

I wagged a finger at him. 'I can see the difference in you already. And somebody is here to cheer you up. My nephew, Athelstan, cannot wait to hear you tell him of your campaigns and victories.'

'Edward's boy? Haven't seen him since he was a baby.'

'He's growing up fast and needs a hero like you to guide him. I will fetch him.'

I returned to my makeshift meeting room and sent for Athelstan from the scriptorium where I had earlier sent him. I heard him whistling merrily outside before he bounced in.

'Settling in well, I trust?' I asked.

Athelstan beamed. 'Oh yes. I have been reading the history book you told me about. The one by the monk, Bede.'

'Excellent. I have someone special for you to read it to. My husband, Æthelred, likes histories and he is unwell. He needs a companion to amuse him, keep his spirits up whilst he recovers. He likes good riddles, too. I will find you some to tell him. It will help him recover from the shock.'

'Why is he shocked?' asked Athelstan.

'I am going to tell you something you must not repeat to...'

I was interrupted by a bang at the door. Cenwulf came in, catching his breath.

'If I can have a word, m'lady?'

'Lord Cenwulf, I was not expecting you back so soon,' I said.

'A private word, please.'

I shooed Athelstan out.

'Sorry to interupt m'lady, but there's news of Lord Æthelwold.'

'They've found him? He's alive?'

'Very much alive. He's with the Danes in the north. They are calling him king.'

FIVE

'King? King of what?'

I had not expected this. I had been hoping Æthelwold would evade capture and quietly slip into exile, but I never dreamt he would be adopted as a leader by our old foe.

Cenwulf looked tired and worried. 'Titles don't mean much to the Danes. Any petty chief calls himself king. But for sure they will use your cousin to cause trouble.'

'What can we do?'

'Find Beorhsige. If I was young Æthelwold and wanted to challenge Edward as king, I would promise to give Mercia its independence back. And if I had someone by my side who had a good claim to be king of Mercia, I would reckon to draw a fair few Mercian warriors to my banner.'

It took me a few moments to take in the full implications of what he had said. But suddenly, it all made sense. Beorhsige was the grandson of Burgred, the last independent king of all Mercia who had fled before the invasion of Halfdan and his Danes three decades ago. The heathens had been halted by Alfred but one half of Mercia still lay in the Danelaw, the other under the overlordship of Wessex. Beorhsige and Æthelwold may have been thrown together by chance, but they had good reason to be allies. If Æthelwold had somehow convinced the Danes to accept his leadership, Beorhsige might persuade Mercians to join a rebellion against Edward, the new king.

I could even see merit in the idea. It could lead to Mercia becoming independent of Wessex, free of my brother's controlling ways. I quickly banished such thoughts. Cenwulf was watching me carefully, waiting for my reaction.

'Where do we look? Do you have news of Beorhsige?'

He shook his head. 'No. The traders who saw Æthelwold in Northumbria said there were no Mercians with him.'

'Do you think he is back in Mercia?'

'Almost certainly. Too dangerous for him in Danelaw without Æthelwold's protection. If I was him, I would come home to either beg forgiveness for being so foolish, or to raise an army to join Æthelwold.'

Or both, if he's clever, I thought.

'Then we had better go and find him,' I said.

*

I baulked at the idea of an immediate journey in search of Beorhsige. It was mid-winter, almost Michælmas, a festival traditionally spent in church with God and family, not in tents with soldiers on the move. I was finally persuaded to leave Gloucester by boat as our route took us up the River Severn to Shrewsbury, the Mercian estate owned by Beorhsige's family. I became particularly interested in an expedition there when I found it on Cenwulf's list of sites to become fortified as a burh.

'Shrewsbury was the old capital of Powys until King Offa took it from them,' Cenwulf told me. 'It's already protected by earthworks so if you want a burh to stop our enemies using the upper reaches of the Severn, this has to be it.'

We took two boats, each of only twelve oars so that we would be able to navigate the twists and turns of the long River Severn as it flowed from its source in the mountains to the west. Bishop

Wærferth travelled with us for the first day as our route took us through Worcester and he was anxious to return home. The Bishop and I huddled together in the stern of the boat, the rain drumming down on the canvas shelter above us. Wærferth was proudly showing me the relics he had purchased in Winchester.

'I'm glad your church has the wealth to make such investments,' I remarked as he repacked a reliquary containing a fingernail of St. Chad and a hair of St Cuthbert. 'It has given me an idea of how to raise money to build the burhs we need. You remember the charter Æthelred and I recently signed in favour of your church in Worcester?'

The Bishop nodded slowly, suddenly most attentive. 'Yes, but I don't see…'

'We agreed to share the taxes due from the markets and trade of the town with your church,' I continued. 'If we both agree to spend all of that money for one year in laying out new streets and sites for more tradesmen in Worcester, we will recover the coin we spend by collecting more revenues the following year because trade will increase, don't you think?'

The Bishop looked aghast. 'But in the meantime I have to pay for the upkeep of the church and abbey from my share.'

'Yes, but you won't need to buy more antiquities for a while, will you?' I said, tapping the top of one of his boxes. 'We will build more churches in the new burhs to house your treasures.'

The bishops eyes brightened at the mention of new places of worship and he made no more objections. The oarsmen looked mightily relieved when we reached Worcester and he and his heavy luggage were hauled over the gunwales of the boat to the shore.

*

Swollen by the winter rains, the stream was flowing fast against us and it took three further days to reach Shrewsbury. I hoped we might surprise the ealdorman of the estate by our unannounced visit, but Cenwulf thought otherwise.

'Beornoth may have been badly wounded by the Danes, but he's still a sly old fox. He'll be waiting.'

Sure enough, before the boats had reached our destination, scouts appeared on the banks of the river, demanding to know our business. When Cenwulf told them who was aboard, they scampered quickly back to their master. By the time the vessels pulled slowly onto a rough wooden wharf at the foot of Shrewsbury's hilltop settlement, Beornoth was waiting to greet us, resplendent in fur and gold ornaments and surrounded by a retinue of armed guards.

'Welcome to Shrewsbury m'lady, although it is not a good time of year to appreciate our surroundings.'

I used to liken him to a weasel on account of his long thin body and sharp beady eyes. I had not seen him since a Danish axe had sliced into his skull and he had been thought to die. I felt some sympathy when I saw the red scar that ran down his face from forehead to cheekbone, a patch covering the place where his right eye used to be.

He still reminded me of a weasel.

'We have reason to come at an unseasonable time, Lord Beornoth. We are urgently seeking your son, Beorhsige.'

The ealdorman gave a look of surprise or made a good attempt at feigning one. 'Why, he has only just departed on urgent business to the north. Shall we shelter from this bitter weather?' He indicated a pathway that wound upwards to a set of wooden buildings on the crest of the rise. 'Will you be staying? Is there baggage to fetch?'

I glanced at Cenwulf who silently nodded his agreement to a halt. 'That depends on what you have to tell us,' I said, striding along the path.

'There is a horse for you,' Beornoth called after me. 'My legs are too old to climb, so I will ride to the hall.'

'I will walk. I have been sitting for too long,' I said.

As I neared the summit, I stopped to look around. It was as Cenwulf had described: the River Severn made an almost complete loop around the hill, enclosing an area that was more than sufficient for a large town. Yet it contained only a few scattered huts in need of repair. The harbour would have to be improved and walls built to defend the unprotected north-eastern approaches, but Shrewsbury could be strengthened relatively easily. With new streets and buildings, it would make an ideal burh.

I had hoped for a cheery, comfortable hall to relieve the discomfort of the journey, but I was sorely disappointed. The rain did not stop at the door but leaked through holes in the thatch so that I had to avoid puddles and drip-catching cauldrons to reach the fire that spluttered on the central hearth. The womenfolk around the warming pots scurried aside to let my party through to dry our wet clothes. I turned my back to the fire, lifting my damp cloak as high as I dared to warm my legs. Beornoth did not keep an orderly estate; that much was obvious. I would need a trustworthy reeve to oversee the building of the town. As the ealdorman's warriors trooped into the hall, I noted that many were familiar to me. They had been around for a long time; some looked even older than Beornoth.

Where are all the young men?

I was offered a thick broth as Beornoth joined me beside the fire.

'Lord Æthelred is well, I trust?' he asked.

As I had just taken a slurp of the hot broth, Cenwulf growled the answer we had previously agreed on. 'He'd be here but couldn't travel. Seasonal sickness.'

I dropped my spoon with a clatter into the wooden bowl, impatient with the formalities. 'Our business is urgent. Your son is a fugitive from the law.'

Beornoth looked shocked. 'Which law?'

'The law that says you should not rebel against your king. The law that says that you do not disappear without permission when you ride as a royal escort.'

'Ah, he did say that there had been a misunderstanding with the reeve in Winchester and he had been forced to leave to avoid unjust detention. He was going to come directly to you to explain once he had returned here. But on that very day, we had news of the Norsemen.'

I flinched. There had been relative peace from invaders for three years and I had not expected trouble, especially in winter.

Cenwulf leaned forward. 'They've been raiding from the Danelaw?'

'No, these are Norsemen from Ireland. The Gaelic kings have united for once and have kicked the Norse out of Dublin. A fugitive band sailed to Mon where they were beaten away by King Cadel of Gwynedd. We had news they were nearing Chester and we were fearful they might take that fort just as the Danes under Hæsten did.

Cenwulf blanched at hearing the name of the old enemy leader. 'At least that whoreson won't be coming back. Where are these Norsemen now?'

'We had a strange message from them which is why Beorhsige went so suddenly.' He paused and gave his weasel-like smile that showed off his sharpened teeth.

'Which was what exactly?' I was beginning to suspect that Beornoth was playing for time whilst his son slipped away. His answer shocked me.

'They say they are starving and need our help. They want to settle near Chester.'

*

It took a day of hard riding on borrowed horses to find Beorhsige or, rather, his camp. His warriors were huddled around a fire at their base in the woods and they told us that Beorhsige had gone to talk with the Norse leader. When Cenwulf suggested that I should stay behind whilst he took warriors to investigate, I shook my head.

'I've never looked a pagan leader in the eye. I'm coming too,' I insisted.

I had accompanied Æthelred when he visited places that had been occupied by the heathens, but only after they had left. The sight of the destruction and misery they had caused was etched in my memory. But I had never visited an encampment where the northern devils were still in residence. The thought filled my mind with trepidation and curiosity in equal measure.

Even so, the campsite shocked me more than I had thought. It was not hard to find. As we cautiously rode down the escarpment into the valley, we heard the din of hammers beating on metal, axes chopping into logs and babies bawling for their mothers. As I dismounted at the edge of a chaotic collection of tents and open fires, the stench from pits of rotting debris and excrement hit me. The real shock was in seeing so many children, their clothes splattered with filth, their bellies swollen, their eyes appealing. I wondered how many would survive the winter.

As guards led me past staring eyes through slimy mud, I caught sight of Beorhsige in a wooden lean-to in the centre of the camp talking to a fair-haired youth. A look of amazement flashed across Beorhsige's face when he saw us, and he quickly ran over.

'M'lady, what wonderful providence brings you here? I was just telling Ingimund that I would have to consult with Lord Æthelred over his request.'

'If that is Ingimund, you had better introduce me,' I said, looking coldly into his eyes. 'I have my own questions for you, but they can wait.'

'Of course, but I should counsel you his demands are… well, they are unusual for a pagan leader.'

Cenwulf and his guards closed protectively around me as I made my way towards the Norse leader who was staring in my direction.

'Ingimund, please welcome Æthelflæd, Lady of the Mercians, sister to Edward, King of Wessex,' Beorhsige called.

The Norse leader did not hesitate but bowed his head so low that his long, pale hair fell forward to drape on the muddy ground. I took my time, noting the broadness of his shoulders and the bulging muscles of his arms, before I acknowledged him.

'I would rather see your face if we are to talk. What brings you to Mercia with all your kin? Were you bored with the land of the Gaels?'

Ingimund lifted his head, flicked back his hair and smiled. We looked at each other for several heartbeats without a word. The charm of that smile, the appeal of the boyish face on a manly body, stayed with me for years to come.

'It is a great honour to meet you m'lady. I would have come just for this moment. You have many admirers amongst the British as well as the Saxons.' His spoke our tongue with a lilting accent.

I chuckled at his gaze. 'You seek to flatter a lady to make up for the shortcomings of your warriors. I hear King Cadel of Gwynedd routed you on the Isle of Mon, which I presume is why you have fled here. What is it that you want?'

'I did not mean to...' he began, but seemed to think better of it and sighed in resignation. 'I think you see us for what we are, exiles seeking a new start in life. We need food for this winter and land to grow crops for the new year. We would pay you with gold but it was stolen from us. All we have to offer you is our labour and our loyalty.'

His forthrightness took me by surprise. 'You would settle here and give us your oath in return for food and land?'

Ingimund made to grasp my hand, but I pulled it back. 'That is exactly what we want,' he said. 'You have said it perfectly. Look at our children. How can I let them starve? I will do anything to put food in their mouths.'

'So why haven't you raided our farms and stolen what you need, as your forefathers always did?'

He chuckled. 'You're right, my grandfather did go a-viking and took without asking. But my father was not a raider, and nor am I, nor my kin. We settled near Dublin, farming and trading as best we could. Until the Gaelic kings did to us what my grandfather had done to them. They took our land. We escaped in our boats with little more than our clothes and have been looking for a new home ever since. The people of Gwynedd were not at all welcoming and the cold months have not been kind to us. You are our last chance.'

I took a moment to think about his eloquent plea and Cenwulf coughed, indicating with his eyebrows that he wanted a word in private.

'Your request is unusual. We will confer, if you could withdraw for a while?' My eyes followed Ingimund as he bowed low and strode from the shelter into the spitting rain.

I turned to Cenwulf and Beorhsige. 'What is your advice, m'lords?'

Cenwulf did not hesitate. 'Don't trust the Norse and certainly not him. It'll be like breeding wolves if we feed them. They'll be soft as cubs until they're strong enough to tear out our throats.'

'Unless we can use them to tear out our enemy's throats,' Beorhsige suggested.

'Use them as mercenaries, you mean?' growled Cenwulf. 'That can go very bad on you. Would you trust him not to turn?'

I shook my head. 'Maybe not, but we must also follow the teachings of our Lord Jesus. Remember the parable? Are we to act like the priest who ignored the injured man by the roadside? Or like the Samaritan who helped him even though he was his enemy?'

Cenwulf looked down and scuffled his feet in the mud. 'This is not one man. It's an entire kin and if the Gaels have their way in Dublin, there'll be more sailing our way. Mark my words, there'll soon be more long boats dropping anchor in the Dee and the Mersey.'

'Exactly,' I said. 'If Ingimund was on our side, he could persuade them to sail further north. What other way do we have of defending this coast?'

Cenwulf looked at Beorhsige. 'How many warriors do you and your father have?'

'You saw most of them in my camp,' Beorhsige said. 'Less than a hundred men, enough to deter raiders, but not Norse fleets. For that we would need Lord Æthelred and the fyrd.'

'Which would arrive too late. We need local defenders. Let's see how far we can trust this young man.' My mind was made up and I signalled to Ingimund that he could rejoin us.

He reminded me of a puppy rather than a wolf as he stood before me, his eyes bright and expectant. 'My wife has chided me. I did not offer you refreshments,' he said.

Behind him, I saw a tall, striking woman looking on anxiously, her arm around a small child. 'I think it is us who should be offering you sustenance. We are the hosts here on our own lands.'

Ingimund reddened and mumbled. 'Of course. I did not mean to presume...'

I interrupted. 'Our Christian faith requires us to help exiles in need, particularly women and children. But it also requires us to defend ourselves from pagans who wish to exploit us. I need to know which category you fit.'

Ingimund indicated the woman and child. 'This is Finna, my wife. She does not speak your tongue but if she did, she would tell you that she is very much a mother in need. She would beg you, as I have done, to save her son, Jokul. She would tell you that you have nothing to fear from her husband. She will make sure that he serves you loyally.'

I scrutinised the pleading faces of the young Norse warrior and his woman, wondering what my father would have done. He was a devout man yet showed little compassion to his enemies. But I was his daughter, not his son.

'Very well, you will take an oath to serve the Lord and Lady of the Mercians and provide us with warriors. In return, we will give you food for the winter and land to till in the spring.' I glanced at his woman. 'Your wife Finna can indeed make sure of your loyalty. She and your son will live with us as hostages.'

*

It was a relief to return to Gloucester. I went straight to Æthelred to explain what I had done. Cenwulf was still not happy with my decision and I wanted to make sure I told the Lord of the Mercians first. He seemed to understand fully, and his speech was stronger.

'Which land did you give them?' he asked.

'I didn't give them any land. We have lent them some, in return for labour. It was wasteland in the Wirral, hardly farmed by anyone. Ingimund said they lived on a muddy estuary in Ireland so they know what to plant.'

'And what of that rogue, Beorhsige? What have you done with him?'

I smiled. 'I didn't exactly forgive him, you will be pleased to know. I put him to building work.'

'Building work? He's an ætheling. He should be doing warrior work.'

'Well building is warrior work now. For his transgressions, I fined him the sum of money needed to rebuild Shrewsbury and Chester. He hasn't nearly enough money, of course, so he will have to build it himself with his men. Keep them all out of mischief, and we will have two more links in our defensive chain across Mercia.

Æthelred nodded and smiled. 'Maybe God had a purpose in putting me to rest and you taking over for a while.'

'Your rest is nearly finished, my dear. We need to get you back on your horse as soon as the weather improves. We have a journey to take.'

'We do? To where?'

'To Kingston. Edward will receive oaths as king there and it would not do for you to miss that.'

There was a tap on the door and Ælfwyn entered, followed by Athelstan.

'Ah, there you are. I have charged these two with the hostages' welfare,' I explained to Æthelred. 'How are they settling in?'

Ælfwyn shrugged. 'The woman, Finna, seems happy to be warm and fed. But she says nothing, just shies away whenever I approach her.'

'Jokul, her son, talks to me,' Athelstan said proudly. 'He is seven, same as me.'

I was surprised. 'He speaks English?'

'Oh no, he has the British tongue, and my tutor translates for me.'

Æthelred looked surprised. 'Curious for a Norse boy to speak like a Briton,' he said.

I had other things on my mind, but I should have seen that as a sign that Ingimund was not to be trusted.

SIX

It was Twelfth Night and I shivered in the cold church of St. Peter's in Gloucester.

Michaelmas that year marked the passing of nine hundred years since Christ's birth, so it was no ordinary occasion. Yet I had permitted only muted festivities in my household. Æthelred was sitting stiff and gaunt beside me. They had strapped his limp arm to his chest so that it appeared as if it was healing from a break, and his weak voice was explained away as the result of winter fever. A false word or a stumble could start rumours, so I had limited his participation in the seasonal celebrations to religious services such as this.

Besides, I had lost my love of Michaelmas on that dreadful day in my childhood when the Danes came.

As the priest droned through a reading from the Old Testament, I recalled that moment when I was seven years old, and my world was turned on its head.

I was in St Andrew's Church in Chippenham, a day's ride to the south from where I now sat. Edward, then a small child of three, was squirming and fidgeting next to me whilst father knelt in prayer and mother sat to save her aching knees from the stone floor. Behind us, our most trusted thegns snuffled and grunted through the recitals. The service was almost finished and

I was eagerly looking forward to the gift-giving that celebrated the arrival of the Wise Men in Bethlehem, when a bell clanged loudly. The thegns were suddenly all on their feet, knocking over benches, rushing for the door. Father was shouting instructions and mother gripped my hand tightly, telling me to look after my brother whilst she found out what was happening. Edward buried his head in my tunic and I covered his ears to muffle the fearful screams outside. I did not whimper and shake like little Edward, but I stood as calm as I could, waiting and wondering. I wanted my father to be proud of me. That mattered more to me than what the Danes might do. The priest dropped to his knees, clasping his hands in prayer and I did likewise, pulling Edward down to me as he began to cry. Ealhswith hurried back, her face ashen, and ushered us out of the church.

'To the stables,' she shouted above the din of metal crashing on wooden shields and men yelling in anger and pain. 'Quick as you can, and don't look up.'

I tried to keep my head down, but I could not resist a glance towards the noise. It was not the chaotic brawl of warriors that I had expected. Instead I caught the rear view of a tight formation of soldiers desperately holding their interlocked shields against the swinging axes and stabbing spears of an unseen enemy. I never forgot those men. They all died giving their king and his family time to escape.

Edward was still bawling when they thrust him onto a horse with a trusted servant whilst mother and I mounted ponies to ride from the fighting. The King and a handful of warriors joined us as we sped from the town, his face dark and drawn as he led us to the west. I later learned that he had chosen to be near the border with Mercia for Michaelmas in order to keep a watchful eye on the Danes who had set up camp nearby in Gloucester. But he had not reckoned on being betrayed by some of his own ealdormen who had allowed the pagans to surprise them in a winter attack.

Now, twenty-two years later, in the very town where those evil Danes had camped, I glanced at the pew where my own daughter, Ælfwyn, sang in her sweet voice with Athelstan and the young monks.

How innocent they look. I just hope they don't have to suffer as I did.

I still had nightmares of that cold, damp winter when we had hidden in the Somerset marshes, foraging and stealing like outlaws, always fearful of being discovered by a pagan patrol. Edward had made life even more miserable. With both father and mother preoccupied with our very survival, I had to cope with my brother's selfish demands, comforting him when he cried, chiding him when he took too much food, washing his clothes when he wet his bedding at night.

Could it be the same Edward who now imperiously commanded all the principal lords and ladies of the realm to attend his consecration as King of the Anglo-Saxons?

Not just King of Wessex, mind. No, the snivelling brat claims to be king of all the Anglo-Saxons.

Still, that was for another day. I gently supported my husband down to his knees, and together we thanked God for sending His Son to earth nine hundred years earlier to show us humility and forgiveness.

*

During the twelve days of Michaelmas, I spent many hours praying to God on behalf of my family and my subjects. By the time the first spring flowers were appearing in the meadows, some of my prayers were being answered.

Building works had begun according to my design at Gloucester, Worcester, Shrewsbury and Chester. In the Wirral, Ingimund and the immigrants were busy tilling the earth and replacing their flimsy tents with wooden homes. Æthelred's mobility was slowly improving with regular exercise and he was performing more of his duties as Lord of Mercia. I was particularly pleased with the new addition to my family. Athelstan had formed a close relationship with Æthelred through their daily readings, and he had managed to learn some of the British and Norse tongues from Jokul, the hostage boy.

However, one particular prayer went unanswered: Æthelwold remained as a so-called king amongst the Danes in York.

As we rode at the head of the Mercian delegation towards Kingston for Edward's enthronement, I quizzed Æthelred about it.

'What do you think Æthelwold is up to?' I asked, admiring my husband's upright posture in the saddle despite the one limp arm.

'Rumours are that he is gathering a pagan warband to his cause.'

'To what end?'

'Seems he's intent on challenging Edward for the throne.'

'What do we do?'

Æthelred fixed his eyes on me. 'I gave my oath to your father to be loyal to his son as king. I know you have your misgivings about Edward, but I cannot waver in my duty. Mercia will support Edward, not Æthelwold, and so must we.'

I lowered my voice. 'Even if Mercia is offered back its independence?'

Æthelred nodded. 'Those times are past. We must stay together, or the Danes will rule us all.' As he spoke, we crested the summit of a hill and a settlement came into view by the river winding though the valley below. 'That's Kingston, if I'm not mistaken. We've come to give Edward our oath and that is what I intend to do.'

*

We had not been offered any accommodation within the small town, so we set up our encampment by the River Thames. I was ready for some sleep and Ælfwyn, who was sharing my tent, attended to my hair in preparation for the night.

'Athelstan seemed out of sorts today,' Ælfwyn said, untangling the tightly coiled hair at the back of my head.

'How so?'

'He's asking who will be at the ceremony. I think he's hoping to see his mother but he's worried he may have to meet Edward's new wife.'

I sighed, feeling a concern for Athelstan that I could not have imagined when I first took him into my care. 'I doubt very much he will see his mother, and his stepmother will snub him. Poor child. Aren't you glad you don't come from a broken family like him?'

Ælfwyn laid down her comb and frowned. 'What will happen to us if father dies?'

I put my arm around her, squeezing hard. 'Don't worry. I'll make sure we live in the same nunnery.'

Ælfwyn hesitated before she realised it was one of my little jokes, and we both laughed.

'Maybe I should marry soon,' she said abruptly.

On several previous occasions, I had thought of raising this subject with her. She had saved me from that embarrassment, but I still felt flustered. It was a sensitive topic.

'Do you have anyone in mind?' I was almost certain she did not. She was tall and well developed for her age, and I had seen the admiring glances of young thegns, and the leering looks of the not so young. Yet, she had not to my knowledge encouraged anyone's particular attention, although mothers had been deceived before.

'No, no-one in mind.' She turned to face me. 'But I do not want to live in Wessex.'

So that was it. She was warning me away from matchmaking whilst we mingled with the nobility of Edward's court.

'Why ever not?' I asked, curious as to her motives, given that she had hardly ever set foot outside of Mercia.

'I want to live amongst my own people. Not be sent abroad like you and grandma.'

She was right to wish it. It had been hard for me to leave home as a young girl, as I am sure it was for my mother. But Ælfwyn did not have to worry. It was unlikely that Edward would allow her to marry one of his ealdormen. That might lead to a new dynasty to rival his own. The granddaughter of King Alfred would always be a valuable commodity to an ambitious lord. Which is why she could not marry in Mercia either, at least not for the moment. I shuddered at the thought of someone like Beorhsige asking for her hand.

'Then you must not catch the eye of any of the handsome young men who will fawn on you,' I said.

'As if I would, mother,' she said, carefully plucking her eyebrows, the hint of a grin playing at her mouth.

*

On the day of Edward's enthronement, we made our way slowly from our encampment to St Mary's church for the ceremony. I cursed inwardly when I saw the throng of people, knowing that it meant delays. All the leading families of Wessex together with a host of clerics were already there, sprawling from the church into the graveyard. It would take some time for everyone to shuffle through the low door-arch and into the chapel. I was not good at waiting and, to make matters worse, I was conforming to ceremonial dress code by wearing a thick robe and cloak on a hot Whitsunday. Rather than endure the heat and expose Æthelred to the close scrutiny of the Wessex nobility, I signalled to my party to hang back and wait in a shady copse. I used the time to seek out Athelstan and found him sitting on a tree stump, reading a book of psalms.

'You were wise to bring a book. It might be a long wait,' I said.

He scrambled to his feet, looking pleased to see me as he always did. 'Why did the king choose such a small place for the ceremony?'

I smiled at the innocence of his question, knowing that the choice of a minor town such as Kingston over a more important centre such as Winchester was a deliberate ploy on Edward's part.

'Why do you think?' I asked.

He shrugged. 'We're on the border between Mercia and Wessex. Did he want to make our journey shorter?'

Not for the first time, I wondered how this child could come so close to working out the machinations of an adult mind. Edward had indeed picked somewhere on the border, but it was not out of any concern for our journey, but to emphasise his authority over both territories.

'Where would you be crowned?' I asked.

Athelstan wrinkled his brow. 'You think I might be king?'

'Your grandfather did, and he was right about most things,' I said, placing a hand on his shoulder. 'If you are wondering about your mother, I am almost certain she will not be here today. So stay close to me instead.'

For the first time, he wrapped his arms around me, and I felt the pressure of his small hands as he gently squeezed my waist.

*

When we finally gained admittance into the church, I was ushered to one side with the women whilst the men in my party were taken forward to sit behind the ealdormen of Wessex. No-one objected to Athelstan staying with me. Edward would not want to parade his eldest son in front of his new queen, so I took him with Ælfwyn to sit next to my mother, Ealhswith, who was bent deep in prayer, her face gaunt and strained. There was no sign of my sister, Æthelgifu.

I fanned my face with my hand whilst I waited for the assembled leaders of the Anglo-Saxon world to squeeze into the tightly spaced benches, the buzz of their conversation rising to the high wooden rafters above. Athelstan sat at my side intently studying the guests, occasionally tugging my sleeve to ask for someone's name.

Just as I thought I might faint from the heat, a horn sounded and all heads turned expectantly towards the door. I glimpsed Edward's plump face smirking above a white surcoat on a crimson robe as he swept past, followed by three armed thegns. Weapons were not normally permitted in church but Edward had obviously made an exception for his own safety. I recognised the three warriors: one was Osferth, a handsome young man much favoured by King Alfred in his later years; the other two were Edward's close friends, Sigewulf and Sigehelm, ealdormen in the Kentish army that Edward had made his own special force. They were almost identical in appearance with stout bodies, cropped hair, fierce eyes and flat noses. They looked like the thugs they were reputed to be.

*

Plegmund, the Archbishop of Canterbury and Bishop Wærferth emerged from the shadows to welcome the king as he approached the altar. Edward stepped up on a grey stone slab to sit on the highchair. He deliberately arranged his flowing robes around him, and turned to face his audience, his three guards lined up behind him.

Plegmund's voice boomed around the colourful tapestries hanging from the walls.

'I present to you, Edward, your undoubted king. Are you willing to do homage and service to him as your king?'

I watched Edward's eyes flicking around the faces before him and hoped my incoherent mumble would be drowned by the loud 'I will,' from the rest of the assembly.

The Archbishop turned to Edward. 'Will you, Edward, swear to rule according to our ancient laws?'

'I will,' he said, projecting his voice to make sure everyone heard.

'Will you carry out justice and enforce our laws?'

'I will.'

'Will you use your utmost powers to maintain the Church of the One True God.'

'I will.'

As I listened to the oaths, I recognised the hand that had scripted them. The bishops were putting on a show to signify that God had chosen Edward to be king. If anyone disputed his authority from this day forward, they would have to answer to the Lord of Heaven. Æthelwold and his pagan army should take note.

Plegmund gently pulled Edward's surcoat over his head and used consecrated oil to anoint his hands, head and heart with the sign of the cross. As symbols of the royal duties, Bishop Wærferth offered a dazzling crown of burnished gold to be placed on the king's head followed by a bejewelled sword, an enormous ring and a sceptre with a cross on the top. All the time, they intoned prayers and a choir sang psalms to sanctify the new king in God's name.

The moment came for the part of the ceremony that I had been dreading the most: the act of homage. One by one the congregation funnelled towards the highchair to state their allegiance to the new king. Children were exempted so I squeezed Athelstan's hand and filed forward to kneel before my brother, my hand on the bible proffered by Plegmund.

I stumbled through the proscribed words as quickly as I could. 'I give you my oath to serve you, Edward, my king, to be loyal and true, and to carry out everything you ask.'

As I made my way back to my seat, I was almost sick on the stone floor.

*

I held onto Athelstan as we shuffled out of the church, hoping to see my husband amongst the line of guests behind us. Just as I spotted him ducking his head through the door, Bishop Wærferth bustled towards me.

'M'lady, a moment if you please,' he panted.

'Congratulations, Bishop, you performed your duties well. Difficult to remember the right order to drape all that regalia onto the king, I would imagine. Did you have a hand in creating the service?'

'A modest role. It was based on Frankish customs of which I have some knowledge.'

'No wonder it was pretentious. The Franks have emperors rather than kings, don't they?'

The Bishop looked flustered. 'I am instructed by King Edward to invite you and the Lord of the Mercians to join him on the royal barge.'

'How kind. Is he offering to row us home?' I asked.

The Bishop moved closer and lowered his voice. 'It is more of an audience for Mercian leaders. He wants Cenwulf and Beornoth there too.'

'What for?'

'I'm sure he wants to personally greet his most important ally. The barge is at the wharf, down there.' The Bishop pointed towards the river. 'I will bring the king to join you as soon as I can.'

I turned to my daughter. 'Ælfwyn, take care of Athelstan. You should both spend time with your grandmother.' I indicated Ealhswith slowly making her way from the church. 'And see if you can find out what's happened to Æthelgifu.'

*

I was grateful that we arrived at the barge before the king. I would not have wished Edward to witness Æthelred's unfortunate stumbling as he clambered aboard. Whilst I tutted at the opulence of a boat that was clearly not made for fighting, I could not help but admire its elegant lines. The clinker-built hull was wide like a trading boat, yet the prow was upturned in a graceful curve that matched the height of the raised decking in the stern. Young women offered us wine and fruit as we boarded whilst eight muscular oarsmen sat silently in the bows awaiting the tillerman's command. We sat under a canopy, listening to the gentle lapping of the stream against the hull whilst we waited. I relaxed sufficiently to fall into a light sleep.

When I woke, I noticed that shadows were lengthening on the shore.

'Are we to spend the night on board this boat?' I grumbled.

Æthelred was looking at me fondly and put a reassuring hand on mine. 'Stay calm, just like you were,' he said. 'Edward is arriving.'

I stood to watch the king sweep across the gangway from the shore, his three armed attendants close behind, Bishop Wærferth tottering along at the rear. Sigewulf and Sigehelm took up guard by the tillerman whilst Osferth stayed close to his king. Edward was taking no chances.

The tillerman began barking orders, an oarsman attended to the ropes, and Edward sank with a sigh into a chair under the canopy, accepting a cup of wine from a hovering slave.

'Really, you would think a king would be free from petitions on such a day but no, some see it as their chance to win favour,' he said.

'We have no petitions, brother dear, and wait only on your words,' I replied.

Edward paused whilst the tillerman shouted instructions to the oarsmen. 'What did you think of the service?'

I was about to speak when I felt pressure from Æthelred's foot on mine under the table.

'A fine show, m'lord king.' Æthelred rasped, straining to make himself heard above the rhythmic sound of blades through water as the boat pulled away from the bank. 'Sent a message to the pagans as well as our people.'

'Good, that is what I intended. We have to hit the Danes hard before the traitor, Æthelwold, gains too much favour.'

Cenwulf leaned forward. 'How would we be doing that, m'lord king?'

Edward beckoned to his companion. 'You know Osferth, of course, ealdorman of the South Saxons? I will let him explain as he has been promoting this idea for some time.'

When Osferth ducked under the canopy, I had to admire the noble look of his dark, swept back hair and strong aquiline nose. This was obviously someone to be reckoned with in Edward's entourage.

'We will combine our forces into one irresistible army,' Osferth said with a broad smile.

Again I felt my husband's foot press on mine.

'Why's that, Lord Osferth?' Æthelred asked. 'We kept our forces separate under King Alfred, and for good reason.'

Still smiling widely, Osferth glanced at Edward before replying. 'You and I both served under the late king, Lord Æthelred, and know what a great military leader he was. But the situation has changed and we must adjust our strategy accordingly. King Alfred's aim was to defend what territories he had left after the pagan invasion. He had to spread his forces to protect his people. Now the objective is to attack and throw the Danes out for good. They are weak, without strong leaders.' He chuckled. 'Why else would they pick a fool like Æthelwold as a king?'

I shifted uneasily, feeling controlled by my husband's nudges. Æthelred asked another question in his strained voice. 'Do you have a plan of attack?'

Edward tossed the rest of his apple into the river. 'That's what I like about you Mercians. You don't waste words on idle banter. Or maybe it's your throat that limits your speech. How long has it been like this? And when will your arm be strong enough to wield a sword?'

Æthelred cleared his throat. 'I'm at your service, lord king, whatever my health.'

I felt hot, wanting to speak but knowing I should not.

'Good. It will take time to gather the army we need so you have a while to heal.' Edward pushed back his chair and stood, waving his hand at the serving women. 'More wine. We are celebrating here, are we not, sister?' He looked, unsmiling towards me.

'Of course. It is a great day when my brother is pronounced to be king of all the Anglo-Saxons,' I said, raising my cup. 'But before we drink too much, I would hear more of this plan to make the Anglo-Saxons rule over all England.'

Edward laughed. 'Ha, we have achieved something today. We have made my sister listen.' He put his arms on the table, leaning in towards me, speaking quietly. 'We are going to play the Danes at their own game. Explain our plan, Osferth.' He crossed his arms as Osferth stepped forward once again to speak.

'The Danes came here with one great army and marched through our scattered kingdoms defeating them one at a time. First Northumbria, then East Anglia, finally Mercia. That great army no longer exists. It has broken into small units, scattered across the kingdoms it conquered. What do we do? We have shut ourselves behind stonewalls and wait for them to go away. It is time to go on the offensive.'

Edward brought his fist down abruptly onto the table, making the cups and platters shake. 'We will raise one great army, just as the pagans did, and throw them out of our lands.'

For a few heartbeats, no-one spoke. I tried listening to the sounds of the river to calm me, but I could not hold back.

'As I recall, the great heathen army did not come with women and children. Nor did the Danes have farmsteads and crops. Nor monasteries and abbeys. They had nothing to lose. But we do. When you take all our fighting men into your one great army, who will protect our families, our farms, our churches?' My voice was rising and once again, I felt Æthelred's foot pressing hard on mine.

Edward sighed dismissively. 'I don't intend to debate military matters with those who do not understand them. Æthelred, I will need warriors to join my men. When my father gave me command of the men of Kent, I trained them into an elite force. We will do the same with all our warriors until we have an unstoppable army that will sweep the heathens from our land. That is the only way to fully protect our people.'

He smirked at me triumphantly, before shouting to the tillerman in the stern. 'Turn the boat. It's time to go back.'

Æthelred had not taken his foot from mine and I took a deep breath, understanding his meaning. Perhaps it was not the moment for an argument with a new king eager to show his authority.

Edward turned his attention towards Beornoth who was sitting quietly, sipping the wine. 'I have a plan in this for your wayward son.'

Beornoth hurriedly set down his cup. 'I'm sure Beorhsige will be delighted to serve you in whatever way you choose lord king.'

'He did not serve me well during his recent visit to Winchester, but I am told he is penitent, and a fine warrior.' Edward turned to Æthelred who nodded his agreement. 'In which case, you can send him to me. He will serve with the one thousand Mercian warriors I will need for my standing army. You will recruit them and Beorhsige will bring them to Osferth who will command our joint forces.'

Cenwulf looked shocked. 'Are you meaning permanent troops, lord king, not part of the fyrd?'

'Of course. I cannot rely on the part-time farmers of the fyrd. I must have an army that I can take with me on a prolonged campaign. What good is conquering a new territory if my men have to return home for the harvest?'

'We only have half that number of warriors in our feasting halls. How are we to pay for more?' Æthelred asked.

Edward swigged some wine and belched. 'Use the coin you are spending to build stone walls around empty towns. We won't need such defences once we attack.'

I could bite my tongue no longer. 'Our father developed burhs in Wessex for good reason and we are doing the same in Mercia. We have enemies other than the Danes.'

For a few heartbeats, no one spoke as Edward glared at me. 'I may have missed something, sister, but I don't recall seeing you on a field of battle or in a shield wall. When I do, I will ask for your opinion in these matters.'

Bishop Wærferth tried to lighten the mood. 'Let us not forget we are celebrating today. Can we raise our cups to honour our new king?'

When we all scrambled to our feet to join the toast, the boat lurched at the sudden movement of our weight. Æthelred stumbled and tried to stop himself from falling by grabbing one of the canopy posts. That proved too flimsy for his heavy body and he crashed to the decking, pulling one side of the shelter down on top of him. I was caught up in the flapping canvass and could not help my husband who was flaying like a drunkard on the deck. Cenwulf came to the rescue, yanking the fallen post back into position and lifting the canopy so that Osferth could help Æthelred back to his feet. He was red with embarrassment but Edward, who had managed to duck away from the melee, began to laugh loudly.

'Good that we have fallen over, and not fallen out,' he guffawed.

It was the wittiest thing I had ever heard from the lips of my little brother. Pity it was not true.

PART TWO
TWO YEARS LATER

SEVEN

When I look back on my life, I can think of several bleak years, but the year of Our Lord nine hundred and two was the most desperate of all.

It began with a message, scrawled on parchment, the letters so ill-formed that I knew immediately that it was not an official communication. No self-respecting scribe would write like that. The message was simple and short but I had to study it for some time to untangle the words:

I will soon be near. Please meet me. I have a way of making your father's dream come true.

The signature was even more illegible, but I recognised Æthelwold's name without deciphering the letters. His scrawl took me back to my childhood days in the scriptorium where I had spent many hours learning how to form letters. Æthelwold had been a fellow student, but not a very conscientious one. Whenever our tutor's back was turned, he would make faces and flick ink to distract me from my work. I thought he would never learn to write. Yet our father had decreed that every notable person in the land should learn to read and write the English tongue and so the clerics had persisted even with errant pupils like Æthelwold.

What did he want with me now? He had established himself as a king amongst the Danes in York and I had hoped that he would live quietly amongst the pagans. After his abortive revolt and Edward's coronation, I had happily withdrawn from the politics of Wessex to throw myself into fortifying towns to protect Mercia from the Danes and the Welsh. Despite Edward's scorn for burhs and preference for recruiting a large army, I had set about rebuilding Gloucester, Worcester, Shrewsbury and Chester and they were already beginning to attract more residents and trade within their protective walls.

The letter threatened trouble.

I read it slowly to Æthelred later that morning before he had become sleepy as he usually did around the middle of the day. His arm had recovered some of its strength so that he could move it to perform basic functions, but he could never join a battle and hope to survive.

'What's that lad up to now?' he muttered. 'He was always trying to do things different when we were on campaign.'

'What sort of things, dear?' I knew that Æthelwold had fought alongside my husband on several occasions, but I had never heard any details.

'Like always trying to fight on horseback instead of in a shield wall like a proper soldier.'

'He's a good rider, you must admit that.'

'No-one fights on horses if they can avoid it. Horses aren't up to it. They panic as soon as the yelling starts and will as likely take you onto an enemy spear as away from it. Couldn't tell Æthelwold that. He had the biggest, craziest mount I've ever seen, but he managed to ride it somehow. And he fought on it when he could.'

'What do you think his message means?'

Æthelred scratched his beard. 'Surely your father's dream was to defeat the Danes. How's Æthelwold going to do that when he is one of their kings?'

'Father's dream was also to unite all of England under one king. Maybe Æthelwold is hoping to do that.'

Æthelred nodded. 'He will more likely splinter us into warring groups like we used to be until your father came along. Best ignore the letter.'

*

Hard on the heels of Æthelwold's message came news from Wessex. My mother was very ill.

I left at once for Winchester. If, as I feared, Ealhswith was not long for this life, I did not want to miss her final moments, as I had my father's. After several days' hard ride, I was shown into a small room in Nunnaminster Abbey. Wiping the dust of the journey from my eyes, I was surprised to find my mother propped up in bed, looking very much alive and studying her small book of prayers. I was so relieved, I began to cry.

Ealhswith raised an eyebrow. 'Do you weep that you find me well enough to read the psalms?'

'Tears of joy, mother. They told me that…'

'I was going to join Alfred? I will soon enough but first there are a few things I must finish here. Come, sit. Tell me your news. How is young Athelstan faring in Mercia?'

'He is thriving on good company and learning. I am beginning to think father may have been right about him.'

'In what way?' Ealhswith asked.

'Athelstan told me the story of how King Alfred had blessed him with the regalia he had received from the Pope.'

'Oh that. One of Alfred's little whims. Of course, he did not know of Edward's new son when he did that.'

I blanched. 'New son? What new son?'

'You haven't heard about little Ælfweard? The news must have crossed whilst you were travelling here. He was born a few days ago. Such a sweet little boy, full of strength judging by his lungs.'

'My brother does at least seem gifted in providing heirs. Will he disinherit Athelstan?'

'Who can read the minds of kings? But it is even more important that you keep the boy safely in Mercia. Maybe he will rule there one day.'

'Maybe.' My mind turned to the current Lord of the Mercians. I had left him falling asleep in his chair whilst Athelstan read him his favourite passage from Bede's history of how the Angles and Saxons had come to Britain several centuries ago.

*

Tired from the journey, I did not want to be thrust immediately into the commotion of the Wessex court nearby, so I accepted my mother's offer of a bed in the nunnery. I retired to a room shared with young nuns. They kept their distance, and I was glad of their discrete company.

I was at prayers in the chapel early the next morning when I heard the grunting and clanking of men bearing arms outside the entrance – soldiers who were almost certainly waiting for me. Once the service had finished, I walked deliberately to the door and invited the three warriors who were patiently waiting in the porch to take me to their master. As they led me across the meadow that surrounded the Minster, I could not resist a disapproving shake of my head towards the new church being built next to the old.

I was swiftly admitted to the royal compound and marched past the great hall into the king's chamber where Edward was seated on his large throne-like chair, an unwelcoming scowl on his face. Standing beside him were Sigewulf and Sigehelm, stiff as statues, and Osferth who smiled broadly as if he had chosen to offset the king's sourness with a more friendly face. Edward seemed inseparable from his three toadies.

'Congratulations on your second son, brother,' I said. 'You seem to have a talent for picking wives who can produce sons.'

Edward exhaled. 'We have more serious news. Lord Osferth will explain.'

Osferth greeted me cheerily but fumbled at the document on the table. Surely he was not nervous? He seemed so assured with his laughing eyes and curved nose.

'The traitor, Æthelwold, has arrived with a fleet of some thirty ships amongst the East Saxons on the north bank of the Thames. He is still in the Danelaw but close to our borders.' He sounded matter of fact but there was a hint of wavering in his voice.

'Do we know his intentions?' I tried not to think of the note I had received from Æthelwold in case my face gave it away.

'He has made no demands or claims on us, but our informants tell us he is meeting with Eohric, King of East Anglia.' Osferth glanced at Edward who nodded for him to continue. 'We believe he is recruiting an army from the Danes in the south to combine with the force he has brought from the north. We must quickly gather our army to stop his invasion.'

'Invasion? If he has made no demands, how do you know his intentions?' I asked.

Edward could contain himself no longer. 'Military leaders tend not to give away their intentions to their enemies. So, we have to try to second-guess him. We believe he will invade Wessex and claim the kingship. This time, he has a large army behind him so he will hope for more support from our subjects.'

'But surely the thegns and ealdormen of Wessex have given oaths to you and will not join Æthelwold now?'

'Osferth has news about that also,' Edward said flicking his fingers towards his advisor.

Osferth cleared his throat. 'He has evidently sent letters far and wide asking for support. We believe he is most likely to find favour in Mercia. He can appeal to those who may hanker after the full independence of the old kingdom.'

'He may even have a plan to reunite the Danish and English areas of Mercia under one leader,' Edward interjected. 'Which is why we have to act quickly.'

'Which leader?'

Osferth fiddled with his document again. 'Beorhsige, son of Beornoth, recently took sides with Æthelwold so we believe he is the obvious threat.'

'Your visit to mother is convenient to our purpose, so that we can proceed without delay,' said Edward.

'Your purpose being what exactly?' I felt increasingly alarmed at the direction the conversation was taking.

'To apprehend Beorhsige before he joins Æthelwold and takes your army with him,' said Edward.

I felt my legs go unsteady as I stood before these powerful men, all watching me expectantly. Suddenly it became clear. They had exaggerated Ealhswith's illness to induce me to Winchester so that I could not obstruct the arrest of one of my subjects in Mercia.

Osferth held up the document he had been twiddling. 'This is the authorisation for his arrest for breach of oath and public brawling. We have sent riders to bring him here for trial.'

I would have snatched it from his hand had it been within reach. 'Who has signed it?'

As if he understood my intention, Osferth drew the parchment closer to his chest. 'King Edward, to whom he owes loyalty.'

I tried to move closer to the king but Sigewulf stepped forward to block my way.

'You are exceeding your authority,' I shouted. 'The Lord of the Mercians has already punished Beorhsige for his part in the uprising. I demand you cease this folly. If you flout what little remains of our independence, the Mercian thegns may well turn against you.'

'But the Lord and Lady of the Mercians would remain loyal to their oaths and dissuade them, I am sure,' Edward smirked. 'Although I do hear your husband's indisposition makes him weaker than we would wish at this time.'

My cheeks felt as though they were on fire. He must have heard of the seriousness of Æthelred's condition.

'He and I will manage the situation in Mercia together. I will return home as soon as I can,' I said.

'Don't worry, we have sent messages to Lord Æthelred informing him of our intentions.' Osferth's smile had not left his face throughout the exchange.

Edward stood and indicated the door. 'In the meantime, I would be grateful if you would stay with us here in Winchester. In case mother's condition deteriorates.'

He meant in case I was tempted to join Æthelwold.

I almost ran from the building.

*

I went straight to my mother's room. Ealhswith was dozing in bed but her eyes flickered open when I sat at her side.

'Whatever's the matter, dear?' she said, struggling into a sitting position. 'I can feel you shaking from here.'

'Sorry, mother. It's Edward and Osferth. They are riding roughshod over Mercian laws. When did those two become so close?'

'Ever since…' Ealhswith stopped and held out her hand. 'There is something I have been meaning to tell you about Osferth,' she said as our fingers intertwined.

'What?'

'He is your half-brother.'

'Say that again. Are you feeling quite well?'

'I am in sound mind, if that's what you mean,' Ealhswith said. 'Before we were married, Alfred had a child by… well let us just say by someone quite lowborn. He was christened Osferth and raised amongst the South Saxons. He proved quite a determined and intelligent young man and made his way to court to become one of Alfred's advisors without knowing that he was the king's son. Do you remember your father's stomach pains?'

I nodded. How could I ever forget the first time I had witnessed the sight of my father, one moment calmly listening to my reading, the next doubled over, crying out with pain, servants rushing in to carry him off. I later discovered it was something that happened regularly.

'Alfred said the pain was God's punishment for his wrong-doing in siring an illegitimate child,' Ealhswith continued. 'I could hardly believe it when it first happened at our wedding feast.'

That shocked me further. 'It happened at your own wedding?'

'Yes, the celebration was an elaborate affair. After all, Alfred was the king's younger brother and I was a highborn Mercian princess. Everyone was there and the feasting went on for days. You should have seen the meat and fish. Not just pig and sheep, but deer, boar, hare, duck, geese, lobster, crab, even porpoise. We gobbled them all down with wine and mead until we could eat no more. I was feeling sick myself when, suddenly, Alfred groaned next to me and clutched his stomach, bending over double. I thought someone had poisoned him or cast a spell on him. He gasped and put his head on my lap while we waited for the physician.'

'What a start to your marriage. Did it last long?'

Ealhswith chuckled. 'You mean our marriage?'

'No mother, you know what I mean. Father's pain.'

'At first, we thought it was all the feasting on rich food, but the sickness never left him. He would be in agony for days and then it would become a dull ache and disappear. But it always came back. He lived in dread of it, always worrying that it would strike him at an important gathering, or worse, in battle. The pain was either with him, or he was in fear of it being with him.'

'Poor father, he hid it well.' I wiped at the perspiration on mother's brow.

'Yes, after a while, he did. Once he realised that it was the hand of God at work, he would thank the Lord for reminding him of his sins and redouble his efforts to make amends.'

'Part of which was to reward his bastard son with lands and titles. Does Edward know?'

'Alfred told him as he was dying and bade him accept Osferth into his family.'

'Which he has done in abundance, it seems,' I sighed. 'The two of them rule us all now. Osferth has convinced Edward of a strategy that will end badly, I know it. Why could you not have made me a boy, mother? I would be a much better king.'

Ealhswith looked offended. 'It is the Lord who decides who we are and he made you a woman for a reason.' She patted my hand. 'A strong woman who always knows best.'

*

I hardly slept that night. I was desperate to return home to prevent Beorhsige being dragged off for trial in Wessex. He may have been the grandson of the last Mercian king, but that did not make him a traitor. Yet I didn't want to leave my mother. Although she had seemed cheerful enough when I first arrived, I could see that she had lost weight and the physician told me that there was blood in her stools.

When I woke the next day, I decided that the affairs of Mercia were more urgent than mother's health. I threw my possessions into a saddlebag before going to say farewell.

I found a row of nuns intensely praying at her bedside.

I ran forward seeing Ealhswith's white face on the pillow and blood on the sheets. 'What's going on?' I asked.

One of the nuns stood and led me back out of the room. 'Sister Oswald found her out of bed, lying on the floor, bleeding between the legs. We have sent for the physician.'

I resigned myself to staying with mother, frantically sending messages to my family and advisors back home. Over the next few days, Ealhswith's health steadily deteriorated. The physician said that she had developed dysentery and ordered spells and herbal infusions, but they did no good. I watched helplessly as mother emptied her bowels and vomited until there was nothing left except colourless bile. It was a mercy when she slept, clinging onto me with a sweaty hand, but I knew that, sometime soon, she would never wake.

*

There was no news about Æthelwold until he did the unexpected.

It was early morning and I was kneeling in prayer in the chapel, when I heard the door bang and loud footsteps approaching my pew. I sensed a sweaty presence near me and I opened my eyes to see Edward's head bowed next to mine. He grunted, indicating the door, and I reluctantly followed him from the chapel. I noted he was dressed in thick leather even though the late-summer weather was warm.

'Æthelwold has invaded Mercia,' he said quietly.

'What?'

'Our cousin is plundering your land with a Danish warband. He crossed Watling Street three days ago and is now north of London, heading west. They are doing what the pagans always do, taking everything they can carry and burning what they can't.'

'You are sure this is Æthelwold? What are our armies doing?' My mind was racing with the possibilities.

'My main forces are in the east guarding the crossing of the Thames into Kent. I have ordered them to move along the river to cut off the bridges further west. I leave today with the Hampshire fyrd to join them. I have ordered Lord Æthelred to raise his forces and move south towards the enemy. We will crush Æthelwold between us like the claws of a crab.'

'Any news of Beorhsige?' I asked.

'Your friend Beorhsige was not at home when my men called. His father claimed he was recruiting warriors in the north and we have not caught up with him. Not yet.'

I glimpsed a nun hurrying towards the infirmary with a bowl and clean linen. 'You should say farewell to mother. She may not be with us when you return.'

He nodded. 'You will stay with her, I trust.'

'Yes, I will be with her until the end.'

*

I watched from the door of the nunnery as Edward led his thegns over the bridge by the mill and out of the east gate to a ringing of bells and cheering from the cluster of townsfolk who waved them farewell. The king's warriors looked like boys to me, too young to have been in any real battles during the long peace. I did not join the cheering. So many times, I had watched my menfolk ride to war knowing that not all would return. A nun tugged at my gown to draw me back into the tranquillity of the convent and, without speaking, led me quickly to mother's room.

Æthelgifu was kneeling at the bedside and stood agitatedly, holding back tears. I had sent news of mother's illness to Æthelgifu's abbey, and to my relief, she had arrived soon after. I leaned as close as I could towards mother's mouth and nose, hoping to sense her breathing. There was nothing. I kissed her cheek and gently stroked her eyelids until they were fully closed.

'Send for the physician,' I ordered to the nun and went on my knees to pray.

Æthelgifu burst into tears but quickly composed herself. Together, we prayed silently to the Lord above to accept our mother's soul into heaven.

The physician arrived and quickly confirmed our diagnosis. I took Æthelgifu aside. 'I must leave immediately. You must see to mother's funeral. Edward's mausoleum is not yet finished so she can be buried next to father in the Old Minster.

'Will you meet with Æthelwold?' Æthelgifu asked.

'I might,' I said, surprised that she had news of our cousin. 'Why?'

'I have a message for him.'

'A message? You want to communicate with him after what he has done?'

Æthelgifu reddened. 'Just tell him that I have returned to my first love, Jesus Christ. And ask him to return Saviour to me.'

It took a moment for me to recognise the name. 'You want me to ask for your horse back?'

'She's such a sweet pony and I have missed her dearly.'

I patted her hand. 'In that case, sister, I will make a special effort to deliver your message. In the meantime, take care of affairs here in the nunnery now that their Abbess is no more. I may be away for some time.'

I looked at mother's face one last time and strode away to find my servants and horses.

*

Finding Æthelwold was easier than I expected.

I had received a message from home telling me that Cenwulf was leading the thegns of Gloucester to join Beorhsige at the head of the warband newly recruited for Edward's army as instructed by the king. They were not strong enough to challenge the invaders alone as Æthelwold's forces numbered over two thousand men advancing west along the north bank of the River

Thames. Cenwulf's aim was to track the invaders until Edward arrived south of the Thames when they would attack the enemy in a pincer movement. But there was little news of Edward since he had departed eastwards to meet the Kentish contingent.

That was all I knew as I urged my small party northwest from Winchester to join up with the Mercian forces. Our horses would travel much faster than Cenwulf's troops who would be moving mainly on foot. I calculated that I would cross the Thames to the west of Æthelwold's warband and meet the Mercian army south of Gloucester. With their protection, I would seek a meeting with Æthelwold to dissuade him from his foolish venture.

I would have done well to remember my husband's remark that Æthelwold loved to fight on horseback.

EIGHT

It took two days to arrive at the upper reaches of the Thames, the river that delineated the border between Wessex and Mercia. Our horses were tired and I was curious to see the improved defences of the nearby burh of Cricklade, so I announced to my small band of companions that we would be stopping there for the night.

'They must have seen your flag, your ladyship. Looks like they have sent a welcome party,' my scout said, pointing to a group of riders descending from the tree-lined ridge ahead of us.

The newcomers did not look particularly welcoming. As they approached, they brandished spears and axes and used their horses to form a tight ring around us. One rider edged forward from the circle, blond hair curling up from under his leather helmet.

'You fly the royal flag of Mercia. Who do I have the honour of addressing?'

I tossed back my hood and urged my mount forward. 'I think you know me, cousin. Or should I say m'lord king?'

Æthelwold threw back his head and laughed. 'The Lady of the Mercians! I might have known you would be here to protect your borders.'

I eyed the warriors who had surrounded us, noting that they wore the fur-trimmed surcoat that was favoured amongst the

Danes. 'We come in peace. I trust your companions understand,' I said.

'The way to make that clear would be for your men to throw down their weapons,' Æthelwold said.

'As soon as yours have done the same, we will. I come at your request for a meeting.'

Æthelwold laughed again. 'I think not. You've come from Wessex, where you've no doubt been plotting with your worm of a brother.'

'No, I have been caring for my mother.' I bowed my head. 'That duty is sadly now over.'

'She is dead?'

I nodded.

Waving to his men to lower their weapons, Æthelwold slid from his horse, inviting me to do the same.

I shook my head. 'First, I would know your intentions towards us.'

Æthelwold took off his helmet and swept back his hair. 'Come, let us share a moment of grief together. Ealhswith was like a mother to me, you know that. I will take you to my camp where we can talk.' He took my palfrey by the halter. 'Your guards will be safe enough as long as they remain peaceful.'

I dismounted and joined Æthelwold in a slow, deliberate walk ahead of the riders. He asked only of my mother and how she had died, not mentioning his own actions. When we came to the top of a rise, I looked down and saw a cluster of colourful tents stretching along the bank of a meandering stream between marshland at one end and woodland at the other.

'See how my following has grown. Isn't it strange how a great river like the Thames can begin as a stream like that,' Æthelwold said, pointing to the valley. 'I feel my destiny is the same. My restoration began as a trickle in Wimborne and has become a torrent that will cut through Wessex and Mercia, just as the Thames does.'

I pointed to a tiny brook that ran beside the trail. 'I would liken your fate more to this tributary. It will soon be swallowed up by the great river into which it flows.'

He laughed loudly. 'I have yet to meet a woman who likes the last word as much as you do. We should have children. They would be the marvel of the age.'

I blushed. As we were first cousins, any offspring of ours would have been the talk of the age.

I hitched up my skirt to avoid the mud as Æthelwold led me down the hill past curious guards to the edge of the encampment.

'Welcome to my temporary abode. My men will take your horses over the ford to the paddock,' he said indicating a makeshift enclosure across the stream.

'Do you intend to steal my horse as you did Æthelgifu's?' I asked. 'She gave me a message for you. She wants her horse, Saviour, back.'

Æthelwold hesitated before chuckling. 'She will have to find salvation elsewhere. We ate that one during our escape to the north.'

He gave orders for my companions to be given food and drink, and led me to the centre of the camp. We stopped outside a tall pavilion and Æthelwold ducked inside whilst I waited apprehensively by the entrance, trying to avoid eye contact with the guards staring at me.

'Come,' Æthelwold finally beckoned, waving me through. 'Meet my new companions.'

I peered at two lanky figures dressed in leather that reeked of the animals it was made from.

They grinned as Æthelwold introduced them. 'This is Ysopa and Oscytel, grandsons of Guthrum, the late King of East Anglia. Your father knew him well.'

That was an understatement. Guthrum was King Alfred's nemesis, the Danish leader who had almost conquered Wessex, the last independent kingdom of the Anglo-Saxon world. The story of how my father hid in the marshes to evade Guthrum before finally defeating him at the Battle of Edington, was still a favourite in the mead-halls.

I noted that both young men displayed Thor's hammer amulets dangling from neck-chains. They had obviously not respected their grandfather's conversion to the Christian faith. Guthrum had been baptised at Alfred's insistence as part of the peace process. As a child of eight, I had watched the mighty figure of the pagan chief taken to the river's edge to receive initiation into the Church of the one true God. Guthrum had made a formidable sight that day with his flowing hair and bare chest as he accepted the blessing of the bishop.

Pity that his grandsons were such scrawny heathen brats.

'You are truly the daughter of Alfred?' the one called Ysopa said, eyes bulging in his fresh face.

'I am. Why have you broken your grandfather's oath of peace and plundered my land?'

Oscytel sniggered and spoke in broken English. 'Like you said Æthelwold, she's a fireball.' He took a pace towards me so that I could smell his sour breath. 'We hear you want to join us. Get rid of your brother.' He pulled a finger across his throat.

Æthelwold must have been making false promises to his Danish allies. I would have to disabuse them.

'Whoever gave you that idea?' I turned to Æthelwold. 'It's a lie, isn't it, cousin?'

Æthelwold held up his hands in mock surrender. 'We heard it from the lips of one of your own ealdormen.'

'Who?'

'Let me explain the proposition first.' He looked around the interior of the pavilion. 'I would offer you a seat but as you can see, we have none. We travel light with no luxuries. There is water or beer if you need refreshment.'

'Thank you, but I am happy to stand and fast for a while. So is this small troop that you call an army led by these clowns?' I asked, indicating the two bemused Danes.

He looked at me in astonishment. 'You have been away from Mercia too long. This is a cavalry unit that I lead. It strikes quickly, taking the plodding Saxons by surprise, just as the long ships used to do. Our main army is under King Eohric and follows on foot.'

I had badly miscalculated his strength. The East Anglian king was a serious threat. His smirk told me that he knew it.

'And your proposition?' I asked.

He twirled a lock of his blonde hair around his fingers. 'Quite simply, to unite the old Anglo-Saxon lands into one England, as your father wanted. I am King of the North. If I become King of Wessex, the Danes of East Anglia will bend the knee to me. That just leaves Mercia which can be reunited under one king, providing he also bends the knee to me as his overlord.'

It was almost an enticing prospect, but I knew it would not work. 'Lord Æthelred would never break his oath to the King of Wessex,' I said.

'I would not ask him to,' he retorted. 'I hear your husband is sick, too sick to rule.' He paused, eyebrows raised quizzically. My throat tightened and I could not speak. He smiled at my hesitation and turned to Ysopa. 'Could you ask the future King of Mercia to join us?'

Ysopa grinned and disappeared. I had badly underestimated my cousin. No, we had all underestimated him. Edward, Osferth, Æthelred, all of us had taken Æthelwold to be a rash adventurer, a nuisance but not a serious threat. If his so-called 'future King of Mercia' was who I thought it was, Æthelwold and his allies would pose a very great threat indeed. He was watching me carefully, his charming smile unsettling me further.

'Maybe you would like some refreshment now?' he asked.

Before I could reply, Beorhsige walked casually though the entrance and bowed. 'Pleased that you made it safely here, m'lady.'

My worst nightmare had come true. Edward was right. Beorhsige had betrayed us. I wanted to slap the inane grin from his face.

'So you have broken your oath. Unless you are about to protect me from these trespassers,' I snarled.

Æthelwold stepped between us. 'Lord Beorhsige has joined us with a large cohort of Mercian soldiers. Your brother ordered him to recruit them. Wasn't that fortunate? Now we can make your father's dream come true.'

'My father never dreamt of treachery and betrayal.' I turned my glare from Beorhsige to Ysopa and Oscytel. 'Nor of allowing pagans to rule parts of England.'

Æthelwold shook his head. 'Let me explain my proposition. You and the remaining Mercian forces join with me to defeat Edward. Once that is done, the Danes who control the other half of Mercia will submit to Beorhsige who will become King of all Mercia, his rightful inheritance. You and the Lord of the Mercians can continue as members of the Witan and to govern your estates. England will be united into one peaceful land, and you can worship your favourite saints undisturbed.'

'And if I don't agree?' I was rapidly trying to think what father would have done in my position.

Æthelwold sighed. 'Beorhsige will go himself to bring the rest of the Mercian army to join us.'

I snorted. 'Your arrogance astounds me. Cenwulf will never agree to that.'

Æthelwold and Beorhsige looked knowingly at each other. 'It seems you have not heard the other sad news,' Æthelwold said. 'Cenwulf is dead.'

That stunned me most of all. I badly needed to sit down. 'How?' was all I could say.

'Not our doing. He died peacefully in his tent three days ago. Maybe, the same day as his sister, Ealhswith. Our informants are reliable.'

The mention of my mother, who had herself faced moments like this when all must have seemed lost, strengthened my resolve. 'I still have no intention of joining your rebellion. I will go to my family immediately and grieve for my uncle as well as my mother.'

'Unfortunately, that will not be possible,' Æthelwold said, running a hand thought his hair. 'If you refuse to be our ally, you must be our prisoner instead.'

*

The next day, I peered out of the small tent I had been given. Together with my companions, I was confined in a compound thrown together by the Danes from earthworks and wooden barricades to house slaves – the main booty that they were taking from their raids. I looked at the forlorn figures huddled around the embers of a fire in the chill autumn air. Only a short time ago, they would have been farmers, weavers and merchants, peacefully plying their trades. They had been brutally snatched by Æthelwold's raiders to be sold into some foreign market, never to see their homes again. A handful of young women were amongst them and I had offered to share my tent with them. They preferred to stay with their menfolk, knowing it would not be long before they would be forced to do whatever some strange new master bade them.

Soldiers were bringing horses across the ford from the paddock and mounting up. When I spotted Æthelwold amongst them, I scrambled out of my shelter into the spitting rain.

'You have no right to detain me. I demand to go to my family and bury my uncle,' I shouted after him as a guard prodded me away from the fence with his spear.

'Save your strength, cousin. You will soon need that for your brother's funeral. I am going to raise my supporters in Wessex whilst Beorhsige here rides to bring us the Mercian army,' he said, indicating my ealdorman who grinned back at me from his mount. 'Oscytel and Ysopa will look after you in our absence.'

I kicked at the ground and sat down, hands around my knees, trying to think. What was Æthelwold up to? He had taken his forces through Mercia following the Thames from its mouth in Essex almost to its source in the west without fighting any battles or taking any towns. They had plundered and taken slaves, but to what end? Could it all be simply to reward his Danish allies and make a show of force? Why had he not crossed into Wessex and challenged Edward? He must be short of men. That was why he was going to Wessex and sending Beorhsige to Mercia. No doubt they would say King Alfred's daughter had joined their cause to give them more credibility. Somehow, I had to stop him raising more troops by getting out the message that I was their captive, not their ally.

I strolled over to my companions who were crouched around a pot that sizzled on the fire. I greeted them cheerily and took a bowl of the greasy broth that they offered me. Glancing around to make sure the guards could not overhear, I leaned forward and quickly whispered instructions. My plan was dangerous but necessary. After slurping down the stew, I sauntered back to my tent.

Autumn was upon us and I was grateful that nightfall came early. As soon as it was dark, I left my tent and wandered towards the river where guards protected the bank.

'Toilet,' I called. 'I need privacy.' In case they did not understand my language, I reinforced the message by imitating the sound of passing wind.

The guard nodded and pointed to the pits that had been dug for the purpose in the compound.

I shook my head. 'No, thank you. I am a lady. I need somewhere private.' I pointed to a more secluded spot by the stream. 'I need to wash also.'

He shrugged and turned away. 'Ysopa and Oscytel have ordered you to treat me well,' I said, raising my voice. 'They will punish you if you do not.'

The guard looked towards a second soldier who grunted an instruction. Saying a prayer under my breath, I allowed the guard to grab me roughly by the arm and lead me to the edge of the stream. I loosened my belt, waving my hands to make him turn his back. As soon as he was looking away, I waded into the stream and began splashing hard at the water.

'Help, help!' I screamed, going down onto my knees and floundering in the fast-running stream as though I was drowning.

The guard reacted quickly, bounding through the water, grasping my arm, but I clutched him around the waist, pulling him down on top of me.

'Assault! Rape!' I yelled, as the guard slipped and stumbled, trying to free himself. I clung on, screaming and sobbing as loudly as I could. Other men were soon running towards us, some yanking at me, others seizing the guard who was shouting at the men who were holding him.

'Fetch Ysopa. Fetch Oscytel,' I cried as I was carried from the river, trying to keep the commotion going as long as I could. A circle of men looked interestedly down on me as I lay panting on the bank, my clothes soaking, my hair dishevelled. Ysopa's face appeared amongst them.

'You think we are fools that you can escape like this,' he sneered.

'I know you are a fool! A smelly, misguided fool who will die soon in a futile battle,' I shouted, trying to tug my sodden tunic down to cover my legs. He shouted some orders and men roughly gripped my wrists and ankles and half carried, half dragged me along the track towards my tent.

As we passed my companions who were looking on interestedly, I gave silent thanks to God. One was missing. A scout had slipped away in the confusion, as I had instructed.

*

It felt like the middle of the night when I heard men shouting and cursing, horses whickering and stamping. I thought I was dreaming but when a grizzled face appeared in my tent doorway and ordered me up, I knew that the army was on the move.

The departure was well managed, I had to admit. By dawn, the camp was packed into bags that hung from the sides of the horses, and the cavalry troop, which I estimated to number about five hundred riders, was ready to move out. Oscytel and Ysopa led the formation to the south, away from the Thames, further into Wessex.

Was this the start of Æthelwold's invasion? He had presumably scouted ahead and given the all-clear for the advance. He must have raised some local support. We were moving towards his family's forfeited estates around Wimborne where his cause might attract sympathy. He was no doubt spreading the word that the Lady of the Mercians was backing his rebellion and had joined his troops. I just hoped that my scout would make it through to my husband in time. Now that Cenwulf was dead, Beorhsige would try to mislead the rest of the Mercian army into joining Æthelwold's cause

After a few hours riding, I heard a shout up ahead and the column halted. I was directed towards a copse where some soldiers began setting up camp, lighting fires, erecting tents. Most of the cavalry formed into rows and trotted urgently to the south towards densely wooded land, which I recognised as Braydon Forest.

Although I was crammed in with the other captives and watched over by guards, I managed to rest, even to sleep fitfully. Towards the end of the afternoon, I opened my eyes to see several black plumes rising in the distance, smoke that meant farms and homesteads were burning. Æthelwold had begun plundering Wessex as well as Mercia. Maybe he was probing to see how loyal Edward's ealdormen would prove to be.

If he was, the answer came quickly. Horsemen appeared on the skyline, riding swiftly towards us. The flowing blond locks of the leading rider told me that Æthelwold was returning. He slid from his mount and men around him were soon barking orders and the camp, which had so recently been set up, began to disappear rapidly around me. Something was causing them to leave in a hurry.

Several of the returning riders towed bedraggled prisoners behind their horses. I tried not to look into their desperate faces, not wanting to see the suffering of fellow Saxons. Soldiers began to throw the prisoners onto the backs of mounts to travel two, even three, to a horse. I felt small arms grasp my waist as a whimpering girl was thrust up to sit behind me on my palfrey. I touched her hand in reassurance, but we did not speak until the melee of horses had settled down into an orderly line, travelling back the way we had come.

'What's your name, child?' I asked.

The girl did not reply.

'I admire your courage, but I am a prisoner too. I am Æthelflæd, daughter of your late king, Alfred.' I heard a gasp and the girl cleared her throat.

'I am Cwen, daughter of the Reeve of Braydon, m'lady,' she said.

That surprised me. The family of a town reeve would normally be well protected. 'What happened? How were you captured?'

Cwen sniffed. 'I was helping my father prepare food for the ealdorman when a fight broke out.'

'Which ealdorman?'

Cwen pointed towards the head of the column. 'That one.'

I gripped her hand. 'You mean Lord Æthelwold, the one with the long blond hair?'

'Yes, that's him. I wish I had never set eyes on him. He was so charming when he arrived. He even said he might marry me if my father supported him. What a liar!' Cwen sobbed. 'He didn't know that we were expecting Lord Ordlaf and his men and, when he found out, he went mad. His men killed my father and he took me.' She laid her head on my back and began to cry.

So that was it. Æthelwold had gone to the reeve of Braydon who had deceived him into thinking he might receive support because he knew that Ordlaf, the ealdorman of Wiltshire, was about to arrive with his soldiers. The reeve's loyalty to King Edward had cost him his life and the freedom of his family. Once Æthelwold had realised that he would soon be confronted by the Wiltshire fyrd, he had pillaged Braydon and beaten a hasty retreat.

*

That retreat was back towards the misty valley of the Thames, but we did not stop when we had crossed the river back into Mercia. Instead, we rode hard and long into the early evening before we rested. The next day the pattern was the same. We rose early and travelled all day with only short rests until the light faded in the evening. Something was driving Æthelwold on at great speed.

I looked for landmarks as we progressed east across the southern boundary of Mercia and saw a wooden tower I recognised as that of St Mary Magdalen's church in Oxford. I hoped the men of that burh had closed the gates of the newly walled town to deny the Danes easy plunder. I need not have worried. Our onward journey continued apace. Except we no longer followed the path of the Thames as it looped south towards Reading but continued due east towards the boundary of the Danelaw.

Cwen clung resolutely to my back as we rode, constantly praying for revenge for her family's slaughter. Her spirit moved me almost to tears: I knew that a young girl like her had little chance of justice in a world dominated by cruel men.

On the third day, we saw fluttering banners and the smoke of campfires in the distance, the unmistakable signs of a warband. My hope that it might be an army from Mercia or Wessex were dashed when I saw three golden crowns on a blue flag, the symbol of the Wuffingas, the ancient ruling family of East Anglia, now usurped by the Danes. In the centre of the scattered tents and pavilions was a farmstead, and my fellow prisoners and I were quickly pushed inside a large barn and the doors slammed shut.

The stench hit my nostrils before my eyes adjusted to the dark. At first, I thought I had pigs or cows for company, but gradually I made out human shapes crouched in the straw, their eyes wary and forlorn. The East Anglian Danes had been stealing human treasure as well as gold and silver. And these humans, who had been cruelly snatched from their homes, were my subjects. I felt like weeping but I knew that I had to give them hope, not tears. It took me a few moments of deep breathing before I could stand tall in the centre of the hall and speak.

'Fellow Christians, I am Æthelflæd, Lady of the Mercians, daughter of King Alfred.'

I looked around as eyes widened and men and women began scrambling to their feet, some bowing, others looking on curiously in disbelief. I chuckled. 'I must confess, I did not choose to come amongst you like this, but I rejoice in our companionship now that I have. Like you, I am a prisoner of these foul demons.'

I moved towards a couple with two young children. 'This may seem like hell for a family such as yours but let us not forget that the Lord Jesus was born in a cowshed like this.' I patted the children on the head as the mother fell at my feet weeping. 'Hold firm in your belief in God. Our armies are close by and we will soon prevail over the heathen enemy.' I paused as heads nodded in agreement. 'Is there a priest amongst us? No? Then I will lead our prayers for the forgiveness of our sins and of those that sin against us.'

Everyone in the crowded cowshed fell to their knees and loudly responded to my devotions and supplications.

'May the Lord watch over you,' I said finally, standing once again. 'We must count our blessings. We seem to be lodging in a grand hall.' I indicated the high walls around us. 'We must amuse ourselves whilst we live in this palace. Who knows some good riddles?'

There was muted laughter and a young lad piped up. 'I know one.'

I held up my hand. 'And what is your name and origin, lad?'

'My name is Osric, m'lady, from Hertford.'

'What is your riddle, Osric of Hertford?'

The lad cleared his throat and looked around awkwardly. 'I am a creature with one eye, two ears, two feet, two shoulders, a back and a neck. And twelve hundred heads. What am I?'

Whilst everyone was debating the meaning of the riddle, I moved closer to Osric.

'How'd you come here, lad?' I asked.

'I'm from a merchant's family, m'lady. My father and I traded metalwork, pots, knives, and the like. Seeing how we lived in Hertford, we bought and sold across the border. The Danes treated us well enough until the day…' The lad swallowed and his lip began to tremble. 'The day the one they call Ysopa came with a band of warriors and said he wanted all the axes we had. My father asked for payment, but he said he had to try the axe first. When my father offered him a handle, Ysopa just swung the axe at his head. If he'd had warning, my father could have thrashed that skinny devil, no problem, but he hit him without warning, killed him stone dead. Took everything we had and shut me in here.'

'How many days ago?'

'This is the seventh day, m'lady.'

That was strange. Why had a Danish army marched a few miles over the border and not moved for seven days?

Discussion on the riddle had reached a hubbub, so I clapped my hands. 'Who has got the answer?'

A mother pushed her little girl forward. 'If you please, m'lady, is it a monster with many heads but only one eye?' She smiled sweetly, showing the gap in her front teeth.

'Indeed it could be,' I said, wondering what fate awaited such a brave young captive. 'Osric, do you have an answer that betters this sweet child's?'

Osric shook his head. 'Just a different one m'lady. My creature is a one eyed garlic-seller.'

The crowd groaned, before clapping their appreciation, just as the giant door of the cowshed swung open and guards stepped inside, carrying an urn.

'Food,' one grunted. 'And don't make a mess.' His companions laughed gruffly and slammed the door shut as the prisoners formed a quiet queue and I picked up the ladle to serve the greasy broth.

*

Early next morning, I lay curled on the straw when I saw light penetrate the darkness as the door swung open once more.

'The Lady Æthelflæd?' a guard asked, looking around.

I scrambled to my feet. 'Who wants me?'

'You'll see,' came the curt reply.

I followed the men into the brightness outside and towards a thatched lodge that must have served as the feasting hall of the farmstead. When I was shown through the door, I was confronted by an enormous figure draped in fur and leather with a craggy face that I half-recognised.

'Well, what have we here?' the giant said. 'Can this really be Alfred's little girl?'

NINE

At first, I thought I was face-to-face with Guthrum, my father's old rival. He had the same wide nose and enormous frame. But Guthrum had died a decade before.

'They told me it was you and now I see it is.' He was grinning widely, peering down to examine me more closely.

I was astounded that he recognised me. My hair was lank and my tunic covered in mud and whatever else I had picked up in the cowshed. Besides, I had last met him when we were both children. He had fooled around like an annoying puppy trying to attract my attention. Now, he was King of the Danes in East Anglia and I was in his power.

I straightened my back. 'Yes, Eohric, I do remember you from the time your father submitted to mine. I also recall that, although you had been defeated, you were treated kindly like a human being, and not locked in a shed like an animal.'

Eohric looked shocked. He bellowed at a figure behind him in the shadows. 'Do not tell me that you put this royal lady in the cowshed?'

It was Oscytel who came forward, cowering before his king. 'There was no other space…'

'We must treat this lady like the daughter of a king, not a slave. When we camp tonight make sure Lady Æthelflæd has suitable quarters,' Eohric said.

Oscytel raised his eyebrows and I smiled at him. 'A tent and some blankets would do. You will find Cwen of Braydon in the cowshed. She can join me as my attendant,' I said.

Eohric nodded and Oscytel sloped away to carry out the command.

'Thank you,' I said. 'Perhaps you can also explain why your army is trespassing on my lands, pillaging and robbing my people.'

Eohric roared with laughter. 'You haven't changed. Do you remember when you jabbed me with your elbow and told me to stop belching after the feast? A proper little tyrant you were, even then.' He beckoned towards the table behind him. 'Why don't we sit down and have a cup together like old friends.'

He poured dark wine into a goblet and offered it to me. I hesitated before accepting. 'Stolen from the unfortunate crofter who lived here?' I asked.

Eohric tutted. 'No, this is better than your local wine. This one came from a trader from Frankia destined for Edward's court.'

I sipped the wine which was indeed more mellow than that produced from local grapes. 'Since when did you Danes become particular about what you stole?'

Eohric looked hurt. 'We have learned much since our forefathers came a-viking to these lands. They may have lived roughly in their boats and taken what they needed, but now we prefer to farm and trade and live under warm thatch.'

'So why have you brought a warband across my border to steal and plunder?'

He swigged from his cup and wiped a dribble from the thick beard around his lips. 'Our fathers made an agreement, right?'

I nodded. I knew in detail about the treaty King Alfred had signed with Guthrum establishing a dividing line between the Danes to the east and the Anglo-Saxons to the west.

'When I became king, I accepted that treaty so that we could continue living peacefully side by side,' he continued. 'That lasted whilst your father was alive, but once Edward took over, things changed.'

'Like what?'

'Started with raids across the border,' he said.

He could hardly blame Edward for that. 'Bandits from the Danelaw have been stealing our cattle for years,' I reminded him.

'No, these weren't cattle thieves. They were Edward's men. Even before he was king, he was sending raiders from Kent, probing our defences.'

That was different, if it was true. 'How do you know that?'

He banged down his goblet and leaned towards me. 'We're not fools. We know what he is up to, and so do you. Your father was hardly cold in his coffin before Edward had gathered an army on our borders.'

'Strange then that you have invaded Mercia, not Wessex.' I took a slow sip of the wine, my eyes not leaving Eohric's.

'That was Æthelwold's idea. He said that once we crossed your border, you would join us.'

I smiled. 'And here I am. Covered in dung from your cowshed.'

'That was... it was unfortunate. But we've had confused messages from your side. First your ealdorman Beorhsige assured us that Mercia was with us in overthrowing Edward. Then your husband returns our envoys' horses without their riders.'

I silently gave thanks to God but tried not to show my delight at this news. Æthelred must have received my message.

'So now you know. Æthelwold is getting no further support from Mercia or Wessex. Why don't you just release the prisoners, hand back whatever you have stolen and go home? I might forgive you for the misunderstanding.'

'You don't know our ways,' he scoffed. 'My warriors followed me for the treasure, not because they fear your brother. Winter is setting in so we will go home, but we will take what we have.'

If, as I now suspected, Æthelred had recovered his health sufficiently to hold Eohric's envoys as hostages against my own safety, my negotiating position had strengthened. 'Alright, I will take the prisoners back with me, but you can keep the gold. And I will make sure that Lord Æthelred and King Edward do not pursue you too hard.'

Eohric stared at me. 'It is too late to bargain. Edward has crossed into the Danelaw ahead of us, so we will be pursuing him. And we have sent a message to Æthelred saying that if he wants to see his wife alive again, he had better keep his troops in Mercia.' He grinned and poured more wine. 'That way, you and I have more time to get to know each other.'

*

Later that day, Eohric's army broke camp and travelled east. Guards marched the prisoners out of the barn and tied them to the baggage carts pulled by oxen. Drivers whipped the powerful beasts along at a good pace and the journey was hard for the women and children who were relentlessly dragged along. I was grateful to be given my palfrey to ride and willingly shared her with Cwen and any of the youngsters in need of a rest. I deliberately travelled near the young lad, Osric, as he was a trader's son and knew the territory we were passing through.

Before long, we were in the Danelaw.

It was the first time that I had crossed the line that divided my world from that of the enemy. At first, it did not look so different to Mercia or Wessex. I only realised that I had crossed the boundary because Osric assured me that we had. Soon after, the terrain looked less familiar, or inviting. The land became flat and featureless with few trees, and an interminable expanse of grey cloud loomed large above me. The soil turned dark and heavy underfoot and we made frequent detours to avoid boggy wetlands and shallow lakes.

'We call this the Fenlands, m'lady,' Osric explained.

'Where do you think we are going in this godforsaken land?' I asked, my mood dampened by the cold mist blowing in.

'We are travelling north on Ermine Street, m'lady. The town of Cambridge is somewhere over there.' He pointed to the east.

I set Cwen and Osric the task of finding out all they could from the servants who marched nearby. They garnered contradictory information: some said we were chasing the army of Wessex, others that it was a separate, smaller warband ahead of us. Whoever it was, they were leaving a trail of burning homesteads behind them.

For three days, we endured a cold hard trek, not knowing where we were headed nor why. When a halt was called on the fourth evening in a muddy field surrounded by ditches, I discovered the truth of our situation.

A unit of mounted warriors rode into camp, the horses' hooves throwing up clay as they thundered past. I caught sight of Æthelwold and Beorhsige as they jumped from their horses and made for Eohric's quarters. They were in a hurry. Something was up.

Osric and Cwen were setting up my tent next to the rest of the prisoners who shivered under their coats in the exposed countryside.

'This mist is freezing,' I said to Cwen, hugging myself with my arms. 'We have our tent to keep us warm, so give our blankets to the young ones.'

'Thank you, m'lady.' Cwen looked towards the pathway that ran through the encampment. 'I think your escort has arrived for your evening appointment,' she grinned.

I peered into the gloom and saw a soldier waving and shouting in my direction as he picked his way through the tents that were going up in the fading light.

'Yes, you're right. The king wants to see me, again,' I sighed, brushing at the dirt on my tunic.

On several evenings as the army pitched camp for the night, I had received a summons to join Eohric in his pavilion where he had shared his supper with me. I was grateful for the food but suspicious of his intentions. On each occasion, he had begun with reminiscences about the past and how, he claimed, our fathers had become almost like brothers.

That evening when I joined him at the table, he went even further.

The food was cold, and I grimaced as I chewed the tough salted meat. He chuckled and poured wine into my goblet.

'Can't cook tonight. No fires. Too close to the enemy for that,' he said.

I sensed the need to be alert, so I resisted tasting the wine. 'I'm amazed anyone would willingly come to this wet wilderness, especially my brother,' I muttered.

Eohric gulped down his cup and refilled it. 'Surprised me too, especially...' he hesitated and took another gulp. 'Maybe it's the cold that has infected his mind.'

I tried not to look too interested. 'He's not as experienced or clever as you are. What's the idiot done now?'

'He's done something that would make your father turn in his grave. The worst tactical blunder you can make,' Eohric guffawed.

I risked patting his hand in an affectionate manner. 'You men and your military talk. I'm afraid I've not heard of a... what do you call it? Tactical blunder?'

Eohric grabbed two wooden plates from the table. 'Let's say this was his army,' he said, putting one plate on top of the other. 'And this is us.' He held a single plate in his other hand. 'He has twice as many men as we have, right? I nodded and tried to smile innocently. 'So we have to keep our distance. Unless we can somehow attack only one part of his army at a time.' He put one of the two plates on the table. 'In which case we are not outnumbered, and everyone knows that one Dane is worth more than any Saxon, so we will win.' He clashed two plates together, triumphantly dropping one to the floor.

'I see,' I said, frowning as if I was completely ignorant of such matters. 'So how will you separate Edward's plates… I mean men?'

'He's done it for us. I couldn't believe it when Æthelwold told me, but he has seen it with his own eyes.'

I had been wondering why Æthelwold had returned in such haste. 'Is he here?'

Eohric grinned. 'He's close by in his shelter with Beorhsige, but don't worry, he won't disturb us. They're both exhausted from following Edward around.'

'Watching him make a tactical blunder – is that the term?'

Eohric clapped his hands. 'We'll make an army chief of you yet! Edward has withdrawn his main force to the south west, leaving his vanguard behind, over there.' Eohric pointed forward, through the door of the pavilion. 'He has divided his forces and we are now between the two of them.'

'Poor Edward. What will happen?'

Eohric poured more wine. 'What do you think?'

'I'm just a woman, but wouldn't it be better if we all made peace and went back to living how we were? You can't really enjoy all this marching around in the cold and wet can you?'

Eohric grabbed my hand and pulled me towards him across the table. 'If you really want peace, there is a way.'

I tried not to flinch as I felt his hot breath on my face. 'What would that be?'

'We can unite Mercia and East Anglia and keep Edward in his place, Æthelwold too, if you…' He paused, suddenly uncertain.

'If I what?'

'Marry me,' he blurted out.

I reddened at his sudden change of direction. 'I am not sure what my husband would say about that.'

'If he is as sick as some say, he will not be a problem for long.'

Eohric sat back and picked up his goblet. 'You and I could forge a territory more powerful than Wessex, whoever rules there.'

I took a deep breath. 'You make an interesting case, King Eohric, which I will consider carefully. In the meantime, what will you do to my brother's men?'

He gulped down more wine. 'We'll teach Edward a lesson he will never forget. We've trapped his vanguard, his favourite troops from Kent, in the marshland. We will destroy them at dawn.'

*

I cursed softly as I tripped on a tent rope. The thick mist had turned the evening gloom into a wall of darkness, and finding my way back to my shelter, even with a guard to guide me, was difficult. The prisoners' enclave was to the rear of the army at the opposite end to Eohric's pavilion, so I had to walk the length of the encampment. Osric's boyish face appeared in the fog as he scrambled to his feet outside my tent.

'Osric, tell me I'm still somewhere on earth and not gone to purgatory.'

'Yes m'lady. I'm fairly sure the Holme Fen is that way.' He pointed in the direction from which I had just come.

I ducked into the tent. 'Then pray for the men of Kent who are trapped there.'

Cwen sat up in the far corner. 'The men of Kent m'lady?'

'Yes, child. They form the Saxon vanguard. You know of them?'

'Yes m'lady. My brother married a Kentish girl and fights with the fyrd of Kent.'

'You best pray for his soul. Our brave King Edward has allowed the Danes to trap them in the fen that lies ahead of us.'

I could not believe the poor girl's misfortune. She had already lost her father to Æthelwold's foolish rebellion and tomorrow she would almost certainly lose her brother.

When I finally managed to fall asleep that night, my head was full of wild imaginings, of raging tempests and stormy waterways that engulfed me. I heard a rustling that seemed more real than my dreaming and I opened my eyes to catch a glimpse of Cwen creeping out of the tent.

'Something wrong?' I asked.

'Just need a pee, m'lady' she said.

I turned over and went back to sleep. Sometime later, I woke and looked towards Cwen's bedding. It was empty.

I crawled from the tent to poke Osric awake. 'Have you seen Cwen?'

Osric rubbed his eyes and shook his head.

'She must be lost in this fog. Come with me,' I said.

I followed my nose towards the cesspits at the rear of the camp. Apart from dozing guards, the area was deserted. I retraced my steps of earlier that evening to the headquarters of the army where Eohric held court. A guard loomed out of the dark to challenge us.

'I'm looking for a young girl,' I explained.

He chuckled. 'I'm always looking for young girls.' He pointed to the line of tents behind me. 'Keeping some lucky sod warm, I should…'

He did not finish his sentence. At that moment, a spear thudded into his back.

*

I did not look at the guard as he fell writhing to the ground. I was held spellbound by the sight behind him. A ghostly wall of shields was advancing silently through the mist. The yelling of the wounded warrior served as a signal for the eerie formation to move more rapidly and suddenly the shadowy shields materialised into a phalanx of running warriors.

I felt a tug at my arm. 'This way, m'lady.' It was Osric who was pulling me hard to one side, out of the path of the advancing warband. It was too late. Suddenly, I could see the helmets and grim faces behind the shields as they closed in on me. I stumbled as I turned, expecting a sword thrust into my body at any moment.

None came.

Instead, the shields parted and the warriors charged around me. I slipped in the mud as I scrambled out of their way and felt Osric's grip on my arm loosen as he was knocked over by a shield. I crouched by his body as wave after wave of solders sped past, yelling war cries in a tongue I knew only too well.

They were Saxons.

I watched in awe as they maintained a tight formation that swept into the camp behind me. I recognised one of the fighters as either Sigewulf or Sigehelm – they looked identical in helmets. The men of Kent must have realised they were trapped and, in a desperate attempt to break out, they had sprung a surprise of their own.

The Danes had begun to appear from their tents to offer disjointed resistance, but the attackers drove on until they reached the very pavilion where I had dined that evening. They swarmed around it like hornets, overwhelming the guards and slashing the fabric sides to gain entry. Rather than attack the body of the army, the Kentish warriors were trying to cut off its head. How did they know where to find the king?

I scrabbled up from the wet mud to see the scene more clearly. Eohric's giant figure emerged from the flapping canvas, quickly followed by the slimmer forms of Ysopa and Oscytel. Eohric's bellow of rage echoed through the fog as he flayed at his tormentors with an enormous sword. His sons desperately tried to protect his back as the Saxons surrounded them, jabbing them with long spears as if they had cornered a bull and its calves. Danish warriors were arriving in more numbers, but the Saxons had formed two circles, one around their isolated prey, the other facing the warriors who were trying to reach them. Eohric made a desperate attempt to break out, rushing at a short soldier, bringing his sword down like an axe towards his head. Raising his shield against the blow, the man staggered back and it seemed as though Eohric might force his way through. With their backs to the king, Ysopa and Oscytel did not see his forward drive and Saxon warriors used the chance to separate them from Eohric, knocking them backwards with sharp blows of their shields. Another warrior darted behind the king and slashed at the back of his legs. Eohric threw back his head with a roar to the heavens and slumped onto one knee.

A groan reminded me that Osric was on the ground at my feet and I glanced down. He was sitting up, holding his head.

'You alright?' I asked.

'Just a little knock, m'lady,' he muttered, trying to stand.

'We must go,' I said, watching the nearby battle reach its climax. Ysopa and Oscytel had disappeared beneath a ring of stabbing soldiers, and spear after spear thumped into Eohric's mighty frame. I hauled Osric to his feet and was about to skirt around the fighting when, out of the corner of my eye, I glimpsed a willowy figure staggering out of the mist. I'd found who I'd been looking for.

'Cwen, over here,' I called and ran to catch her before she fell.

'M'lady, I…' Cwen stuttered.

'Save your strength. Osric, help me if you can.'

We linked arms to support her and slowly made our way around the fighting towards the dyke that marked the edge of the encampment. It had been lined with guards but now there were none.

I looked at the empty field beyond. It was tempting. We only had to cross the dyke and we would be swallowed into the mist and could escape.

No, I cannot just leave the others.

'Cwen, where have you been, child? Are you hurt?'

'No, m'lady, sorry m'lady. But I had to warn them.'

'You went to the Kentish soldiers?' I asked, amazed.

Cwen hung her head and nodded.

Osric's eyes were wide with wonder. 'You're only a girl. You should've asked me.'

Cwen put her hand on his. 'Sometimes it's easier for us girls to get past the guards,' she said, with a knowing look in my direction.

'You did well, Cwen,' I said. 'But, although they seem to have killed the king, our troops are outnumbered.' I glanced over to see the state of the fighting. 'And now they are surrounded. We need to free the captives and go.'

Slowly, we made our way around the encampment, hoping the battle would draw any attention away from us. When I finally saw the huddled forms of the prisoners in the compound, I cursed under my breath. They had been roped together and a sentry stood nearby. He was looking in our direction and I recognised him as the guard who had taken me to Eohric's pavilion on several occasions.

'Why are you still here and not following your king's orders?' I called to him.

Although it was not yet daybreak, he obviously recognised me. 'What do you mean, m'lady?'

'The Saxons have attacked, and we are struggling to hold them. The king needs every man at the front, including you and your men.' I saw his frown as he glanced towards the prisoners. 'King Eohric sent me to look after them. They will obey me. I'm their queen after all.'

The guard called behind him and three men appeared out of the dark. I could not catch what he was saying to them but I saw them hesitate.

'Hurry! Or your fellow soldiers will think you cowards for loitering in the rear,' I said.

They shrugged their shoulders and scrambled towards the sounds of battle.

I breathed with relief. Now I just needed a knife.

'Osric, come with me. Cwen, go to the prisoners and tell them what is happening. Keep them quiet.'

With Osric following at a respectful distance, I strolled into the small enclave where servants and kitchen staff were huddled together for warmth, looking anxious as the sounds of battle drifted towards them. They proved easy to convince. A mixture of Saxon peasants and slaves, they had little loyalty for their Danish masters, and I soon persuaded them to give me what I needed. Osric cast an expert eye over the cooking knives and sharp tools before carrying back his selection in a sack.

There was an air of expectancy in the prisoner's compound, and I heard mutterings of thanks to God as Osric emptied his sack and began hacking at the hemp ropes. He cut the men loose first so they could help him with the task of freeing the women and children.

Just as they were cutting the last few free, I heard men running towards us.

'Sit down and look as though you are still tied. Hide the knives,' I hissed.

Four warriors appeared out of the gloom and headed for the makeshift paddock where the horses were tethered, ignoring us. They seemed intent on finding mounts for themselves; whether it was to rejoin the fight or escape from it, I could not guess. But I did see that one of the warriors had bright blond hair that curled up at the ends. Someone who preferred to fight on horseback.

Æthelwold.

He took a horse by the halter and heaved a saddle onto its back. Next to him I could make out the upright figure of Beorhsige, who waved at one of the other men to help him mount up.

I closed my eyes to pray that they would not recognise me. So, I did not see Cwen hide a knife beneath her tunic and move quietly towards the paddock.

Until it was too late.

'Have you not time to say goodbye to an old sweetheart?'

I turned abruptly at the sound of Cwen's voice and gasped when I saw her appealing to Æthelwold from the edge of the paddock.

What is the child doing! She will give us all away.

I sat petrified as Æthelwold smiled in Cwen's direction and walked over to her, stooping as if to kiss her.

The eerie atmosphere was broken by a high-pitched scream as Æthelwold staggered back, clutching at his stomach, before he fell thrashing to the ground, where he yelled and thrashed some more.

Beorhsige reacted quickly, running to where Cwen stood trembling, a long knife in her hand. He snatched the knife from her grasp and slashed the blade across her neck. A red stain coloured her grey tunic as she crumpled onto Æthelwold's twitching body. Beorhsige bent over her, struggling to pull her away from his lord.

The shock that had transfixed us all suddenly wore off and we rose as one to charge to the paddock. Osric got there first and threw himself onto Beorhsige's back, wrapping his arms around his neck and his legs around his waist, pulling him away from Cwen. Beorhsige still held the knife which he used to jab wildly at the unexpected arrival on his back. I winced as I saw the blade stab into Osric's neck. Soon, men were grappling with Beorhsige, forcing him to the ground by weight of numbers, kicking him, punching him and shouting "Traitor!" A horse reared up on its hind legs and lashed a hoof into one of the other soldiers who took fright and ran off, followed closely by his comrade.

In what seemed like a few heartbeats, it was all over.

I looked down on the bloodied bodies of the two traitors and the two youngsters who had killed them.

The world had surely gone mad.

TEN

I pulled the fur cover to my chin and tried not to wake. After sleeping on uneven, damp surfaces for many days, it felt so good to doze in a familiar bed. Yet there was something that dragged me into wakefulness, a sweet scent in the air, the occasional snuffle that did not sound like my husband's. I forced my eyes open.

'Ælfwyn, what are you doing here?' I said, surprised to see my daughter sitting on the bed.

'Waiting for you to wake, mother. You've been sleeping like a baby.'

'Oh, my sweet child, I can't tell you how wonderful it is to be home.' I wrapped my arms tightly around Ælfwyn and wept quietly. Cwen would have been the same age as my daughter and, hard as I tried, I could not banish the terrible images of her last moments from my head.

We drew apart at a tap on the door and Athelstan bounced into the room and flung himself onto the bed.

'Hooray! You're awake,' he shouted. 'Can you tell us about the battle now?'

I smiled. 'Wouldn't you like to know how I am first?'

'Sorry, yes, of course. How are you, aunt? What was it like being a prisoner?' he asked in a rush.

127

'I'm a little tired but unhurt. Unlike many who perished in the fens.'

'Is it true that all of father's enemies were killed even though he lost?' he asked, wide-eyed.

I had tried to push the violent scenes of the conflict to the back of my mind. Yet I knew everyone would be talking of little else.

'It was not just the highborn but almost all the Kentish troops who were killed. Some very brave prisoners too. But yes, King Edward is safe on his throne now that Æthelwold and his ally King Eohric are dead,' I said.

Athelstan frowned. 'Why did so many Saxons die if the Danish King was killed?'

'That is a question you had best ask your father,' I said, brushing the hair out of his eyes.

Ælfwyn jumped up. 'That reminds me. He's coming here as soon as the weather improves.'

'Who?' I asked.

'King Edward. I heard the messenger telling the clerk this morning.'

I sat up straight in bed. Edward had never been to Gloucester before. Why now?

'Has Æthelred returned yet?' I had seen him fleetingly at the border of the Danelaw when I had escaped there with the prisoners. After a brief reunion, he had sent me swiftly home whilst he stayed to help sort out the aftermath of the battle.

'He sent word that he will be back in a few days.' Ælfwyn tightened her grip on my hand to make her final point. 'And he said to make sure that you rested until he returned.'

My mind was too full of thoughts to rest. I could not forget the despairing faces of the prisoners in the cowshed, nor the killings by the paddock. I had always accepted that warriors had to fight to protect the land and repel invaders. But why did God allow innocent women and children to be harmed as well?

Once I was dressed, I asked Ælfwyn and Athelstan to accompany me on a walk. We went to the east gate set into the ancient walls built by the Romans centuries ago. I noted that construction had begun, as I had ordered, to lengthen the old wall down to the river to form a more complete protection for the township. Yet no one was working on it now. Similarly, when we reached the River Severn that curved around the northern end of Gloucester, I saw that work had been started to repair the old bridge, but nothing was being done that day.

Maybe I had slept longer than I thought. 'Is it Sunday?' I asked Ælfwyn, who sat beside me on a slab of rock that lay abandoned by the track leading to the bridge.

Ælfwyn looked concerned as she turned towards me. 'No, it's Saturday. Did you lose track of the days when you…'

'No, each morning, I gave thanks to God that I was still alive and I made careful note of the day. I know it's Saturday.' I stood and pointed towards the bridge. 'But when I saw there were no workmen, I thought I must be mistaken, that it was Sunday, the day of rest.'

Athelstan was hopping from one foot to the other whilst listening carefully. 'It was thegns doing the work and Lord Cenwulf took them with the army when he left,' he said.

Cenwulf. How I would have dearly liked his thoughtful advice at that moment. It was hard to belief he was not there, nor would be ever again. I put an arm around Ælfwyn and signalled to Athelstan to sit next to us.

'When I was a prisoner, I saw for myself how people change when they are distressed. Nice, thoughtful people acted foolishly. Peace-loving folk became bitter.'

I paused to choose my words. 'I made a promise to God that, if I survived, I would not be like that, that I would change how I am sometimes. I know that I am… well, I can be… maybe a little hasty in what I say and do.'

I paused, looking first at Ælfwyn and then at Athelstan, half expecting at least one of them to protest that what I was saying was not true. Yet they both remained silent with the same stunned, mouth-open expression.

I cleared my throat. 'So, I am praying to God that he might make me more… even more thoughtful than I have been, so that I can promote harmony, not conflict.'

The youngsters looked dumbfounded, and I felt my cheeks burn. Maybe I had gone too far.

I slid from the rock. 'These walls and this bridge need building with more urgency, but I will try to remain calm whilst I see to it that they are.'

I strode off to inspect the bridge one more time.

*

Three days later, Æthelred returned with his thegns late in the afternoon. Alerted that he was coming, I had prepared a welcome for my lord. I prised him away from the customary drinking and ribaldry with the retainers in the great hall and ushered him to our own chamber for a quiet meal for two. I had ordered the cooks to prepare his favourite dishes: a pie stuffed with pork, onions, turnips and carrots, copiously flavoured with pepper, followed by warm bread, cheese and apples.

When he saw the spread on the cloth-covered table, he grunted his appreciation before drinking deeply from the silver goblet brimming with cider and falling ravenously on the oozing pie. I watched with satisfaction whilst he ate and drank his fill, trying not to notice that he had to rely on one hand to do most of the eating and that one side of his mouth seemed insensitive to the liquid that dribbled from it.

He gave a satisfied burp and wiped at the remnants of food caught in the hair around his mouth. 'I feel better for that. Must thank the cook for remembering the food that I like.'

I stopped myself from telling him of my part in the choosing of his meal. 'Much has happened, my lord, since we last ate together like this.'

'You can say that again.' He looked at me with concern. 'And you have suffered much. First your mother, Ealhswith, then your uncle, Cenwulf.'

Not to mention my Cwen and Osric, I thought.

'As for this episode with the Danes,' he continued. 'Your brother should be grateful that it's Eohric that's dead and not him. If it hadn't been for the warning that you sent, the Kentish vanguard would have been taken by surprise, and not the other way round.'

'It was not me but a very brave girl who surely will be in heaven for what she did to help her people.' I reached across the table to put my hand on his. 'How do we put a stop to this killing of innocent folk in our wars?'

Æthelred brushed my hand gently with his giant fingers. 'I don't know. Nor do I know exactly how we are going to fight our wars anyway. We have no generals left. Your uncle is gone, that fool Beorhsige is dead and his father Beornoth is too old. We are left with a bunch of young thegns. And me.' He loosened his grip of my hand to lift up his limp arm. 'A cripple who can't fight any more.'

I shook my head. 'You're much improved. Your voice is stronger and you led the army to the borders of Danelaw, didn't you?'

'I can ride, clinging onto the horse with my knees and steering it with my good hand. But I cannot fight.'

'But you can still direct and inspire our young warriors. Can you not train one of our thegns to take charge during the actual fighting?'

'That will take time, time that we may not have. I hear King Edward is paying us a visit. Now he is secure on the throne and East Anglia is no longer a threat, he may be looking to take control of Mercia.'

'He can look all he like. We are in command here, are we not?' He nodded and I put my hand back into his. 'We should eat together like this more often.'

'You're right. I can't remember the last time I dined alone with a lady,' he chuckled.

'I, on the other hand, have been dining frequently with a king for company. He even asked me to marry him.'

Æthelred sat back. 'Did he now. And how did you reply?'

'I told him I would ask my husband.'

Æthelred threw back his head and roared with laughter, just as he used to do.

*

The weather became cold, colder than many could remember, and it snowed for days on end. Edward's visit was put back until after Michaelmas and he finally arrived when the daylight hours were lengthening and green shoots were showing in the fields.

I had expected the king to ride into Gloucester at the head of an army of attendants, but he came accompanied by only a small force of warriors and a handful of servants. I stood on the steps of the great hall with my family and the remnants of Mercian nobility to greet him. As he dismounted and walked towards us, I thought I detected a change in his demeanour. His old swagger was more of a regular stride and his smile could almost have been genuine.

When the welcome party bowed, he pulled the leather helmet from his head. 'It is I who should be bowing to recognise your service to our cause,' he said.

I was lost for words. What game was he playing? Osferth followed closely behind the king. Had he devised a new scheme for Edward to gain control of Mercia?

Æthelred stepped forward. 'Welcome, our lord king.'

Edward acknowledged his words with a nod but moved towards me. To my surprise, he enveloped me in a swift embrace, patting my back awkwardly as if it was a horse's neck. It was as close as we had come to physical affection since he was a baby. I felt tears welling, and, as he stepped back, I wiped a sleeve across my face, grateful for the stiff breeze so that I could feign rubbing dust from my eyes.

When Æthelred turned to lead the king's party into the great hall, Edward pulled at my elbow.

'We need a private audience before we proceed too far,' he said quietly in my ear. 'If possible, before any festivity you may have prepared.'

I began to regret our decision to mark the first visit of the new king to Mercia with a sumptuous banquet and entertainment. But I took a deep breath and walked quickly to the overseer of the cooks around the hearth. The wizened woman looked less than pleased to hear my instruction, clapping her hands sharply to relay the change of plan. The womenfolk bustled in and out of the hall, returning with ale, oatcakes, cheese and fruit to satisfy the immediate appetites of the travellers whilst waiting for the delayed feast.

I gestured for my husband and the king to leave the hubbub of the hall. In turn, Edward beckoned to Osferth and we four made our way to the receiving room next to the great hall. I ordered out a minstrel who was using the room to tune his lyre and a bard who was rehearsing his lines.

'Shall I send for some refreshments? You must be starving after your journey,' I asked.

Edward munched on an apple he had taken from the hall. 'Another of these would be welcome. It has preserved well since the harvest.'

'The goat's cheese and mead looked good,' Osferth said.

I shouted instructions from the door. For some reason, I felt quite faint, and took a few moments to gulp in some fresh air.

'You may wonder why the secrecy of this meeting,' I heard Edward say as I turned to rejoin the men. 'But after the betrayal by your ealdorman Beorhsige and others, I felt the need for caution.'

'I think we can trust those with us today, m'lord king,' Æthelred said.

'I noticed Beornoth is not here,' Edward said, taking a bite of his apple.

'He is in Shrewsbury, mourning the loss of his son. He professes allegiance but we are watching him all the same,' said Æthelred.

A guard tapped on the door and ushered in a woman bearing cheese, fruit and mead which she placed on the table as all conversation stopped. I studied Osferth carefully as he sliced into the cheese.

His nose looked like my father's. I wondered if he knew that I knew his lineage.

When I had told Æthelred of my mother's revelation that Osferth was Alfred's bastard, he had not shown much surprise. Perhaps it was more common knowledge than I thought.

Edward washed down the apple with a swig of mead. 'The question is what do we do about the Danes,' he said abruptly.

I glanced anxiously at my husband. At least it wasn't what do we do about Mercia.

'Osferth and I have been talking of little else,' Edward continued. 'We have some plans and before we become befuddled by your excellent wines, we wanted your advice.' He smiled at me. 'Especially now that you have had first-hand experience of our enemy.'

This was not the old Edward speaking. Something had happened to him in the fens.

Æthelred cleared his throat. 'Perhaps we can hear these plans, m'lord king,' he managed to say in a steady voice.

Edward looked to Osferth. 'Why don't you begin?'

Osferth needed no further invitation and put down his cup. 'King Alfred once told me that we should begin the next campaign by learning what we can from the last one.'

He looked directly at me as he spoke.

By mentioning our father, was he telling me that he knew that I knew?

'What I learned is that the Danes now fear us,' Osferth continued. 'They avoided battle because they knew we were stronger. But we cannot defeat them in the way we thought. Gathering one large army to attack the Danish fiefdoms, one after the other as we had planned, will not work.'

Edward pushed back his chair to stand. 'It's the old problem you and I had before, Æthelred,' he said, clapping him on the back. 'You remember how we had Hæsten trapped at Thorney Island only to have half our army march away.'

Æthelred nodded, looking pleased at his acknowledgement of the part he had played with the young Edward in stopping an earlier Danish invasion. 'Ah yes, we had him cornered alright, but the duty time of the fyrd was up and our men went home for the harvest. We had to let the bastard escape.'

'Exactly the same happened in the fenland of East Anglia,' continued Osferth. 'We had Eohric in a pincer between the armies of Kent and Hampshire, but we ran out of time, as well as provisions. The Hampshire fyrd had to turn away, but somehow our messages to the Kentish vanguard did not get through. They advanced when they should have been retreating.'

Edward slumped back into his seat. 'And we know what happened to them. Only good fortune and your quick thinking, sister, saved us from complete disaster,' he muttered. 'But Sigewulf, Sigehelm and my brave warriors of Kent paid the price for our problems.'

It was the first I had heard confirmation that Edward's friends had died in the battle. That might explain some of his deflation. He had been very close to those two in his youth.

Maybe he blamed Osferth for the tactical blunder, as Eohric had called it.

If Osferth had been at fault, it did not show in the confident way he continued to explain the proposal. 'King Alfred had a way of containing the Danes that I believe we can now use to attack them. First, we fortify our towns on the frontier with Danelaw. Then we push forward and build new burhs on the land we have gained. That way, we can protect our gains when our armies return home.'

I nearly fell from my chair. He was presenting it as his idea. Yet he was using Alfred's strategies, just as I had been doing. Only he had added a new element. They would build burhs in Danish held territory. I had to admit, it was a good idea.

'I told you...' I began but bit my lip. Maybe this was not the moment to quibble about who thought of it first.

'Before we push east into Danelaw, we have to cover our backs in the west,' Æthelred interjected. 'We have the Welsh to consider.'

'Not just the Welsh,' Edward said. 'I hear that Norwegians are fleeing towards you from Ireland.'

My face burned at his words. Had he heard of the pact I had made with Ingimund and his Norsemen?

'Perhaps we should reinforce Chester,' I said quietly. 'It would protect our Welsh frontier and give us a northern base to move against the Danelaw. We did begin some building work there.'

'Makes sense to defend the northern end of Mercia as well as the south,' Æthelred agreed.

Osferth looked disgruntled. 'We cannot let our advantage slip. The Danes are leaderless. If we push forward now, they will crumble.'

So that was it. Osferth wanted an aggressive policy, but Edward's confidence had been knocked in the fens. I waited on Æthelred's words and, for once, I was praying he would agree with Edward.

'No point in moving east into the Danelaw if we are invaded from the west. Let's secure our borders before we seek to extend them,' Æthelred said.

I wanted to kiss him, but Osferth looked as though he could kill him.

Edward grunted. 'So that settles it. We'll make peace with the Danes and see to our defences.'

Osferth clenched his fists. 'If that is your wish, lord king. But let us use the peace to make ready for war.'

*

The feast that evening followed the traditions of our forefathers. Leaving their weapons at the door of the feast hall, the king's retinue and our Mercian thegns squeezed together onto the benches with much jostling and bawdy greetings. As Edward took his place next to Æthelred at the high table, they all stood to bang their fists on the tabletop as a salute to their king.

But custom held that the lady of the household should greet menfolk into her home. So it was I, the Lady of the Mercians, dressed in a flowing red robe and adorned with a golden neckpiece and glittering rings, who came forward to serve the warriors who had noisily assembled in my feasting hall. I carried a large silver pitcher engraved with fighting figures and filled to the brim with foaming ale. I moved as gracefully as I could towards Æthelred, my lord, curtseying and smiling, before filling his ale-cup. He gulped a mouthful and passed the drink on to his visitor, the king, who took a sip and raised his glass to acknowledge that it was good enough for the assembled guests to drink. The roar of their approval echoed loudly around the rafters. When the din had died down and the men had all taken their seats, I looked kindly towards Edward and spoke in a clear voice that I hoped all could hear.

'Lord king, welcome to our humble home.' I turned to face the tables. 'And welcome to all our guests. We hope you enjoy our modest offerings and amusements.'

With that, the hall-women appeared, carrying Mercia's finest silver salvers brimming with steaming pork, cabbage, carrots and sprouts and more jugs of ale and mead. It was scarcely spring so that the stores were depleted and the feast was not as varied as I might have wished, but the men fell upon it like wolves. When the toasting and feasting was done, the minstrels and bards appeared to entertain the gathering with coarse songs and sagas of heroic deeds.

I was happy to slip away with the women and retire to my room, although the sounds from the hall kept me awake for some time. I knew that Æthelred would not be joining me in our chamber as, like as not, he would fall unconscious with his thegns in the hall and remain there until dawn.

*

The next morning, I was up early to check the arrangements for the day. I avoided the great hall where I knew the men would still be snoring, half-drunk from the night before, and made for the stables by the walls of the town. We had arranged one of Edward's favourite pastimes for late morning: a hunt for deer and boars in the surrounding countryside. I questioned the hunt master on the availability of mounts and equipment and the likelihood that they would find prey to ride down, and returned, satisfied that all was ready. By the time the befuddled menfolk emerged blinking into the light of day, I had made sure that an early meal of thick barley stew boiled with vegetables, or grilled trout if they preferred, was ready for them.

I sighed with relief when they rode off to hunt as it gave me time to attend to the many other tasks that I had had to neglect during the king's visit. The weather was fine so the hunt did not return until darkness had begun to fall. When I went to greet them, I asked politely about their day and admired the slaughtered animals that they laid before me.

'The wolf's pelt will make fine trimming for a war-coat, m'lord,' I said to Osferth with a cheery smile, but he just nodded and turned away.

I left the men to eat, drink and brag about their kills, and sat weaving a tapestry with Ælfwyn for a while, before making for the bedchamber.

To my surprise, Æthelred came in just as I was finishing my evening devotions at the small altar by the bed.

'Is something wrong?' I asked.

He looked tired. 'We have received news of Norsemen landing near Chester. I have to take my thegns to investigate. Edward has agreed to cut short his visit so we can counter the threat quickly.'

'Shame,' I said. 'I was almost enjoying his company.'

I watched, smiling, as Æthelred struggled to take off his close-fitting riding breeches with his one good arm. 'Let me help you with those, my old bear,' I offered.

'Thanks. You think he has changed, do you?' he said, sitting on the bed so that I could tug at the trouser bottoms.

I was kneeling on the floor, admiring my husband's muscular legs as I pulled the trousers around his ankles. 'Yes, the rebellion seems to have made him... well, more modest, less arrogant.'

'I've seen it happen to other men, especially the young ones,' he said. 'They start off cocky and confident. Think they can beat anyone, conquer the world. It's all a show really and they are as nervous as anyone. Except when they take a knock, maybe something that suggests they are not the best there has ever been, they collapse and loose all confidence in everything they do. I think Edward is a bit like that now.' Æthelred wandered across to the other side of the hut and pulled a fresh tunic over his head. 'He's been asking my opinion on all manner of things, all day. Annoyed Osferth like hell.'

I followed him. 'Opinion on what?'

'Military matters mainly. Although he did ask me about women.'

I cocked an eyebrow. 'Which women?'

'Don't worry it wasn't you, dear. He talked mainly about his new wife. She's very ambitious for their son and wants Athelstan disinherited. Edward says he will talk to him tomorrow, before he goes.'

'It seems as though you and my brother have become close friends in just a few hours. You're sure this is not a ploy for him to gain a firmer grip on Mercia?'

'Maybe, but war does alter people. It seems to have changed you.'

I folded the trousers one more time than was strictly necessary. 'Me? How have I changed?'

'You seem more mellow, more agreeable, since you came back.'

'Really? In what way?'

He pointed to the leggings. 'I can't remember the last time you pulled my trousers down,' he laughed.

'Men!' I snorted, throwing the trousers in his face.

*

Æthelred's snoring woke me the next morning, and reluctantly I had to accept that I would get no further sleep. Splashing cold water from the wooden tub onto my face, I dressed in a simple tunic and opened the door to see what weather to expect that day. The rising sun dazzled me as a cold wind whipped at my thin dress. I was about to shut the door hastily when I saw a stocky figure outside the entrance to the great hall, buckling on a sword.

'Good morning, Edward,' I called.

He hurried across at the sound of my voice. 'You've heard I will be leaving today?'

When I nodded, he looked past me into the hut, lowering his voice to a whisper.

'I think we both know there is something important to discuss before I leave,' he said.

My mind whirred. 'Yes, I'm sure... but Æthelred is still asleep.'

'Good. We need to be alone.'

I slipped a cloak around my shoulders against the bitter wind and joined Edward in the courtyard. Slaves and servants were scurrying in and out of the feasting hall, loading bags and weaponry onto carts in preparation for the king's departure.

'It will be impossible to find a quiet corner around here. It might be easier to talk as we walk,' I said. 'Did you want to discuss Athelstan?' I knew that the boy was waiting in some trepidation to talk to his father.

'No, I have a gift for Athelstan which I must remember to give him before I leave. But I wanted to talk with you about Æthelred.' Edward looked behind him. Two of his personal thegns were following and he waved them away.

I felt my heartbeat quicken. I had known for some time that this difficult moment would come, and I had rehearsed various words over and over in my mind during many sleepless nights. I still did not know what to say.

We turned into the main street that ran towards the river. It was still too early for the merchants and tradesmen who would normally have been using the road, so we walked in solitude to the sound of our footsteps on the recently laid river-cobbles. I wanted to tell my brother of the improvements I had overseen in the town and of my future building plans, but his mind was on another matter. He did not look at me but walked slowly.

'Æthelred is a brave man and he hides his sickness well. But I know how serious it really is.'

I did not deny it. Our old story that Æthelflæd had broken his arm and had a sore throat was no longer credible. I took a deep breath.

'He has rallied strongly since he was first stricken with the palsy. We did not want the Danes to think us weak at a time of change.'

There, I had said it, and given a good reason why we had concealed the truth. I felt almost lightheaded with relief but readied myself for Edward's wrath.

'The deception may have worked on the enemy, but not on me. Ever since I realised Æthelred had palsy, I have been wondering how we can replace him.'

'Replace? But he is still improving and will soon be back to his old self.'

Edward stopped and held my arm. 'After you'd left for Mercia, father insisted I study medicine. At the time, I resented anything that took me away from hunting but, as usual, he was right, and I am grateful now for what I learned from the leechbook he gave me. One of the things I remember about palsy is that it rarely strikes only once.'

I tried to hold his gaze but looked down when he continued in the calm, direct manner that I was finding particularly disconcerting. 'We need to work out what to do if he should suffer from a further bout.'

The possibility that Æthelred might suffer a further attack had, of course, occurred to me but I had not wanted to face it.

'I checked the leechbook for myself and it says to take coriander and crush it in woman's milk and put it in the healthy ear,' I gabbled.

'Which may improve the patient, but it will not cure him. Æthelred will never stand in a shield wall again, we both know that,' he said. 'We need someone ready to take command here.'

'Someone like who?' My mind was racing through the possibilities.

'Before the rebellion, I would have wanted to promote Beorhsige or one of your younger ealdormen to take his place. Today, I would only trust someone very close to me. Someone like you.'

I felt like laughing. That is exactly what I had decided when Æthelred had first fallen ill. For a while, I had enjoyed the power of making decisions myself. But now that I had seen war at first hand, I had been happy to hand back the reins of power to Æthelred.

'I am no warrior. I can hardly pick up a shield, let alone wield a sword,' I said.

'You do not need to fight. You just have to inspire others to fight for you. And they will. I have heard how you lifted the prisoners out of despair in the Danelaw so that they rose up and killed their captors. Without you, our enemies would still be alive.'

'It was just luck. We owe it all to brave young people who were less fortunate than me. You've told me how little I know of military matters, and I think you're probably right.' A gust of wind whipped up from the river so that I had to grab at my cloak to keep it around my body. 'I'm cold. Can we shelter in St Peter's?' I pointed to the church ahead.

We walked briskly towards the sturdy wooden doors and Edward pushed them open. A young monk was sweeping the vestry and he gawked at us, his broom clattering to the ground as he bowed low.

'Good morning, Brother. We would contemplate in the pews, if you can give us privacy, please?' I led the way to the bench reserved for my family by the pulpit.

As we knelt side-by-side in prayer, I found myself thinking of our father, Alfred. What role would he expect of me now? Surely he would wish me to follow a devout life building churches and helping the poor?

Edward coughed and pushed himself up onto the seat and waited for me to finish my devotions. When I finally sat by him, brushing the dust from my tunic, he turned and took my hand.

'We have not always seen eye-to-eye, have we? Not unusual for brother and sister, I know, but now we have to be different. You and I must fulfil father's wish,' he said.

How strange, that he was thinking of father too. 'Which wish would that be? He had so many. He wanted us to read and write in our own language, to believe in the One True God, to be humble and kind...'

'And to create one united kingdom of the English-speaking people. That's the wish I mean,' Edward interjected.

'I can understand why that might be attractive to you men who would rule such a kingdom, but it does not hold a special appeal for me, nor for most mothers and children who would be caught up in the war to create this great realm.' My voice reverberated around the empty church more loudly than I expected and I turned to check that no-one was there. I slid along the bench to distance myself from him, still wary of his temper when his wishes were denied.

He just chuckled. 'And I thought you would jump at the chance to rule Mercia. I will just have to ask Osferth, after all.'

I closed my eyes for a heartbeat longer than normal, cursing myself for not seeing the trap. Osferth, Lord of Mercia. Of course, he must have planned that all along.

'You would put a bastard over the proud people of this kingdom?' I blurted.

'So, mother told you about Osferth. I hoped she would so that you would believe it. Before he died, father made me promise to treat him like a brother. I do, and he serves me well.'

'For the present,' I said. 'But would you trust his ambition if he ruled here?'

He studied me carefully, forcing me to avert my gaze once more. He had an intensity in his eyes which I had not seen before.

'Not entirely. I would rather keep him close to me in Wessex. But if the worse comes to Æthelred, you will give me no choice.'

I wanted to say, 'I have changed my mind. Osferth cannot rule here. I will do it.' But for some reason, the words would not come and were left unspoken.

It was something I came to regret very soon.

ELEVEN

Once Edward and his entourage had departed to the south, Æthelred and his thegns hurriedly prepared to ride out to the north to counter the threat of the Norsemen who had landed on the coast near Chester. I suggested that I would accompany my husband as far as Shrewsbury to inspect the building works that I had commissioned there, and he readily agreed.

Going in search of my family to say farewell, I first sighted Ælfwyn laughing with a group of young thegns who were preparing to ride out with the warband, many of them for the first time. I walked quickly on, knowing that a mother's presence would not be welcome there, and made for the scriptorium where Athelstan was normally to be found. He was seated at his customary desk in the corner by the bookshelves, examining a vellum parchment.

When he saw me, he jumped up, grinning.

'See what father lent me.' He looked flushed with delight, pointing a finger excitedly at the parchment.

As I bent over it, I recognised the map that I had studied for many hours with my tutors as a young girl. It had been one of King Alfred's favourite possessions, a representation of the entire world originally drawn many years before in Rome. Edward must have inherited it and was encouraging his son to think big.

Athelstan pointed to the bottom left-hand corner to the land labelled 'Britannia.' My tutors had told me that our monks had updated that section to include details unknown to the Romans.

'This is where we are, and this is where the invaders are coming from.' He indicated a large island labelled 'Hibernia' that lay on one edge of the world. 'That's Ireland, where our hostages are also from.'

'You mean Finna and whatever her son is called?' I had not given much thought to Ingimund's wife and child I was holding as a guarantee for the good behaviour of the Norsemen in the Wirral.

'Yes, Jokul.' Athelstan lowered his voice. 'Except he is not his son.'

'What do you mean?'

'I am learning the British tongue which Jokul speaks with his mother. I heard them whispering about someone who must be his father. His name was not Ingimund.'

I blanched. If the Norseman had tricked me with false hostages, it was for a reason. And that could only be that he intended to break his oath. I had even more reason to travel north.

*

I decided to go by river to Shrewsbury and convinced my husband to save his strength by accompanying me for that part of his journey whilst his soldiers travelled by land. Æthelred proposed that Athelstan should travel with us to Chester as part of his education. I had insisted that we should also take the two hostages with us. I wanted to see what value they might have with the Norse if we needed to negotiate.

At the end of the first day, we rested in Worcester. Bishop Wærferth was away but he had arranged to make our stay comfortable. We left early the next morning and after another day on the River Severn we arrived in Shrewsbury.

146

Lord Beornoth was on the quayside in person to greet us. I thought he looked even older and the long scar on his face seemed to burn even redder than when we had last met. The treachery and death of his son Beorhsige must have weighed hard on him. He greeted us warmly but said very little as we made the steep journey up to his hilltop home.

Æthelred pointedly rejected Beornoth's offer of a mount to ride to the top of the incline and marched so strongly at the head of his companions that even I could hardly keep up. When he made it to the courtyard outside Beornoth's hall, he looked delighted to be the first to the top, but I noticed the redness in his face and his heavy breathing. I paused outside to admire the view over the surrounding town and noted that some progress had been made to improve the fortifications, but not enough. I would need to chastise Beornoth for that.

I heard a cry and a crash of timber behind me.

Trembling, I dashed into the hall where everyone was crowding around an overturned table. I felt my mouth go dry as I pushed my way through and saw Æthelred lying in a heap on the floor.

'Stand back! He needs to breathe,' I yelled, kneeling beside my lord. I laid my ear to his chest and exhaled with relief when I detected a flicker of a heartbeat. Cuddling his great hairy head in my arms, I tried not to cry.

*

The local healer seemed to know her business and soon had Æthelred in a bed lying on his side so that she could administer potions into his ear. He had not stirred much since his collapse, but his breathing was regular and he occasionally made faint sounds as if he was trying to speak. As the healer held my husband's hand and mopped at his brow, Beornoth touched my arm.

'Can I interrupt you for a moment, m'lady?'

I followed him to one side of the stark chamber. 'I had urgent news for Lord Æthelred but ...' He gave a resigned glance towards the bed where Æthelred lay. 'I thought I should tell you.'

I found it hard to focus on his words as he continued. 'We have informers amongst the Norsemen who settled in the Wirral. They have reported that Ingimund had a secret meeting with the leaders of a Norse fleet from Ireland and a warband from Danelaw. They agreed to form an alliance and attack Chester.'

I tapped my forehead, trying to think. We had thought we were dealing with only a few Norse ships, not a combined army of Danes and Norwegian settlers and invaders. 'How many warriors? Where are they?'

'We think they are gathering their forces in the Wirral. They could move on Chester anytime ...' His voice trailed away as I walked to the door and went outside.

He found me sitting on a large boulder, gazing north over the river.

'Somewhere out there, warriors are preparing to plunder our land and enslave our people, and we have no-one to lead our army against them.' I turned to look into his battle-scarred face. 'Do you have one more campaign left in you, Lord Beornoth?'

He lowered himself gingerly onto one knee. 'I would dearly love the chance to redeem the name of my family in your service, m'lady. But these old bones can hardly move around my own property, let alone defend it. And I can't think like I used to. The elves are taking away my mind. I fear it would be a disaster if I led our soldiers into battle. The young thegns will happily give up their lives for you though. They will do as you direct.'

'What are you suggesting?' I asked.

He struggled to stand and I took his arm to help him up. 'I am suggesting that you take your husband's place at the head of the army,' he said.

'What if I'm tired of war and do not wish to send young men out to kill each other.'

He narrowed his one good eye to glare at me fiercely. 'Then we must hand over our land to foreigners and surrender our subjects into slavery.'

I sighed. 'I know. I have little choice. I will do it, just this once. We must keep the nature of Æthelred's condition to ourselves. Tell the men he will resume command as soon as he is better.'

He nodded his agreement. 'There is one thing I can do for you. You should not be in the thick of any fight so you will need to direct our soldiers from a distance. For that, you will need an adjutant who knows the language of war and can take your commands to the men. They must trust him enough to do his bidding, and he must be swift and brave enough to find his way through any struggle.'

I nodded. 'Thegns' sons are used for such a role, I believe. Do you know of a good one?'

'My youngest son, Merewalh, is almost old enough to stand in the shield wall, and I have schooled him all his life in military matters. He would make an excellent adjutant for you.'

I studied the man I used to call the weasel. It took courage to offer me his last son. But should I trust another of his brood?

'Merewalh. Wasn't that the name of a former king whose daughters were sainted hereabouts?' I asked.

'Yes, he was son of the pagan King Penda of Mercia but a Christian himself. His namesake will serve you well.'

'He had better. Look after my husband and Athelstan whilst I go to Chester. And put the local fyrd on standby. We may need reinforcements.'

With the threat hanging over me that Osferth might take over Mercia, I knew that I could not fail.

*

The sun had already set, replaced by a bright full moon, as I urged my horse to splash across the ford of the River Dee. Glistening in the moonlight on the other side, I saw the white-stone wall that surrounded the town of Chester. Before that stood a line of guards, shields up, spears at the ready.

Good, they were vigilant. But even in the dim light, I could see the poor state of the walls. They had been built into a horseshoe bend of the river, like those at Shrewsbury. The Roman army had made the walls thick and tall, the height of three men in places. But now there were gaping holes where the stone had collapsed or been taken by builders for other purposes.

The captain of the guards looked surprised to see a woman at the head of the cavalry troop when we arrived at his gate. I sent him scurrying away to find the town reeve as we dismounted and loosened the riding straps of our horses. The reeve arrived immediately and gave orders for the horses to be taken to the paddock by the river. He looked young for his position, his face still marked with the spots of adolescence, his body willowy with seemingly little muscle on his prominent bones.

'Wiglaf, son of Wigmund, at your service m'lady,' he said bowing low. 'We have quarters for your men in the main hall and for yourself in my humble abode, if that suits.'

'I am sure it will. We have little time for sleep. There is much to be done before the enemy gets here. Have you done any repairs to the walls? I instructed them to be strengthened a year ago.'

'Lord Beorhsige did come with his thegns and began some rebuilding, but soon after, he took his men and many of ours to the war.'

So that was it. Beorhsige had not only left the defences unfinished but had taken defenders away too. 'How many men have you left?'

'Less than a hundred. Not much experience among us either. We're mainly the sons of those who went with Beorhsige and didn't come back.'

'Including your father?' I asked, trying to study his face in the light of the torch that flickered on the wall.

He hung his head. 'My father would've killed himself rather than fight against the King, but Beorhsige gave him no choice. He was killed in the battle.'

I put a hand on his shoulder. 'Wiglaf, tell your young warriors that they have a chance to make amends for Beorhsige's treachery. There is much to be done if we are to save the town.'

*

The work started at dawn the next day. I had my new design of the town chalked onto a large stone so that the builders could refer to it. The Romans had given their original square fort extra protection by building it into a tight bend of the River Dee. I did not have time to repair all four of the original walls, so, instead, we extended the north and east fortifications down to the river, leaving the Dee to protect us to the south and the west. The design was similar to the developments I had instigated at Gloucester, Worcester and Shrewsbury and gave the towns space to grow into trading centres as well as a fort.

Time was short and I ordered every available man, woman, and child to help with the rebuilding effort. I had the great hall emptied and bade local farmers to bring in their cattle and stores. Women dug up vegetables and picked fruit from beyond the defences to store inside the town. Everything was done not only to build up our own stocks but also to deny food to the attackers.

On the third day, Æthelred's foot soldiers arrived and filled the town with their tents, weapons, cooking utensils and bad language. I calculated that our defenders now numbered four hundred, but informants in the Wirral had reported news of three separate warband encampments. I needed more men if I was to stand a chance of holding the makeshift stronghold.

That evening I called the troops and the townsfolk together. They put aside their hammers, chisels, spades, saucepans and kettles and made their way to the grassy meadow in the bend of the river. There, they eagerly feasted on a good but not extravagant spread of eggs, cheese and bread washed down with flagons of ale. It was a warm, light evening and I walked amongst them offering food and drink to families and soldiers alike, as I would have done for a royal feast. I welcomed farmers, artisans, merchants, priests, housewives and children as well as war-hardened warrior-thegns. All were equally important to me in defending the town against the gathering storm of Norse and Danish warriors.

When we had all eaten and drunk our fill, I stood on a flat rock so that I could be seen. My new reeve, Wiglaf, banged the hilt of his sword on the rim of a shield to call for quiet.

'People of Chester, soldiers of Mercia!' I called, lifting my arms. 'We are here to defend this town against wicked invaders. This place was a ruin with few inhabitants until recently and even now it is only half-built. So why does it matter so much? This town is a refuge, that's why. Just as Noah built his ark against the floods, so we have built this burh to keep us safe. Here we can protect our loved ones, our animals, our homes, as Noah did. We will never give them up!'

Men began banging their fists on the food trestles that had been set up in the meadow so that I had to shout to be heard. 'If we build strong towns, the pagan devils will not dare to raid our homesteads. Defend Chester and our enemies will know they can never violate or steal from us unpunished ever again.' I smiled at the expectant faces all listening attentively to my words as I tried to finish with a flourish. 'That is why we must succeed here, whatever it takes!'

They were all cheering now, pumping fists into the sky, clapping each other on the back. The reeve helped me down from the slab.

'Well said, m'lady.'

'It will take more than fine words to succeed here, Wiglaf, but they may help.'

I caught sight of Merewalh and called him over.

'You have met my adjutant, I hope?'

When Merewalh and Wiglaf greeted each other, I noted that they both had the long dark hair of the border people and the same youthful build.

'You will need to work closely together,' I said. 'I am returning to Shrewsbury for the next few days, but I will be back with reinforcements. Wiglaf, you will take charge here in my absence, and you, Merewalh, will bring me news as soon as anything changes. I leave at first light.'

*

It was a long day's ride and dark clouds brought an early end to the daylight as I crossed the bridge over the River Severn into Shrewsbury. As I passed the old church of St Chad that dated from the time of King Offa, something drew me in. I was desperate to see my husband to make sure that he was still alive, but I stopped by the tumbledown chapel, wondering if I should pray for him. Seeing a warm light shining from the narrow windows, I found myself pushing open the low door. The wall torches spluttered in the draught and the light of the flickering flames picked out a congregation bent over in prayer. It was not the normal hour for devotions and my astonishment grew when I saw Athelstan sitting on a bench next to Beornoth.

Heads turned towards me in surprise. Athelstan jumped up with a squeal and ran over.

'You're back, Aunt! Has there been a battle yet?'

'Not yet,' I said, putting an arm around his shoulders. 'What are you all doing here?'

'It's St Chad's day. Did you forget? The service of celebration has just finished.'

I breathed deeply. That explained it. The priest hurried over to greet me, his long white tunic brushing the straw on the floor. He blessed me and stood by the door as the worshippers filed out. Helped by a retainer, Beornoth struggled to his feet and slowly made his way over.

'How are preparations in Chester?' he asked.

'Much still to be done. What news of my husband?'

Beornoth glanced over his shoulder and spoke quietly. 'Same as you left him.'

'I must return to Chester, and I need to take more men. Is the fyrd ready?'

Beornoth shrugged. 'We lost many men to the rebellion. They are hard to replace and the farmers are busy.'

'Tell your farmers that they cannot hide in their barns. Without reinforcements, Chester will fall and the heathens will come south to burn their homesteads, ravage their wives and carry off their children. I return north the day after tomorrow and I expect every available man to follow. Those with mounts can ride with me.'

He nodded and made to go, but I grabbed his arm. 'A tactical question, lest I forget.'

I hesitated, realising that I should not talk of war in a House of God.

He'll understand. I'm fighting pagans, after all.

I lowered my voice. 'We are extending Chester's walls to use the river as part of our defences, as you are doing here. But we do not have enough soldiers to man the added length. What do we do? Spread the defenders more thinly or concentrate them at key points?'

Beornoth did not hesitate. 'Post lookouts so they can survey the entire area and group your men into units that can go where they are needed. Have ladders at regular intervals so men can quickly reinforce the wall where it is attacked.'

Athelstan had been listening to the conversation intently. 'What about a tactical withdrawal?' he said quietly.

I stared at him. 'What exactly is that?' I asked.

'The Greeks and the Romans used it all the time. I've been reading about it in Caesar's Gallic Wars. You pretend you are losing the battle and retreat. The enemy follow and you ambush them.'

I took his hand. 'I wish you were old enough to come with me. We would surely defeat the pagans…' My voice trailed off as I caught sight of a tall young woman with white-blonde hair, a child at her side. 'If indeed we are fighting pagans. What is Finna doing in church?' I asked.

'I know, I know!' Athelstan could hardly contain himself. 'She's Irish, and the Irish are Christians.'

'You mean Ingimund married an Irish woman?'

'Yes, and the son is hers but not his.'

'How do you know this?' I asked.

Athelstan looked at his me warily. 'Promise you won't tell her I told you?'

I nodded.

'She thinks Ingimund has betrayed her by attacking you and that you will kill her.'

'She told you this?'

'No, I overheard them talking about it, so I told Jokul I would help him escape if he told me who he really was. So he did.'

'And?' I was becoming angry at his presumption.

'You have to promise not to kill him first.'

'I am hardly going to kill a child.'

'Or his mother?'

'It depends on what she has done,' I said.

'She and her son were for sale in a slave market in Dublin. Ingimund bought them and married Finna soon after. Jokul says there are many other Irish with the Norsemen.'

And they would all be Christians too, I thought as we made our way out of the church.

I had nearly made it back to Chester at the head of a small column of mounted troops when I saw someone riding fast in my direction. I watched him take his mount skilfully across the ford before galloping towards me. He did not dismount but called to me from his horse. It was Merewalh.

'I was coming to warn you,' he said. 'They're here.'

I scanned the area but could not see a single enemy warrior.

'On the other side of the walls.' Merewalh pointed, and I caught sight of a thin trail of smoke that must have come from fires beyond the town. 'Danes as well as Norwegians. We shut the gates and they've set up camp outside.'

I felt a shiver run through my body. I had a troop of thirty horsemen behind me and a hundred or so soldiers would follow on foot, assuming Beornoth could persuade them to leave the spring harvest. With the defenders in the town, I might have five hundred men at my command. Most lacked experience of war – including me as their leader.

I silently prayed for a miracle.

*

I led my men across the ford and noted that the water level had increased with the recent rains. That would make the river more difficult to cross, but easier to navigate for the Norse ships. I was sure that, once word went out that there were easy pickings to be had in Chester, more of the Norsemen expelled from Ireland would sail up the River Dee.

As I rode into town, I looked to my right to make sure the old town wall had been extended as I had ordered. I saw an earthen embankment running down to the riverbank at a much lower height than the stone fortifications built by the soldiers of Rome centuries earlier. It would have to do. At least, they had managed to repair the walls and I could no longer see any gaps in the original stonework. The people scurrying along the streets that criss-crossed the town seemed in a sombre mood, but I paid them scant regard. I was anxious to see the enemy.

Once I reached the north wall, I nodded to one of the guards, indicating that I would climb to the top of the parapet. He checked that the wooden ladder was secure, and I gingerly clambered up the rungs. When I stepped onto the narrow walkway around the top of the wall, the view made my blood run cold. A sprawling mass of colourful tents and cooking fires lay in the open fields that ran down to the river. In the distance, I could see the upturned prows of long ships dragged up onto the banks. Everywhere, I saw foreign warriors, some eating around the fires, some honing blades, others joking and jostling with their comrades as if it were market day. Their leather jerkins, full-length leggings and warm cloaks told me they were prepared for a long stay.

'Welcome back, your ladyship.'

I glanced around to see my town reeve energetically scaling the ladder behind me.

'Good to see you, Wiglaf. How many of the devils do you think there are?' I asked, turning back to study the forces outside the walls.

He climbed up the last rung to stand beside me, breathing heavily.

'Difficult to say exactly. We think that lot over there are Danes.' He pointed to the camp closest to the main gate. 'Maybe four hundred of them. But the biggest group is over there, by the ships.' He indicated a more distant camp by the riverside to the north west. 'That's the Irish Norse. More than five hundred of them plus three ships that arrived today. More on the way, I expect. Must be a thousand men in all.'

I listened carefully to the reeve and studied the disposition of the forces ranged against us. My mind went back to the discussion during one of the evenings that I had been obliged to spend with King Eohric in East Anglia. He had derided the way that Edward had divided his forces, calling it a tactical blunder. Had the Norsemen committed the same mistake?

I pointed to the nearby camp. 'Is there any reason why the Danes are camped apart from the rest?'

Wiglaf scratched his chin. 'I can only say what I would do if I were them. I'd have one force positioned to stop the defenders getting in and out of the gates too easily, and another to guard my ships, my means of retreat. And that's what they seem to have done.'

The young man impressed me with his grasp of detail. He would serve me well – if he survived the fighting to come.

An idea, partly inspired by Athelstan's mention of the withdrawal tactics used by the Romans, had formed in my mind.

'I have a plan,' I said after a few moments. 'We should attack. Tomorrow, at dawn.'

TWELVE

I hardly slept that night, tossing and turning in my narrow bed, wondering if my strategy was too bold, imagining all the things that could go wrong and the men who would die because of my decision.

When I'd explained the idea to Wiglaf and Merewalh, they had not seemed as eager as I was to take the fight to the enemy. Yet, when I woke in the early hours of the morning and pulled on a thick woollen robe and cloak, I was certain we should stick to my plan.

Before first light, I hurried into the courtyard where sleepy warriors were shuffling into line. A hooded priest stood before them, intoning prayers and reassuring them that God would be with them because they did His work. I studied the men carefully, assessing their mood.

They were a mixed crew. Some confidently jostled with their comrades; others constantly fiddled with their gear, adjusting their leather helmets or checking the points of their spears. Their leader was Cearl, one of my husband's retainers who had survived more than a decade of warfare; he might be slow of wit but he could be relied on to do what he was ordered until his last breath. Behind him were younger men, the sons of thegns, like Cuthberht, son of Cnebba, who had recently won his spear but had yet to see a real battle. To the rear were local men dressed in makeshift war-gear, looking grim and nervous as most knew not what to expect. Some, like Merfyn of Gwynedd who had recently been recruited to our ranks with a band of Welsh exiles, were not even Saxons.

Wiglaf greeted me quietly and gestured to the sky. The stars were disappearing in the first blush of dawn. It was time to go.

The warriors trooped in single file towards a small gate in the eastern wall. As I had ordered, they did not carry shields. This was not to be a fight of attrition, battering toe to toe with an enemy behind a shield-wall, but a lightning strike on their camp to prick the Danes into a compulsive act they would regret. As the guard opened the postern gate in an arch of the wall, I peered out and saw the flicker of fires in the distance. Even at night, enemy lookouts were observing our town like predatory owls. The north entrance, the main gateway into Chester, would be visible to them, but I hoped they might not see the smaller exit we were using.

Standing by the gate, I acknowledged each warrior as he left the safety of the walled town. Whatever their status, I wished each one of them well as they jogged through the arch to clamber across the ditch outside. I counted one hundred men, not enough to overwhelm the Danes but sufficient to cause them a problem if they caught them by surprise. They ran silently, one behind another, weaving across the field like a long serpent slithering towards its prey. As the last one disappeared into the gloom, I silently asked God and my ancestors in Heaven to go with them. The survival of the town and the people within it depended on their success.

I hurried back through the postern and into the courtyard. Grooms were leading horses into the square and cavalrymen were adjusting their gear, preparing to ride. I waved to Wiglaf who gave the signal for the riders to swing up onto their mounts. The horses seemed eager to go, whickering and pawing the ground, but the riders reined them back towards the high wall on either side of the north gates until their tails swished against the stonework. Their turn for action would come, but not yet.

I scaled the ladder to the top of the wall and peered into the half-light. I could make out the shadowy outlines of my men running through the enemy camp, stabbing at the tents with their spears as if trying to stick a boar in a hunt. I also heard the shouts and screams of Danish soldiers, rudely woken by the taste of sharp metal.

The attack had begun.

*

I strained my eyes, trying to assess the right moment to call for the retreat. If I sounded the horn too early, the Danes might be insufficiently provoked to follow. If I left it too long, the enemy might catch my warriors before they had time to run. And run they must if the rest of my plan was to work.

Wiglaf joined me on the parapet. He pointed away from the skirmishing amongst the tents, towards a group of warriors who were forming up around a standard hanging limply from a tall pole. A warlord seemed to be rallying his men. One of them waved the standard and I glimpsed the crude depiction of a large black bird – the raven, symbol of death, so beloved by the pagans.

'Now, m'lady?' Wiglaf asked.

I nodded. It was the moment to recall the troops.

The deep blast of a horn sounded from the top of the gate. The skirmishing around the tents intensified but no one broke away from the fighting. I looked anxiously at Wiglaf who narrowed his eyes and stared hard towards the battle.

'Again!' he shouted. The horn blasted at a higher pitch as the hornsman blew harder.

I felt a sense of rising panic. I could lose a hundred men for little gain if they did not turn soon. I waved at Merewalh who sat ready on his horse by the gate.

'Go! Instruct them to retreat,' I yelled, cursing when I saw that the guards were still struggling to open the heavy gates. 'Hurry there! Let him through.'

The horn sounded a third time as Merewalh galloped across the earthen bridge over the ditch, mud flying from his horse's hooves.

'No, leave them open until my command,' I shouted to the guards who had begun to close the gates.

'Look m'lady. They're coming,' Wiglaf said, indicating the enemy camp.

My warriors seemed to have got the message and were now running wildly away from the enemy encampment. But not all. Others were too engrossed in their individual battles to flee.

My heart beat faster when I saw the emblem of the raven carried high, beckoning on a howling band of heathens who were streaming towards my men.

'Have they not heard the horn? Why do they not return?' I looked fretfully to Wiglaf, who pursed his lips.

'When you fight man to man as they are, it is difficult to break off without endangering yourself, even if you do remember that you should. But look, Merewalh is there and more are coming now.'

His eyesight was evidently better than mine because, at first, I could make little sense of the blur of figures. Finally, I did see the outline of a horseman gesticulating keenly. Merewalh was proving to be as plucky as his father had promised.

My soldiers were in full flight, streaming across the field towards the north gates which stood invitingly open. Roaring with triumph and anger, the Danes rushed after them in close pursuit. Too close in some cases. I grimaced as I watched a man crumple as an axe thumped into his back. The bloodlust of those whose sleep had been so rudely disturbed was evidently running high. The warriors following the raven saw their chance to intercept my raiding party and lowered their shields to run full tilt after them.

I studied the unfolding action carefully, assessing my warriors' chances. They were closer to the town now and I could make them out more clearly. I caught sight of Merfyn amongst the first group of young warriors who easily outpaced their pursuers and would soon make the safety of the gates. Most of Æthelred's thegns, including young Cuthberht, had stuck together and were retreating in an orderly fashion.

Bringing up the rear was a band of slower men who were coming within range of enemy spears. I could unleash my cavalry to help them but I preferred to hold them back for another, more deadly purpose. Amongst the very last, I saw Æthelred's faithful retainer, Cearl, who seemed to be limping. It didn't look as though he would make it with that wound. What would Æthelred do, I wondered. Leave him to his fate or rescue him and jeopardise the plan?

I looked towards Wiglaf, thinking I might ask his advice, but he was busy organising the courtyard to receive visitors. A line of warriors, shields and spears at the ready, stood facing the gates awaiting their fleeing comrades and the pursuing enemy.

The Danes converging towards the fortress were urging each other on, redoubling their efforts. They had seen the bigger prize presented by the open gates. They had a chance to establish a foothold inside the town.

Cearl and his comrades were close to being engulfed in the onward rush. One was pulling Cearl by the arm, encouraging him on, but he shrugged him off and instead turned to face the oncoming enemy alone. I saw the first man to reach him stagger back under a deft thrust of Cearl's spear and another drop from a slice of his sword. But he was soon overwhelmed and, in a few heartbeats, he had fallen, trampled under Danish boots. But his stand was enough to secure the safety of his companions who now had the extra yards they needed to make the safety of the gates.

Relieved, they staggered into the courtyard, expecting the thick wooden doors to swing shut behind them. Yet the gates stayed open and they heard their comrades inside urging them on, to take more steps and shelter behind the wall of warriors who faced them. Most managed the final effort and stumbled through the friendly shields and into the streets behind where womenfolk were waiting to give them bread and ale.

Some still hesitated in the courtyard, not understanding the urgency of the situation. From the parapet above, I yelled at them to move on but it was too late. The first wave of pursuing Danes hurtled through the gates, whooping and bellowing as they scythed into my men.

Their triumphant roars were soon muted when they saw the menace of the deadly defensive wall facing them. The leading Danes had little in the way of shields or body armour; they must have leapt from their tents dressed as they slept. They knew they were no match for the formation ahead and quickly span around to retreat the way they had come.

As they turned, they were pressed back by the arrival of the warriors following the raven who were fully equipped and eager to take possession of the town. They poured through the gates in such numbers that, from my position on top of the wall, I worried that we would not be able to close the thick doors. I heard the horn again, this time two sharp blasts as Wiglaf ordered the closure. Danes were still streaming through, knocking back the guards who came forward to heave at the heavy gates which remained stubbornly open.

My eye was caught by movement in the field outside. Glancing over my shoulder, I caught my breath. More Danes were coming and worse, the Norwegians had left their boats and were also streaming towards the town. The entire enemy army was rushing to take advantage of the open gates. I waved frantically towards Wiglaf who was now directly above the gates shouting down instructions.

To this day, I can vividly recall what happened next. It was the moment the tide of the battle turned.

The cavalry charged.

The horses hit the rear of the enemy like an avalanche of rocks. Until that moment, they had stood patiently waiting against the north wall. The Danes did not see them as they rushed into the town, but they soon felt their impact. Riders stabbed spears into their unprotected backs and hooves trampled them down as they wilted under the weight of the assault. The surge of the charge threw the Danish warriors forward and gave Wiglaf's guards the space to close the gates, which they slammed shut and locked with a heavy iron bar.

There was nowhere for the enemy to run.

I stood transfixed as the final act of the battle was played out below me. Like two milling stones grinding corn, the shield wall and the cavalry crushed the foe between them. The foot soldiers advanced steadily, an unbroken line of fresh warriors eager to fight. The cavalry charged again, forcing the Danes onto the spears that protruded from the shield wall like the spines of a hedgehog. The enemy were falling rapidly and those that fought on were slipping and stumbling on the bloodied bodies of their comrades. Crushed into a confined space, the Danish warriors could hardly raise their weapons as the men of Chester systematically cut them down.

A tall warrior in a leather helmet waved the banner of the raven, screaming to the men around him to form a circle of interlinked shields. Some did as he instructed but many could not reach him and fought individually before they were struck down. Where their weapons did find their mark and one of the men of Chester fell back, he was quickly replaced by a fresh soldier stepping into the line of shields.

To my surprise, I heard the sound of my name from one of the enemy in the courtyard below. He was gesticulating and calling to me, but I could not understand his words above the din.

'He wants to surrender,' Wiglaf said.

I hesitated. Keeping prisoners in a town under siege was a complication I could do without. I looked down into the upturned face of the warlord below. He plucked a silver cross from around his neck and waved it towards me. He was a Christian.

I nodded to Wiglaf. 'Tell him they will not die if they all lay down their weapons now.'

*

We had little time to deal with the prisoners and the bodies before a dull thud reverberated around the courtyard and the main gates shuddered as if a quake had struck the town. Wiglaf ordered men to place the ladder back against the wall and he quickly scaled up to the parapet.

'The Norwegians are battering at the gates,' he shouted down to me.

I gesticulated to soldiers nearby. 'Take up spears, stones, anything heavy to hurl down on the enemy.' As men scurried up the ladder to the top of the gates, I scanned the courtyard.

Where was my adjutant when I needed him? 'Merewalh, find archers, anyone who can shoot a bow. Send them to the parapet. Quickly!'

He jumped from his horse and ran off to do my bidding. I ordered more ladders to be placed against the north wall and used one to clamber up myself. The scene at the top reminded me of the brawls I had witnessed after a long feast. Men were hurling rocks and wooden beams at a group of sweating warriors below. They were shouting abuse back as they used a large log to batter at the wooden gates, whilst other soldiers held shields over their heads to deflect the objects that were showering down.

The gates shook under another heavy blow. 'Get ropes and winch up some bodies,' I shouted down to the courtyard. 'Only their dead, mind. Not ours.'

Archers began to arrive and trained their arrows onto the men carrying the log.

'No!' I shouted. 'Shoot at the shield-bearers.'

They were easy targets with their shields held high and howled as a volley of arrows tore into their sides. They instinctively lowered their guard, exposing the log-carriers. Those men had evidently been picked for their strength and not for their bravery: as soon as the archers trained their arrows on them, they dropped the log and retreated out of range. The respite did not last. A second tier of shield bearers was added to protect the first line and the formation returned to pick up the heavy tree trunk and swing it against the gates again.

'The bodies! Throw down the bodies,' I ordered.

I almost vomited as I watched soldiers throw crumpled human forms, some still twitching and moaning, over the parapet. A few fell senseless to the ground, others landed on top of the shields, and one hit the log itself, splattering blood and entrails onto the Norsemen. It did not take long for the attackers to realise they were adding to the carnage of their comrades. They retreated once more, this time back to their boats.

*

Later I questioned the Christian warlord we had captured. He sat facing me on a bench in the feast hall, his hands bound tightly behind his back, his muscular chest thrust forward in a defiant manner. A deep scar across his forehead marred his youthful face and the combination of brown eyes and flaxen hair gave him the exotic look of a man of mixed race.

I tried not to seem impressed. 'What's your name?'

'I am Halfdan, son of Ragnar.' His deep voice resonated around the hall and the other prisoners slumped against the wall raised their heads at the sound of their leader.

'And where do you hail from, Halfdan Ragnarson?' I asked.

'I am from Jorvic.' The name rolled proudly from his tongue.

That surprised me. 'York? Why are you so far from home?'

He smiled and spoke our language with only a slight trace of accent. 'Your cousin invited me. We made him our king and he promised us land, Saxon land. I came here to collect what he gave me.'

'You made a bad choice. Æthelwold had no right to offer you what is ours and he has paid the price for his treachery.' I leaned across the table between us. 'As will you and your men.'

He sat back, studying me in a way I found unsettling. 'I have never fought against a woman before. I did not enjoy it. Maybe I would like it more if I was on your side.'

I met his eyes and, for a heartbeat, I was tempted. He was a fellow Christian and I needed more men.

'I have learned not to trust young warlords like you,' I said finally.

He laughed. 'You mean Ingimund!' He lowered his voice and leaned forward. 'I do not trust him either. My fellow Danes in Jorvic are not fond of these Norwegians from Ireland. They are taking our land too.'

I made a mental note of his comment but, for the moment, I was not prepared to put my faith in any of my enemies, Christian or not.

'We will release your men on condition they return immediately to the Danelaw. You will remain our prisoner and will forfeit your life if any of your men take any further part in this battle.'

I felt Wiglaf, who was sitting next to me, touch my arm and I leaned towards him so he could whisper in my ear. His suggestion was a good one. 'Your followers will be branded to ensure we can recognise them if they do return.'

Halfdan raised his eyebrows. 'You would treat fellow Christians like cattle?'

I glanced at his warriors, estimating there were about fifty of them, enough to make a difference in the battles ahead. I had no choice but to eliminate them from the conflict. Besides I doubted that many were Christian.

'My other option is to kill them now,' I said, nodding to Wiglaf who stood and walked deliberately from the hall. I turned back to Halfdan. 'You will remain our prisoner until your ransom is paid.'

'Ransom? I was tricked by the false promises of your cousin. I am worth nothing.'

'I'm sure your family will raise the one hundred silver pennies for your release.'

He laughed loudly, wriggling his hands behind his back. 'You've the wrong man if you think you can make a fortune from me. I have no family to pay even a one penny ransom.'

'Warlords must have wealth to reward their followers, and you command many men. Tell one of them to return with the payment for your sins and you will be free to return home.'

'Then I fear I will rot in your custody. My followers' reward was to be the land they are now sitting on.'

Wiglaf returned. 'The smithy is ready, m'lady,' he said.

I stood. 'Do it quickly for we have many other matters to attend to.'

When Wiglaf ordered the prisoners to their feet, one of the captives protested loudly in the Danish tongue.

Halfdan called over to me. 'He asks that you treat him as a Christian and not have him branded by Wayland like a pagan.'

'Tell him our smithy is a good Christian who will not harm his sons or daughters,' I replied. I knew the Norse legend of Wayland the Smith. He was enslaved by a king and took revenge by killing his two sons and raping his daughter, before escaping by magical flight.

Halfdan tried to stand. 'Ask your smithy to mark me first. I always lead by example,' he shouted.

My opinion of the young man rose. 'So be it. Brand him with the letter C if you have it. It is the only part of Chester that he will keep.'

*

As I walked through the town to inspect our defences after the attack, I detected the sharp smell of burning flesh. The smithy was doing his work on Halfdan's men. Had I been too cruel to the prisoners? What about the dying men, tossed like rubbish from the walls? How would God judge me for that?

A woman followed by three children scurried along the street, acknowledging me deferentially as they passed. I shuddered to think what the pagans would do to families like that if they took the town. The Danes deserved the punishment I had given them. And I would be even less lenient to the Norwegians who had broken their oaths to me. Any sign of weakness on my part would only encourage them to try harder. If they thought they were up against a feeble woman, I would prove them wrong.

Ingimund and his men were only here because I'd allowed them to settle. I'd thought my compassion for them was justified, that I was saving their starving women and children. But there was no end to man's greed, it seemed. Not content as a farmer, Ingimund lusted after easier pickings and was now threatening my own families. Father had once told me that the path of true righteousness was difficult to follow. How right he was.

Merewalh hurried towards me, interrupting my musings.

'You sent for me, m'lady?'

'Ah yes, I want you to ride to Shrewsbury. Bring the hostage, Finna, here to me. Straightaway.'

She and her treacherous husband would find out just how weak I really was.

THIRTEEN

After the massacre within the town and the repelling of the attack on the gates, I hoped the enemy would cut their losses and withdraw. But it seemed that the Norsemen were made of sterner stuff. They quickly devised a new scheme to enter the town.

The restoration work on the ancient defences had been hurriedly done, rocks and slabs piled up loosely to fill gaps in the crumbling stonework. The cunning Norsemen soon spotted these weaknesses and sent men to unpick the hasty repairs. Using spare planking from their ships propped up on thick posts, they created a shelter to protect them from the arrows and stones sent down by the defenders above. It reminded me of the horse built by the Greeks to enter the town of Troy in ancient times. But I was not going to be beaten by such ploys.

It became a war of attrition.

The first day that the Norsemen burrowed into the wall, they laboured all day under their shelter but did not break through. Retiring, exhausted, in the evening they took their equipment with them, but not the stones they had dislodged. When they returned the next day, they found the stonework neatly replaced. My warriors had worked through the night to do that. There was some shouting and disagreement amongst the enemy, but they quickly learned from their mistake. They set to and tunnelled into the walls once again, only this time they dragged the rocks well away from the town and guarded them.

I realised that it would only be a matter of time before the walls were breached, so I devised other ways to deter them. I ordered buckets of beer and water to be hauled to the top of the wall and emptied into large cauldrons heated by fires. Once piping hot, it was poured over the edge of the parapet and onto the protective shelter below. I had noticed that the Norse builders had saved wood by leaving small gaps between the planks that formed the roof. Arrows might not penetrate, but boiling water could. I raised a fist in triumph when I heard the shrieks from below as the tunnelers ran out, screaming from burns to their skin.

Not much wall was removed that day.

The following morning, the mobile shelter returned, covered in thick hides. This time, the scalding liquid ran harmlessly from the sides of the roof and the stone workers remained resolutely underneath, scrabbling and hauling away at the rocks.

That evening, an elder of the town came to me with her daughter. 'My family are beekeepers,' she explained. 'Maybe our hives can be used against the invaders.'

I smiled when I heard their proposal. It was quite ingenious. That night I ordered my men to carefully conceal beehives amongst the stones when they replaced those that the Norsemen had dismantled.

The next day, the town won another respite.

When the Norsemen began pulling out the slabs, they were greeted by an angry swarm of bees. From the parapet, we all jeered as the enemy below dropped their tools, dancing and flapping their arms to escape from the stinging bees. Work was halted for the day, and the spirits of the townsfolk rose when the news spread of how bees had joined in the defence of Chester.

The sight of savage warriors discomforted by such small creatures cheered me enormously. But my mood did not last. I knew that the Norsemen would find a way to storm the broken walls sooner or later. I had to do something different.

That evening, I was on the parapet, overseeing the nightly repairs to Chester's defences. I felt the chill of the wind in my position high up on the walls and pulled my woollen cloak closer to me.

'More stone over here,' I called down to men arriving with a cartload of rocks.

Whatever the Norsemen tore down during the daylight hours, we would replace during the night. 'When your cart is empty, fetch more. There's more openings,' I said to the foreman of the gang.

'Beggin' you pardon m'lady, but we've little left, unless we…'

'I know. You will just have to pull down more buildings. You have my permission to take whatever you need. You know that.'

I scrambled down the ladder and walked briskly to the hall. Wiglaf and some of his retainers were eating, but they quickly pushed back their bench to stand when they caught sight of me in the doorway.

'All's well outside, m'lady?' Wiglaf asked.

'As well as can be expected without enough stone. We're having to use wooden barriers to keep the devils out.'

I noticed the meagre portions of pork, bread and vegetables on the table and tried not to feel hungry. 'Any news of Merewalh?'

'Why yes, m'lady, he returned earlier this evening with a woman. A hostage I believe.'

'They're here? Why wasn't I informed?'

'Apologies m'lady, I…'

'No matter. Have her sent to my chamber straightaway.' Ignoring the tempting smells of cooking from the hearth, I strode from the hall.

When I had first lodged in Wiglaf's modest home, I had shared it with his household, but as my stay stretched from days to weeks and into months, he had diplomatically moved out, allowing me to turn his family dwelling into my headquarters.

I hardly had time to take off the long scarf that covered my hair, when there was knock at the door and Finna timorously entered behind a guard.

'Fetch us some wine, would you,' I said to the guard. 'And some pork if your friends haven't wolfed it all.' I took Finna's arm and led her to a chair. 'You must be tired and hungry after your journey.'

Finna half-smiled but said nothing.

'And bring Merfyn or another of the Welshmen here,' I called after the guard, remembering I would need some form of translation.

We sat in silence, smiling at one another across the rough-hewn table, strewn with rolls of manuscripts. Her normal proud bearing was subdued, and she did not look me in the eye. Finally, she cleared her throat.

'Sorry, my husband bad,' she said haltingly.

'Ah, you do speak our tongue,' I said, surprised.

'Speak only Gaelic.'

'So my nephew told me. How long have you been with the Norwegians?'

'Yes, speak Norwegian,' she said.

A girl appeared with a platter of food and a jug. As she set it down on the table, she curtseyed briefly. 'Beggin' your pardon, m'lady, the wine butt is empty so I've brought ale.'

I peered into the jug. 'Mouldy ale by the smell of it.' I looked up as Merfyn entered the room. 'Taste this for me, would you. Will it poison me?'

Merfyn's eyes lingered on Finna before he bowed to me and took a swig from the jug. He smacked his lips. 'Shouldn't kill you, m'lady, though it's hardly fit for a queen.'

'It's good that I'm not a queen, then,' I said, indicating to the maid that she could pour the drink. 'Merfyn, I'm told your Welsh is close enough to the Gaelic language that you can understand it. Is that so?'

'For the most part, yes.'

'Good. This is Finna and I want you to translate what I say to her and what she replies to me. Make sure you understand our words as accurately as possible. Is that clear?'

'Yes m'lady.' He turned towards Finna. 'As long as she don't gabble fast like some of the Irish do.'

'If she does, instruct her to speak more clearly. First, ask her how she regards her husband now that he has broken his oath to me. And tell her to help herself to food,' I said, indicating the plates on the table.

I tried to eat whilst I watched Finna during the lengthy exchange with Merfyn that followed. When Finna began to talk, her face lost its downcast expression, and became animated and rather beautiful. It was no surprise that Ingimund had fallen for her, even if she was lowborn. Merfyn seemed to be enjoying her company, beaming and smiling, not taking his eyes from her.

Finally, he turned back to me. 'She says she is ashamed of what her husband has done and begs you to forgive her for his sins.'

It seemed a short message from such a long conversation. 'Is that it?' I asked.

'Apart from pleasantries, yes, m'lady,' Merfyn replied, grinning sheepishly and pushing a plate of food towards Finna.

'Then ask her how many Irish Christians are with the Norsemen and whether they are all enslaved, as she was.'

I watched Finna's blue-green eyes narrow when Merfyn posed the question. Her face became even more expressive as she replied.

Merfyn seemed taken aback at what he heard. 'She says she was not a slave, although her husband treated her like one. There are about fifty Irish amongst Ingimund's followers, some slaves, some fosterlings sent by their families to live with the Norse. She thinks other warlords who have come here from Dublin would also have Irish slaves in their crews.'

'Are they all followers of Christ?' I asked.

Finna looked surprised and replied emphatically.

'She says that all the Irish follow the True Faith and despise the pagans who took their lands,' Merfyn translated.

'Ask her what she will do to atone for the sins of her husband and his Norse pagans,' I said without taking my eyes from her.

The reply came quickly. 'Anything you ask.'

I smiled and patted Finna's hand. 'Good. I like your spirit.' I raised my goblet in salute. 'If you do what I ask, I will free you and your son to live wherever you wish. The other Irish too.'

*

An hour before dawn, I walked carefully across the meadow towards the river with Finna, Merfyn and Wiglaf. It was a misty, moonless night so we took the footpath next to the newly constructed wall that had extended the old defences down to the riverbank to the south of the town. When we reached the waterfront, we made our way to the small harbour where several boats were moored, guarded by a handful of warriors.

Wiglaf pointed to a shabby vessel that floated close to the waterline. 'She can take that one. It's no loss if it don't come back.'

I turned to Merfyn. 'Finna has to have a convincing story for Ingimund. Ask her how she would evade the guard if she had to steal the boat.'

Finna looked thoughtful, then lay on the moist meadow grass, rolling around until her dress was thoroughly wet and muddy. She scrambled back to her feet, grinning and shaking leaves from her long red hair as she replied.

Merfyn translated hesitantly. 'She says she would persuade the guard to give her the boat by lying with him in the grass. He would report that the moorings must have come loose and the boat drifted away.' He frowned, for once looking away from Finna.

Wiglaf chuckled. 'And you would volunteer to be the guard, no doubt,' he said to Merfyn, gingerly scrambling aboard the boat, bailing out some of the water that swilled around his feet. 'Pass the sack. It's full of knives for her friends. It's all we can spare.'

'It's all she can carry by the weight of it,' said Merfyn, swinging the sack from the shore to Wiglaf who stowed it in the bows.

'Tell her to hide the sack in some reeds as she approaches their ships, and come back for it later,' Wiglaf said. 'Otherwise they might find it when she lands.'

Finna approached me and tentatively held out a hand before throwing herself forward, embracing me firmly with both arms.

I held her for a few moments. 'God be with you. I will look after your son, Jokul, should anything happen to you. You are a brave woman.' I brushed at the mud on my cloak and laughed. 'Next time, we should embrace before you roll on the wet ground.'

Finna put her hand to her mouth to stifle a giggle before accepting Wiglaf's hand to step into the boat. He began showing her how to position the shaft of the oars between the wooden rowlocks, but she waved him away.

'She says she can row a curragh which is more difficult to handle than this,' Merfyn translated.

'God be with you then,' Wiglaf muttered as he stepped ashore and pushed the small craft out into the stream.

Finna looked over her shoulder to check her position and dipped her blades smoothly into the black water before disappearing downstream towards the Norwegian boats.

*

I waited three long days for a sign from Finna. Our defences were in a parlous state. When the Norsemen withdrew to their boats on the third evening, they left a gaping hole in the walls.

Another day, maybe two and we would not be able to plug all the breaches, however hard we worked.

Something had to change if we were to save the town.

As darkness fell, I watched the town gates swing open and a cohort of Saxon troops file out of the town. Once they had crossed the earthen bridge over the ditch around the wall, they formed up into a long shield wall and advanced a hundred or so paces towards the Norse camp.

There, they stopped and waited, as I had ordered.

Ahead of them, a Norseman was silhouetted in the flames of a campfire, no doubt wondering what the men of Chester were up to this time. He may have guessed that their intention was to take back some of the stone they had taken from the ramparts that day, because he could be seen hurrying in the direction of the stack of rocks before disappearing into the gloom.

I looked down from the ramparts, praying that a sign would come from the enemy encampment by the river. It was close to midnight and a half moon had risen to brighten the night sky. My warriors looked cold as they huddled silently on the grass.

Still no sign from Finna.

I climbed wearily down the ladder and said softly to my adjutant: 'Merewalh, give the order to withdraw. We must repair the walls as best we can.'

*

The next day, the Norsemen broke through the east wall.

It was a narrow passage and they dared not risk sending their troops through one by one. Instead, they began to widen the opening, and only nightfall prevented them from making a larger breach. When they withdrew for the night, jeering and hurling threats at the guards on the ramparts, I knew they would be back the next day to mount a full-scale attack. All I had left were wooden hurdles and beams to block up the holes, and they would not take long to dismantle or burn.

Once again, I ordered fighting men to march through the gates out of the town and form up in the darkness and await my orders.

This time, the moon did not cast any light through the clouds and the wind began to rise, blowing smoke from the enemy fires towards us.

I stood on the palisade, straining my ears for the slightest sound. All I could hear was the whistling of the wind. Only the occasional flicker from the far-off fires penetrated the darkness that enveloped the fields.

'There!' Wiglaf was beside me, pointing in the direction of the river. 'I heard a cry over there.'

I stared into the black night but saw nothing. Yet my warriors beyond the wall had begun to stir, rising to their feet, checking their shields and spears.

Something was happening out there, but what? Maybe they had misheard the howl of a fox or wolf.

A piercing shriek made me jump. That was no animal, but the unmistakable sound of a human in distress. More cries and shouts came out of the darkness. The volume of noise rose quickly and soon became a general clamour of hollering and screaming.

I clutched Wiglaf's arm. 'It's time.'

He nodded and shouted down to where Merewalh waited by the gates. 'Order the advance!'

Involuntarily, I put my hand to my mouth as our men stepped forward and disappeared into the darkness.

I could not bear it. I had to find out what was happening and started towards the ladder, but Wiglaf took my arm.

'M'lady, we agreed you would stay out of the fighting, did we not? You will see more from up here.'

I looked into his earnest young face and felt the firmness of his grip. He was right. There was nothing I could do but wait.

*

I could clearly hear the clashing of metal on hardwood, the roars of triumph and curses of pain from unseen men fighting in the darkness. Yet it seemed like an eternity before I could see who was making the hubbub in the dark.

A group of men burst through the gloom, stumbling towards the gates. They carried no shields nor spears and some stopped to double over, hands on knees. They had been running hard.

I stifled a shout. These were not my warriors. The sound of fighting grew louder behind them, but, however hard I stared, I could not see if my men were winning or losing. Should I be closing the gates in case the enemy had overwhelmed my forces? Or should they stay open to ensure their safe return?

Wiglaf was shouting down to the guards by the gates to encourage the men through into safety. Had his young eyes seen something I had not? I peered again into the noisy gloom.

There they were at last! I glimpsed the shield wall moving slowly back towards the gates in an orderly formation, preventing the enemy from breaking through.

I made for the ladder and this time Wiglaf did not stop me.

'What happened?' I shouted to the first man who panted through the gates. He looked up, exhaustion on his face, but managed a torrent of words of which I understood not one. More fugitives were arriving, some dropping to their knees to pray, others hugging their comrades with relief.

'We need a translator. Where's Merfyn?' I asked Wiglaf who had followed me from the wall. He just pointed through the gates. I had forgotten; he was in the shield wall.

'Archers to the walls!' I shouted to the bowmen who stood ready in the square. Glancing through the gates, I could see that the shield wall had made it to the outer mound of the ditch and had halted there. Pushing aside an archer who was about to mount the ladder, I climbed swiftly up to the parapet. From constant practice, my feet had become more assured on the rungs, and I could scale the ladder as fast as any man.

The scene below me seemed confused. My warriors looked outnumbered, but the shield wall remained unbroken. The enemy had fallen back, but were not retreating, just watching and waiting. Maybe they were regrouping for a final charge. Wiglaf joined me on the parapet, waving the archers into position.

'Time to sound the retreat?' he asked.

For a heartbeat, I was unsure. Even though they were outnumbered, my soldiers looked secure enough. To withdraw, they would have to break their solid formation to cross the narrow bridge or risk moving down into the ditch around the wall and up the other side. Yet I could hardly leave them outside the gates hoping the enemy would go away.

'Time to retreat,' I confirmed, inwardly chiding myself for my hesitation. An experienced warrior like my husband would have made that decision immediately. Maybe, in time, it would become like that for me.

The horn sounded loudly in the night air and I held my breath. Yet the shield wall did not dissolve into soldiers running individually for shelter as I had imagined it would. Instead, it folded back on itself, keeping its cohesion. One half of the wall moved purposefully back to form a second row. This newly formed rear line remained in place to judge the enemy's reaction, and when there was none, the rows divided again. Once the manoeuvre was completed and the Norsemen still did not attack, those in the rear line turned and made their way across the bridge and through the gates. The process was repeated several times until all that remained was a short, but intact, defensive wall. This gradually fell back towards the bridge where it paused briefly before the overlapping shields finally separated, and the warriors calmly made their way into the town. As soon as they did, the archers let loose a volley towards the enemy, some of whom had already begun to withdraw back to their camp. From my position on the wall, I heard the great cheer of greeting as the last of my men made it through the archway, and many willing hands pushed shut the heavy gates.

I scanned the newcomers below, looking for Finna amongst the throng but there was no sign of her distinctive figure. What exactly had happened in the Norse camp that night? Other than to free a few Irish slaves, maybe my mission had failed.

FOURTEEN

I caught sight of Wiglaf hurrying down the ladder to the courtyard.

'Find their leaders and take them to the hall. I need to question them,' I called over to him. 'And we'll need Merfyn to translate.'

I searched the faces of the newcomers for clues as to what had happened. There were females amongst the men, some more like girls than women. Once Wiglaf had grabbed three of the older looking men and sent them towards the feasting hall, I hurried after them.

Cooks were busy around the fire, preparing a large cauldron of soup for the hungry warriors who would soon be spilling through the door. I gestured to the three Irishmen to fetch some bread and broth and follow me to the high table.

One of the Irishmen moved closer to the serving maid who was holding out a wooden bowl, his hands uncertainly searching for what was in front of him. 'Is that potato and leek I can smell?' he asked.

I regarded him in surprise. 'You speak the English tongue?'

'Why yes, who is asking?' the man said, turning towards the sound of my voice.

I could tell by his cloudy eyes that he was blind. 'Æthelflæd, Lady of the Mercians.'

He bowed low, broth dripping from the bowl. 'Bless you, m'lady, I am Father Fintan of Kildare and honoured to be in your presence.'

'Here, let me take that,' I said, rescuing the bowl and leading him to a seat. 'You're a priest?'

'A monk, or rather I was until I became a thrall – a slave, in your tongue.'

'How did that happen?' I asked. I had heard that Christian monks were being enslaved, but it was a shock to meet one.

'I belonged to the community of Kildare Abbey. The Church of Oak, some call it, because our founder, St. Brigid, loved the ancient tree that stood by the abbey. Hundreds of people came from far and wide to be blessed at Brigid's shrine. I was at prayers when the pagans stormed the church. When they found no gold, they went berserk, killing elderly monks, ravishing young nuns. They ransacked every corner but found little of value. So they took us to Dublin market and...' He shook his head. 'I couldn't believe it even of the pagans, but they sold us. They sold the servants of God to be the slaves of men. We fetched twelve ounces of silver each, the women eight.'

'There're nuns with you?'

'No, I can only pray for our Sisters, for they were shipped from the slave market to some foreign land. The girls with us are from poor farming folk. The Norse took them when the farmers could not pay their dues after a bad harvest. We all lived in despair, but they felt it the worst, treated like whores by their masters. Then, like a miracle, Finna came to us and offered us hope.'

'Where is Finna now? What exactly did happen last night?'

'I can only tell you of my part. My eyes don't see much,' he said, feeling the bench with his hands and lowering himself carefully. 'My companions will know more. Are they here?'

I turned to see the two other Irishmen slurping broth and chatting happily with the hearth-women. I waved agitatedly. 'Over here. I need you over here.'

As they ambled over, I touched Father Fintan's arm. 'Tell me what you know.' I'd noticed that there were smears that looked like blood on his sleeve.

'As I said, it seemed like a miracle when we heard that Finna wanted to free us. We knew her only as Ingimund's wife and, although there were rumours she'd been a slave, she'd behaved like a warlord's wife until that moment.'

'How did she say she would free you?'

He frowned. 'Why, she said she came from the Lady of the Mercians. Isn't that you?'

'Yes, yes, but what did she ask you to do?'

'We were to kill the Norse leaders as they slept. She said that was what you had asked in return for our freedom.'

'And did you?'

'No, we dare not. They had guards and we're not fighting men.'

My heart sank. It seemed I had rescued the Christian slaves for little gain for them or us. The pagans would surely return with a vengeance and recapture them all when they took the town.

We were interrupted by the arrival of Fintan's companions, who greeted me eagerly and dragged out a bench to sit with us.

Fintan turned towards the noise. 'If I have not mistaken the sound and the smell, these rascals are Brother Cormac and Brother Cadman, both from Kildare. We've been rowing the Norse boats together for over seven years, haven't we boys?'

They both looked blankly until Fintan spoke to them in their own tongue, when they nodded and began a torrent of conversation.

I banged on the table. 'Stop! Just tell me what happened.' I grasped Fintan's hand. 'Briefly, please.'

'We devised a different scheme,' he said, leaning forward. 'Although as Christian brethren we obey the commandments, we contrived a way to kill. Or rather Finna did. She told Ingimund and the other Norse leaders that there were certain folk within Chester who would open the gates and deliver the town to them. But, in return, these folk would need the Norse leaders to take an oath to guarantee their safety and reward them with land and property.'

Fintan groped for the bowl before him and noisily swallowed a mouthful of broth. 'The clever part of this plan was that we said that the oath had to be witnessed by fellow Christians. Otherwise, we said, the townsfolk would not trust the Norse.'

My impatience grew as he picked at some gristle in his teeth. 'A cunning plan, Father. Did it work?'

He wiped his mouth on the sleeve of his tunic and gave me a toothy grin. 'I have yet to tell you the really clever part. When Norsemen take an oath, they don't do it on the bible like we Christians do, but on what is most precious to them – their weapons. They lay their swords and shields down before them and swear to their false gods. This was known to Finna, so she told us to conceal knives under our robes when we stood amongst the Norse leaders to witness their oaths.'

As Fintan took another slurp of soup, I studied the three monks before me. Seven years of rowing had given them powerful bodies, but they looked unlikely killers, if indeed that is what they had become.

Fintan continued, 'Ingimund laughed when I came forward, saying that no-one would believe what I had witnessed because I could not see who was speaking. I explained I was there only to translate the oaths for the townsfolk as I could speak their tongue. With that, Ingimund insisted I stand next to him so that I could hear his words more clearly,'

I felt anxious for him. 'Did you have a knife?'

'I did, but it was not planned that I would use it because my aim is not so good.' He chuckled and spoke to his two companions, who began talking garrulously.

I held up my hands. 'I just need to know if you managed to kill them.'

'Sorry, m'lady, I was asking my companions that same question.'

'And what did they answer?'

'They're not sure.'

I exhaled loudly.

'Ingimund was not expecting to be stabbed, especially by me. I heard the shock in his voice when I pushed my knife into his belly, but he fell back so I couldn't press it all the way. Someone – Brother Cadman I think it was – pulled my arm and we began running away from the pandemonium I could hear around me. I'm used to running in the dark so that was the easy part for me, especially when I heard your soldiers banging on their shields to direct us.'

'What about the other Norse leaders? Were they stabbed too?' I asked.

Fintan shrugged and spoke with his two companions. There was laughing and shouting from the entryway as soldiers came looking for sustenance after their long night.

I saw Wiglaf and waved him over. 'Any sign of Finna or Merfyn?' I asked. He shook his head. 'Then sit and listen as best you can. I am trying to get this trio of monks to tell us what happened.'

I cleared my throat to make myself heard above the hubbub. 'Father Fintan, this is my reeve, Wiglaf. We need to know urgently what happened to the Norse leaders so that we can deploy our troops accordingly.'

'It's hard for us to say for sure as there was so much commotion last night.' Fintan's dull eyes swivelled in my direction and he grinned. 'But at the very least, they'll have stomach pain or neck ache.'

Wiglaf looked at me with a resigned expression. 'I think we can assume the enemy leaders are wounded, but no more.'

I agreed. We would just have to wait and watch. It was not for long.

When I left the hall, the sun had risen. My warriors were all accounted for, except for Merfyn, and the town's population had swollen by over thirty fugitives. Their stories of what had happened out there in the dark were vivid but confused. Knowing that the assassins were monks, and that one was blind, had dampened my hopes that they had killed the Norse chiefs. I headed for my chamber, determined to rest until there was more definitive news. It had been a long night.

I was halted by a shout from a sentry on the ramparts.

'Ship leaving!' The sentry was pointing towards the river.

Somehow I found the energy to sprint to the ladder and climb the steps to the viewpoint. I could clearly see the Norse longboats dragged up onto the riverbank, but none appeared to be moving.

The sentry was one of Wiglaf's captains. 'What did you see?' I snapped.

He pointed towards the furthest ship. 'They're dragging that boat towards the waterline, m'lady. It's low water, so they're having to pull it on logs. Must be keen to leave.'

I could see tiny figures carrying tree trunks from the stern of the boat towards the bows. I watched with mounting hope as they heaved the vessel onto the logs that rolled it over the mud towards the fast-flowing water.

As he seemed knowledgeable of marine matters, I asked the captain why the Norsemen had berthed their boats so far onshore.

'Probably fearful of damage to their ships during the bore tides, m'lady,' he explained. 'Tides are strong for the moment. If they boat now, they'll have a following current, whereas if they delay, it'll be a strong flow against them,' he said.

Norse warriors defeated by monk's knives: could it be true? The sentry interrupted my musing.

'Someone approaching, m'lady!' He pointed towards the area where the town's defences extended down to the river.

I followed the line of his arm. A stocky figure was stumbling from the reedy bank towards the wall. He seemed to reach out to touch the stonework before slithering to the ground.

I glanced back at the enemy encampment. All activity there was concentrated around the boats.

'Fetch whoever that is. Probably another Irish fugitive. Unless...' The man had rested his head on his knees, and I thought I recognised that shock of black hair. 'It might be one of our soldiers. Hurry and take him to the infirmary.'

*

I was right. It was Merfyn.

I waited impatiently as he was laid out on a board and healers applied poultices to a flesh wound on his leg. He winced as a bundle of seaweed was pressed against the skin, but he managed a brief smile when I bent over him.

'How did you come by this?' I asked.

'Making a pagan talk, m'lady,' he grunted.

'What did he tell you?'

'Died too quick to tell me everything, but...' he paused and squeezed his eyes shut for a moment.

'But what?'

'Ingimund still lives and has Finna with him. He grabbed her when he fell with a knife in his gut.'

I saw the sweat on the young man's brow as the healer stood back, her work complete. 'You went to save her, didn't you?' I said quietly.

He said nothing but nodded, grim-faced.

'A brave but foolish act, and one for which the reeve may well punish you. I presume he did not give his blessing to your sortie?'

'No, m'lady, but I found out that four of the Norse leaders are dead, and two, including Ingimund, are badly wounded. They're sailing to find healers.'

I smiled. 'In which case, I will tell Wiglaf that you have been punished enough by the departure of the woman you risked your life for.' I took a towel and mopped his brow. 'Thank you, brave Merfyn. Hopefully this will be the end of Ingimund, but not of Finna. As you seem so fond of her, you can help me look after her son.'

*

Two days later the ride from Chester to Shrewsbury was a delight. The sun shone but a breeze kept me cool. My head was still singing from the sight of the departing longships and the cheering of my warriors who had crowded onto the ramparts as the Norsemen rowed back the way they had come.

I had seen the thrill of victory on my husband's face many times when he returned from battle, but I had never experienced it for myself. When warriors celebrated by drinking themselves into a stupor, I soberly mourned for those who had not returned. Yet today, I rode hard, leaving my hair free to blow in the wind. I hadn't done that since I was a girl in Winchester.

My small group of companions struggled to keep up as I crested a grassy hillock. Below me, the town of Shrewsbury nestled into a great loop of the River Severn. What I saw abruptly changed my mood. An army encampment had sprung up. Row upon row of tents and shelters sprawled between the walls of the town and the banks of the river.

Norsemen must have sailed up the Severn!

I caught sight of a banner emblazoned with a half-dragon, half reptile wyvern, the symbol of Wessex.

Edward! What is he doing here?

I urged my horse on, strangely eager to see my brother. I wanted to tell him what had happened at Chester, and the part I had played – despite my ignorance of military matters.

But it was not my brother who greeted me as I rode through the town-gate. It was my stepbrother Osferth – the bastard as I had come to think of him, although I would not care to call him that to his face.

'Hail to the conquering heroine,' he called to me as I slid from my horse. The smile that perpetually adorned his face seemed even wider.

I brushed a tangle of hair from my eyes. 'If you've come to help, you're too late.'

'Your brother will be proud of you.'

'Which one?' I asked mischievously, knowing that he had yet to admit to me that we shared the same father.

For a heartbeat, he hesitated. 'I was sent by King Edward.' He indicated the encampment behind him. 'With an army to secure our borders.'

'We need more burhs to prevent these incursions, not your army.' We were having the same old argument about strategy all over again, and my exasperation probably showed.

The smile left his face. 'We have much to discuss and I don't have much time. I need to pursue these Norse settlers and make sure they never return.'

'They took to their longships and will be far away by now. You will never catch them.'

'That's for me and my captains to decide.'

'You are subject to our advice while you are in Mercia,' I snapped.

'If by that you mean the Lord Æthelred, you had best visit him,' he said, turning on his heels and striding away.

Breathing deeply, I watched him go. Why did the powerful men of my family always rile me?

A voice nearby reminded me that I was still holding my

horse. 'Shall I take her now, m'lady?' the groom asked nervously.

I handed him the reins and went in search of my husband.

*

Athelstan found me first. He bounded down the steps of the hall and threw his arms around me.

'You're back at last, Aunt,' he said. 'Everyone is talking about you. Is it true you defeated the Danes with bees?'

I felt tears in my eyes as I held him tight. 'Yes, bees did help. Many brave people as well.' I knelt to look into his eager face. 'You too.'

His eyes widened. 'How?'

'You remember you told me about some Roman generals?'

'Like Scipio and Caesar?'

'Yes, I used some of their tactics.' I kissed him on the forehead. 'So keep up your studies.'

'Did you lure the pagans into a trap?'

I nodded. 'I will tell you all about it later. First, I must see Lord Æthelred.'

Athelstan stared at the ground.

'What? What's happened to him?' I asked.

'Lord Beornoth says he is half-dead.'

'Then I will go and see the half that lives.'

*

I was directed into a small chamber, away from the hall, in a quiet area close to St Chad's church. He would like the view over the river from the doorway, I thought.

When I said his name, he reacted very slowly. His head hardly moved and he didn't blink. Only his eyes swivelled slowly towards me.

'It's me, your wife,' I said.

'Ætte.' His voice was an indistinct rumble.

'No, it's Æthelflæd.'

'Ætte,' he repeated.

I turned to the portly servant who had been assigned to look after him. 'Is your name Ætte?'

'No, m'lady. He calls me that too.'

I took one of his hands, gently trying to straighten the stiff fingers that curled claw-like into his palm. 'How does he eat?' I asked the servant.

'I feed him broth with a spoon, m'lady. And I clean him afterwards.' She paused, meaningfully. 'All over.'

I wanted to cry. My old bear was in a sorry state, and I loved him even more, for all that. But I didn't want him to see my tears.

'I'll look after you, don't worry,' I said, wiping my eyes. 'I'll be back soon.'

'Ætte,' he said as I left.

*

Osferth was waiting for me by the church.

'Desperately sad end for a brave warrior,' he said.

'Sad, but not the end,' I replied.

'The physician is not hope…'

'He is alive, and whilst he lives, there is hope.'

His smile returned. 'Of course.' He indicated the low door of St Chad's church. 'We are gathered here, m'lady, to discuss what needs to be done. Will you join us?'

I was too deflated to argue and followed him into the vestry.

When I saw who was there, I realised something sinister was afoot.

The room was full of Mercian elders.

Bishop Wærferth bustled towards me and kissed my hand effusively. 'My dear lady, words fail me in expressing the grief and the joy that I feel simultaneously for you.'

I touched his sleeve. 'Thank you. It's good to have you here.'
Behind him, a number of elderly figures were struggling to
their feet to greet me. Lord Beornoth was amongst them, as I
would have expected, but others, such as Æthelred's old retainer,
Cnebba, must have come from a considerable distance.

Why had they all assembled?

Osferth waved an arm towards the table. 'Please, let us all
be seated. King Edward asked me to convene this meeting to
discuss the future governance of Mercia.'

Suddenly, the trap became clear.

Osferth was taking over.

*

My head span and for a moment I could not think straight.

Fortunately, it took some time for the frail old men in the
room to be seated. I remembered a past moment when I was
sitting at my embroidery whilst Athelstan read to Æthelred. As
ever it was a story of warfare when a Roman general had won
against the odds.

'You see, m'boy,' Æthelred had said when Athelstan finished
reading. 'Sometimes attack is the best form of defence 'specially
if they have outmanoeuvred you.'

I certainly felt outmanoeuvred. I would have to attack.

'How convenient,' I said, taking the chair at the head of the
table where Osferth was about to sit. 'I planned to call a meeting
of our Witan myself so that I would receive the advice of our wise
councillors on how we should proceed, now that Æthelred is infirm.'

Osferth stopped smiling. 'Exactly, I ....'

'Do take a seat, m'lord,' I said to Osferth, waving him towards
the back of the room. 'I think it appropriate for you to be here
as an observer so that you can report back to the King on our
decision. Is that so, Bishop? You are more informed on these
matters of protocol than I am.'

I looked hard at Bishop Wærferth, hoping he would understand my predicament. All eyes around the table were on him and he looked a little flustered.

'If this is to be a meeting of the Witan of Mercia, as you suggest, m'lady, we should give notice to all its members to attend. The Lords Cenwulf and Beorhsige are no longer with us, so in fact all surviving members are here.' He paused to look directly at me. 'Except, that is, for the Lord of the Mercians.'

'Whose authority I now carry,' I said quickly.

'How so?' Osferth had reluctantly moved to one side but remained on his feet.

'Why, I received that authority from Lord Æthelred himself, did I not Bishop Wærferth? It was on the occasion of his first bout of palsy and he thought it prudent to delegate his authority to me, should he become incapable for a period. The Bishop and Lord Cenwulf were witnesses.'

I breathed out quietly when Wærferth nodded his agreement.

'Why was this not reported to the King?' demanded Osferth.

The Bishop seemed to be gaining confidence. 'It was before the new king's coronation, so we had yet to swear our allegiance. By the time King Edward had officially become overlord of Mercia, the Lord Æthelred had recovered sufficiently to resume his duties. Unfortunately, that is no longer the case, and Lady Æthelflæd has, rightly in my view, resumed the authority she was previously given. And I think we must all agree,' he said, pausing to give his words more impact, 'she has used it to great effect thus far.'

He tapped lightly on the table and Beornoth joined in, drumming more loudly and calling, 'Rah, rah, well done, m'lady.' Cnebba took up the rhythm and soon the vestry was reverberating with their banging and cheering.

I held up my hands. 'Thank you, my lords. What little I have been able to achieve, I have done by following your wise advice and with the help of your noble families. Whatever we choose to put in the place of Lord Æthelred's leadership, we must not lose the precious ingredients provided by this counsel,' I said looking straight at Osferth, who was definitely not smiling.

Beornoth cleared his throat. 'M'lady, although he is sadly diminished in powers, the Lord Æthelred still lives, so could we not continue as we are? You have proven a most able deputy, so I would suggest you rule in his place as Lady of the Mercians.' He glanced at Osferth. 'Whilst continuing to acknowledge the overlordship of King Edward.'

Osferth shifted from one foot to another. 'Naturally, the King expects to be consulted in these matters. In fact he sent me as...'

He hesitated and, in that moment, I knew he had lost the argument.

'... as his representative at this Witan, and as someone who might now lead the Mercian army.'

Silence greeted his words.

Beornoth finally spoke. 'We must thank the King for his generous offer.' He turned to his colleagues. 'It is most noble to send his very own general to serve under our Lady, is it not?'

The sight of Osferth's squirming stayed with me for many years. Everyone began thanking him for suggesting that he might serve me. It was an offer he clearly had not intended when he had set out for Mercia, gathering up the elders en route to Shrewsbury so that the Witan would endorse his takeover.

I put him out of his misery. 'You cannot waste your military talents with our paltry forces. Edward was clearly expecting you to have territory to administer here in Mercia.' I was enjoying the moment knowing that it was all of Mercia that he was expecting to rule over. 'Lord Cenwulf, God rest his soul, was responsible for our southern lands from London to Oxford. That would be a fitting responsibility for you now, would it not?'

I believed I had made a good compromise. Edward had clearly promised him Mercia, and I had at least given him a part of it to govern.

It worked, for a while. Yet I came to regret it in the end.

*

So it was that I became the first woman ever to rule over an Anglo-Saxon realm.

I began with acts of compassion. That evening, I sent commands to Chester to free the Irish slaves in return for their ambush of the Norwegian leaders. Wiglaf quickly reported back that Fintan was so humbled by my actions that he asked if he could pray for me and my family from a monastery in Mercia. I replied that he would be welcome at the new abbey that I was founding in Gloucester where more monks would be needed.

I also ordered the release of Halfdan, the Danish leader, even though his ransom had not been paid. I knew that would be a difficult decision for my followers to accept, but I wished to show mercy to a fellow Christian, even if he was an enemy.

It was another decision that I came to regret.

PART THREE

FIFTEEN

By the year of Our Lord 910, I had lived for forty years and the aches and pains in my body told me I was getting old. Yet I felt I had done little with my life thus far. My father's arrangements to share the land with the Danes were intended to be temporary, but half of Mercia still lay under the control of the pagans. Since assuming authority from my sick husband, I had not taken back a single inch of our former territory. Nor had I provided any obvious heir to succeed us, normally the first duty of any ruler.

Fortunately, the Good Lord works in wondrous ways that we poor mortals seldom understand. Many of my actions had consequences I could never have imagined at the time. I little thought that the abbey that I founded as our family church in Gloucester would have the impact it did. Yet so many events that followed had their roots in that simple decision to build a monument to God.

We sited the abbey by the river, between the residence I had built for the family at Kingsholm and the newly repaired walls of Gloucester. The fields around the town were scattered with the ruins of buildings left by the Romans and we used the plentiful stone to create a church. From the rubble of past generations, the masons skilfully raised majestic walls and gracious arches, and constructed a most beautiful House of God. We named it after St Peter but, as I will recount, we had cause to change that later. When my earthly toils are done, I have chosen to lie there, in my own modest chapel, rather than the grandiose mausoleum that my brother has built in Winchester.

I had thought it an act of charity to give Fintan a living at the abbey, but he turned out to be more useful than I had thought. My father, King Alfred, had insisted that all highborn children should read and write in the English tongue, and I was determined to follow his example. Although he could not see to read, Fintan could recite the histories and the Gospels from memory, and he took on the role of tutor for the young people in my care. That included not only Athelstan and Ælfwyn but also their companions amongst the sons and daughters of my household. Fintan listened attentively whilst his pupils read to him, correcting any who wavered too far from what was written as their voices echoed around the spacious nave. The new priory became a centre for learning as well as worship. I never imagined it would also become a destination for pilgrims.

It was Fintan who asked the question that began it all. On a sunny day, I had decided to walk to the abbey that had risen so gloriously above the grassy meadow by the river. Fintan greeted me in his nonchalant manner as I paced around the perimeter, checking the recently finished stonework, admiring the workmanship of the masons and carpenters.

'I'm told it's a beautiful abbey,' Fintan remarked. 'Did you have any particular relics in mind to keep here?'

It was a sensible enough question. I always tried to find holy relics to bless the churches that I founded. I had recently acquired the bones of St Werburgh from a trader who had rescued them in Hanbury when the Danes invaded that town, but I had allocated those to the new church I was building in Chester in celebration of our victory there.

'I will ask Bishop Wærferth if he has anything suitable,' was all I could think of saying because I did not know of any relic with sufficient status for such a fine abbey.

'What about St Oswald?' asked Athelstan, who had joined us after his studies. He seemed to spend as many hours with the monks of the abbey as he did with the warriors in the hall. He had grown swiftly in recent years and now stood as tall as I did, and, at nearly seventeen years old, his piercing eyes and wiry frame still reminded me of his grandfather. Yet aspects of his face must have come from his mother's side. She was a great beauty and had given him her flaxen hair mingled with golden threads and a fine bone structure to balance the more rugged looks that he had inherited from my family.

Fintan shrugged. 'Some of Oswald's bones are in Bardney, but they might as well be at the bottom of the Irish Sea.' He was referring to the fact that Bardney was an abandoned abbey in Lindsey, part of Mercia that now lay well inside the Danelaw.

'Can we not buy them from the Danes?' asked Athelstan.

'I've tried that,' I said. 'I have told merchants who trade with the Danelaw that I will reward them well for such relics. But they return empty-handed.'

'I have a friend, a monk who was at Bardney Abbey,' said Fintan, who seemed to have friends everywhere. 'He says that the bones have great healing powers especially the hands which, as I am sure you know, are buried apart from the head.' He was referring to the dismemberment of Oswald's body by his killers who had put his head and limbs on separate stakes.

Athelstan looked thoughtful. 'There must be another way of acquiring the relics. Mercia owes King Oswald the honour of a holy resting place in a Christian community.'

He was right. If Oswald could not rest safely in Northumbria, the land of his birth, then he should be brought to Mercia. Oswald had been killed by Penda, a pagan king of Mercia and

I would have liked nothing more than to make amends for the slaughter of one of our first Christian kings by Mercians.

But I had more urgent things to do. I had the living to take care of. It was five years since the successful defence of Chester, and we had been at peace with the Danes for all of those years. Edward still seemed to be dazed from the battle at Holme Fen that had simultaneously secured his throne and shattered his confidence. Likewise the Danes had lost some of their warlike ambition and were more content to plough than to plunder. They were increasingly distracted by the constant threat of the Norsemen from Dublin who were looking for new territory to replace what they had lost in Ireland.

I had been using the years of peace to improve our defences and was determined to complete the ring of walled towns along the main routes into Mercia. Some objected to the expenditure and effort; churchmen had joined ealdormen in questioning my strategy. But I ignored their complaining and, instead, drew up plans to build new burhs close to the border. I thought the Danes would never dare to invade us again.

Yet they did, prompted by the bones of St. Oswald.

*

Athelstan and I left the abbey with the issue of the relics unresolved, but I could sense it troubled him. He was an intense young man who took life very seriously. He must have been awake most of the night, for the next morning he came to me with a plan.

When Æthelred was incapacitated with palsy, I became responsible for a realm that ran from London in the south to Chester in the north, a triangular wedge of land between the Danelaw in the east and the Welsh kingdoms to the west. I needed clerks, scribes and messengers alongside me, so I had moved my place of work to a small hall within the royal residence.

Normally, I required visitors to give warning before they entered to see me, but I made an exception for Athelstan. My fondness for the young man had grown to such an extent that I allowed him to come and go freely in my presence and I increasingly used his fine mind to test my ideas.

This time he came with an idea of his own.

'If I ride north of here, to the border with the Danelaw,' he said, 'I am just two days ride from Bardney. Maybe less if I had a team of horses.'

'And this is important to me because of what exactly?' I had been pouring over a summary of taxes that were still uncollected and the figures did not please me.

'Because I can bring you St. Oswald's relics.' He smiled in his disarming way. 'If you just give me enough men and horses.' He produced a rolled parchment on which he had drawn a rough map. 'See, Bardney is here.'

I shuddered when I looked at its location. It was almost on the east coast of Lindsey, north of the Wash, and close enough to the Fenland to remind me of the events at Holme Fen.

'*You* will bring me the relics? Have you negotiated a safe passage with the Danes to do that? Do you think a King's son, worth a fortune in ransom, can just wander across their land and take what he wishes?'

For the first time in my presence, he raised his voice.

'It is not *their* land. It is our land!' He almost banged his fist down onto the map but slowed his hand at the last moment. 'If grandfather was here, he would agree with me.'

'I'm sure he would. But what do you think he would be doing about it? Risking all by rashly attacking the enemy, or patiently building our strength until the result was in no doubt?'

I felt the intensity of his look as he paused for a moment, breathing hard. 'Grandfather would have a plan. He wouldn't just be building walls. He would be working out how to use them,' he said.

I slammed shut the book of ledgers and stood up. 'You think I don't have a plan? Follow me.'

I swept past the clerks, who wisely kept their eyes on their work, and stood on the top of the steps outside of the hall. Pointing to the walls of Gloucester in the distance, I turned to Athelstan as he hurried to my side.

'When you arrived here as a child, do you remember what it was like inside those walls?'

'Ruins,' he said, head bowed.

'Exactly. The place was a ruin. No people, just rubble, rubbish and weeds. Now it's a thriving town full of merchants, artisans, and most importantly, warriors,' I said, indicating some soldiers hurrying towards the town gate. 'Enough men to defend this town if it was attacked without calling on some distant army for help. In your grandfather's time, an army of Danes camped here. It was from here that Guthrum attacked us in Chippenham. King Alfred would be amazed and proud to see that Gloucester is now a secure and thriving Mercian town. And he would see the same at Worcester, Shrewsbury, Chester, Oxford, London and many more in a few years from now. So don't tell me I have no plan.'

He shifted from one foot to the other. 'Sorry, I didn't mean... that is, I know you and my father have agreed to make sure we cannot be caught unawares again.' He looked up, his eyes bright. 'And I think that is a good plan. But it doesn't win back our lost territory.'

I put an arm on his shoulder. 'Come, I'm hungry. Let's find some food and I can tell you the next steps.'

We strolled towards the hall, and I told him of my discussions with Edward. I liked my brother more since he had lost some of his arrogant bluster. He and I had managed several meetings without once shouting at each other. During the years of peace, we had agreed that we would first complete our ring of defensive burhs, and then we would begin encroaching into the Danelaw and establishing fortified encampments there.

'Soon we will be ready to make our first move across the borders and set up strongholds in their territory,' I said.

'When?' Athelstan said eagerly. 'And how can you be sure of holding them if they counter-attack?'

I did not have a good answer for that, so I told him of an idea Edward and I had discussed at our most recent meeting. 'Before we set up a new burh over the border, we will raid the farmland all around, burning their crops, stealing their cattle. Without provisions, they will have fewer men to attack us.'

He fell silent for a few moments. 'Now would be a good time for that. When the calves and lambs are young and before they can begin harvesting,' he said.

I nodded my agreement, and we went into the hall to find food.

Edward and I had yet to agree to this strategy so I should not really have been discussing it with the king's son.

*

The next day I went to the chamber where Æthelred spent his days. I was leaving on one of my tours of Mercia to make sure that justice was being done, taxes collected, coins minted, and defences built according to my specifications. It was always difficult to say farewell to him, for I was never sure I would see him alive again. He had not improved since he had been stricken with his second, most serious bout of palsy. Every winter his condition deteriorated, and we would think we might lose him. But he was a tough old bear, and every spring he would manage to twitch his mouth into a hint of a grin, and I would know he would live a while longer. Now that he resided in some seclusion away from the town, we could occasionally take him outside to sit in the sunshine and read to him from his favourite histories. But mostly he sat in his room staring vacantly ahead, only the tremors in his hands showing signs of life. Still, it was a comfort to me to know that he was there. And whilst he lived, we could avoid the dispute over who might succeed him.

'Ætte,' he said as I hurried into his room, using the name he had chosen to call me. Ælfwyn was with him, as she often was, wiping the remains of his morning food from his face.

'I am going north,' I said and, when I saw a flicker of interest on his face, I continued. 'I will see your old companion, Beornoth. His health has deteriorated. I am taking his son, Merewalh, with me.'

I took particular note of Ælfwyn's expression as I continued. 'He has been away from his father for too long and should be with him at this time.'

Ælfwyn shot me a vexed glance before lowering her eyes.

'Come, bid your mother farewell,' I said to her, standing and opening my arms. 'Are you not sorry to see me go?'

'Of course, Mother.'

'Or will you miss someone who is going with me even more?'

'I don't know what you mean,' she said, but her reddening cheeks told me that she did.

That was something else I had to resolve on my journey.

*

We had planned to go first to Chester and the settlements on the borders of Danelaw to the north, but en route we heard that Beornoth's condition had deteriorated further. We decided to go to him whilst there was still time. When we arrived at his dwelling in Shrewsbury, Beornoth did not rise from his bed to greet me, so I knew he was gravely ill. He did manage to sit up and his face flickered into a smile when he saw Merewalh standing behind me.

'I am returning your son to you, thankfully all in one piece,' I said, taking a stool beside the bed. 'Since you generously offered him to me as my adjutant during the defence of Chester, he has served me courageously and skilfully. But I think you need him by your side now.'

Beornoth nodded his appreciation and coughed to clear his throat. 'Thank you, m'lady, he will be of comfort to me. But he will be restless here. Not much to do except watch an old man die.'

I had other motives for wanting Merewalh away from my own household, but I did not want to burden Beornoth with such family problems.

'You are right,' I said, putting my hand on his withered arm to reassure him. 'He has inherited many of his father's fine qualities, and I do have a particular role in mind for him.'

I stood so that I could look at Merewalh, as I had not told him the details of what I was about to announce.

'As we have expanded the number of burhs, our chain of command has become fragmented between the garrisons of the towns and the standing armies of the fyrd. I am therefore creating new military commands to include the garrisons and the fyrd of a given area. Wiglaf will take command of the north from his base in Chester. Cuthberht, who leads my personal thegns in Gloucester, will command that area, and we have Osferth in the south.'

Beornoth was nodding. 'My young reeve, Thurston, now has two hundred men under his control in Shrewsbury, yet he has little experience of battle and is more used to building bridges than standing in a shield wall. What are you proposing to do here exactly?'

'I have decided to put Merewalh in charge of the local fyrd and the garrisons of your towns. One unified command so there is no confusion.'

Merewalh was bowing low in gratitude, but his father seemed confused. 'I am pleased for my son but my reeve is not going to be happy at being replaced.'

'Not replaced. Thurston remains as reeve but will be overseen by Merewalh who will soon have other garrisons to worry about.'

'Other garrisons? Where?' Beornoth was looking troubled, and I feared I might be overtaxing his strength.

Merewalh stepped forward to speak in his ear. 'Father, her ladyship has ideas for more burhs over the border. Stafford, Tamworth, Warwick. We need shield walls of forts, as well as of warriors.'

I could not have put it better myself. Beornoth fell back onto his pillow, breathing hard. 'Burhs into the Danelaw. If only I could live to see it. What about Woden's Fort?'

I had not heard of the place, although I could tell from the use of the Norse god in the name that it must be in the borderland.

Merewalh saw my blank look. 'It's a day's ride to the east, m'lady. A hill fort used by the ancients before the Romans came. It has a fine view of the area towards the Danelaw.'

Wherever I could use existing fortifications to make new defences, I did. Anything to save the toil of digging new ditches and the timber to build new walls.

'Take me there tomorrow if you think it a good location,' I said.

That was one of those seemingly small decisions that was to have consequences so profound that I truly believe the hand of God was at work that day.

*

Merewalh did not have the swagger and boldness of Beorhsige, his treacherous elder brother, and I liked him all the better for that. Quiet and thoughtful, he normally kept his own counsel unless I asked for his opinion. It was something of a surprise, therefore, when he drew his horse alongside mine as we rode away from Shrewsbury the next day.

'M'lady, may I beg the favour of a word with you,' he said.

I was in a hurry to see this hillfort and the brisk pace of the horses made it hard to hear. That made it a particularly unfortunate moment for him to ask what followed.

'Yes, what is it?'

He cleared his throat. 'It would seem I am to be separated from your royal household for some time.'

'Quite so.'

'I have made many good friends there. I will miss them.'

'You belong here, with your family. I'm sure you will rekindle the old friendships you had.'

'There is one particular person I cannot replace in my affections.'

I knew what was coming, and my heart sank.

'No-one is irreplaceable.'

The wind rose at that moment so the poor man had to almost shout the words he was finding so difficult to say.

'It's your daughter, Ælfwyn. I would ask your permission to marry her so that we can always be together.'

That took courage. As a mother, I wanted to put my arms around him and welcome him warmly into my family. His calm thoughtfulness was the perfect foil for my daughter's headstrong passions. And she so needed a good husband to keep away the unwanted attentions of every up-and-coming thegn she met.

But I had to answer as Lady of the Mercians, not as a mother.

'Ælfwyn cannot marry. Certainly not to someone like you with a claim to the old kingship of Mercia.'

For a moment he lost his composure. 'I make no such claims! I will take oaths to renounce my ancestors' rights in Mercia. I do not want any advancement in this. I just want Ælfwyn.'

'What of your sons, will they renounce all claims? That is a risk we cannot take.'

He did not answer so we rode in silence for a while. Whenever I heard whispers of men vying for my daughter's favours, I wanted to whip them. It was not to protect my daughter's innocence; it was to safeguard the delicate balance of power between the royal houses of Wessex and Mercia. I could never allow new claims for power to arise through some upstart lord's dalliance with King Alfred's granddaughter.

Merewalh was different. He was sincere in his affection; I could see that. So my anger turned to pity, and I made the mistake of giving him hope.

'I am grateful that you care for my daughter, but please understand that we cannot entertain any serious relationship between you two. Certainly not until we have firmly established dominion over all our lands.'

The beginnings of a smile on his face should have warned me that I had gone too far.

'You mean I can ask you again when we have defeated the Danes?'

What could I say? For once it was the mother, not the Lady, who replied.

'You can ask, but I make no promises, and Ælfwyn may have tired of you by then.'

I urged my horse on, hoping that would be the end to the matter and that I would not have to face my daughter over it.

*

The view from Woden's Fort went some way to compensate for that difficult conversation. On the valley floor below me lay a golden carpet of spring barley edged with white borders of blackthorn blossom. I little imagined it would soon be stained red from the slaughter of countless men.

Smoke rose from homesteads in the distance. 'That way lies Tettenhall,' Merewalh said pointing to a hamlet in the west. 'And the Danelaw border is over the horizon to the east.'

Woden's Fort was situated on the route between the River Severn, which gave access to the heartlands of Mercia to the west, and Watling Street which ran along the boundary of the Danelaw to the east. It was ideal for fortification, as Beornoth had suggested. The hill would provide a military vantage point so we would build the burh around its base. Merewalh and I set about pacing out the distances and planning where walls and buildings would be best situated.

Designing settlements where families could live securely in peace was the work I loved best. I came to believe that this above all else was what the Good Lord intended me for. It was certainly something that came easily to me and I readily became engrossed in it. I lost count of the days that we took to plan out and measure the positioning of the fortifications and the layout of streets. It would not be a grand town on the scale of Chester but it would be an important military base.

When we had finally finished our drawings and estimations, we travelled southwest to the crossing of the Severn at Quatford. For Mercia, the River Severn is both a blessing and a curse. It pulses like a blood-route through our land carrying trade and people from Shrewsbury in the north, through our heartlands at Worcester and Gloucester, and out into the Celtic Sea to the south. Yet like the veins of our body, it can become infected. Our enemies also made use of our great river. The longships of the Danes were once a frequent sight on the Severn until we fortified towns along its banks to block their passage. Now it was also becoming a protective wall, shielding western Mercia from the Danes to the east.

In a campaign fought by my husband, Æthelred, the Danes under Hæsten had used the ford at Quatford and made camp there. I wanted to make it impossible for them to do that again. However, there was little suitable ground to build defences around the ford, so I judged it was not a good position for a new township. Scouting around the area, we found a better place two miles to the north, with soft rocks ascending above the river that would be easy to mould into defences. The river was deeper and would need to be bridged, so I set about pacing and mapping the area to find the best crossing point. I wanted to leave Merewalh in no doubt about how to build the new burh.

I asked a local farmer if the place had a name, other than Quatford. When he shook his head, I asked Merewalh what we might call the new township.

'If we are to build a bridge to the north of the settlement, then maybe it could be called Bridgnorth, m'lady?'

It was not the most creative of names, but I liked it and that is what it is called to this day.

*

We were swigging some warm ale on the grassy banks of the river when the messenger arrived. He was in a hurry and hardly stopped his mount before he jumped from its back. I was sure he came with news of Beornoth and would therefore address Merewalh.

Yet he ran towards me. 'M'lady, I have a message from King Edward.'

'Take some ale. You must be thirsty. It's a long ride from Winchester, if that is where you are from.' I studied his travel-worn appearance. A deep scar from his chin to where his right ear should have been made his face memorable, but I did not recognise him.

'Yes, m'lady. Longer still as I was directed to find you in Chester.'

I nodded, realising I had not been exactly thorough in leaving word of the changes to my journey plans. 'You have done well to find me. What would the king have me know?' I waved at a servant to pour more ale and retire, as the messenger caught his breath.

'He sends news of his intention to invade the Danelaw, m'lady.'

I almost spat out the ale I had just sipped. 'What do you mean invade the Danelaw? Did the King really say *invade?*'

The messenger fumbled at a bag hanging from his saddle and held out a document.

I saw that the seal had been broken. 'Was this intended for me?'

'Urgent message for the Lord and Lady of the Mercians explaining King Edward's intention to invade the Danelaw,' he intoned. 'That's what I was ordered to say, m'lady.'

I carefully unfolded the parchment. The message was brief; Edward had never been a man of words. It told me that he was sending a force into the Danelaw to lay waste to homesteads and crops before returning to Wessex. He was probing the Dane's strength, testing their resolve to defend the land they had conquered.

I wanted to tear the message up and pretend it did not exist. We were not ready for this. Our defences were still vulnerable and if we struck too early, a counter-attack could unravel all our careful preparations. When I read Edward's last sentence, I groaned audibly.

This is not a campaign of war. It is a raid, a chance for young warriors to prove their manhood by riding with my spears.

'Who did you give this to?' I shook the document at the messenger as if it were a weapon.

'The Lord Athelstan received me at your Gloucester residence, m'lady. He told me you were away so he took it to Lord Æthelred.'

'How long ago?'

The messenger looked puzzled.

'How many days since you were in Gloucester?' I asked.

His hands trembled as he counted his fingers. I watched with alarm as he used all his digits and began a second round.

'Fifteen, m'lady.'

I looked at the date of the message. It was nearly three weeks old. Even if I could have prevented this act of folly, it was too late. The raiders would have already left.

I imagined Fintan's young scholars eagerly swapping their books for swords, ready to pillage Danish farms. I knew that Athelstan would seize the chance to go.

'Merewalh, find me a fast boat. I must return immediately to Gloucester. You can return to your father.'

SIXTEEN

The boat was small and had rotting timbers, but my four oarsmen and the fast-flowing stream pushed it along at a good pace. By the afternoon, we reached Worcester, where I called a halt to rest and ask Bishop Wærferth for further news. The wharf was bustling with trading vessels and we were not flying a royal flag to indicate our priority, so, at first, the harbour master waved us away. My captain soon bellowed out who was on board, and harbour-men hurriedly rearranged the cluster of moored boats to give us a berth. As I stepped onto the quayside, I noted that the timbers had been repaired with strong oak and the storehouses lining the waterfront smelled of fresh thatch and wood. Trade in Worcester was obviously thriving.

If I had to choose just one place to spend the rest of my days, it would be Worcester. As I walked along the grassy banks of the Severn, the scene resembled my idea of Paradise. A blackbird sang from an orchard of apple, pear and plum trees, beyond which I glimpsed the handsome buildings of the bishop's palace, surrounded by lawns and a thorn hedgerow. Overlooking it all was the ancient church of St Peter's, its graceful wooden tower soaring to the heavens. Wærferth had been Bishop of Worcester for almost as long as I had lived and, as a loyal servant of the rulers of both Mercia and Wessex, he had been well rewarded. Assembling the finest craftsmen that money could buy, he had restored the church and built a handsome residence, scriptorium and library next to it. I particularly liked his hall; it was modest in size but rich in decoration with crossbeams carved with the images of angels, and colourful tapestries adorning the walls.

Wærferth himself stood at the entrance to greet me, an unusually large smile on his face. 'Your ladyship, we have found you, praise be to God.'

'I was not aware I was lost. Am I too late to stop this latest nonsense?'

'Nonsense, m'lady? What would that be?'

'Edward's foolish raid that will soon bring a pack of vengeful Danes to our door.'

'But we were told that you had agreed the idea with King Edward.'

'Who by?'

'Why, Lord Athelstan. Was the Witan misinformed?'

'The Witan? You called the Witan in my absence?'

'You could not be found, m'lady, and we had to respond to the king's request for warriors.' The bishop dabbed his brow with a cloth. 'Can I offer you refreshments?'

'So in my absence you decided to send youths to plunder like Norsemen.'

Wærferth breathed deeply. 'We complied with the King's wishes by dispatching one hundred warriors to join the harrowing of the Danelaw.'

It was my turn to take a deep breath. 'And you allowed Athelstan to go with them?'

'Yes, his lordship was most adamant that he should go. His tutors said he was ready for the restricted military action of a foray rather than a full-scale invasion.'

'Then let us go in before I cry at the eagerness of men to kill each other,' I muttered.

The bishop stood aside and I walked under the golden cross above the doorway.

*

Wærferth's cooks produced a welcome meal of baked river trout served with an interesting apple sauce. As I ate, the bishop told me the details of the raiding party. Edward's men had ridden north from London and a mixed Mercian warband of experienced and novice warriors had gathered in Gloucester to join them. Ten days ago, they had passed close to Worcester on their journey eastwards, to receive the Bishop's blessing.

The news took away my eagerness to return to Gloucester. It could be a long wait to see how many of our young warriors returned home. I despaired at the thought of Athelstan riding to fight the Danes; it hardly seemed yesterday that his voice had deepened and he had taken to washing in private. My only consolation was in learning that Cuthberht, who had fought with me at Chester, was leading the troop and that Athelstan's trusted companions, Jokul and Merfyn, were with him.

I needed to pray. It was nearing the hour of vespers so I interrupted Wærferth, who was ordering more wine, and asked him to take me to church.

'Gladly, m'lady, but it is Sunday. Would you not prefer my private chapel rather than join the townsfolk at prayer?'

'No, I would like to pray with the people of Worcester.'

My mind went back to a happier time some fifteen years earlier when I had come to the town with Lord Æthelred and King Alfred. We had met with the bishop and other elders to witness a charter that had set out the rights of the church in Worcester. We had agreed to endow St Peter's with half of all the dues from the land tax and the market, as well as the fines for fighting and theft. In return, Wærferth had agreed that Æthelred and I would be remembered in future services at the church. It would be interesting to see how he was keeping his side of the bargain.

When I entered the vestibule of St Peter's with the bishop, we paused to allow those ahead to be seated. Someone whispered and pointed in our direction. As one, the heads of the congregation turned to gawk at me before looking down to pray as though they had seen nothing. Wærferth walked me down the knave, past the rows of farmers, artisans, traders and their families, and into the empty front pew. I sat there in lonely isolation whilst the bishop took his seat in the chancel. The priest who took the mass was young yet word perfect, and the choir of monks sang in such harmony that I almost wept at the beauty of the sound. Finally, at the end of the service, the moment came when I would discover how our charter agreement was being honoured. The priest looked to Bishop Wærferth who rose and came to the pulpit. I had noticed before that the bishop used a booming voice when he spoke in church, yet today he used softer tones, more like the ones he used privately.

'Those of you who regularly attend this church will know that it is our custom to sing the psalm, De Profundis, to conclude our service. The younger ones amongst you may not know why we do this. Well, many years ago, the Lord and the Lady of Mercia generously endowed this church and, in return, we agreed to sing this psalm in their honour as long as they shall live. Happily, we welcome the Lady Æthelflæd amongst us today, so I ask you to sing even more heartily than usual for our kind benefactor.'

Tears welled in my eyes as the psalm resonated around the rafters and I joined the good folk of Worcester in singing the words:

Out of the depths, I have cried unto You, Lord. Lord, hear my voice.

I was soon to discover that He had.

*

When I woke the next morning, it was hard to force open my eyes and stir my body from the bed. Not even a splash of cold water on my face could invigorate me. The thought of another day of travel to add to the many I had undertaken over the past few weeks made me feel weak. Returning to Gloucester to inspect ledgers and to listen to the aggrieved was the last thing I wanted to do. I decided to send word that I would rest in Worcester for a few days.

Taking my morning meal of eggs and cheese to the orchard, I admired the diligence of the gardeners who were cutting back raspberry canes and clearing weeds from the orchard. Tranquil though the scene was, I found it hard to sit idly by and watch men work. I sent a maid scurrying to find the town reeve. I would inspect the fortifications of the town.

I had known Wulfhad, Worcester's reeve, since I had first arrived as a girl in Mercia. Like my husband, he was of the Hwicce people who used to rule these parts before they were subsumed into Mercia. He was a tall upright man and I noticed flecks of grey in his hair as he bowed before me when he arrived.

'Master Wulfhad, I trust you and your family are in good health.'

'They are m'lady, and I trust you and yours are likewise.'

I wanted to say that my husband was near death of the palsy, my daughter distressed that I had banished her lover, and my foster-son in mortal danger on a foolish raid, but instead I forced a smile.

'We are, and I am impatient to see what exactly you have been doing to the town.'

'It would be an honour to show you, m'lady. Would you walk or ride? We have lengthened the walls to a total of some five thousand feet now.'

'I am weary of the saddle. I will walk.'

Wulfhad's long legs took us at a good pace to the walls that formed three sides of the ancient fortress with the river providing the fourth to the west. To the north, a new section had been added to the defences that almost doubled the size of the burh, but it was built from stony earth with a wooden palisade on top, not solid rock. It was lower than the old wall, so we had to scramble down steps to the walkway that ran along the new rampart. I looked down into the outer ditch, calculating that from the bottom to the top of the defences, it was still more than the height of three men, enough to deter a direct attack.

'How do you prevent the earth from sliding when it is wet?' I asked.

'Reinforced with oak timbers on the inside as well as those you see on the outside, m'lady,' Wulfhad said.

We had reached the north-east corner and were strolling west to the point where the defences met the river. I pointed to a heap of old boats that lay on the riverbank outside the wall.

'What are those doing there?' I asked.

'We'll sink them to block the river if enemy ships—'

His reply was cut off by a shout from a nearby lookout.

'Horsemen approaching!'

I squinted into the sun in the direction of the sentry's arm. All I could see was a bright haze over fields and trees.

'There on the crest,' the man shouted.

As my eyes scanned higher, they caught flashes of brightness like the flicker of a flame. I cupped my hands to form a shield against the low sun and saw the outline of riders and horses, the metal of their weapons and riding gear shimmering in the light. They must have ridden into the shade for I lost sight of them. I shook my head and rubbed my eyes in exasperation.

'There!' shouted Wulfhad, and I looked once again to clearly see warriors cantering down a grassy slope towards us. As they came nearer, they halted, regrouping into a more orderly formation. I still could not make out if they were friend or foe, but they unfurled a flag and waved it vigorously in our direction. It was a golden saltire on a blue cloth, the symbol of Mercia. I had to restrain myself from not running to greet them.

'Open the gates,' yelled Osric, as I tried to count the riders as they approached the town walls.

'Around thirty men, sir,' the lookout reported to Osric. That made me search their ranks even more thoroughly. Why so few? One hundred warriors had been sent from Mercia. Where was Athelstan? Even from a distance, I was sure I would recognise the upright posture of his handsome figure, but, as yet, I could not be sure of anyone.

As they neared, I began to identify several of my young thegns. I saw the unmistakable black hair of Merfyn, the leading rider. Jokul's tall frame was recognisable next to the flag bearer. But hard as I tried, I could not make out Athelstan. I became desperate as they approached the northern gate, their smiling upturned faces in full view and not one of them my foster-son. He must have stayed behind with his father, unless...

The wind dropped and suddenly, there he was, holding the drooping flag that had concealed him thus far. I waved vigorously and wanted to shout his name. But, as if from nowhere, a crowd had gathered in the square by the gates. I had to be the Lady of Mercia rather than a mother, and welcome home all our returning warriors.

*

I was rewarded with a brief hug from Athelstan before the rest of the troop descended on me, grinning and laughing as I congratulated them on their successful return. Amongst the celebrating, I did manage to ask what had become of Cuthberht and the rest of the Mercian warriors. Evidently, they had stayed with Edward who was continuing to harry the Danelaw. Everyone seemed very pleased with themselves, and I was so relieved at their safe homecoming, that I did not ask why they had returned before the others.

Merfyn was evidently in charge of the troop. I had picked him for promotion to my body of companion thegns after his bravery at Chester, so I watched with some pride as he began to organise the stabling of the horses and provisions for his men. Bishop Wærferth appeared and invited them all to his residence to refresh themselves and recount their adventures. I was desperate to talk to Athelstan alone, but I could not deny him his moment of glory. Word of their arrival had quickly spread and the townsfolk cheered them all along the main street towards the hall. Once there, the ale was poured and the stories began.

Merfyn told me that they had crossed into Danelaw and met with King Edward who had come north with his forces from Wessex. He described how the air was thick with smoke from burning fields and thatched farmsteads as they plundered Danish settlements. Yet when I pressed him, he gave me few precise details of where they had been or what they had done.

I finally made my way through the throng to where Athelstan was standing, his face flushed as he gulped down ale and held out his goblet for a refill. I had rarely seen him take strong drink, let alone at such speed.

'M'lady, can I announce to all what we have been doing in the Danelaw? Our undertaking was no ordinary raid and I want to make plain what we have done and why,' he said between swigs.

'My ears have never been more eager to hear your words,' I said, not exaggerating in the slightest.

Athelstan disappeared for a few moments and reappeared carrying a manuscript and a silver casket. The casket was discoloured and the hinges looked rusty, but the elaborate motifs on the lid hinted at its former glory.

'You have brought us an ancient hoard?' I inquired.

'Of sorts,' he said. He banged on the table for silence and jumped up onto a bench. The audience, myself included, gaped at the golden-haired apparition who now addressed us.

'When we joined the expedition into the Danelaw, I asked King Edward's permission that the thirty brave warriors you see standing here today should undertake a special mission, and he agreed to my plan. Not for us the burning of crops and the looting of farmhouses. We had a much more important task, one that had become dear to my heart and to that of my beloved stepmother, our Lady of Mercia.'

I tried to stay calm as I acknowledged his kind gesture, but my heart was racing. I had an inkling of what they might have been up to.

'Merfyn was our able leader as we rode away from the Wessex warband near Bedford. We were a cavalry troop and rode fast, skirting around Peterborough where we saw Danes gathering men to march against the King. We did not want to be seen so we took to the Fenland that few men use for fear of flooding and the evil spirits that are said to live in the marshes. A Saxon crofter guided us to the north-east along causeways known only to the local folk. With God's help we made good speed, unseen to anyone except a handful of peasants fishing in the dykes. We made our destination in just two days, and in the twilight we had our first glimpse of the Abbey of Bardney.'

I felt weak at the knees and looked around for a chair as Athelstan reached down for his goblet. I caught sight of Wærferth whose stunned expression told me that he also knew of what was kept at Bardney.

Athelstan drank deeply and continued his account. 'I knew that the Danes had plundered the Abbey, but I was shocked at the extent of the destruction. Many buildings had been burned and walls pulled down so that I began to fear that what we had come for could not have survived. But the small church stood undamaged and, on the breeze, we caught the sounds of the chanting of nocturnes so we knew that some monks were still in residence. We knelt on the hard ground outside the church to join them in prayers.'

He paused to pick up the rolled document that he had placed on the table alongside the casket.

'I wanted to remember the exact circumstances that had led to our journey to Bardney, so, before I left Mercia, I copied out the relevant passage from the history of our land written many years ago by the venerable monk, Bede.'

He waved the scroll towards us as a teacher might his pupils. 'I will not tire you by reading all the passages, but just to remind you, Bede tells us how the bones of King Oswald – St Oswald – were taken to Bardney Abbey. You will recall that when the saintly king was killed in battle, his body was dismembered but his brother, King Oswiu, later collected the parts and buried the head in the monastery of Lindisfarne, and the arms in Bamburgh Castle. Oswiu's daughter, Oswald's loving niece, Osthryth, the Queen of Mercia, took the remaining bones to Bardney Abbey. She sent the relics on a cart to be buried in the monastery, but the monks would not accept them into the church, because they still resented Oswald for conquering their lands.'

The ale was making him gabble, but the audience was hanging on his every word.

'So, when we pitched our tents to rest in the field outside the Abbey that night, we recalled that the cart bearing St Oswald had also remained outside the abbey on the night it had arrived, also covered by a tent to protect the bones. However, a miraculous sign had proven the saintliness of the relics. All that night a pillar of light had stretched up from the cart to the heavens so that in the morning the monks willingly admitted St Oswald's remains, washing the bones and laying them in a casket. We had only moonlight that evening, but we were sure the monks would welcome us the next day.'

Athelstan paused as all eyes turned to the casket on the table. I held my breath as he lifted it in the air, wishing he had not drunk quite so much.

'This is the casket of St Oswald's bones. May this holy relic protect us and help us defeat our pagan enemy!'

A mighty roar went up from the warriors who had recovered those most precious remains, and we all joined in, banging on the tables and shouting praises to heaven. Athelstan shakily descended from the bench and handed the casket to Merfyn who stood beside him.

'I now ask Merfyn, the leader of our troop, to present the casket as we have all agreed.'

I half expected Merfyn to turn towards the bishop as the representative of the Church, but instead he walked slowly towards me, carefully holding the casket before him, and clearing his throat to speak.

'The bones of the saintly King Oswald were collected by a Queen of Mercia, so it is fitting that they should now be given to another,' he announced in his singsong tone.

I grasped the casket, eager to be near such powerful relics. The din that followed was so loud and so prolonged that I could not speak, which was probably just as well, because tears that I could not wipe for fear of dropping the casket, were streaming down my cheeks.

*

By the next morning I had abandoned all thoughts of resting in Worcester and joined those thirty brave warriors on their triumphant return to Gloucester. Like Athelstan, I was convinced that the taking of the holy relics from the heart of the Danelaw was a heavenly sign that we were now ready to take back our lands from the pagans. My mind raced with plans of how we should begin to encroach into our former territories. With St Oswald to protect us we would be able to return to Tamworth, the ancient capital of Mercia, and protect it as a burh. The expedition to Bardney had made a man of Athelstan, and I realised that he could now fill the void that I had felt at my side ever since Æthelred's infirmity.

However, as we rode side by side on the trail that wound down the hills from Worcester, he showed none of the enthusiastic joy of the previous night. He had lost his upright bearing and was slumped on his horse with a drawn, tired look on his face. My attempts at conversation had been met with grunts and frowns. As our horses scrabbled up an incline, he suddenly moaned and leaned over to vomit into a grassy bank.

I slid from my mount and held his horse whilst Athelstan was sick again.

'Water, bring us water,' I shouted.

Jokul was quickly by his side and helped him into the bushes where he retched again and again.

'Did no-one teach him about drinking ale, m'lady?' It was Merfyn who came to stand beside me as I tried not to watch my poor stepson suffer the ignominy of being sick before his fellow warriors.

'I left that to his friends,' I said, turning to him. 'Companions like you and Jokul.'

'I've never seen him drink like that,' he said. 'But I suppose everyone deserves to celebrate their first kill.'

'Kill?' I could not contain my surprise. 'What kill?'

Merfyn looked down. 'Sorry, m'lady, maybe I should have reported to you more fully last night. There were guards as well as monks at the Abbey.'

'And you killed them?'

'We'd searched around the ruins but found no one, so we decided to enter the church before morning prayers. There was a guard just inside the door. I went in first and, I admit, I was surprised by him. I did not think to have a weapon in my hand going into a church. The man just lunged out. I think he must have been sleeping and did it instinctively. I managed to avoid his sword, but he swung it back for a second try. Luckily

Athelstan was alert and he had his blade in the man's neck in a flash.'

I looked at Athelstan's white face in the bushes. 'He killed someone inside a church?'

Merfyn nodded. 'Yes, but he was a pagan, m'lady.'

'How many others were there?'

'Nine more Danes and four monks. They must have been sleeping in the aisles because they all scrambled up when they heard us. The guards quickly grabbed the monks as hostages when they saw our numbers, so we had to let them go.'

'Where did you find the relics?'

He grinned and pointed to the ground. 'We were standing on them. They were in a crypt under the flooring.'

The sight of a bedraggled Athelstan emerging from the bushes and being helped back onto his horse interrupted Merfyn's account. As we restarted our journey, I could not help but smile at Athelstan's embarrassed look.

'Feeling any better?' I asked.

'God has reminded me of my sins,' he muttered.

'Drinking too much? Or killing a man in church?'

He blanched. 'You heard about that? I do not think it wrong to kill a disbeliever who strikes first at your companion, do you?'

'No, you had no choice. I would not have expected guards either. Why would pagans have sent so many men to watch over Christian relics?'

Athelstan shrugged. 'I have been puzzling over it ever since. All I know is that the Danes would value St Oswald's bones in gold, not in miracles.'

'Yet when I tried to buy them through a trader, I was refused,' I said.

'There must have been another buyer,' he said.

Athelstan was right, as he often was. There was another buyer – someone who was so incensed that the relics had been snatched away that he sent an army to retrieve them.

SEVENTEEN

I met the rival owner for the relics of St Oswald the following summer. It was not a pleasant meeting.

I had journeyed north to Chester, the town I had omitted from my tour the previous year and was discussing military matters in the hall with Wiglaf when the news arrived. Wiglaf was now my commander in northern Mercia, a powerful lord who controlled much land. Yet he was little changed from the humble reeve I had first met before the siege of Chester. He wore everyday clothes with little ornamentation. Only the imposing silver cross and chain around his neck spoke of his status. The walls of Chester were now fully restored and within them, the town had grown prosperous. The market and the harbour thrived and a royal mint produced coins bearing the head of the king on one side and a tower to represent the fortified town on the other. Wiglaf had more than repaid the trust I had placed in him.

We were interrupted by the sound of raised voices outside the door, and we saw a scout, bespattered with the grime of hard riding, push past the guards to bow before us.

'M'lord, m'lady, I bring urgent news.'

'Then speak it,' said Wiglaf waving away the attendants around the table.

'A warband approaches from the east, from the Danelaw,' the man said.

I froze. It had been six years since the Danes had dared cross into our territory and we had thought them to be living submissively on their farms.

'How many?'

'Two hundred riders, maybe more. And reports of many more foot soldiers in the area.'

'How far away?' I asked, wondering if I was to be besieged in Chester once again.

'I have ridden hard for a night and for what has passed of this day,' the scout replied.

Wiglaf jumped up from the table. 'They will be here in the morning. I must see to our defences m'lady.'

He began issuing instructions to his thegns in his calm way to bring everyone inside the walls of the town and for the gates to be closed.

'Did you see anything to identify these raiders?' I asked the scout.

'I did glimpse a banner, m'lady. Sign of the raven.'

My mind flashed back to the siege of Chester, when men bearing such an emblem had entered the town before we tore down their flag and captured their leader, Halfdan Ragnarson. Was he back again? The Danish jarls were fond of ravens, so it could be one of many. But if it was Halfdan, I might have cause to regret my decision to release him.

*

I went outside, expecting to see signs of panic from the townsfolk. Yet the tradesmen who scurried to their homes and the soldiers who hurried to the fortifications seemed more purposeful than fearful. After all, we had beaten off such an attack once before and we could do it again. Wiglaf strode back to my side.

'M'lady, should you and your family leave whilst you can?'

I had not considered leaving. If I were seen to flee, what would that say to the brave warriors and townsfolk who I would leave behind? But Wiglaf had reminded me of a complication. I had my family with me. Athelstan had become my adjutant since his heroics in the Danelaw and now accompanied me on all my tours. I had also given Ælfwyn a new role.

The previous year, I had returned triumphantly to Gloucester bearing the relics to their new resting place in St Peter's Abbey – which Fintan had rightly insisted we rename as St Oswald's. I had received a joyous reception from everyone.

Except my daughter.

I saw her glance in my direction as I approached the Abbey but scan those riding behind me more thoroughly. She must have seen that Merewalh was missing, because she had turned her back and walked quickly away without a word of greeting.

Later, I had sought her out in her chamber. Her red eyes and downturned mouth told me that Merewalh's absence had confirmed her fears that I had rejected his request to marry her. As I tried to explain my reason, her misery turned to anger. She railed that I had condemned her to a life as a spinster and that I was effectively forcing her to become a nun against her will. I had not wanted to tell her so soon of my plans for her future, but I had little choice.

I told her that she was to be my heir.

The idea had come to me as I rode from Worcester, the casket of St Oswald's relics strapped to my saddle. Mercia could never be truly independent whilst it needed the support of Wessex. Neither would it accept direct rule from a foreign king like Edward. Having what amounted to a queen in Mercia had proven to be a good compromise, so why not continue with the arrangement after I was gone? I had no son to complicate the succession, but I did have a daughter, and a capable one at that. I was confident I could win the approval of the Witan.

It had taken Ælfwyn some time to come round to the idea that she would gradually take on more responsibility in the running of the realm. However, by the time we had reached Chester that spring, she had begun to adopt her role more enthusiastically. That very morning, I had taken her on a tour of the town to explain the defensive works we had undertaken. I little thought that we might see them in action so soon.

Wiglaf was waiting for my reply, looking as impassive as ever, but I knew that beneath that calm exterior, his mind would be racing with all the preparations he had to make to defend us from the invading Danes. He did not need my help, yet I wanted to send a message to all the people of Mercia that we should have confidence in our newly fortified towns.

'You are in command here, Wiglaf, but I will be staying with Lord Athelstan. Lady Ælfwyn will ride south with our messengers to warn the burhs of the pagan invasion. If you organise the horses and riders, I will tell her ladyship.'

*

Ælfwyn needed no second bidding to ride out with the troop of scouts that afternoon. After all, their first stop would be to warn our new commander at Shrewsbury – a certain Merewalh. I did warn her that the messages they were taking were urgent, so their reunion would have to be brief as well as discreet.

Troubling news came in the next morning. The Danes were close to Chester, burning and looting as they approached, which was no surprise. The shock was that a second warband had been sighted further south heading for Shrewsbury – the same direction as Ælfwyn and the messengers. I cursed myself for sending my daughter into the path of danger. The Danes of the middle-lands had been peaceful for many years, so I wondered what had provoked them into joining the Norsemen of the north in an attack on Mercia.

I discussed the situation with Athelstan and Wiglaf as we took our morning meal.

'I sent scouts to warn the Lady Ælfwyn, m'lady. I'm sure she will make it safely to Shrewsbury this morning,' Wiglaf reported.

I was not so certain. The Danish warband could easily have come between Ælfwyn's troop and their destination, cutting them off from the safety of the burh.

'Could this be part of a general assault on King Edward's territories?' Athelstan asked. 'The Danelaw kings may have all combined to seek retribution for his raid last year.'

He was right. If the Danes were also attacking Wessex, their timing was perfect. Edward had gone to the south coast to celebrate the launch of a great fleet of over two hundred new ships. The king had confided in me that he wanted to test the seafaring skills of his field army, so he had taken a substantial force with him. If the Danes somehow knew that most of Wessex's warriors were far to the south, it would have emboldened them to attack us here in the north. It certainly meant that we could expect no quick help from Edward.

'We need to prevent the Danish forces joining together if we can,' I said. 'What are our total forces here in the north, Wiglaf?'

'Our garrison in Chester totals one thousand and two hundred men. Merewalh has another thousand at Shrewsbury, two days march away,' he replied.

'I can send for my campaign troops from Gloucester,' I said.

'They may not be here in time, and they may be needed in the south if other warbands attack,' Athelstan said.

Shouts from outside brought us to our feet. The Norsemen were in sight.

As we hurried from the hall, I looked to the skies and asked for help from my father, Alfred. I begged him to keep his granddaughter safe.

*

As I waited before the barred town gates, I remembered the great slaughter we had inflicted on the Danes in the very square where I now stood. Had their leaders returned for vengeance? Wiglaf waved to me from the ramparts.

'They send a flag of truce, m'lady. They want to parley.'

'Send for my horse and my purple cloak,' I said to Athelstan who stood beside me. 'If I am to talk to the enemy, I best look the part of a queen.'

'Is it wise that you should go?' he asked. 'We should not trust these thieves until we know more of them.'

'We women like to judge a man by looking him in the eye. But you are right to be cautious.' Wiglaf had descended to the square and was organising a guard to ride out. 'Find out who wants to speak with us,' I called over to him.

It did not take long for a guard to ride out and report back to Wiglaf.

'They say that King Halfdan Ragnarson and the Eorl Ingimund demand the presence of the commander here,' he said.

I swallowed hard. I had shown compassion to both men and now they returned with impressive titles that spoke of their increased power. Maybe the merciful ways of a woman were not always wise.

'Athelstan, wait here and do not reveal yourself on any account. Wiglaf, you and I will speak with our old acquaintances,' I said.

I held back as our group rode out of Chester, not wanting to be seen immediately. Halfdan sat waiting impassively on his horse with a small entourage of guards. Even at a distance, I could make out the long scar on his cheek and the cross that hung at his neck. He had changed little from the day he had stood before me as a captive, except for the wide golden belt around his waist and the cascade of silver rings around his arm. I wondered if the brand mark I had ordered on his forehead still showed, but a metal helmet covered the area. I did not recognise the hunched frame of the man next to him who called to us as we drew nearer.

'Who amongst you has authority to agree to our demands?'

It was Ingimund's strange accent. His once boyish face was thin and lined and his body was twisted and deformed. Fintan's knife had damaged him badly, it seemed.

I kicked my horse forward to halt beside Wiglaf.

'Ingimund, I presume you have returned to pay homage for the land you were given,' I shouted, pleased to see the astonished look on his face. 'And you, Halfdan, you must have come to pay the ransom for the release that I granted you.'

The two men glanced briefly at each other.

'The Lady of the Mercians, why are you still here, building your walls?' Halfdan said. 'They will not serve you now. It is not your town we want. We have come to take back what you have stolen from us.'

'Thieving Norsemen complaining of theft. Next you will be asking us to protect you.' I turned to Wiglaf and laughed.

'I am King of Northumbria,' Halfdan growled, 'and only return to this forsaken land to collect the relics of St Oswald which rightly belong in my kingdom, and yet were stolen from Bardney Abbey.'

I should have known he was my rival bidder for the bones. He had converted to the cross as some Danes had, God be praised. If, as he claimed, he ruled in Northumbria, he would already have Oswald's head and arms in his possession. With the relics in my possession, he would have the entire body, and he would no doubt claim that the saintly Oswald demanded revenge on Mercia whose pagan king had killed him.

I looked at him as contemptuously as I could. 'Alas, I have no ancient bones for you, only the flesh and blood of countless warriors anxious to fight you, should you trespass further on our lands.'

Halfdan drew himself up, scowling. 'Return the relics that I know you have, or you will be burying the bones of your warriors. Old bones in a casket, or fresh ones in graves. The choice is yours.' He laughed, and the men around him joined in his little joke.

'And you Ingimund, what are you offering? A new hostage to replace the one who prefers to live with me now?' I was referring to Jokul, his so-called son whom he had given to me as a guarantee of his word, which of course he had broken.

He flicked back the hair that still hung long down his back, but he did not smile as he used to do when we first met. 'I have come to take new wheat from your farmers to replace the crops your men burned in my land last year.'

You are concerned for your farmers but not your child? What of Finna, your wife?' I was hoping that she still lived.

'The traitress met a suitable end. We told her as she died that you had killed her son. So don't disappoint us.'

That changed my mood. The thought that poor Finna died believing I had betrayed her trust was too much. I edged my horse forward.

'You will take your stinking, rotten bodies off my land before nightfall, or we will kill you all. If you think you can play with us as you once did, you will find my patience with boys like you has run out.'

I backed my horse away, and, when I saw they did not follow, I turned and rode back to the town.

To my surprise, they seemed to do as I had bid them. By next morning, there was no trace of them or their army.

*

Wiglaf had been diligent in positioning his scouts and their reports dashed my hope that the Norsemen had fallen back. On the contrary, we heard that they had moved swiftly, using the long sunlit hours of mid-summer to travel south, deeper into Mercia. I was surprised that they were prepared to leave the garrison of Chester to their rear as we could now cut off their line of retreat. Yet the warband would be burning homesteads and wreaking havoc on the Mercian countryside. They left me no choice.

'We must follow them,' I announced to Wiglaf and Athelstan, as we listened to the latest news from the scouts that morning. 'Athelstan and I will take our mounted warriors and move towards Shrewsbury, as they have done.'

Wiglaf frowned. 'The reports suggest they will soon meet the second warband. They will be uniting their forces whilst we separate ours.'

'We cannot just sit behind fortified walls whilst our people suffer,' I said. 'Soon we will have enough burhs to protect everyone, but not yet. We cannot abandon half the land.'

Athelstan was rubbing his chin. 'If we are to give battle on open ground, we need to gather our forces together and choose where we are to fight.'

He liked to think deeply about military strategy, but this was not the moment for that.

'First, let's find the Danes. Then we can work out how to defeat them,' I said, sweeping from the hall.

We rode hard, but the dry weather had turned wet and heavy rain soaked through our capes and made our horses stumble on the slippery slopes. We saw no sign of the enemy; the homesteads we passed stood unmolested, the cornfields unburned. The Danes had not passed this way.

It was dark when we finally made our way into Shrewsbury. I had taken two hundred cavalrymen with me and whilst Athelstan took care of our horses, I gave thanks to God in St Chad's church for our safe journey. I left the monks to mop the puddle of water that had dripped from my clothes in the pew as I knelt and walked as briskly as my aching limbs would allow to the great hall. Thurston, the town reeve, was waiting for me.

'What news?' I said curtly, surprised that Merewalh was not there in person to greet me.

'Not good news, M'lady. My Lord Beornoth is gone from us.' Dampness glinted in the eyes of the young retainer as he beckoned me into the hall.

Beornoth had chosen an inconvenient moment to die. I had thought he would not survive the winter, but the old weasel had outwitted death for longer than anyone had expected. He was the senior ealdorman of Mercia whose passing deserved respect and ceremony, yet we were at war and short of time for mourning.

I closed my eyes and crossed myself to ask for his spirit to be taken into heaven, although, from what I knew of his life, I doubted he had much chance of passing through St Peter's gates.

'Is Lord Merewalh with his father?' I inquired.

'No, M'lady, he departed with the Lady Ælfwyn,' Thurston said.

I felt relief at the news. My daughter had evaded the Danes on her journey to Shrewsbury and had continued her journey south with a strengthened escort.

'When did they depart?'

'This morning m'lady.'

'Only this morning? Are you sure?' By my reckoning, she should have left two days ago.

'Yes, m'lady. Lord Beornoth died almost the moment she arrived. She sent her messengers on ahead and delayed here to mourn with Lord Merewalh. They took a boat today to speed their passage.'

That comforted me somewhat – until I learned that the Danes had moved even quicker than we thought.

*

I took prayers with Beornoth's grieving household the next morning whilst Athelstan instructed the reeve to follow us with foot soldiers and reinforced our troop with as many horsemen as he could find. I also sent a message to Wiglaf in Chester ordering him to bring his forces south. Riding out of Shrewsbury at the head of over three hundred cavalry, we crossed the bridge and followed the west bank of the Severn. If we could keep Halfdan and Ingimund to the east of the river, it would protect much of Mercia from their ravages. I just hoped the messengers would reach Worcester and Gloucester so that more of my troops would be mobilised.

The valley floor was muddier than the hilly uplands we had ridden the day before, so our progress was slower. By nightfall, we were nearing Bridgnorth, the place where I had decided to found a burh the previous year. We were stopped by a scout who rode hard towards us, one hand held high to halt us.

'The enemy is camped but ten furlongs to the south,' he called, his mount splattering mud towards us as he drew up sharply.

'Which side of the river?' I asked.

'On the east bank, m'lady.'

I silently gave thanks to heaven. They had not yet crossed the river to our side.

'How many men do they have?' asked Athelstan.

'Difficult to count in this light, m'lord. Many more than us, to be sure.'

'We have enough men to block the ford,' I said, urging my horse on.

We camped by the ford where we could see the enemy's fires but kept ourselves hidden. They would find us in the morning, but I wanted to surprise them.

There was a surprise – but for us, not for them.

*

At daybreak, we made our way to the riverbank at Quatford where the Severn was sometimes shallow enough for foot soldiers to wade to the other bank. When Athelstan saw the disposition of the ford with a relatively narrow crossing area, he nodded.

'With three hundred men on horse we can prevent a much bigger force from crossing here. But not forever. They will find ways of going round and forcing us back. We'll eventually need reinforcements or we'll have to retreat.'

'Ælfwyn's messengers should be alerting the standing army in Gloucester as I instructed,' I said. 'And more warriors from Shrewsbury should soon be with us.'

The whickering of our horses soon alerted their scouts to our presence, as I knew it must, and before long a group of a warriors stood opposite us on the east bank.

'Who dares to bar our way?' one shouted.

'The owner of this land,' I replied, throwing off my hood so they could see who I was.

They turned and hurried back towards their camp. Athelstan busied with our formation whilst we waited, positioning men with bows and spears on either wing, with a solid phalanx of horsemen barring the exit of the ford. He wanted to conceal our true numbers from the enemy so he advised me to spread out our men, with some standing on hillocks in the distance as if we had foot soldiers waiting to advance as well as cavalry.

Before long, a group of horsemen appeared on the other bank, Halfdan and Ingimund at their head together with another warrior whose impressive mail coat and helmet told of his high status.

'Lady Æthelflæd, you are a most diligent hostess. Wherever we travel, you arrive to welcome us,' Halfdan called across the river.

'Our welcome will be of sharpened metal if you trespass further on my lands,' I shouted back.

Halfdan laughed. 'You accuse us of trespass! My friend, Eowils, King of Lindsey, guardian of Bardney Abbey, would like to speak with you of trespass.' He indicated the warrior at his side.

Finally, I met the man who refused my offer to buy St Oswald's relics.

I could see enough of Eowils' lined face to know he was an old warrior whose best days were behind him, yet he spoke in a gruff, authoritative voice.

'I am told your Christian God forbids stealing. Yet you have stolen from me. We are the wrath of your God, sent by your saint, to punish you.'

A Dane lecturing me on the ways of my God! For a heartbeat, I did not know what to say. My hesitation must have shown because Halfdan rose in his saddle and pointed at me.

'You are cursed by God for your sins against us. He has sent us a sign that you must repent and meet our demands.'

Before I could utter my rebuff, he turned in his saddle and shouted to the guards behind. 'Show the prisoner.'

I had to grip tightly with my knees to prevent myself from falling from my horse.

Ælfwyn!

She looked pitifully at me across the river as a guard pushed her forward.

'The Son of God sent us the daughter of a queen. She meekly sailed into our midst – a sign that *our* cause is just. Give us back what is ours and we will return your daughter.'

EIGHTEEN

My mind and body froze, unable to function. Ælfwyn and I stared at each other across the river. I could see the fear in her eyes, just as she must have seen it in mine. I tried to give her a reassuring smile, but my lips would not move. She was made to kneel in supplication on the muddy bank, her hands bound, a spear at her neck.

I urged my horse forward and yelled, 'Harm my daughter and I will kill you all!' Athelstan moved with me and reached across to place a restraining arm on mine.

Halfdan wagged his finger at me as if he was admonishing a child. 'I see you do not like having things taken from you. Nor do we,' he said gesturing to his two companions who sat grinning, no doubt enjoying the spectacle of a tormented mother and daughter. 'I want my casket of bones. King Eowils wants the casket filled with silver in recompense for the theft of his relics, and Ingimund wants to replace the grain that you burned. And you want your daughter. You, Lady of Mercia, can make us all very happy by giving us what we want.'

He stuck out a boot from where he sat on his horse and shoved the kneeling Ælfwyn over into the mud. 'Or, if you don't agree, you will make some of us very angry, some very sad. And one very dead.' He kicked out again at Ælfwyn who was bravely struggling up with her hands tied behind her back. The Danes jeered as she fell face down in the mire.

In that moment, I made my decision. I would no longer be a lady of mercy.

I will kill them all.

Halfdan swept off his helmet. 'When we first met you gave me something to remember you by,' he smiled, indicating the scar on his forehead that still resembled the C of Chester. 'In return, I have something for you.'

He fumbled at a sack that hung from his saddle. Grasping it in one hand, he whirled it around a few times before letting it fly high in the air across the river. It landed close to me and my horse skittered and reared back.

A bloodied head rolled out of the neck of the sack. I heard Ælfwyn scream as I looked down at Merewalh's blue eyes and red stained hair.

'A severed head in exchange for the engraved one you gave me,' Halfdan sneered and turned to Ælfwyn who had collapsed onto the grass. 'The fool was caught sneaking towards your tent. Perhaps someone you know?'

Until that moment, I had felt some bitterness towards Merewalh. His feelings for Ælfwyn had caused him to dally with her in Shrewsbury on the excuse of his father's death, and that had led her to her capture. But that resentment turned to anguish now that I realised he had bravely sacrificed himself trying to rescue her.

I shivered. Was this a sign from God? King Oswald's head had also been severed from his shoulders. Maybe the saint had sided with this Christian Dane who was, after all, king in Oswald's native Northumbria. If I had angered St. Oswald over the resting place of his relics, I should return them and make amends just as Halfdan was demanding. Besides, I had no choice.

'Very well. I will bring you the relics and exchange them for my daughter,' I said as calmly as I could. 'And you will go back to your lands and stay there.'

Halfdan smiled triumphantly. 'We will return to the Danelaw when you have met our demands. Bring the relics and a chest of silver coins to a place close to our boundary.' He thrust the helmet back on his head. 'Meanwhile, we will enjoy your Mercian hospitality.'

Eowils grinned whilst Ingimund slid from his horse and grabbed Ælfwyn by the hair, jerking her to her feet. From his belt he took a knife and held the blade to her throat.

'This is the knife that a mad monk shoved into my guts on your orders. I want to use this same knife on your daughter to repay you for that moment, but my friends hold me back.' He pulled up Ælfwyn's long hair and hacked into it with the knife, holding up the severed strands as she slumped back to the ground.

'If you should try just one trick to deceive us, I will be cutting into her guts, not her hair, and I will leave her to watch while animals eat into her entrails.' He threw the strands of her honey-brown hair into the river where they swirled downstream.

I got the message. I had to work fast to save my daughter. Halfdan seemed to be in charge of this army but, if he lost control, Ingimund was not interested in the bones so I would lose what bargaining power I had.

'I do not have the relics nearby but let us meet in seven days to make this exchange.'

Halfdan looked at me curiously. 'An interesting choice. If I am not mistaken that will be on St Oswald's feast day, the fifth day of August.'

'An appropriate day for him to meet his new owner, don't you think?' I said, trying to smile.

I also intended it to be a test of which side the saint would favour in this dispute. I glanced down at the mutilated head of Merewalh that lay before me, remembering the happy time he and I had spent designing a new burh not far from here. It would make a fitting place for our meeting.

'There is a place called Woden's Field about a hundred furlongs to the east of here, close to the border with Danelaw. Let us meet there on the saint's feast day and go our ways in peace. It's near a hamlet called Tettenhall.'

*

I watched the Danes slowly ride away from the riverside, my daughter stumbling behind Halfdan who had tied her to his horse by a long rope. They had completely outwitted me so far. Ignoring my fortified towns, they had plundered the countryside unimpeded. Their forces were united in one strong army; mine were divided in the burhs. Worst of all, I had allowed domestic issues to cloud my judgement. To appease my daughter's disappointment in love, I had encouraged her to take on responsibility that had led to her capture and the death of one of my most able warriors.

Father would have done things differently. But what would he do now?

I turned to his grandson who had said nothing during the entire exchange. 'I trust you agree with my decision, Athelstan. I had no choice.'

As he looked towards me, I saw the tears in his eyes. 'This is my doing isn't it? If I hadn't have taken the relics...'

I had not expected this. He was usually so certain in what he was doing. 'We are paying the price for underestimating our enemy,' I said.

He brushed his eyes and dismounted, walking towards Merewalh's head that still lay staring, open-eyed on the ground. Carefully placing a hand on each gory cheek, he picked it up. I flinched when I saw the damage that had been done to Merewalh's handsome features as Athelstan spoke.

'Dearest Merewalh, I know you will soon be in heavenly bliss, but you deserved a happier fate here on earth. I have played a part in your misery, and I Athelstan, son of King Edward, vow that your death will not be in vain. Just as King Oswald lost his head in battle but returned to heal the wounds of others, I will carry your relic with me until the wrong that has been done to you and the woman you loved has been made right.'

He carefully placed the head into the sack and tied it to his saddle.

The tears were in my eyes now, but his words had cleared my mind. We needed to act swiftly and decisively.

'Well spoken. Now let us make sure your vow is realised. You must ride immediately and retrieve the relics. We have to quickly consolidate our armies, so bring our forces from Gloucester and Worcester back with you, but concealed at a distance. I will send word for the men of Chester and Shrewsbury to move towards Tettenhall, and I will ask Osferth to march north with his men and any of Wessex that he can muster.'

Athelstan was looking at me in disbelief. 'You intend to sacrifice Ælfwyn and attack them?'

I swallowed hard. 'No, I intend to rescue her. Then attack them,' I replied, trying to believe my own words.

*

Watching the enemy forces despoil my lands was one of the hardest things I have ever done. I could not lose sight of my daughter so I trailed the marauding Norsemen as they marched south in search of plunder. With minimal forces at my command, I could do little to protect those in their path. For seven long days, we rode past burning fields and farmsteads, our lungs filled with the smoke of smouldering crops, our clothes spattered with ash blown from burnt-out thatch. We saw few people; most had managed to escape to the safety of the burhs, warned by our messengers of the approaching apocalypse. Some, mainly older folk, had ignored the warnings and stayed in their homes. Their corpses lay scattered in the villages that they had tried in vain to defend.

On the fourth day, the pagan horde turned north and began to make their way back towards the Danelaw and our meeting place at the border. As they did, I caught sight of two Danes who tarried too long in a homestead, one slaking his thirst on stolen ale, the other his lust on an unfortunate woman whose screams finally broke my self-control.

I turned to Merfyn. 'Teach those barbarians to respect my subjects,' I ordered.

With several warriors, he raced to the homestead to rescue the poor woman, cutting down her tormentor whilst the other Dane took flight.

'What shall I do with her?' Merfyn asked when he returned.

'She can share my tent,' I said. She looked young to have stayed behind, no older than Ælfwyn. I just prayed they were treating my daughter more kindly.

The next day came a sign that they were not.

Riders approached our camp bearing a flag of truce. 'A message from King Halfdan,' one shouted from a distance. 'For every man that I lose, your daughter will also lose something. Here is the first item.' He threw down a small object that glinted in the sunlight as it fell.

Merfyn ran to pick it up but hesitated when he neared.

'What is it?' I called.

'A finger, m'lady. A little finger with a silver ring.'

'Better a finger than a head,' I said, trying not to show the fear and anger that churned in my stomach as the messenger laughed and rode away.

*

At least we had time to accurately count our enemy. In total, the three armies of Halfdan, Eowils and Ingimund numbered almost four thousand warriors on foot with some two hundred on horse. Provided I could unite all my forces, we would be equal in strength to the enemy. If only Edward could send troops from Wessex, we would outnumber them. But the latest news I had of him was that he was sailing along the Kentish coast with one hundred ships full of seasick soldiers. Nevertheless, I sent messages imploring the ealdormen of Wessex to send whatever support they could.

Finally, the day approached when I hoped my torment would end: August 5th, the day that St. Oswald had died in battle, two and a half centuries earlier at a place called Oswald's Tree after the ash tree on which they hung the saint's dismembered body. My chosen place to meet the enemy was Woden's Field, an area I had explored with Merewalh the previous year. There I would finalise our trade: a dead saint for a live daughter; the past for the future.

Athelstan returned, grim faced, bearing the casket which he handed to me without saying a word, no doubt still feeling guilty about the pain its capture had caused us. With him he brought a troop of cavalry and the news that my standing army of two thousand men under Cuthberht was moving rapidly from Gloucester and should reach us at the appointed time. One side of my trap was ready to be sprung.

'Where are they?' he asked of the enemy as we rested in a shady wood.

I took him to the edge of the trees. To the north, we could see smoke rising from their campfires.

'They have taken up position in Tettenhall, just where I thought they would,' I said pointing towards a tree-covered outcrop. 'That ridge rises above Smestow Brook, a stream named after the smithy who owns the homestead, but in truth it is really a river at that point with high banks.'

'So they are protected by a wooded ridge on one side and a steep-sided river on the other. Why did you want them there?' he asked, shielding his eyes from the glare of the sun as he tried to assess the lay of the land.

'To make the exchanges we have agreed, they need to feel secure in a good defensive position.'

'Which we can't attack,' he said scratching his head.

'No, but we will withdraw, and they will begin their journey home. That will take them into open land where we will attack them. They will be caught between our forces arriving from Chester and Shrewsbury to the north, and our army from Gloucester in the south,' I said, demonstrating the pincer movement with my hands.

'Who commands the soldiers from Shrewsbury, now that...' Athelstan obviously still found it difficult to say Merewalh's name.

'Thurston, the reeve. He is young and inexperienced but the only choice after all the fatalities in the family that he served. His role is to block the enemy's route north once our forces move up from the south.'

'Surely they will go east towards the Danelaw, not north,' Athelstan said.

'You are right, which is why I ordered Wiglaf and his forces from Chester to occupy Woden's Fort, over there to the east.' I pointed to the horizon to my right, where I could faintly make out the hill I had climbed the year before and looked down on this very spot. 'The plain you see between Tettenhall and the Fort is Woden's Field. That is where we will trap and destroy the Danes.'

'Woden's Field,' Athelstan repeated. 'Our family is descended from Woden, so they say.'

'Maybe the pagan god will favour us now that his followers have become besotted by the relics of a Christian saint,' I chuckled, but stopped when I saw the shock on Athelstan's face and quickly added, 'but I know St Oswald will give us victory. My plan is to surround the enemy on three sides. Cuthberht will attack from the south, Wiglaf will surprise them by descending from his fort to the east, and Thurston will come down on them from the ridge in Tettenhall behind them.'

Athelstan smiled for the first time since his return. 'An excellent plan. Although I have read that every plan can only be judged by what happens on the day. And especially how well you recover from what goes wrong.'

He was right, as he often was. Events did not go according to plan.

*

I hardly slept that night and was out of my tent to watch the sun rise over the plains where I hoped to slay our foes before it set that evening. I had received a message from Wiglaf that he was safely encamped in Woden's Fort that was catching the first rays of dawn to my right. I knew from Athelstan that Cuthberht was arriving from the south behind me, but I had heard nothing from Thurston who should be making his way towards the far side of the ridge ahead of me. Much would depend on the timing of the assaults by each of my three armies. Yet, I could not risk sending out messengers for fear the Norsemen would intercept them and uncover my trap.

I glimpsed a movement ahead and strained to see into the glare. To my surprise, a group of riders were making their way from Tettenhall towards us. They were much earlier than I thought. I called for Athelstan and Merfyn and rapidly finished my ablutions before the delegation arrived.

I recognised the man who came forward to speak with a youthful warrior at his side. He was the one who had delivered Ælfwyn's finger.

'I carry a message for Lady Æthelflæd of Mercia,' he called, stopping a spear-throw from us.

'I am Lady Æthelflæd. What is your name now that you know mine?' I shouted back.

'I am called Anlaf the Swart,' he grinned, his teeth bright amidst the blackness of the beard that covered his face, 'And my companion is Ragnall. He has been taking good care of your daughter.'

'If you have harmed my daughter again, Anlaf the Swart, I will darken your days until they are blacker than your name,' I glanced at Ragnall, the warrior beside Anlaf, who looked a similar age to Ælfwyn. His face was striking, his eyes piercing as he studied me. 'And you, Ragnall, I will cut off your balls if you have defiled her.'

Ragnall showed no expression. 'Why not ask your daughter how she was treated? She is with King Halfdan by the ford over there.' He pointed towards the river where it flowed into Tettenhall.

'She is alive and will remain so, providing you bring what you have promised, with no more than six of your men,' Anlaf continued.

The timing was unexpected and would allow the Danes to slip away before I could fully gather my forces. 'Why so early? I have not yet eaten.'

'The King presumed you would want to see your daughter as soon as you could,' Anlaf smirked.

Danes were never so considerate. Something was causing their haste.

'Will you share some refreshments before we meet your king?' I asked.

He shook his head and patted his stomach. 'I have fed so well from your farmsteads, I have no space for more.'

I could think of no other reason to delay us. We took our time over fetching the relics and the silver and preparing the horses. Yet at the hour when I would normally be stirring from my bed, I found myself riding towards the river to meet the villains who had invaded my lands.

It was the beginning of a day that would define my life like no other.

*

Halfdan sat on his horse flanked by Ingimund and Eowils. Behind them, under the watchful eyes of Anlaf the Swart and Ragnall, stood Ælfwyn, her face eagerly seeking mine.

252

I smiled and nodded encouragingly in her direction. After seven days of marching around Mercia, she looked thinner, her hair shorn and her hand bandaged, yet her expression was cheerful.

'We have enjoyed our journey around your territories,' Halfdan said. 'And your daughter has entertained us well.'

'Don't tell me she cut off her own finger,' I said.

'It could have been worse,' Halfdan said, turning to his companions. 'Eowils wanted to cut off her breast.' He threw back his head and laughed.

I shifted uncomfortably in my saddle. I had almost liked this Dane when I first met him, but now I hated him and his vile companions with a vengeance. He was peering behind me.

'I see you have the casket,' he said. 'Please bring it forward so I can see it.'

Athelstan swung from his horse, unstrapped the silver box next to his saddle and gently placed it down.

'You have me at a disadvantage,' Halfdan said. You know that this is your daughter, but how do I know if this is really St. Oswald? If I return your daughter, how can I be sure to receive the true relics in exchange?'

That was a good question and one that I had anticipated. 'I will swear an oath that these are the same relics we received from Bardney Abbey. Beyond that, it is for King Eowils to confirm they are genuine. He had them before me.'

Eowils looked tired. 'Bones are bones,' he said. 'I would not know one set from another. I prefer silver and gold which I am hoping are in that chest there.' He indicated a second coffer that Merfyn had placed next to the relics.

'I will fetch my holy book and swear on that,' I offered. That would take up some of the time that I so badly needed.

Halfdan jumped from his horse. 'No need. I have mine here.'

He dragged a heavy book from his saddlebag and I almost gasped. The cover was exquisitely decorated in gold lettering and vividly illustrated with a picture of a saintly monk working at his desk in a scriptorium.

'Where did you get this?' I almost said 'steal'.

'The Bishop of York gave it to me. Northumbria is full of such psalters. I have to restrain my countrymen from burning them on their fires. It should serve our purpose.'

He held it towards me and my hands trembled as they touched the beautiful tome. I cleared my throat and swore that, to my knowledge, the casket contained the true relics of St Oswald. As I did, the thought struck me that I had not looked inside; I did not know what was there. I glanced at Athelstan for some reassurance, but he was steadfastly looking down. I finished and reluctantly handed back the psalter, running my fingers over the spine.

Halfdan was looking at me strangely. 'Perhaps you would prefer to keep the book and leave your daughter with us.'

'Let us do what we came to do,' I said.

Ragnall brought Ælfwyn forward and he carefully hacked through the bonds on her wrists. I heard Halfdan say something to Eowils and wondered if they had arranged a trap of their own. It would not be difficult. They had four thousand men waiting on the other side of the ford under the ridge. My men were over an hour's march away.

'Tell your companions to withdraw twenty paces and you and I can make the exchange,' Halfdan announced.

That would leave me alone with a powerful warrior. He carried no weapons but he had proven untrustworthy before. *Can I trust him now?*

Merfyn and Athelstan were waiting for my command. Ælfwyn was watching me, her eyes wide with expectation. I nodded my agreement and shivered as my escort retreated.

Standing next to Halfdan, I could make out the faint trace of the letter C that I had ordered to be branded onto his forehead. He had reason to hate me. His eyes were on the casket next to me. Mine were on Ælfwyn who stood transfixed and expectant next to him. The three of us stood like that that for a heartbeat or so, and he looked about to speak.

A throaty roar reverberated like thunder behind him.

I stared at the ridge above the river in disbelief. Warriors were hurtling down the slope towards the Danish camp that occupied the narrow strip by the river. Above them swayed a banner, a blue cross on a yellow background.

The flag of Mercia.

NINETEEN

I should have known it would be an inauspicious time and place to fight my enemies: St. Oswald's day in Woden's Field, the celebration of a Christian saint in a place named after a pagan god. Thurston, the reeve of Shrewsbury, had panicked on the hillside above the enemy and ordered his men to attack too early.

Halfdan and his companions spun round at the commotion behind them. That gave us a very brief chance.

'Run!' I shouted.

Ælfwyn did not hesitate and rushed towards me. Grasping her hand, I turned and sprinted away, expecting a spear in my back at any moment. Glancing over my shoulder, I stumbled and Ælfwyn had to yank my arm to keep me on my feet. I glimpsed Halfdan's men charging after us, closing the gap rapidly. I silently prayed.

O Holy Oswald, please save us. We did this for you.

As if in answer, I felt reins thrust into my hand. It was not Oswald but Athelstan and Merfyn who saved us by bringing our horses forward so we could grab them and mount up. No spears came as we galloped away, and I turned to see Halfdan, standing by the casket, yelling at his riders, caught between chasing us and returning to his beleaguered army.

We rode hard towards our base in the woods. Once there, I wanted to hug my daughter, but had no time to even dismount. Halfdan's group were busy loading the casket and chest onto their horses whilst a battle raged on the other side of the crossing. Thurston's men had come down through the trees and caught the enemy on the narrow strip between the wooded slopes and the river. If only they had more numbers, they could push the Danes back into the brook. But Thurston was fighting not one, but three armies spread along the riverbank. We had to act fast if we were to salvage something from the mistimed attack.

'We need men over there, now,' I said, indicating the battle. 'Ælfwyn, take two men and ride like the wind to Cuthberht. Order him to bring his army here immediately.'

I could see from her weary face that she did not relish the task, yet I wanted to get her away from danger. She gave me a wistful glance whilst Athelstan gave her hurried directions, and she rode off.

Merfyn was rubbing his chin. 'Reinforcements will be of no use if they cannot cross the river,' he said. 'We need to secure the ford.'

Athelstan rejoined us. 'What about Wiglaf's men? If they attack from the other side, we will have the enemy bottled up at both ends.'

I knew that Wiglaf would wait patiently in his hilltop fort to the east, according to our original plan. 'Yes, send orders for him to come quickly.'

But can Thurston hold out that long? I shielded my eyes to study the tiny figures battling in the distance. Thurston's men had used their initial advantage well and driven the rear of the Norsemen's forces back to the edge of the river. But the enemy armies were stretched out in a long formation from west to east, many untouched by the fighting. I could see Danes at the eastern end of the encampment, scurrying into the woods of the ridge to work back to the assault on their rear in the west. It was as though Thurston had attacked the rump of a wild animal, and the shoulders and head of the beast were turning to bite him.

'We have two hundred good horsemen with us,' I said, indicating the warriors who were waiting around us in the woods. 'Merfyn's right. We need to secure the ford.'

*

As we galloped back towards the spot from which we had so recently fled, Athelstan shouted and pointed ahead. His sharp eyes had seen that the battle across the river was taking on a different shape. The enemy was outflanking our warriors: the jaws of the beast were closing around them. Thurston had seen the danger and his men were falling back, wheeling around to form a shield wall in the narrow gap between the wooded ridge and the river.

In doing so, he was unwittingly isolating Halfdan and the enemy leaders who were riding back to rejoin their men carrying the relics and the silver. Thurston's sudden manoeuvre blocked their route.

I watched as Halfdan faltered and reined back his horse, gesticulating and pointing, before making a dash for the rapidly closing gap between Thurston's men and the river, the precious casket of St Oswald's relics balanced before him on his saddle. Ingimund, Eowils, Anlaf and Ragnall took a different route and turned north to head for the ridge and the safety of its wooded slopes.

Merfyn needed no further encouragement.

'After them,' he yelled.

'Leave ten men with me at the ford, and God be with you,' I said, waving him forward. 'Athelstan, you will stay as my adjutant,' I quickly added, knowing he would want to go with the others. He reluctantly joined me and together we watched the action across the ford.

It was St Oswald's Day, and the saint was about to have his say in the outcome of the battle.

Halfdan was almost through the fast-closing gap between Thurston's forces and the riverbank, when I heard his despairing howl. The possession he prized above all else slipped from his grasp. The casket fell to the ground.

Halfdan pulled up and, for a heartbeat, I thought he might even dismount to rescue the relics. His hesitation cost him the chance of reaching his own forces. As Thurston's soldiers raced down to take up position on the riverbank, he could have turned and ridden away but he seemed mesmerised by the casket, staring at where it had fallen. Perhaps its contents had spilled out and he was in awe at seeing the very bones of the saint. He was jolted from his reverie by Thurston's foot-soldiers who were snarling around him like wolves around their prey. Sitting up tall on his mount, Halfdan swept his long sword in a wide arc, desperately attempting to ward them off. They ducked away from his blade and threw spears. One narrowly missed him but another sank into the flanks of his horse. His mount shied and stumbled yet Halfdan somehow managed to retain his seat. The next spear took him in the back and, as he crashed forward onto his horse's neck, eager hands pulled at his legs and dragged him down. He must have fallen close to the casket and the relics.

I had little time to wonder at his fate. Merfyn and his troop were across the ford and riding hard in pursuit of the others. Like Halfdan, Eowils had taken his prize with him. The chest of silver was strapped to a horse led by Anlaf. Whilst Ingimund and Ragnall galloped ahead, Eowils and Anlaf followed at a slower pace with the treasure. It was only when they realised that Merfyn's cavalry was closing fast that they urged their horses into a gallop.

They left it too late. My cavalry steadied their mounts, rose in their stirrups and hurled spears forward. Most fell short or wide, but one struck the rump of Eowils's horse. The animal leapt forward at the shock and for a few strides it seemed to recover but stumbled as its rear legs sagged to the ground. Anlaf might have escaped but he stayed to protect his king. As Merfyn and his cavalry caught the two Danes and savagely cut them down, I had to ask the Lord's forgiveness for my joy at seeing the two men die. They paid the full price for cutting off my daughter's finger.

Merfyn rode after Ingimund, keen no doubt to avenge the death of Finna, Ingimund's Irish slave-wife, who had died at her husband's hands. Merfyn was a skilled rider and soon caught up with his quarry, but Ragnall warded him off, forcing him into combat. It took Merfyn several thrusts and parries to swat him away before he could ride after Ingimund, by which time he had slipped into the woods. Danes were coming that way to outflank Thurston's shield wall and Merfyn was forced back as they emerged from the trees.

Thurston's army from Shrewsbury now occupied the gulley between the ridge and the river with a line of men almost two hundred wide, standing four or five deep. The shields in the front line took the brunt of the attack, supported by a second row of men who reached over to spear their assailants or stepped into the breach if a man before them fell. To the rear, archers shot their arrows through any gaps or upwards to land on enemy heads. Merfyn's cavalry harried any Danes who tried to outflank the line.

Against them, heaved a host of Danes who must have stood ten deep, using their superior weight to shove Thurston's shield wall back. They did not seem aware of the fall of their two kings and continued to attack full-heartedly and savagely. Yet it was not easy to push against men who used swords and spears to thrust and stab between their shields. My men were holding — just. It was only a matter of time before the extra weight of the Danes gave them the advantage over the brave men of Shrewsbury. We had sent messengers to Wiglaf to bring his men down from the hillfort to the east, and to Cuthberht to join the battle from the south. But there was no sign of them yet.

Athelstan sat on his horse beside me, scanning for movements in all directions.

'Soldiers approaching from the east!' he shouted, pointing into the sun.

Surely, it was too early for Wiglaf's men to have made it that far. I followed the line of his arm and saw warriors on our side of the river. They were not our men, but Danes moving fast in our direction.

They must have found another crossing point. From my previous visit to the area, I could not recall any ford to the east of Tettenhall. I remembered that the brook disappeared at one point, thinking it was the trees that obscured the view. Yet, fast flowing streams sometimes found weak points in the earth's crust and went underground. I cursed myself for not taking better note of the terrain.

Athelstan looked anxious. 'They're coming around the river to get behind Thurston.'

He did not mention the other problem that we were in their path and would soon be exposed with just a handful of men.

'Bring back some cavalry and we will stop them here at the ford,' I said.

He nodded and splashed through the water.

I waved my handful of guards after him into the ford. 'We will wait on the other side,' I said.

Horsemen amongst the enemy galloped forward to secure the ford and quickly reached the opposite bank where they stopped to assess our strength. We were six and they numbered ten, but we had the advantage of defending a dry bank.

'Withdraw and save yourself,' one growled. 'We have many more coming.'

We said nothing but stared resolutely back. I tried not to turn to see where Athelstan was, but I thought I heard hooves in the distance behind me.

They charged.

It was a sight that haunts me even now. Ten fierce warriors galloped into the ford, yelling to their false gods, their faces contorted like demons, their horses snorting and spraying up water in plumes. I drew my short sword knowing it would be woefully inadequate against the spears that were pointing menacingly my way. My six guards moved ahead of me to take the brunt of the attack.

One of the charging horses must have hit a hidden rock for it stumbled, its forelegs giving way, throwing its rider into the stream. Either side, horses reared up and shied away from their onward dash. As riders desperately tried to pull their mounts under control, five horsemen reached the bank and the waiting spears of my guard.

It is surprisingly difficult to fight on horseback. Controlling a weapon in one hand and a mount with the other is difficult on dry land. In a flowing stream strewn with concealed stones, it proved fatally impossible for the first of the Danes who crashed into my men. He ran his steed's neck into a waiting spear and was thrown as his mount reared up. His companion was knocked off course and stabbed by a blade as he fought to control his horse. A third urged his mount up the bank, but my man was on him as he scrabbled in slippery mud and knocked him from the saddle with a straight blow of his spear to the chest. The fourth managed to parry one blade thrust at him but did not see the next until it was buried into his shoulder and he was screaming in pain.

The fifth rode a small horse, almost a pony, and made it through where the bank was low, somehow evading my guards. He was riding straight for me. I was surprised by the shrillness of the voice that hurled insults at me and the fresh look of his face. He was but a boy, yet he was threatening me with a man-sized axe. I raised my sword to parry the blow, but it did not come. His yelling turned to screaming as one of my guards thrust a spear into his side, and his young face contorted in pain as I watched him slither from his mount.

Shouts from behind told me that Athelstan was returning and the Danes, who were still able to ride, turned their steeds around and fled. I closed my eyes and thanked God for sparing me. I opened them to see my soldiers slitting the throats of the wounded Danes in the river and I wanted to shout stop when they dragged up the young lad who writhed on the bank. Instead, I prayed for his soul as they drew a knife across his neck.

The next wave of the enemy arrived on foot, breathing heavily from the exertion of moving fast in war gear. Yet they did not hesitate to plunge into the ford with a roar. The waters in the middle came to the waists of the pagan warriors, making it difficult to wield a weapon, and Athelstan was quick to take advantage. He ordered a wave of horsemen forward to attack them as they crossed.

I do not normally take pleasure in watching men kill each other, but that day I cheered loudly at every blow that struck an enemy body. I even clapped when a horse reared up and kicked its hooves into an attacker's face. It was a short violent encounter. Two of our horses went down, their riders clawed from their backs. But more fell on the Danish side as my horsemen thrust and slashed their blades into unprotected flesh. The Danes fell back to their side of the river.

For a moment, both sides caught their breath, glowering at each other. More enemy warriors were arriving and they formed up, several lines deep, spears thrust forward, ready for their next assault.

I sensed that their numbers would tell the next time they charged. 'We should withdraw,' I said quietly to Athelstan.

'We could retreat to the rear of Thurston's line and harry the enemy as they attack,' he said. 'Cavalry would be more effective in the open than in this treacherous river. Now is the moment, before they come again.'

I nodded, watching the enemy carefully whilst Athelstan quietly gave the order. We turned and trotted back to the battle by the ridge.

I have never stood in a shield wall and never wanted to. Imagine being the thickness of two shields from some brute who is heaving against you, trying to thrust a wicked blade through your defences so that it tears into your exposed neck or face. Or the horror when the comrade at your side is stabbed and slips to the ground, exposing your flank, until someone stands over his writhing body to take his place.

That was the spectacle that confronted me when we arrived behind the lines of Thurston's men. The wall was holding, but only just. The four lines had reduced to three and I was glad to be watching it all from horseback, although the spectacle of men dying still made my throat retch.

We found the tall figure of Thurston in the middle of his troops, cajoling and encouraging them as best he could. We quickly warned him of the impending attack from behind his lines so that he could turn a section of his warriors to face the new onslaught.

'If you can hold out for a short while longer, reinforcements will be here,' I shouted to him and he nodded, grim-faced. It was a tough assignment for an inexperienced young leader.

Athelstan was urging me away, to distance myself from the fighting so that I could escape if I needed to. But there was something I wanted to do before I withdrew any further. I took a guard towards the river and pointed to the body I had seen lying to the rear of Thurston's formation. I was sure it was Halfdan and, as we neared, I saw the gleam of the casket. In the heat of the battle, no-one had rescued the precious relics.

'Sever the head,' I ordered, pointing to Halfdan's body. I jumped from my horse and ran to the casket searching for the bones in the churned soil of the field.

'What are you doing?' Athelstan shouted down to me from his mount. 'You shouldn't endanger yourself like this.'

'We need St Oswald on our side,' I said.

Athelstan chuckled. 'Do you think I would give up the relics so easily?'

I looked more closely at the bone I was about to carefully replace into the casket. 'These are not St Oswald's?'

Before Athelstan had time to reply, we heard the shouts of the enemy soldiers who had crossed the ford and were now pouring towards us, eager to attack the rear of Thurston's men. We had to move fast to avoid being trapped.

The guard held up the head he had cut from Halfdan's body.

'Show it to the Danes so they realise their leader is dead,' I shouted, remembering the shock of Merewalh's head spilling before me from a sack.

'Help me, Athelstan,' I said, picking up the casket and hastily filling it with what bones I could find. 'Place this near Thurston and tell him he fights with St Oswald beside him.'

'But—'

I cut him off. 'It's what they believe that counts.'

I mounted and rode along the ranks of Thurston's men who were turning to face the new threat, waving and shouting reassurance to them. They had need of encouragement. As I scrambled up the slope, I could see their predicament more clearly. They were about to be battered from both sides. Thurston's warriors stood back-to-back with a rapidly depleting third line between them to step into breaches on either side. To the east, several ranks of Danes continued to press them hard, whilst increasing numbers had crossed the river and were now engaging them on the western flank. They could not hold out for much longer.

I heard a roar and saw Halfdan's head held aloft on a spear. The men of Shrewsbury were taking heart that the enemy king had suffered the same fate as Merewalh, their leader. Maybe the sight disheartened the Danes or maybe they wanted to regroup, for a horn blew and gradually both sides of their forces pulled back, cursing and shouting insults at us from a distance. Thurston's men were still trapped but grateful to take words rather than blows from the enemy for a while.

A group of Danes gathered behind their men, pointing and arguing. Looking down from the ridge where I had taken refuge, I studied them closely and my heart sank. Standing amongst them was the unmistakable figure of Ingimund. He had somehow managed to escape into the woods to rejoin his forces, and he was now redeploying them. I could understand why. His forces were unable to use their superior numbers to sweep away Thurston's wall. On the eastern side of our shields, he had men standing four or five deep who could not engage us because of the narrowness of the gully. Yet Thurston's men were more exposed on the western flank where the ridge fell away and offered less protection. He made the obvious decision and ordered more men to trek around the river to the east and return along the southern bank to the ford. Once across that, they could join their attack on the western side, and Thurston's beleaguered wall would be crushed like flour between a miller's stones.

*

There was an eerie pause in the battle as warriors on both sides grimly helped wounded comrades back through the lines. Those near the riverbank pushed those beyond help into the water so they would not impede the fighting when it recommenced. Bodies lay twitching on the banks or floated, half submerged, reddening the waters as the life-force spilled from their wounds.

Athelstan was directing cavalry to protect our wing when I saw him stand in his stirrups, looking south, before waving excitedly in my direction.

Had he seen our forces from Gloucester?

We would still be outnumbered. My mind went back to the previous battle I had witnessed in the dank marshes of Holme

Fen. Edward had lost that battle because he had divided his forces in two. Mine were separated into three.

Athelstan was gesticulating wildly and, in the distance, I caught a flash of the sun reflecting on metal.

At last! It was Cuthberht.

Just as I saw our reinforcements arriving from the south, I heard shouts from a different direction. Ingimund's redeployed forces were running towards us from the east.

'See there,' I shouted to Athelstan over the din of the battle below, stabbing my finger towards the Danes.'If they arrive before Cuthberht, they can seal off the ford and stop us reinforcing Thurston.'

Athelstan looked east and then to the south. 'It will be a close-run thing,' he said.'We have to delay the Danes. I will take the cavalry.'

'No,' I said firmly.'I will take the cavalry with Jokul. You will ride to Cuthberht and direct him to secure the ford above all else.'

So it was that I rode forth with one hundred cavalrymen to stop five hundred Danish warriors.

TWENTY

I consider myself neither brave nor cowardly. I had lived to a reasonable age and had played my part in securing the Anglo-Saxon lands, but the future lay in the hands of youthful leaders like Athelstan and the others who directed my troops. I had Jokul with me to direct the men in the heat of combat, but I was under no illusion about my chances of surviving the encounter by the river at Tettenhall. I commended my soul to the Lord and rode forward with my brave horsemen who I knew would fight even harder with a woman at their head.

'We don't have to defeat them, just hold them up,' I shouted to Jokul beside me.

He grinned. 'We're doing that already,' he said, indicating the enemy who had halted to form into a shield wall ahead of us.

'I will try talking with them,' I said, thinking it would waste more time.

They had begun to hurl insults towards us as we drew up to face them in a line that matched the length of their wall, except they stood five or six deep and we were a single line of horsemen.

'Men of Danelaw,' I shouted, suddenly aware of the shrillness of my voice over their snarling jibes. Still, it had the effect of quietening them; they were clearly confused by a woman addressing them before a battle.

'Men of Danelaw, your kings are dead. Halfdan and Eowils are rotting on the ground, but that does not have to be your fate. Take your spoils and ride across the border. Turn and go home to your women and children. We will not pursue you.'

To my surprise there was a pause, as if they were seriously considering my offer. A loud guffawing towards the back of their formation broke the silence and a figure that I knew only too well pushed himself through the shields to stand before me, hands on hips, laughing loudly.

It was Ingimund.

'Now we can kill the Mercian queen to honour our fallen–'

He had no time to finish his words because Jokul charged at him, spear outstretched. Ingimund had killed his mother and his rage must have overcome his senses. For a heartbeat, I thought Jokul's blade would make its mark but Ingimund staggered back, somehow managing to deflect the spear, anger in his voice.

'Get off your horse you cowardly pup and fight me like a warrior, not a woman's runt.'

Jokul took the challenge, jumping from his saddle, trying to use the length of his spear to get through Ingimund's defences. Ingimund may have lost his fine physique, but he soon proved he was still an able swordsman. He used his shield to ward off the spear and continued its forward movement to crash it into Jokul's skull. As he fell back, stunned, Jokul did not seem to see the blade that Ingimund was now aiming at his neck. Yet somehow, he twisted away, using his sword to half-parry the thrust, but the blade sliced down his chest, ripping into his leather jerkin.

It was one thing to fight on horse without a shield but quite another on foot. Jokul had little left to defend himself against Ingimund's counterattack. He stumbled, breathing hard, his eyes no longer showing rage but fear as his heavier, taller opponent strode forward. The Danes began to shout for their leader, urging him to finish off his young challenger. Ingimund needed little encouragement and swung a scything blow. Without a shield,

Jokul could only partly parry the blow which cut deep into the slashes in his jerkin. I saw the redness as blood seeped through, but Jokul summoned up the strength to draw himself back up and made a movement that surprised me – and his opponent.

He swopped over his sword and spear so that he now held the spear in his left hand. He lunged with the sword which Ingimund blocked with his shield, and, as he did, Jokul took a huge risk. He threw his spear.

He had drawn Ingimund's shield away with his sword thrust and the spear flew straight at Ingimund's unprotected chest. I heard Ingimund howl as it struck him on his arm as he desperately tried to fend it away. Ingimund's arm fell limp at his side and his shield crashed to the ground.

They eyed each other, breathing hard. Both were wounded and held but one weapon. I wanted to ride between them and tell them that honour had been done and they should fight no more. But duels do not end in stalemate.

Jokul found the strength to attack, forcing his opponent back, which gave him the chance he must have intended. He quickly picked up Ingimund's shield and rushed forward again. It was the turn of my soldiers to yell encouragement as Jokul used the shield to knock aside Ingimund's sword whilst thrusting his own blade towards his opponent. Ingimund twisted to avoid taking the sword in the neck and it struck him in the shoulder.

The Danes in the shield wall began to roar even louder. At first, I thought they were urging their leader to one more effort, but when I saw some pointing behind me I turned, and gasped.

Athelstan rode towards me, followed by a host of running warriors. Cuthberht and his army had arrived.

*

Jokul's reckless attack on Ingimund had bought us the time we needed and to this day I blame myself for not saving him.

When I saw reinforcements arriving, I could have immediately ordered my cavalry forward to protect Jokul and begin the assault on the Danes. Instead, I breathed a sigh of relief and closed my eyes to say a prayer of thanks. In that moment, Ingimund must have used the distraction of Cuthbert's arrival to hurl himself on Jokul. When I opened my eyes, both men were down, locked in a desperate struggle in the dirt. I urged my men forward as I dismounted and ran towards the combatants on the ground. Jokul lay still underneath Ingimund who convulsed and groaned. I stabbed my short sword into the back of Ingimund's neck and he let out a groan and went limp. I was desperately trying to pull him from Jokul when Athelstan arrived.

'What happened here?' he cried, throwing himself from his horse to help me heave Ingimund aside. We both stared speechless at Jokul's lifeless body, before I commended his soul to heaven and tried to compose myself for the battle ahead.

*

When Cuthbert's army reached us, we withdrew the cavalry and ordered the footsoldiers to attack the Danish shields. Outnumbered and dispirited by the fall of their leader, the Danes soon turned to hurry back the way they had come.

They ran straight into Wiglaf's forces. He could not have timed his arrival better. I did not see his army for the melee of men ahead of me until the retreating Danes stopped and suddenly we were upon them. Wiglaf had blocked their path. Ingimund's men resisted stoutly, as trapped warriors always do, but the result was not now in doubt.

My attention turned across the river to where Thurston and his men were making a valiant last stand, close to being overrun.

I shouted towards Athelstan and Cuthberht who were directing the battle ahead of me. 'Send men to support Thurston. He cannot hold out any longer.'

I watched as Athelstan made the arrangements to redeploy our forces, sending men to attack the Danes from the east and the west. It was hard to believe he was just reaching his full manhood. All this seemed to come naturally to him, even though he must be grieving badly for the loss of his friend, Jokul.

I rode with Cuthberht's men back across the ford and, as we splashed through the river, it looked as though we had left it too late. The Danes attacking our shield wall had broken through at the riverside end. Thurston's wall was collapsing, allowing the enemy to pour through the gaps. I could see Thurston's tall figure in the centre, waving and shouting, trying to direct his soldiers into a circle now that their lines were breached.

One thousand of Cuthberht's soldiers ran hard at the rear of the enemy who were so busy hacking at Thurston's shields, they did not notice our charge until we were upon them. Caught on two sides the Danes were pressed back and it did not take long for us to break through their ranks and join up with Thurston and his men.

There were loud shouts from the other side and I guessed it was Wiglaf's forces and the balance of Cuthberht's men attacking from the west. Until that moment, the Danes believed they had trapped Thurston between them. Now they were caught between my armies. We had two thousand troops pressing them from the eastern side, and nearly as many from the west. In trying to get around Thurston's wall, the Danes had divided their forces in a way that had given us the advantage. Yet, although they were without leaders, they still numbered over three thousand men caught between the ridge and the river, and it would not be easy to finish them off.

Cuthberht rode up beside me. He had left Wiglaf to take charge of the eastern front and joined Athelstan and I to discuss our next moves. His youthful face was creased, his mouth unsmiling as he took off his helmet to bow and greet me.

'My men ran here, m'lady. Hope we're in time.'

'Only just, but I think we have them now.'

His frown deepened. 'At what cost? We'll lose many men.' Cuthberht had a habit of speaking curtly in short bursts, like thunderclaps, but I respected his judgement.

'If we deplete our armies here we may not have the men to take back the Danelaw,' added Athelstan. He was thinking ahead. We needed to conserve our forces for future years.

'What do you propose?' I asked.

'Offer them a truce. Send them home,' said Cuthberht.

'That will leave more of them to return another time to attack us,' I said.

'I think they will be very wary of us in future,' Athelstan said. 'They have seen how we fortify our towns and they have lost their leaders.'

'Very well, but they must return home without their spoils,' I said.

*

The Danes will tell you that I tricked them that day, but I did not intend it to end the way it did.

Leaderless and trapped on both sides, they quickly agreed to our terms when we offered to let them go. We escorted them to the end of the ridge and watched as they trudged across Woden's Field, leaving their baggage train and all that they had stolen behind.

Cuthberht sat on his horse beside me and I was about to ask him where he had left Ælfwyn, when I heard shouts from the wooded area to the south. Horsemen were pouring from the trees, galloping hard after the Danes. A stream of foot soldiers followed, intent it seemed on catching the retreating enemy. The flag of Wessex fluttered from their midst. Edward had finally arrived.

'Stop them!' I shouted to Cuthberht.

He looked at me, puzzled. 'Stop who, m'lady?'

I pointed towards the men who were almost upon the Danes. 'Stop them breaking the truce.'

Cuthberht looked unmoved. 'They're from Wessex. I can't stop them.'

He was right. He had no authority over Edward's soldiers. I kicked my horse forward.

'Bring some men and come with me,' I called over to Athelstan and rode towards the skirmishing that had already begun as some Danes turned to face the danger behind them, whilst others began to run.

Athelstan drew level as I urged my mount on.

'Over there,' he shouted, pointing towards a group that had drawn up at the rear of the Wessex army. It was Edward. He wouldn't be risking himself in combat. By the time we reached the group, the slaughter had already begun as the Wessex cavalry harried the retreating army, and their foot-soldiers finished off any stragglers.

Edward waved to me. 'Looks like we arrived just in time, sister.'

'No, you're too late. We agreed a truce. Call off your men.'

He grinned at Osferth beside him. 'Truce? We haven't agreed to a truce, have we?' He chuckled. 'But fear not, sister, we will not need your men. We can finish them off ourselves.'

For a moment, I was tempted to go along with the deception. Destroying the enemy completely would make our task of reconquering the Danelaw easier when the time came. But I remembered the stern faces of the men who had made the deal with me. They had trusted my word. Some spoke our tongue perfectly and were almost certainly of Anglo-Saxon stock. When we took back control of the Danelaw, we would need their support.

'We are in Mercia so we should honour Mercian agreements. I said that they could go home. Order your men to withdraw, or my word means nothing.'

Silence followed my plea. Edward was surrounded by a large number of advisors who looked at each other but did not speak. I recognised one of the priests amongst them.

'Bishop, did not the apostle Matthew say we should love our enemies and do good to those who would harm us? Do you not think it is time to show compassion towards our enemy?' I asked. 'There are Christians amongst them. Should we not be showing them how good Christians behave?'

The Bishop nodded. 'It is true, lord king, that more Danes might convert if, in their hour of need in battle, they feel the force of God's love.'

Edward turned to look towards the slaughter over on Woden's Field, and I followed his gaze, listening to the growls of the victors and the howls of the vanquished. He was no doubt desperate to play some part in the victory so that his chroniclers could record it as a triumph for Wessex as well as for Mercia. But I believed that the number of priests in his entourage spoke of a new religious zeal in my brother, and I proved right

'Very well. Sound the withdrawal,' he ordered. 'Release any captives, but only on condition that they are first baptised.'

*

When I hear the story that my husband, Æthelred, died of his wounds at the battle of Tettenhall, I smile and do not deny it. He would have liked nothing more than to have met a warrior's end as a result of that most important of victories. I recounted every detail of the campaign many times to him by the fire that winter. Whenever I sat with him in his chamber, he would become agitated and say something that sounded like 'bat' and I knew that he wanted me to go over the battle once again. I could tell by the expression on his face that he understood much of what I said. I just wished he could tell me what he was thinking. His long experience of warfare could have given me new perspectives on what happened that day. Instead, I had to make do with his cries of 'Ætte, Ætte,' whenever I was about to play a part in the action.

In truth, the battle did kill him, for I was just recounting once again the fight between Jokul and Ingimund when he began to choke. At first I thought it was a sob. He had been very fond of Jokul who, as Athelstan's constant companion, had often listened to Æthelred's accounts of his campaigns with King Alfred. But soon it became apparent he was gasping for air, a raw rasping coming from his throat. Quickly I sat him fully upright and thumped his back thinking he had something stuck in his throat, but blood began to trickle from his nose. The choking subsided and he lay on his side, breathing in laboured gulps, until the healer came. She shook her head when she saw the red stains on his pillow and told me to call the family and the priest.

We sat with him all night, Athelstan, Ælfwyn, Father Fintan and I, listening to his rasping breaths until they slowed and eventually stopped. I had been expecting him to die for many years but it was still a shock when he did. He had been a constant in my life ever since I had left home and come to Mercia. I had not loved him at first. I thought I was too young and good-looking to be given to a hoary older warrior as his prize for helping my father. Yet I had grown to love him. He was as kind and gentle to me as he was merciless and brutal to his enemies. When I arrived in Gloucester as a young girl, nothing was too much trouble for him in making sure that I was comfortable in my new home. He was devoted to me, always seeking me out immediately when he returned from his campaigns against the Danes and the Welsh, recounting to me each battle in great detail. I think that is why I took to commanding soldiers so naturally. My husband had somehow given his years of experience to me through his vivid descriptions. Although he had not been able to speak a complete sentence to me for several years, I felt an emptiness in my life from that day forward that has never left me.

The death of a lord or a king is always doubly hard. The sorrow at losing a loved one is soon engulfed by the struggle of who is to succeed him. So it was with Æthelred. He left no sons, only a daughter. He had no surviving brothers or nephews and the old Mercian dynasties had been wiped out in the successive wars that had swept through our lands. I had ruled since his infirmity, but I had done so in his name. Widows do not succeed their husbands as rulers in Anglo-Saxon kingdoms. Other women in my position had retired quietly on their estates or, like my mother, spent the rest of their days in a nunnery.

That was not my intention.

I knew that when Æthelred drew his last breath, he would want me to succeed him, to carry on the work of rebuilding Mercia that he had made possible by defending it so stoutly from complete extinction.

What did I want?

A part of me did want to take the easy path and live out my days without the burden of leadership. Yet I knew that was not God's path. Nor would it have been the wish of my father. I had lived through too many struggles to give up now, and I was determined to reunite Mercia as one Christian land. However, to become its ruler in my own right would not be easy. I would need the authority of the Witan to continue. That august body had changed much in recent years as the older nobility had died off and younger men such as Cuthberht and Wiglaf had joined it who supported me. Yet they were still all men and they had never elected a woman to lead them in the hundreds of years the Witan had been presiding over our affairs.

I would also need the blessing of our overlord, King Edward, and that, as I was to discover, would only come at a price.

*

It was spring in the Year of our Lord 911 when we completed the arrangements to assemble all the nobles and bishops to honour the passing of Æthelred and appoint his successor. We all squeezed into the minster of St Oswald's, as St Peter's in Gloucester was now known. We had created a shrine for the relics in a splendid crypt supported by columns on the eastern end of the church. I could not help smiling as I prayed to St Oswald and gave thanks to him once again for our victory at Tettenhall on his saint's day. I had thought his bones were with us that day in the casket, as had Halfdan and his Danes. But Athelstan had carefully replaced the saint's with some unknown bones from the cemetery and returned with the casket, leaving the relics safely in the shrine. Now they were back in the casket and Æthelred was buried beside them.

Edward knelt beside me in the church. He had arrived with his entourage only the day before and I had little time to talk with him before the service in honour of Æthelred's life. As Bishop Wærferth read the eulogy, Edward took my hand and squeezed it. Whether he would continue this support for me in the Witan that was to follow, I could not yet say.

As was the custom, I walked slowly from the church before the mourners, except for Ælfwyn who took my arm. She had not been the same since Merewalh's death. I had thought her fondness for him was an infatuation that she would soon forget, but she had withdrawn from almost all company and had lost weight. To the guests who watched us make our way along the knave of the church, she may have looked more of a grieving widow than I did with her gaunt figure and pale skin.

'I would make them walk. It's a fine day,' I said, knowing that, however I made my way to the feasting hall, everyone else would have to follow. It would also be an opportunity to talk with her. 'We'll miss him, won't we?'

Ælfwyn nodded. 'I have lost both the men most dear to me and I miss them both terribly.' She paused before she continued. 'And soon I am to lose my mother, I suppose.'

I stopped. 'How so?'

'When you become queen, you will have no time for your family.'

I put an arm around her and squeezed. 'Not so. I will give all the work to the men, and we women will enjoy ourselves again.'

She smiled wanly at that, but I knew she did not believe me.

I heard a cough behind me and I turned to see that Edward had caught up with us.

'A word if I may, sister,' he said.

Ælfwyn raised her eyebrows as if to say, 'I told you so,' and dropped back.

'Æthelred will be hard to replace,' Edward said. It had not taken him long to get to the topic that was on everyone's mind.

'He is irreplaceable,' I replied.

'At least, not by another man,' Edward said. 'But I am hoping his wife will continue to take his place, as she has done successfully for several years.'

This was going more easily than I had anticipated. 'I thought you might want your son, Athelstan, to rule here.' It was an obvious way for Edward to take more control in Mercia and he was someone I would support myself. Just not yet.

Edward rubbed his chin. 'Athelstan is too young. Besides politics in Wessex would not favour him.' By that he meant his wife. She was keen to support her son over his elder brother and was already spreading rumours challenging Athelstan's legitimacy.

'You will support me and advise the Witan?' That would almost guarantee my confirmation as ruler.

He nodded. 'Together, we will take back the conquered lands. We will finish the work that our father began.'

I smiled, waiting for the condition.

'Our attacks must be co-ordinated more smoothly than the recent campaigns. I need Osferth back under my command,' he said.

I could only agree with the need for better co-ordination and Osferth had been an unwilling subordinate of mine. 'That seems reasonable. He was your close advisor,' I said.

'Good. His estates will remain with him, of course.'

That was the condition. Edward was taking London and Oxford and all the lands in between. His price for supporting me was a quarter of Mercian territory.

*

The Witan spent much time in debating the succession. But rather than discuss who was to succeed, the argument was over my title. Even when men agree, it seems they have a need to debate the details at great length. Cuthberht wanted me to take the title of Queen. This, he said, would indicate I was the sole ruler, equivalent to the ancient kings of Mercia. But Bishop Wærferth pointed out that this was not the reality of our situation. Our territories were but a shadow of what they had been and we had an overlord, the King of Wessex, who provided us with protection that we still needed despite our most glorious victory at Tettenhall. He, like King Alfred before him, would not want Mercia ruled by a separate king or queen. They decided to invite me to give my opinion in the matter.

I did not hesitate to speak forcefully. I wanted to set the tone for the future.

'Edward was crowned as King of the Anglo-Saxons and I took an oath to serve him as such. This is not the moment to divide our loyalties. This is the moment to unite all Anglo-Saxon people and drive the enemy from our lands forever. I will be called, as I am now, the Lady of the Mercians.'

PART FOUR

TWENTY ONE

The battle at Tettenhall changed everything. It changed the Danes, who had lost their leaders and their powerful armies. It changed Edward, who, from that day on, respected me as a leader and even began to see me as a threat to his kingship.

And it changed me.

I saw men slaughtered in the thousands in just a few hours, and from that day, I no longer fear death. Instead, I see it as a necessity to make the world better for the living. Ælfwyn tells me that I am less of a woman since Tettenhall, whatever that means. She also says that I have become a workhorse blinkered to the needs of my family. I tell her that my family extends beyond her, to all the Anglo-Saxon people whether they live in Mercia, Wessex or even the Danelaw. She complains because she is afraid of losing me, poor child. She shuns all other company but mine and the priests around me.

Edward and I agreed a plan to take back our land from the Danes. We would not seek another encounter like Tettenhall to decide it all. Why should we chance the future of our people in one single battle? I had seen for myself how things in war can so easily go wrong. Edward finally conceded that we would reclaim the Danelaw by stealth. Along the borders, we would develop a line of fortifications, his to the south, mine to the east, like two great claws of a crab that would gradually crush our enemy between them.

He no longer cowered south of the Thames with the occasional raid into the Danelaw. He crossed the river that had defined his territory for so long and began building burhs, just as I was doing.

First, he went to Hertford where he built a fortress on the banks of the River Lea, threatening the Danish encampments at Bedford and Cambridge. The following year he moved his ships into the Blackwater estuary at Maldon and built earthworks at Witham so that he controlled the ancient road that ran from London towards the Danes of East Anglia.

I made simultaneous inroads into the Danelaw further north. But unlike Wessex, Mercia had a potential enemy to the west as well as to the east. The Welsh were rarely content to live in peace and constantly raided my lands before retreating to their hilltops. I had to secure my frontier with these troublesome tribes. Immediately after I became ruler in my own right, I returned to Bridgnorth to complete our defences of that important river crossing. Together with Shrewsbury, it would control the upper reaches of the Severn against incursion by both the Welsh and the Danes.

I wanted to take Ælfwyn with me, to try to purge the memory she had of the area where she was taken prisoner, but the thought of returning to the spot where Merewalh's severed head had been thrown across the river was enough to make her wail. Near to Shrewsbury, I ordered the construction of another small fortress by the Severn at Scargeat. It was the third of May, the holy day of St Helena who had discovered the True Cross, so I bade my men kneel by the gurgling river and pray with me that we might defeat our enemies just as her illustrious son, the Emperor Constantine, had defeated his.

*

In the following year, 913, I was ready for my boldest move yet against the Danes. I marched on the ancient royal centre of Mercia. I took an army to Tamworth.

It was not just an army. I took workmen to rebuild what had once been King Offa's great hall and residence. I took my household of clerks and priests. It was to be my permanent camp on the frontline of our struggle to reclaim the middle lands of England that my ancestors had ruled for centuries. It was in Tamworth that King Offa had received vassal kings and lords from far and wide and I was determined to reinstate it to its former glory. Those who lived in the surrounding Danelaw would see that there was now an alternative to being ruled by the Danes.

Tamworth is sited on the juncture of two rivers, the Tame and the Anker, which protect its southern boundary. I was first to ride my horse across the ford near the confluence of the rivers and up the incline towards the ancient buildings. We had sent scouts ahead, so I knew there was no danger and I wanted to show that the Mercian royal family was returning to its home. When I caught sight of the ancient palace and the church, tears sprang into my eyes. I looked upon a desolate ruin of rotten wood and crumbled masonry overgrown with weeds. The inhabitants had long gone and rats scurried around the fallen timbers.

I dismounted and walked to the charred remains of the church. I could see it had been deliberately burned, whereas the great hall had fallen into disrepair through neglect. Poking among the remains, I hoped to see signs of the original ceremonial items but found nothing.

Athelstan joined me, kicking amongst the ashes. 'The pagans would have plundered anything of value,' he said.

'We must rebuild it, and the hall,' I said. Seeing one of the scouts nearby, I waved him over. 'Where are the people? Does no-one live here?'

'The farmsteads are a mile or so beyond that forest,' he said, pointing to a thickly wooded area to the north. 'Only an old hag lives here.'

'Bring her to me,' I said. I signalled to Cuthberht that he and the thousand warriors he commanded could set up camp. 'Tell your men to be ready to start work on building the fortifications here tomorrow. We will need a ditch and an earthen bank topped by a timber palisade. I will discuss the layout with you later.'

He nodded and began giving instructions to his men as the scout returned, dragging an old lady covered in filthy rags.

'She calls herself Editha, m'lady,' he said, shoving her towards me.

I was intrigued. Editha was the name of the daughter of King Penda of Mercia, the very king who had defeated and killed St. Oswald.

'Welcome, Editha. How did you come by such an illustrious name?' I asked.

She looked at me, squinting, clearly not able to see well. 'Sorry m'lady, but I do not know your name.'

'I am Æthelflæd, Lady of the Mercians.'

She fell to her knees, clasping her hands together in prayer. 'Thanks be to God! A saviour has come at last.'

I touched the matted hair on top of her head. 'I am flesh and blood, like you. But I will drive the pagans from this land.'

I helped her to her feet and she stood close to examine my face. 'You are the one who snatched St Oswald's bones from the heathens?'

'Yes, my dear, and you have the name of the saintly daughter of his killer.'

Her eyes widened. 'I have more than just her name.'

'How so?'

She looked suspiciously at the warriors around me. 'You are safe with me. You have my word,' I said.

'I was but a girl when the pagans first came all those years ago. We lived here, around the great hall. I was baptised in this very church that now lies in ashes,' she said, her eyes brimming with tears. 'They called me Editha after its patron saint. We fled to the other side of the forest when we heard the Danes were coming.' She stepped even closer so that I could smell her breath. 'But not before I had taken a souvenir of my namesake.'

I stepped back as my eyes could not see her plainly at such close range. 'You have a relic of St Editha?'

She nodded. 'A lock of her hair.'

I grasped her bony hands. 'Your relic will have back its home. I will rebuild this church in St Editha's honour.'

'God bless you, m'lady. I've lived for this moment. The cowardly priests may have abandoned this church, but I never did. The pagans burned everything and moved on, and I've lived here praying for our salvation ever since. Not like my family.'

'What happened to them?'

'They sleep under the same roof as the barbarians. Some even share their beds.' She spat on the ground.

'Will they fight for the Danes?' I asked.

She snorted. 'They have grown fat from the years of peace. They will grovel to whoever is strongest.'

'Then I will show them my army.' I waved over one of the guards. 'Make sure she has blankets to keep her warm and plenty of food.' I drew him nearer, lowering my voice. 'And see she does not leave.'

I had learned to trust no one, especially in times of war.

The following day, I agreed the outline of the new fortifications of Tamworth with Cuthberht and left him to begin the work. I took Athelstan and two hundred men to visit the homesteads on the other side of the forest. We found prosperous farmers and their households scattered around the fertile countryside. They offered no resistance but seemed alarmed at the prospect of a Mercian army in their midst. I ordered the elders of each group to meet with me in the largest of the lodges. Around thirty men and women filed into the small hall in the early evening, their faces unsmiling. I had not expected a euphoric welcome but I found it hard to believe these were Anglo-Saxons, not Danes.

They listened in silence as I welcomed them and began to explain my plans. 'The Danes stole this land from your forefathers and I intend to return it to you,' I began. An older woman who stood to one side, arms folded, interrupted.

'With respect m'lady, no-one stole this land. We have owned it and farmed it for generations. We pay dues to the Danes. Are we to pay dues to you as well now?'

'You will pay nothing to the Danes. You will owe your allegiance to Mercia only, as you did in days gone by.'

She looked around the room. 'I see no one here who has ever bent the knee to Mercia. When you and your army leave, what do we say to the lords who bring their army from Derby to collect what we owe?'

I felt Athelstan bristle beside me. It seemed they had grown too used to being Danish subjects. I tried to smile.

'After forty years of subjugation, I can understand that it must be difficult to recognise your true allegiance. Yet your forefathers were Mercian and proud to be so. From this day on, you are Mercian once again. We will not be leaving. We will fortify Tamworth and drive the Danes from Derby for ever.'

My warriors lined the walls and they banged their spears on the ground in approval. I had hoped the farmers might also show their appreciation but they did not. Instead, they turned and discussed the news with their neighbours.

I turned to Athelstan in exasperation. 'What is wrong with these people?' I muttered.

'It will take time for them to adjust to the new situation. Besides some are half-Danes with fathers from the army in Derby. We will have to overcome that to be secure here. That will take more time.'

*

It actually took four more years before we were ready to go to Derby. Even then I was not prepared for what happened there.

That was the day I learned that taking back land from an enemy was very different to defending it. It was a lesson I learned too late to save my friends. Even now, my hand tremors to write about it.

I will tell you first of happier times when I was building my burhs. I have said before that I believe God made me to build towns. I know of no other leader who has created as many as I did in such a space of time. The same year that I began building Tamworth, I also went to Stafford. When I arrived, it was an empty peninsular of sand and gravel surrounded on one side by marshes and on the other by the River Sow that gives into the Trent. Now it is a fortified town that produces pottery for which it has become famed and it processes meat and bread for my armies. I gave it a church, dedicated to St Bertelin who had a hermitage in the marshes.

The following year, in 914, I turned my attention to the north where Norsemen from Ireland continued to trouble us. I led Wiglaf and his men out of Chester and we marched ten miles towards the very tip of Mercia at Eddisbury Hill in the Delamere Forest. On the summit, we strengthened the earthen defences of the fort that the ancients had built there. It gave good views towards Cumbria and Northumbria so that we would have warning if the Norsemen should dare to invade again.

Yet my main mission lay to the south where I returned in the late summer of that year. I chose a wonderful site for a burh at Warwick near the Fosse Way, a road which gave me direct access to the Danes of Leicester and Lincoln. A trading settlement had already developed on the sandstone cliff overlooking the crossing point of the River Avon, an ideal site for fortifications. My men were busy building an oval-shaped palisade to encircle the existing homesteads, when some visitors came calling. They were Danes.

Six horsemen bearing no flag to indicate their allegiance sat watching us on the far bank of the Avon by the ford. Their leader sat tall on his horse but wisps of grey hair in his beard told me he was not young. Athelstan had already exchanged greetings with him when I arrived from the far side of town where I had been measuring the ditches we needed.

'He is the Jarl Thurketel from Northampton. He wants to know our intentions,' Athelstan reported.

I chuckled and shouted down from the cliff top to him. 'Have we killed all your kings that I have to speak with jarls, now?'

To my surprise, he bowed his head and smiled. 'M'lady of the Mercians, I had hoped to meet you. Your renown has spread throughout our land.'

His tone surprised me. 'Maybe you would like to cross the ford and kneel before me. I would accept your allegiance now that you have no king.'

His grin disappeared. 'And take my lands and kill my children as soon as I lay down my sword, no doubt.'

'Once you submit, you will have my word and of King Edward and all our followers that you will live in peace under our protection. You and your warriors will be welcome to stand alongside us against our common enemies.'

His smile returned. 'I've heard you have the reputation of a lady who likes to command men. I will think on what you have said. We will meet again.' With that he rode away, no doubt to report to his fellow warlords in the Danelaw.

I turned to Athelstan. 'Send a messenger to King Edward and tell him the Danes are soft and ready to be plucked.'

My missive must have emboldened my brother, for that autumn, he advanced on Buckingham where he built fortresses either side of the Great Ouse that flowed into the heart of the Danelaw. We were tightening the noose around the necks of the Danes.

They choose not to hang.

On a cold day in December, Thurketel and many warriors from Bedford and Northampton rode to meet Edward and submitted to him as their king. Many were originally our subjects, forced to serve a foreign master and willingly came back to us, pledging loyalty to our cause. Some were pagan Danes who bridled at what they regarded as surrender. Even so, when Edward advanced on Bedford in the following year, 915, the town submitted without a fight.

For so many years, the Danelaw had seemed a lost land to us, only visited by merchant traders. Now we rode freely across the frontier. I sometimes think that the ease with which we made those early inroads softened my mind to possible disasters ahead.

*

Whilst Edward was taking Bedford, I continued to fortify my borders. Confident in our strategy, I increased the pace of my programme, building three new burhs in one year. Whilst we had been advancing east into Danelaw, Norsemen from the west had been encroaching closer to our borders. Ingimund was dead but a new Norse leader, Ragnall, had captured the Isle of Man and was raiding the nearby mainland. I countered by building defensive positions in Runcorn and Warburton near the River Mersey.

The Welsh rarely miss opportunities to cause trouble and when they heard I was busy in the Danelaw to the east, they began nibbling at my borders in the west. Although I had already built two burhs to the north that year, I summoned up the strength and resources for a further effort and identified a defensive position close to the Welsh border by Offa's Dyke at Chirbury. We threw up earth ramparts on a hill where the church of St Michael's stood. The siting of a church within the burh tempted me to appoint one of my priests, Ecgberht, as abbot to help with the development of the town. I encouraged him to seek settlers from the neighbouring areas to live around the burh to strengthen its position commercially as well as militarily. Ecgberht worked within my household and had shown himself adept at administrative matters.

Unfortunately, his mastery of numbers in ledgers did not transfer to worldly matters, and, once he had left the sanctuary of the scriptorium, he proved unskilled at dealing with people. When I returned to the eastern front, this priest took it upon himself to visit Welsh chieftains and reprimand them on the slow payment of their annual tributes. Welsh kings are a notoriously quarrelsome bunch and one of them, Hwgan, King of Brycheiniog, was a difficult man if sober and positively dangerous when drunk. Ecgberht went to visit him in his small kingdom in the south of Wales, and, after a disorderly supper, he apparently chastised the king for fornicating with a maid before him in the hall. Hwgan flew into a rage and struck out at Ecgberht who fell against a hard post and cracked his skull, never to regain his senses.

I too flew into a temper when I heard the news of my unfortunate priest. Abandoning my plans to go to Tamworth, I straightaway took a sizeable cavalry unit under the command of Merfyn to teach this vassal lord a lesson. His palace was on an island in the middle of Llangorse Lake accessible only by a narrow causeway. As we approached this land-bridge, I searched for signs of guards, but seeing none, I waved Merfyn and his men forward. To my surprise, they charged across unhindered, and I strode after them. My soldiers were everywhere, running into outbuildings and banging though rooms, but there seemed no sign of occupants. I made my way into a courtyard at the centre of the complex and there we finally found what remained of the king's household.

A cluster of young women dressed in flowing robes cowered against a wall, wailing entreaties of mercy. Maybe my renown had spread, as Thurketel had suggested, or maybe Hwgan was a coward, for he had evidently fled, leaving his wife and her companions to fend for themselves. I ordered Merfyn to pursue the king with his cavalry, and I took his queen and her household as hostages for their runaway lord. Our journey back to Gloucester revealed the gentler side of my hardened soldiers. They willingly shouldered the baggage of our female captives, seemingly entranced by their dark curly hair and olive-skinned features.

I sometimes wonder if what followed was God punishing me for uprooting those defenceless women from their home.

Hwgan and his followers led Merfyn a merry dance around the hills of Wales before heading north and crossing with his warriors into the Danelaw. I sent a messenger to order Merfyn to break off the pursuit and not risk entering hostile territory. Developments on the eastern front with the Danes demanded my attention and I could ill afford the distraction of chasing Welsh fugitives.

*

By the spring of 917, Edward and I were ready for our next foray against the Danes of middle England. We had discussed the tactics of the campaign over the winter, and it all went according to plan – for a while.

Edward instructed Osferth to bring his troops from London and march north towards the burhs I had already established on Watling Street at Tamworth and Warwick. They reached Towcester, which they fortified by repairing the old Roman walls. The Danes finally woke up to the threat posed by our armies in the line of forts on their borders and gathered their forces to attack Osferth at Towcester. In anticipation of such a response, I had been concentrating my strength, ordering Wiglaf, Thurston and Cuthberht to bring their men to Tamworth. From there, I made my boldest move yet.

I invaded the Danelaw and took my army towards Derby.

*

The news that soldiers from the Danish army around Derby had marched to join the assault on Towcester came as no surprise. It is what Edward and I had anticipated. We had sent enough men under Osferth to defend Towcester, and, when the Danes left Derby, I marched across the border with a large force to take their base from them.

Derby was a full day's march from Tamworth and the sun was beginning to set behind us when my scouts brought some surprising news. They had seen a warband of several hundred warriors also making for Derby.

'Do they fly the raven's flag?' I asked, thinking it might be the Danes of York coming to the aid of their compatriots.

The scout scratched his beard. 'No flag nor emblem of any kind, m'lady.'

Athelstan stood by me as we heard the news. 'How did they look?'

'More like the Welsh. Swarthy and short,' the scout replied.

Athelstan turned to me. 'It must be Hwgan and his fugitive army.'

My heart sank. Just as we thought we had outmanoeuvred one foe, another took their place. 'Let's catch them in the open before they reach the town,' I said.

We increased our marching tempo and Merfyn and the cavalry went on ahead to seek out the enemy.

When we approached the great flood plain of the River Trent, I would have dearly liked to stop at nearby Repton where many of the ancient families of Mercia lay buried. The heathen army had camped there when it had first invaded our lands, and there are tales that a deadly plague killed many of their soldiers in retribution for violating the mausoleum of our ancestors. Yet I had no time to dwell on the past.

A messenger galloped back with a report from Merfyn. 'Enemy force engaged ahead, m'lady,' he called as he dismounted.

'Thank the heavens, Merfyn has caught them,' I said, waving Thurston forward. 'Tell your men to leave their baggage and move with all speed,' I yelled to him. 'We must support Merfyn.'

In a few minutes, I was galloping after my warriors as they hurried over the bridge of the Trent.

*

As we emerged from a copse, we clearly saw the fortress called Derby ahead of us on the River Derwent. I could tell instantly that Romans had built it; it was a compact fort well positioned on the banks of a river with perimeter walls of stone.

Yet the stout wooden gates looked invitingly open.

A glance around the surrounding area told me why. Warriors were streaming across a field, dropping bags and even shields, running hard towards the entrance of the fort. It was the fugitive Welsh army judging by the dragons and red crosses that adorned their weapons and clothes. Behind them rode Merfyn's cavalry. They reached the stragglers and began chopping and cutting at the backs of the men as they tried desperately to keep ahead by zigzagging though the grass. A group of those fleeing turned and locked their shields together in desperate defence. The horsemen checked and I saw Merfyn wave his sword to direct some of his men around the wall and others to make a frontal attack. They soon swept the wall aside and charged on, but the delay was enough for the front-runners to make it through the gates.

I ordered Thurston to take his foot-soldiers in support of the cavalry, and they roared as they ran across the meadow towards the fort. I saw Merfyn turn to see that he had help close at hand.

I fear that my command was his undoing.

He must have realised he was not going to prevent many of the enemy escaping through the gates, but with an army of foot soldiers behind him he decided to take a fatal risk. He led his men up to the gates and into the town, catching some of the fleeing men just as they thought they had reached safety. I watched in horror as the gates began to close as the last of the cavalry charged through. Thurston and his men were close to the walls but arrows from the bowmen above forced them to crouch under their shields.

I do not know exactly what happened next. I still have a vivid picture in my mind of the gates inching together and Thurston looking hard at me, as if awaiting my command. Then there is a blank, a void in my memory as if my body froze. The next thing I knew, Athelstan was shaking me.

'Tell Thurston to follow them, now!' he shouted, pointing to the gates.

'On! On!' I yelled at Thurston, trying to think clearly through the fog that had clouded my eyes. Warriors rushed forward and clawed at the narrow space that remained between the stout doors, desperately trying to squeeze through. But enemy axes hacked at their hands and arrows and spears poured down on them from the ramparts above. One warrior fell writhing between the gates, blocking their progress, but he was dragged into the fortress, and the gates slammed shut. We had no option but to retreat, leaving Merfyn and his men locked within the walls.

TWENTY TWO

I fear that my moment's absence before the gates of Derby might signal the beginning of the end for me. The healers reassured me that the hot sun blazing that day caused my dizziness and gave me jugs of herbal liquids to drink. But it has happened since when the weather was cold. I have much to do before my Maker claims me, so I have less time now to write my story. Forgive me if my account is incomplete.

Once I had taken in what had happened before the walls of Derby, I acted more decisively.

'See if there's another way in,' I yelled at Athelstan who was still looking at me curiously. 'Cut logs to batter at the gates,' I shouted to Thurston.

The sounds of fighting from within the walls encouraged me to believe Merfyn and his men would survive if we could enter the town quickly. We worked frantically and soon were pounding at the oaken doors with a stout tree trunk, protecting the warriors who wielded it with a makeshift shelter of shields and branches. Wiglaf and Cuthberht arrived with the remainder of the army and their soldiers surrounded the walls searching for weaknesses.

Having inspected the defences, Athelstan ran towards me. 'We should fire the gates. They are the only way in and they are not yielding,' he said.

He was right. The gates showed little sign of weakening and men were dying from the deluge of arrows and stones from above as they hammered at the thick oak.

Wiglaf nodded his agreement. 'Wood should be dry from the hot summer. Burning would be quicker than that,' he said, indicating the men who were falling back after another unsuccessful assault, dragging their fallen comrades with them.

It did not take long to assemble a substantial pile of branches against the gates. When it began to burn, I saw that the wind was in our favour, taking the flames onto the wooden planking.

I was increasingly anxious about Merfyn and his men behind the walls. 'How long will it take for the doors to burn?' I asked Wiglaf.

'I can go forward, m'lady, and watch for signs they are weakening. Perhaps Thurston and Cuthberht can stand-by ready to order men to hit the gates with the log through the flames when I indicate,' Wiglaf said, touching the large silver cross on his chest. 'By the Grace of God it could be over in a few minutes.'

I nodded and in turn felt for the cross around my neck, knowing this would be a dangerous venture. Wiglaf ran forward with soldiers to protect him and stood as near as he could to the gates that had already become engulfed with flames. I cupped an ear but could hear no sounds of battle from within the walls above the crackling of the fire. Time slowed as we all watched for Wiglaf's signal. Thurston and Cuthberht were inching forward with their most experienced warriors, ready to rush forward as soon as they could. Merfyn could surely not hold out if we waited for the fire to die down, so we had to break through the raging fire once the gates were broken.

Through the smoke, I saw Wiglaf signal to Cuthberht and Thurston to lead their men into the inferno. The warriors had tried to protect their bodies with as much dampened leather as they could, but I winced as I saw them carry that log into the flames. It crashed into the gates and I heard a splintering sound but the entrance was still barred. They pulled back from the heat, one beating at flames that had caught hold of his clothing, and waited.

Wiglaf went forward to inspect the damage and waved the men forward once more. The flames were higher now, licking up to the very top of the walls, preventing the defenders from firing down on us. I heard the log thump into burning wood and the sound of timbers cracking and splintering, but the gates did not yield. The battering team retreated from the heat and Wiglaf ran forward to see the problem. The log seemed to have jammed into the woodwork and Wiglaf and his guards began heaving at it, levering it up and down. A flaming timber came crashing down from the top of the gates and I saw men leaping aside to avoid being crushed. Several screams told me they had not all escaped but I did not see who had survived in the flames and smoke.

More beams splintered and fell just as Cuthberht and Thurston reached the inferno. I saw Cuthberht's distinctive frame outlined against the blaze just as one of the great doors collapsed around him in a cloud of sparks and flying timbers. When the smoke cleared, I could not see Cuthberht, but my soldiers were streaming into the fortress.

I called to Athelstan to advance rapidly with the remainder of our forces and together we ran towards the town. The heat was intense as we approached the fire still raging in the entrance and I wondered how my brave soldiers had endured it for so long. Many had not survived the blaze and I tried not to wretch when I saw their charred bodies half buried by smouldering timbers. A glint of metal halted me and I ran towards a body that was trapped beneath a beam. A large silver cross lay on the blackened corpse.

'Over here!' I shouted to one of my guards as I desperately tried to get closer over hot ash and burning embers. His face was badly burned but I knew it was Wiglaf. My guard grabbed at one end of the beam and heaved it aside in a shower of sparks.

I gasped when I saw that another body had been trapped by the beam and lay next to Wiglaf's. His head moved as the weight of the timber was lifted from him, the blonde hair instantly recognisable.

'Cuthberht!' I yelled, rushing to him, somehow not feeling the heat in my feet.

His eyes stared up at me and his hand reached for mine. I grasped his fingers just as he opened his mouth to speak. No words, but blood gurgled forth from his lips and his hand slipped away from mine, his eyes closing.

I commended their souls to heaven. I could only suppose that Cuthberht had come to Wiglaf's aid but had been crushed by a beam that fell on them both. The intense heat forced me to leave my fallen thegns to rest in peace, knowing that a commander's first duty in any battle is to the living and not to the dead.

*

Athelstan had already taken his men through the gates, and I hurried over the burning timbers to study the battle for the town. The fortress was small with few buildings, and fighting men seemed to be everywhere. I passed skirmishes in alleyways and hand to hand fighting in doorways as my soldiers tried to take control of the streets. Spying Athelstan up ahead, I followed him around a corner into a large open square where I found the main battle for the town. My warriors were formed up into lines advancing on a foe at the other end of the rectangle.

On elevated ground behind the enemy forces, I made out more men gathered on an earthen embankment against the wall. Standing in their midst was the unmistakable figure of Merfyn, shouting and cajoling his men.

He must have been pinned back to the wall by the town's defenders, who in turn were now trapped by my men. I shoved my way through the ranks of shield-men to reach Athelstan.

'What's happening? Where's Thurston?' I called.

'He's at the front with his men. Must have arrived just in time to save Merfyn,' Athelstan said. 'There's a strong force of Danes and Welsh warriors here. We have the numbers to overcome them, but we must take care not to crush us all in this tight space. Should we offer them surrender terms?'

'Yes, I don't want to risk more deaths,' I said. I was reluctant to forgive the Welsh, but there would be Christian people of our own race amongst the defenders.

*

Organising any sort of truce in the crush of men was difficult but Athelstan and Thurston finally managed to pull back their troops and shout out the offer of an honourable surrender to our opponents. Some men held up their arms and made their way forward to give up their swords. The Welsh contingent stood firm and one of them took off his shiny helmet to shout at us in a tongue I did not understand.

'He must be the Welsh leader, Hwgan,' Athelstan said. 'He says that he would rather die than surrender to an ugly Saxon woman.'

'Then tell him to prepare for an ugly death,' I said.

Whilst we shouted back and forth to Hwgan, Merfyn stood on his mound, still trapped on the far side of the enemy. Once the Danes who wished to surrender had laid down their arms, we prepared to make our final assault on Hwgan and his Welsh followers.

Merfyn then made an unexpected move.

I thought he would stand his ground and let our fresh troops do the final work, but that had never been Merfyn's style. He waved his sword above his head and led his men down the slope and threw himself on the rear of his fellow Welshmen. It might have been his frustration at not capturing Hwgan before or maybe he was stung by the insults they had made about me.

Unfortunately, at the very instant that Merfyn charged, Thurston commanded his archers to fire on Hwgan's formation. Arrows can be deadly at such close range and many thumped into Welsh warriors who fell screaming. But one flew above their heads and curved down on the other side. I watched in disbelief as it tore into Merfyn's neck and he dropped to the ground like a deer hit by huntsmen.

It was the turn of Thurston to lose his composure. Seeing what his archers had done, he bellowed at his men and led a furious charge into the enemy shield wall. The Welsh are renowned for their hot-headed charges in battle but on that day it was our turn to act rashly. Thurston burst through the first rank of his opponents and sought out Hwgan, shouting his name and aiming a mighty blow at the shoulders of the Welsh king. Hwgan staggered back but managed to fend off the blow, his personal guards closing protectively around him. Thurston did not relent but used his height to thrust his shield into Hwgan's face so that the king did not see the sword that Thurston plunged into his belly. Hwgan squealed like a pig, falling to his knees.

Thurston could have stood back to watch the king die, but in his battle rage he pushed his sword deeper and smashed his shield into Hwgan's body to knock him over. The Welsh king yelped louder, grasping at Thurston's shield, tugging him towards him. Off balance, with his sword still stuck in Hwgan's guts, Thurston was exposed to the king's guards who were eager to avenge their master. One stabbed a spear into his side, another cut at his neck with a sword. Thurston slumped on top of the Welsh king.

It was over before I could breathe.

*

Four of my bravest and most able thegns died in that fateful battle. Wiglaf had been an inexperienced reeve when he took charge of the defenders of Chester, who included the youthful

Cuthberht and Merfyn. They had served me faithfully and skilfully ever since. Thurston stepped into Merewalh's shoes so nobly at Tettenhall and I had high hopes of him for the future. All had been snatched from me in my moment of triumph. They say I have not smiled from that day to this.

Fortunately, I still had Athelstan who was now coming into his prime at twenty-two years old. Despite the loss of my generals, we took Derby and all the surrounding area it controlled. The news of the loss of a stronghold held by the Danes for over forty years reverberated around the land like thunder signalling a storm. My warriors poured through farmsteads and holdings that all submitted without resistance.

I returned to Derby and sought out the remains of its church. It had been built by my ancestors and dedicated to the murdered Mercian prince, St Alkmund. The pagan invaders had left the church in ruins, but the priests who accompanied my army had brought me some exciting news. They had discovered the sarcophagus of St Alkmund himself. When I saw the stone coffin, wonderfully carved by an ancient craftsman, standing like a heavenly ark amidst the rotting timbers of the minster, I felt the presence of the Lord above. My vision blurred into an orange haze, my knees trembled and my mind numbed. The next thing I knew, a hand had taken a firm grip of my arm.

'Your pardon, m'lady, but I feared you were about to fall.' It was the young priest who had led me to the sarcophagus.

'Thank you. I was overcome by such a divine vision.' I rubbed my eyes and opened them gently, thankful that my sight had returned although it was still blurred. 'Does it still contain the relics of the saint?'

'God be praised, they are preserved within it, m'lady.'

'We must remove them to safety,' I said. Although we had taken the stronghold, enemy armies were close by and I did not want to risk such precious artefacts.

I ordered St. Alkmund's bones to be transported to Shrewsbury, to the church I had already dedicated to his name there. Leaving Athelstan to organise the peace in our newly enlarged territories, I accompanied the relics as far as Tamworth, where I had decided to stay for a while. I was secretly concerned that my body was warning me with these lapses that it was close to breaking point. I sent word to the King, telling him of my plans to rest over the winter.

*

Ælfwyn greeted me when I arrived in Tamworth. I had left her to administer our estates whilst I was away on campaign, still hoping that she would succeed me as Lady of the Mercians. She appeared more animated than I had seen for some time.

'I have interesting news from the north,' she announced whilst I was taking a soothing bath after my ride.

'What's happening there?' I asked. Whilst I had been taking back our ancestral lands to the east, I had had little time to consider the turmoil further north where Norse warriors continued to seek new territory.

'We have received approaches for support,' she said, a little too smugly for my liking.

'Who from? The Christians of Northumbria?' I asked, knowing that the true faith had many followers even in territory dominated by pagans.

'No, from Norsemen recently returned from conquests in Ireland who have taken lands beyond the Mersey.'

Her news potentially threatened Mercia's borders beyond Chester so I immediately sat up in my bath, brushing the water from my ears. 'I hope this is not Ingimund's kin asking for our assistance again.' I still smarted from the memory of the treachery that I had received in return for my kindness in helping that band of refugees.

'No, this is someone I met when I was a captive before the battle,' she said. 'I got to know him well, but you may not remember him.'

'Didn't we kill anyone of any importance at Tettenhall?' I was beginning to tire of her guessing game, but she persisted.

'He was a subordinate then but has grown to pre-eminence since.'

'And his name is?'

'Ragnall.'

She did not elaborate but I have always had a good recall of names and faces, and I instantly recalled the aloof demeanour and piercing eyes of the young warrior I had met briefly before the battle. 'Your keeper when you were prisoner? Didn't he cut off your finger?'

She shook her head vigorously. 'No, no, he argued against it. Ragnall was the only one who showed me any kindness.'

'I see. What favour does he now ask in return?'

'He wants our help against the Northumbrians. He says they have been leaderless since Halfdan was killed and, if we don't act soon, the Scots of Alba will move south and take York from the Danes.'

'No doubt he wants to take it for himself,' I said, sensing that we were faced with a newcomer of ambition.

'Yes, he would rule in York, but he would accept you as his overlord.'

Ælfwyn was clearly excited at the prospect of an alliance with this Norseman and I was beginning to wonder exactly what had happened between them when she was a vulnerable young captive. A few years ago, I would have laughed at the idea of a pagan chief bending the knee to me. But it was no longer an absurd notion. It had just happened in the Danelaw.

'You have met with him to discuss this idea?' I asked.

'Yes, he took the risk of riding here in person.'

'You entertained a Norseman in my absence?'

She blushed. 'You said I should take on more authority, and I could hardly turn him away.'

I stood in my bath. 'I will think on what you have said.'

I did not need to think, for I knew what to do. My daughter's cosy chat with Ragnall would alarm the Danes in York because he already represented a major threat to their independence, and if I sided with him it would tip the balance of power. I could choose which side to support against the other, and demand their submission to my authority in return. It was a choice between Ragnall, an ambitious pagan warrior who seemed to have some hold over my daughter, and the existing elite in York amongst whom I counted Archbishop Hrotheweard as a friend.

I chose the Archbishop.

I had heard the Danes of York were turning in increasing numbers towards the True Faith and I could insist that the word of God was to be openly preached if I became overlord through this alliance. Before long, I would have a vassal Christian state. I despatched an urgent message to the Archbishop, and word to Ragnall that we would talk with him as soon as we were able.

*

Edward thinks I am dying. He must have heard of the strange blankness that has afflicted me on several occasions because he came to see me unexpectedly at Tamworth. It was near to Yuletide and we sat by a fire whilst he prattled on about how he had stormed Tempsford and the ancient Roman town of Colchester, and how the Danes had counter-attacked at Maldon but he had marched to relieve the town, and the army of East Anglia had submitted to him.

'Next year, there is little to stop us reconquering all of old Mercia,' he said. 'If you are well enough.'

I almost railed against his suggestion that I might be weakening, but I chose a different tactic. 'I am ready for a final campaign. But I want your word that Ælfwyn will succeed me whilst you are king.'

We had discussed the succession before and he had agreed to support my daughter as the next Lady of the Mercians, should anything happen to me. I feared the people of Mercia were not ready to be directly ruled by Wessex and might rise up against Edward if he was to take sole power. Ælfwyn would provide an interim solution, whilst not posing a long-term threat to Wessex; she was, after all, a woman without a husband or children. One kingdom of the Anglo Saxons might emerge later, after Edward's reign. He and I both knew there was only one person who could rightfully claim to be king of both realms by birth, and that was Athelstan. But Edward had other sons by different queens, and he was wary of discussing his heirs with me.

He obviously thought my succession plans were more pressing, for he moved closer to me, his voice a whisper. 'Are you close to the end?'

I shrugged. 'I'm closer than I was last year, and probably closer than you. So I look to the uncle to protect and promote the daughter.'

'I give you my word,' he said.

I took his hand and squeezed it hard. There had been a time when I adored and cherished my little brother, but that had come to an abrupt end when he took it upon himself to try to assert his power over me. Since our military cooperation, I had felt more at ease with him and began to feel my old affection for him once again. Yet I still did not trust him.

*

Early in the year of our lord 918, I was ready for the final push to retake Mercia. Edward and I had planned it carefully as we had the previous campaigns. Once again, I learned to expect the unexpected.

Feeling strong both in mind and body, I rode at the head of my warriors as we left Tamworth. I paused at St Editha's to say a final prayer and greet the old woman who had now become a priestess in the church that bore her name. The minster had been finely reconstructed with oaken walls and a slate roof. The local folk who had treated me with much caution when I first brought my army to their land, now came out to greet me and shower me with gifts of food, even silver, as I rode to war once more.

My first target was a Danish warband at Leicester whilst Edward moved on another at Stamford. The first surprise came as I approached Leicester.

The Danes submitted without a fight.

We were prepared for war like never before, but we did not have to unsheathe a single sword. A delegation of Danish jarls met us on the road towards the town and offered to swear allegiance to the Lady of the Mercians. If you had told me when I was a fickle young girl that one day a procession of battle-hardened warriors would bend their knee before me, I would have thought you mad. Yet I watched one after another, some old and scarred, some young and haughty, hand over their weapons and take a bible or the hammer of Thor to commit themselves to my service. I felt I was standing on the shoulders of my father, King Alfred. He had made this possible and he would have been so proud that I was finishing his work.

I was about to turn my attention to the remaining warbands at Nottingham and Lincoln, when more pressing news arrived. I heard that Archbishop Hrotheweard and a delegation from York were hurrying to see me, having received my message. Instructing Athelstan to take charge of my forces and to liaise with Edward over the campaign, I returned to Tamworth. Hrotheweard was waiting to see me when I arrived.

So was Ælfwyn.

She burst into my chamber whilst I was changing into relaxing robes after my ride, and glared at me, hands on hips.

'What have you done, Mother?' she demanded.

'Let me see,' I said, casually. 'Last week I took Leicester. Next week, York.'

'With the wrong ally!' she yelled.

'We will see which one we favour when we have spoken to all the interested parties. At the moment, I would tend to favour the Saxon archbishop over the Norse warlord.'

She shook her head. 'You haven't heard have you?'

'What exactly?'

'Ragnall has crossed from Ireland with an army and defeated King Constantin of Alba at Corbridge. He no longer needs us and will suspect treachery when he hears you are meeting with his avowed enemies.'

That did surprise me. I had exchanged letters with the Scottish king, Constantin about the threat of the Norsemen, but neither of us expected them to arrive in force so soon.

'If Ragnall does not need us, we had better treat with those who do, don't you think?'

She made a growling noise and banged the door on her way out.

The information about Ragnall made my meeting with Hrotheweard and his companions even easier to negotiate. I made it clear that, in return for the protection of my army, I would accept nothing short of submission to my overlordship and a significant annual tribute. The jarls in the Archbishop's delegation haggled only over the tribute. Their submission was not disputed.

I retired to my room to contemplate on what had already been a tumultuous year – and it was only June! I prayed that I could be given the strength to finish the task of reuniting the English-speaking peoples, so that we could all live again in Christian fellowship – and so that my brother would not steal all the credit for it.

EPILOGUE

My mother, Æthelflæd, died suddenly on the twelfth day of June, 918. She was found dead in her room, her last act seemingly to make entries into this manuscript that I have kept ever since. The healers could find no trace of poison or other sign of treachery and concluded that her bodily functions had ceased to work because of the strain she had placed upon them.

Not a day goes by that I do not think of her and the momentous life that she lived. I am still tormented by the memory of the last words between us that were spoken in anger. If only we could have spoken more reasonably, I might have foreseen the disaster that I brought upon myself once she was no longer here to guide me.

We buried her in the east chapel of St Oswald's, her beloved church in Gloucester, next to Lord Æthelred and the saintly relics. The very next day, the Witan assembled to choose her successor. I was the only candidate. King Edward gave me his blessing as the new Lady of the Mercians, provided that he was appointed my guardian, even though I was thirty years old. He returned in haste to the battle front in the east where he quickly received the submission of all the people, Danish and English, who lived in Mercia. Within a few months of her death, my mother's brother finished her lifework, and he naturally claimed all the honour for it.

Athelstan accepted my authority, although he might have expected to have been given the role himself. He too was preoccupied with the reconquest of lands to the east and took command of the Mercian troops who campaigned with those of Wessex.

I was left to administer Mercia as best I could. I realise now that the Lord above had a higher purpose for me and he guided me into a decision that was to relieve me of the burden of involving myself in the treacherous affairs of men.

I agreed to marry Ragnall when he made himself King in York.

I still believe my grandfather, King Alfred, would have approved of the plan, for he knew how to draw pagan lords into our faith and our communities.

Ragnall sent an emissary to offer me his hand in marriage. He would convert to the Christian faith and give me his support against those he called 'overbearing advisors'. When I was a prisoner amongst the Danes, he and I had talked long into the night about how the children of nobility suffered because we were forbidden to follow our hearts in selecting whom we were to marry. His heart, he had confessed, was drawn to me. Mine had been recently broken when his compatriots had killed Merewalh, so at the time I resisted his affection.

However, as the newly appointed Lady of the Mercians, I saw merit in the idea of marriage to Ragnall. He said he could easily take York if we did not support the local jarls, as my mother had planned. Between us, he and I would rule the kingdom of Northumbria as well as Mercia. We could talk on equal terms with Edward so that he would have to temper his overbearing ways. I wanted to discuss the plan with Athelstan, whose advice I respected, but he was away on campaign. I trusted no other advisor. I accepted Ragnall's proposal.

It was mid-winter when Uncle Edward arrived in Tamworth and accused me of treachery. He called the Witan, and seeing his army at their gates, they agreed I had acted above my station and that my guardian, Edward, should decide my fate.

He decreed I was to become a nun and join Aunt Æthelgifu's convent in Shaftsbury.

I have lived in God's service ever since. Perhaps I should not have been tempted by power and withdrawn to serve a higher purpose earlier in my life. My mother and I may have been spared much pain. I know she was disappointed in me during her life and would have been distraught to learn that I had lasted a mere six months as the Lady of the Mercians, when she held the post for seven tumultuous years after her husband's death.

I take comfort that my mother's work has recently attained its greatest reward.

Athelstan has become King of all England!

She fostered him from an early age, raising him as the son she never had, giving him responsibilities beyond his years when he showed his capabilities. His father, Edward, never gave Athelstan those opportunities and when his second and third wife gave him sons, he preferred them over his first born.

I am so glad that, by God's grace, I was given the years to see the end of Uncle Edward. He died eight years after his sister. He achieved little in those years, other than completing the work of my mother. He did nothing to prevent Ragnall from capturing York, but built burhs to protect Mercia from the north, just as Æthelflæd had conceived. He even made peace with Ragnall, the suitor he had found so objectionable. That treaty turned out to be valueless because Ragnall died soon after, and his heir, Sihtric, raided freely into Mercia. Edward's reign ended with a revolt against his rule by the people of Chester who had held Æthelflæd so dear to their hearts.

I held my breath awaiting news of Edward's successor. The Mercians accepted Athelstan as king, but Wessex favoured Edward's second son, Ælfweard. As we braced ourselves for civil disorder, the Lord God intervened. Did my saintly mother guide Him for she must surely be sitting with him in Heaven? Ælfweard died of a sudden disease hardly a month after his father, and Athelstan was crowned at Kingston. He quickly annexed Northumbria and brought all the English-speaking people into one kingdom for the first time.

My mother made all this possible. Yet, power-hungry leeches have tried to deny her legacy ever since. Now that I have become a nun, I can read some of the lies that these men produce in the name of history. In Wessex, monks write a Chronicle on the orders of the king that ignores Æthelflæd's deeds and awards the glory of the reconquest of the Danelaw to Edward. Yet in Ireland, where the monks are independent of our nobility, they proclaim her as the most famous queen of the Saxons.

I trust this account will right the balance and confer appropriate honour on my mother, Æthelflæd, King Alfred's daughter.

Ælfwyn,
Nunnaminster, Winchester, 927

HISTORICAL NOTES

The following notes are aimed to help you understand the evidence-based facts underlying this story, and what is conjecture. The following timeline of events is taken from well-known primary and secondary sources about the life and times of Æthelflæd.

TIMELINE OF EVENTS

865   'Great Heathen Army' of Danes lands. Over several years, it takes the kingdoms of York, East Anglia and eastern half of Mercia.

868   Alfred, youngest of the four sons of Æthelwulf, king of Wessex, marries Ealhswith, a noblewoman of Mercia.

869/70   Æthelflæd is born, first child of Alfred and Ealhswith.

870   Alfred's brother, King Ethelred, is wounded during repeated Viking attacks on Wessex.

871   Alfred becomes King of Wessex when his brother dies of his wounds.

874   Æthelflæd's brother, Edward, is born, the future king of Wessex (known to history as Edward the Elder).

875   Æthelflæd's sister, Æthelgifu, is born (future Abbess of Shaftesbury).

878	Surprise Danish attack on Chippenham at Yuletide (Christmas). Alfred and his family are forced to flee to Atheney and hide in the marshland of the Somerset Levels. (The 'cake-burning' legend stems from this time.)
878	Battle of Eddington – by May, Alfred has managed to raise an army and defeats the Danes under Guthrum, who agrees to become Christian and withdraws to rule over East Anglia.
879	Æthelred becomes ruler of the western part of Mercia not under Danish control and accepts the overlordship of Alfred.
879–886	Alfred uses a peaceful period to fortify key towns as 'burhs.'
886	Alfred and Æthelred recapture London from the Danes.
886	A peace treaty divides England into Danelaw to the east and Anglo-Saxon Wessex and Mercia to the west
887	Æthelflæd marries Æthelred, lord of the Mercians, to cement the alliance between Mercia and Wessex, sometime between 885–7 when she was around 16 years old.
887–9	Ælfwyn, only child of Æthelflæd and Æthelred, is born.
891	The Anglo-Saxon Chronicle begins, originally written in the Old Minster, Winchester.
890s	Worcester is restored and fortified by Æthelred and Æthelflæd in conjunction with Bishop Wærferth. They restore Gloucester and found a priory, initially named St Peter's, later St Oswald's.
892	A Danish army under Hæston lands in Kent and raids into Mercia up the River Severn. Alfred and Æthelred combine to thwart it.
894/5	Athelstan is born to Edward and his wife/consort Ecgwynn. At the age of about six, he is sent to the Mercian court to be brought up by Æthelflæd.
899	Alfred dies and is succeeded by Edward.

899	Æthelwold, son of Ethelred (Alfred's brother and predecessor as king of Wessex), raises his flag in rebellion at Wimborne Minster in defiance of Edward. He takes with him a nun of high birth (suggested by one historian to be Æthelgifu). Edward takes an army to Badbury Rings outside Wimborne. Abandoning the noble nun, Æthelwold flees at night to Northumbria, where he is proclaimed a king.
900	Edward is crowned King of the Angles and Saxons by Archbishop Plegmund at Kingston. He takes a second wife – Ælfflæd of Wiltshire.
901	Shrewsbury fortified and established as a burh by Æthelred and Æthelflæd.
902	Ealhswith, Æthelflæd's mother, dies at Nunnaminster, the abbey she founded and is buried with Alfred in the New Minster, in Winchester. Æthelwulf (Cenwulf in our story to avoid a confusion of Æthels), Æthelflæd's uncle, brother of Ealhswith and an important Mercian leader, also dies.
902	Æthelred, Lord of the Mercians, reported to be ill. Æthelflæd increasingly takes charge of Mercia.
902	Battle of the Holme. Æthelwold, Æthelflæd's renegade cousin, returns to the south with a war-fleet and is joined by Danes from East Anglia. They raid Mercia along the Thames before crossing into Wessex at Cricklade. Harrying south to Braydon Forest, they meet the Wiltshire fyrd and turn back east. King Edward follows them into the Danelaw, spearheaded by forces from Kent. When Edward gives the order to turn back, the Kentish forces are cut off and defeated at Holme, near Peterborough, with many casualties including their leaders, Sigewulf and Sigeholm. However, it is a pyrrhic victory: Æthelwold is killed along with Beorhsige, son of Beornoth, a Mercian nobleman who

had joined Æthelwold's cause, and Eohric, Danish king of East Anglia, and his jarls, Oscytel and Ysopa.

902   Norse Vikings in Ireland are expelled and one of their leaders, Ingimund makes his way via Wales to Chester and seeks an audience with Æthelflæd. She grants him land to settle in the Wirral in return for oaths of allegiance. Æthelflæd begins restoring Chester, a ruined Roman camp.

905   A combined force of Ingimund's Norsemen and Danes from Northumbria attack Chester. Æthelflæd leads the defence, ordering troops to lure the attackers into the fortress where many Vikings were killed. A siege develops and the people of Chester are said to have poured hot liquid from the walls and hurled hives of bees to ward off attacks. Æthelflæd sends secret messages to Christians within the Viking forces to trick their leaders who are slaughtered when they put down their weapons in a traditional gesture of oath-giving.

907   Æthelflæd redesigns Chester and founds St Werburh's church (later Chester cathedral).

909   An Anglo-Saxon raid into Danelaw recovers the bones of St Oswald from Bardney Abbey in Lincolnshire. They are taken to Æthelflæd's abbey in Gloucester which is renamed St Oswald's Priory.

910   Battle of Tettenhall. A Danish army invades Mercia from the north and raids down the Severn valley to the Avon. King Edward is in Kent exercising his troops and a new fleet. The Danes turn back towards home with their booty, crossing the River Severn at Bridgnorth, when they are ambushed at Tettenhall by Mercian and Wessex forces near Woden's Field (now Wednesfield near Wolverhampton). The Danes are routed and three kings killed including Halfdan and Eowils.

910	Æthelflæd founds a burh at Bremesbyrig (location uncertain, possibly Bromsgrove).
911	Æthelred, Lord of the Mercians, dies. He is succeeded by Æthelflæd who takes the title of Lady of the Mercians. Edward takes back control of London and Oxford from Mercia.
912	Æthelflæd fortifies Bridgnorth and Scergeat (location unknown) as burhs.
913	The reconquest of the Danelaw begins with a coordinated Wessex-Mercian attack. Æthelflæd captures and fortifies Tamworth, the historical capital of Mercia, and Stafford. Edward secures land north of the Thames.
914	Æthelflæd fortifies Eddisbury and builds a burh at Warwick.
915	Æthelflæd strengthens defences on the Welsh border with burhs at Chirbury and Hereford.
916	Æthelflæd sends a force against Hwgan, King of Brycheiniog, near Brecon in south Wales, who had killed one of her abbots. They capture his palace on Llangorse Lake and take the queen and her court hostage, but Hwgan flees.
917	Æthelflæd captures Derby, a significant Danish army base, but at a cost. Four of her most trusted lieutenants were killed 'within the gates.' Welsh annals report that King Hwgan had fled to Derby and chose to die by the sword there rather than 'submit to a woman.'
918	The Danes of Leicester, another important army group, surrender to Mercia without a fight. Æthelflæd negotiates with the Northumbrian Danes in York who offer to submit to her in the face of a threat from a rival Viking, Ragnall.
918	Æthelflæd dies at Tamworth on 12th June and is buried in St Oswald's, Gloucester. Ælfwyn is named as her successor by the Mercian Witan.

918	In December, Edward removes Ælfwyn from power and takes control of Mercia and the newly conquered areas of Danelaw.
924	King Edward dies. Athelstan is pronounced King in Mercia. Edward's son by his second marriage, Ælfweard, also dies, leaving Athelstan to succeed to the throne of Wessex as well.
925	Athelstan is crowned King of the Angles and Saxons at Kingston.
927	Athelstan annexes Northumbria, making him the first King of all England, and overlord of much of Britain.

These are the known events that underpin this book. Modern historians have suggested some of the conjectural aspects of my story (e.g. Æthelgifu's part in Æthelwold's revolt; Athelstan's role in bringing back the relics of St Oswald). Others are my own invention (especially Æthelflæd's role as a hostage at the Battle of the Holme and Ælfwyn's capture in the Tettenhall campaign).

CHARACTERS

Most of the names of the characters in this story are taken from the historical records. These are presented alphabetically at the beginning of the book. A few, listed in italics, are names I have invented although their roles probably existed. For example, the Mercian Register tells us that the Danish army at Derby was defeated at great cost to Æthelflæd because *"four of her thegns who were dear to her, were killed within the gates."* Unfortunately, it does not name them. As her husband and his military commanders grew older, Æthelflæd would have appointed her own generals. I have named these four as Cuthberht, Merfyn, Thurston and Wiglaf. Soldiers like these would have played significant roles in her military campaigns.

INTERPRETATION

This book begins in 899 with the death of Alfred the Great and the succession of his son, Edward, as king of Wessex and overlord of what remained of Anglo-Saxon Mercia. It was no surprise that Edward and his thegns committed themselves to both defend their realm and recover what they could of what had been lost to the Viking invaders. What is surprising is that Alfred's daughter, Æthelflæd, should play such an important part in the reconquest of England. Women had significant roles in Anglo-Saxon society, but not military or political ones. They were heads of households and could own land in their own right; some, like Æthelflæd's mother and sister, became heads of religious establishments. But none were war-leaders or fort-builders – except for Æthelflæd.

Historians now recognise that she played a vital role in the creation of an independent England out of a hotch-pot of territories, many of which were controlled by foreign warlords. As the young wife of Æthelred, Lord of the Mercians, she was active in government and helped hold together the alliance that was crucial to her father's success. When her husband became ill, she increasingly took on more responsibility in leading Mercia. After he died, she succeeded him as the 'Lady of the Mercians', the first time that a woman governed an Anglo-Saxon state. If that was not exceptional enough, she used her position to play a crucial part in the counterattack against the Danes that laid the foundations for her foster-child, Athelstan, to become king of all England within a decade of her death.

Why have her achievements been under-played for so long? Part of the reason is to be found in how the happenings of the time were documented. Æthelflæd's life is an early example of how an alternative narrative of events can be spread through state-controlled media. The most important contemporary written source is the *Anglo-Saxon Chronicle*, a year-by-year record of events covering the first millennium AD and beyond. Begun during the reign of Alfred the Great, it was first written by scribes, probably monks, in Winchester using Old English, the language that Alfred promoted over the continued usage of Latin. Copies were made and distributed to other monasteries throughout the Anglo-Saxon world. There, other scribe-monks added not only the official updates circulated from Wessex but, crucially for our story, they also inserted local records of events. One such copy, known as the 'Mercian Register', focuses on Mercian as well as West Saxon happenings. This differs in that it contains details of Æthelflæd's life that are completely ignored in the original 'Winchester Chronicle' that merely records her death in 918.

The Mercian version records more information about Æthelflæd than any other woman throughout all the Anglo-Saxon Chronicles. Acknowledged as 'lady of the Mercians,' she is documented as ordering the construction of many burhs, some of which are now important towns in the West Midlands.

For example, in the entry for 912, the Mercian Register states:

"In this year, by the grace of God, Æthelflæd, lady of the Mercians, went with all the Mercians to Tamworth, and built the borough there in the early summer and afterwards, before Lammas, that at Stafford."

This was not simply fortifying her own boroughs (or burhs) but rebuilding them in territory formerly held by the enemy. Despite their significance, these actions are ignored in the Winchester Chronicle which merely records an unsuccessful Danish raid on Luton that year.

The Mercian register continues to document Æthelflæd's military campaigns against the Danes and Norwegians (they were not called Vikings until later), culminating in the capture of Derby and Leicester.

"In this year (917), Æthelflæd, lady of the Mercians, ... obtained the borough which is called Derby, with all that belongs with it; and there also four of her thegns who were dear to her, were killed within the gates. In this year (918), she peacefully obtained control of Leicester... and the greater part of the army which belonged to it were subjugated."

These are highly significant moments in the reconquest of Danelaw as Derby and Leicester were not just towns but bases of the Danish army. Again, the Winchester Chronicle is silent on both events.

As Æthelflæd reconquered eastern Mercia and Edward invaded East Anglia, the final fiefdom of the Danelaw around York also submitted – not to King Edward but to Æthelflæd:

918 "And also the people of York had promised her – and some had given pledges and some had confirmed it with oaths – that they would be under her direction."

Tragically, Æthelflæd died before she could receive their submission.

"But very soon after they had agreed to this, she died twelve days before midsummer in Tamworth, in the eighth year in

which with lawful authority she was holding dominion over the Mercians. And her body is buried in Gloucester in the east chapel of St Peter's church."

The Winchester Chronicle finally acknowledges her existence with a brief record of her death and her title.

918 "In this year died Æthelflæd, lady of the Mercians."

After her death, the Mercian Register tells how Æthelflæd's daughter, Ælfwyn, succeeded her as lady of the Mercians only to be *"deprived of all authority in Mercia and taken into Wessex, three weeks before Christmas."*

The Winchester Chronicle ignores Ælfwyn's brief reign, recording only that *"all the nation in the land of the Mercians which had been subject to Æthelflæd submitted to him (Edward)."*

The Mercian Register appears to confirm the connection of Athelstan with Mercia when it records that he was chosen by the Mercians as king in 924, where the Winchester Chronicle merely states that *"King Edward died and his son Athelstan succeeded to the kingdom."*

Why should Æthelflæd and her heirs have been written out of the history as recorded by scribes in Wessex? Kings such as Edward would have closely monitored records of events during their reign as they had an important influence on their legitimacy and power base. The differences in the entries in the Anglo-Saxon Chronicles would not have been merely at the whim of the scribe-monks who wrote them. The Winchester scribes would have been under pressure to ignore Æthelflæd's role in order to emphasise their own king's achievements and to downplay the resurgence of Mercia as an independent military power.

It is possible, of course, that the Mercian Register exaggerated Æthelflæd's role. Fortunately, we have some corroboration of her achievements from contemporary sources in Ireland, Scotland

and Wales, where monasteries had a long tradition of chronicle writing. These Celtic sources are more fulsome in their praise of Æthelflæd than any of the English histories. For example, the *Fragmentary Annals of Ireland* give a detailed, if fanciful, account of Æthelflæd's dealing with the Norse chieftain, Ingimund, and the siege of Chester (on which this book's version is based). These Annals also refer to the illness of Æthelred, Lord of the Mercians, during this time, implying that it was Æthelflæd who oversaw the defences. The *Annals of Ulster* call her the 'most famous queen' and her death a 'most significant' event. Welsh chroniclers write of her as a woman of 'most singular virtues' who 'greatly strengthened the kingdom of Mercia.'

Further evidence of Æthelflæd's activities can be found in contemporary charters that documented how land was divided and distributed. These provide insights into her building defences and founding burhs. For example, a charter of 901 tells us she, her husband Æthelred, and other Mercian nobility were in Shrewsbury, probably to witness its development as a burh. Interestingly, Æthelred's last known public appearance is in a charter dated 904, seven years before his death, further evidence that he had a long, debilitating illness.

Some modern historians portray Edward and Æthelflæd as a brother and sister team co-cooperating largely in harmony in the conquest of the Danelaw. There were instances of this, but the absence of Æthelflæd from the chronicle written under the scrutiny of Edward in Winchester indicates he did not want his sister taking any glory. Significant friction is visible, for example, in 911 when Æthelflæd's husband died and Edward annexed the southern third of Mercia, as recorded by the Winchester Chronicle:

> "911 In this year, Æthelred, lord of the Mercians, died and King Edward received the boroughs of London and Oxford, and all the lands which belonged to them."

The accession of Æthelflæd as lady of the Mercians, an event that would have been regarded as exceptional anywhere in Europe, is not even mentioned. Instead, it records Edward taking what he could of the former Mercian kingdom. He had to wait until she died to seize the rest by deposing Ælfwyn who had been selected by Mercian lords to succeed her mother as first lady. Edward did allow his son, Athelstan, to be raised in Mercia, but that was probably because there were hostile forces at work against his son's legitimacy in Wessex.

King Alfred the Great devoted his life to ensuring the survival of the Anglo-Saxons as a sovereign nation. His dream of a united Anglo-Saxon kingdom covering most of modern-day England was completed with no small thanks to his daughter.

FURTHER READING

If you want to delve further into the life of Æthelflæd try the revised 2022 edition of Michael Wood's *In Search of the Dark Ages*, which has a recent chapter on Æthelflæd.

There are more detailed modern biographies:

+ Tim Clarkson, *Æthelflæd, The Lady of the Mercians*, 2019;
+ Margaret Jones, *Founder, Fighter, Saxon Queen*, 2018 (which has a helpful guide to places honouring Æthelflæd including place names and statues);
+ Joanna Arman, *The Warrior Queen: Life and Legend of Æthelflæd, Daughter of Alfred the Great*, 2017;
+ For a shorter summary, try *Æthelflæd: England's Forgotten Founder*, by Tom Holland, 2019.

ALSO BY DAVID STOKES

Angles or Angels?

From the early history of the English-speaking people, a dramatic story that helped define the boundaries of Britain. Compelling characters reenact a saga of love and betrayal that is meticulously researched from historical and archaeological records.

Late 6th century Britain. Regional kingdoms are engaged in a ruthless struggle for supremacy. To the south, Saxon kings predominate but, in the north, British leaders are combining in a final effort to overthrow their two Angle rivals in Deira and Bernicia. To survive, the Angle warlords must put aside their ancient rivalry.

Acha, daughter of one king, is chosen to act as 'peace-weaver' by marrying the rival leader. But when her intended husband kills her father and disinherits her young brother, she has to choose between her lover, her family and her duty to the wider kin.

Against a backdrop of military campaigns that decide the shape of northern Britain, this story follows the personal tragedies that force siblings into rival camps. The outcome may be a united kingdom but families will be divided forever.